ESCAPE FROM UKRAINE

One Man's Journey to the Black Sea

D1738717

WARD R. ANDERSON

Cover Design by Ward R. Anderson

About the cover: The flag of Ukraine carries the blue of the sky and the gold of the wheat in the country's breadbasket. The red sword of Russia descending from the northeast splits the country and graphically presents the annexation of Crimea and occupation of Eastern Ukraine.

Dedicated to the displaced Ukrainians

Contents

Maps iii
Names, Birth Date, Birthplace.................................... iv
Locations: City, Country (known later as) vi
Prologue: Feodosia, Ukraine, 27 February, 2014 1
Part One: A Difficult Decade, 1934–1944 5
Chapter 1: Peasant Farmers, 1934 7
Chapter 2: Little Dmytro 13
Chapter 3: Fishing Together 19
Chapter 4: The Germans, 1941 23
Chapter 5: The Deserter, 1944 32
Chapter 6: Westward Flight at the Summer Solstice........... 36
Chapter 7: Pleasure and Guilt at the Carpathians 43
Chapter 8: Winter Takes its Toll 50
Chapter 9: Uncle Yarik Disappears 54
Chapter 10: Tested by Partisans 57
Chapter 11: More Sadness 61
Chapter 12: Dmytro Becomes a Czech Named Luboš......... 65
Chapter 13: Guests in Slovakia, January 1945 71
Chapter 14: The Trek Resumes.................................... 77
Chapter 15: The Red Army, April 1945.......................... 81
Part Two: Luboš Becomes a Man, 1946-1955 92
Chapter 16: Luboš Alone... 94
Chapter 17: Young Worker, 1948–1955.......................... 98
Chapter 18: Private Luboš Novák, 1955–1956.................. 102
Chapter 19: Elite Bus Assignment, 1957–1967................. 107
Chapter 20: Marcela, Fall 1967................................... 115
Chapter 21: Friendship Evolves................................... 126
Chapter 22: Prague Spring, 1968 132
Chapter 23: The Warsaw Pact Invades and Occupies 136
Chapter 24: Bus to Freedom 143
Chapter 25: Marcela Alone 145
Chapter 26: The Secret Police..................................... 146
Chapter 27: Pilnost je Svoboda, 1969-1988..................... 153
Chapter 28: Life and Death in Kamp No. 12, 1970–1980. 159
Chapter 29: Revenge, 1981 163

Chapter 30: Hope and Slow Change, 1984...................... *166*
Chapter 31: Zuzana, 1987.. *170*
Chapter 32: Correspondence... *172*
Part Three: Change Is Coming, 1988–2014 .... *178*
Chapter 33: Luboš Is Released, 1988 .... *180*
Chapter 34: Transition... *191*
Chapter 35: Wilhelm's Family in Prague, June 1989....... *197*
Chapter 36: Reflection *205*
Chapter 37: Death Throes behind the Iron Curtain.......... *207*
Chapter 38: The Velvet Revolution and Tragedy.............. *210*
Chapter 39: Life Is a Kaleidoscope.................................. *214*
Chapter 40: Immigration to Crimea, 1992 .... *222*
Chapter 41: Lida and Libor Chart Their Paths *231*
Chapter 42: The Fisherman and the Garage.................... *240*
Chapter 43: Return to Vienna and Prague, 1995 .... *244*
Chapter 44: Lida and Libor in Business, 1998................. *252*
Chapter 45: Family... *258*
Chapter 46: Zuzana Visits Crimea, 2005......................... *271*
Chapter 47: Max Grows Up... *276*
Chapter 48: Father and Daughter Discuss Zuzana *283*
Chapter 49: Zuzana Returns to Feodosia, Autumn, 2013. *285*
Chapter 50: Libor Moves On, December 2013................. *290*
Chapter 51: Confrontation, February 2014...................... *294*
Chapter 52: Get Out of Ukraine! *300*
Acknowledgements *305*
About the Author *306*

ii

Maps

1934–2014

Crimea, Ukraine: 1991-2014

Names, Birth Date, Birthplace

Luboš Novák (Táta, Tatínek, Deda, Dedeček), 1934, North of Moldova/Ukraine border between Kamianets-Podilskyi and Chernivtsi

Max (Maksim), 2004, Feodosia, Crimea, Ukraine

Dmytro, later known as Luboš, 1934, North of Moldova/Ukraine border between Kamianets-Podilskyi and Chernivtsi

Anton (Tato), 1895, North of Moldova/Ukraine border between Kamianets-Podilskyi and Chernivtsi

Nadiya, 1896, North of Moldova/Ukraine border between Kamianets-Podilskyi and Chernivtsi

Aunt Alya, 1878, North of Moldova/Ukraine border between Kamianets-Podilskyi and Chernivtsi

Uncle Yarik, 1875, North of Moldova/Ukraine border between Kamianets-Podilskyi and Chernivtsi

Jan (Uncle), 1895, Kadan, Bohemia, Sudetenland

Josef Babiak (Uncle), 1871, Smižany, Slovakia, Austria-Hungary

Petra Babiaková, 1872, Smižany, Slovakia, Austria-Hungary

Marcela Burešová (Máma, Babička), 1932, Prague

Zuzana Burešová, 1931, Prague

Miluše Burešová (Maminka, Babička), 1910, Kojetice, Bohemia, Austria-Hungary

Černy, 1935, Prague

Wilhelm (Vater), 1917, Vienna

Lida Nováková (Máma), 1969, Vienna

Libor Novák, 1969, Vienna

Serhii, 1968, Donetsk, Ukraine

Mila Hellerová, 1972, Prague

Locations: City, Country (known later as)

Feodosia, Crimea: Ukraine (Annexed to the Russian Federation)

Kamianets-Podilskyi, Vinnystia: Ukraine

Chernivtsi: Romania (Ukraine)

Košice, Prešov, Smižany, Nováky, Bratislava: Slovak Region of Czechoslovakia (Slovakia)

Kadan, Bohemia, Prague, Kojetice, Kamp No. 12: Czech Region of Czechoslovakia (Czech Republic)

Vienna: Austria

Simferopol, Crimea: Ukraine (Annexed to the Russian Federation)

Prologue: Feodosia, Ukraine, 27 February 2014

The supreme art of war is to subdue the enemy without fighting.
Sun Tzu, *The Art of War*

Luboš didn't bother checking the morning news. The night before, Ukrainian television announcers had painted an optimistic picture for the country, confident that justice would prevail. The day's plan was set: Max would skip school to avoid bullying from Russian classmates and fish with his grandfather for winter shad on the shore of the Black Sea.

The violence that had resulted in more than 100 dead in Kyiv was over. President Viktor Yanukovych, fearing for his life, had fled the capital before the Verkhovna Rada, the parliament of Ukraine, could remove him from office. The vast Independence Square, the Maidan, was peaceful following days of restrained victory celebrations. Exhausted protestors studied the defaced statue of Lenin, upside down, laying on the cobblestones. The success of the democratic movement that became known as the Euromaidan promised integrity, civil rights, and respect for the law.

Max zipped his hooded jacket against the chill and grumbled like a typical ten-year-old. Luboš pushed last night's braided kalach bread into his pocket, and they set off as purple and orange hues yielded to the rising sun. A light breeze carried the wind offshore—perfect conditions for Max to cast his lure into the waters of the Crimean port of Feodosia. Their route along the narrow pedestrian street began in silence until they approached the coastline.

"What's that buzzing sound?"

Eighty-year-old Luboš, partially deaf from two decades as a political prisoner laboring in a quarry, didn't answer. Machinery noises in the distance echoed against the buildings and grew louder until he finally heard. He raised his chin, adjusted his hearing aids, and twisted his head to identify the racket. The wop-wop-wop of helicopter blades roared and then faded.

They rounded the last corner, stunned to see the Russian Federation Tricolor flying from the Genoese Fortress. Luboš stopped short, while a distraught Max stared straight ahead at the armored vehicles belching blue smoke into the frosty air. *Not again*, the grandfather thought.

Supply trucks with tires taller than Max lined the roads to the pierhead. Large warships patrolled the shore to block access to the Ukrainian Naval Forces port. Russian-speaking men unloaded pallets delivered by the recently departed helicopter.

Luboš pulled Max close when soldiers dressed in new, dark green uniforms without insignia approached. They wore balaclavas over their faces, and their eyes projected menace.

Max and Luboš eased toward the beach, only to see it crowded by inflatable boats disgorging armed men. A noisy hovercraft advanced toward them. An officer, his right hand atop the crisp new holster of his Makarov pistol, ordered them in Russian, "No fishing today. Go home."

They turned from the low winter sun. Luboš paused at the shadow's edge of the granite and bronze monument, "Feodosia Landing, 1941," commemorating the Red Army seaborne counteroffensive in World War II. No shots had been fired, yet the city was overrun. Stepping onto the shadow, he said, "Max, we have passed this statue many times. Today marks another invasion."

Max pulled his grandfather to a halt. "Deda, look!" He pointed to the jumble of sailing dinghies the neighborhood kids had stowed neatly away for the winter, now crushed by the heavy trucks. Luboš shuffled on.

2

"What's happening?" the boy asked his grandfather over the racket of forklifts moving pallets of military cargo.

Luboš held his words for a moment and absently grumbled in his mixed Russian, Czech, and Ukrainian dialect. "I heard that Russia might invade Crimea, like they did Georgia."

"The country near us?"

"Yes, the small country that is now even smaller," Luboš replied sarcastically. They turned to walk the shortest route home through the village green.

A gauntlet of belligerent-looking men dressed in a mix of camouflage pants and unmatched jackets scrolled with "Night Wolves" blocked their passage. They hefted Kalashnikov assault weapons and shiny new magazines.

"Why can't we fish from the pier or the beach?" Max asked.

"We have been invaded by the Russians—once again," Luboš muttered, too loudly. "They are bullies."

"Hey! Old man! What'd you say?" demanded one of the thugs, boots planted.

Luboš had survived the oppression of Communists, collaborators, and Nazis. He suspected the authoritarian President of the Russian Federation, Vladimir Putin, was sending a new message challenging Ukraine's recent parliamentary decisions. Summoning the hard-won strength of a survivor of tyranny, Luboš bristled, faced the leader, and demanded, "Have the Russians invaded Feodosia?"

The agitated man countered, "We are local volunteers, loyal to Russia."

"Why is the hammer and sickle flag alongside the Russian Tricolor? This is Ukraine."

"Old man, I can't understand you. You aren't from Ukraine. Crimea is returned to the Motherland. We are Novorossiya."

"I'm more Ukrainian than you, and so is the boy. I haven't seen such warships, and I have fished here for twenty-two years. What country has uniforms without insignia? When will they leave? When will YOU leave?"

Glowering over them, the leader growled, "If you want to see his next birthday, you better go to Kyiv while you can." He grabbed Luboš's fishing pole, grinned, and slowly bent it until it splintered. Max slipped behind his grandfather as a more aggressive man shouted obscenities, broke Max's new fiberglass pole, and stomped on their bait basket.

The leader yelled, "Get out of Crimea! Get out of Ukraine!"

As they eased away from the village green, Max said, "The television showed dead people in Kyiv. Do we have to go to Kyiv? Will there be shooting in Feodosia?"

"It's too late for shooting."

Familiar despair enveloped Luboš. He flashed back to his army duties during the Hungarian Uprising in 1956 and when Warsaw Pact tanks occupied Prague in 1968.

The Crimean city of Feodosia, 800 kilometers south of Kyiv on the Black Sea where Luboš and Max lived with Max's mother, had been spared the violence that had fractured cities in Ukraine for months. On the dispiriting walk home, church bells from All Saints Church rang eight times, but the day seemed over. He realized the hard-won years of happiness with his family were threatened.

Max dragged his feet and mumbled, "I'm afraid."

Luboš dropped the shattered rods and led his grandson home.

"Max, hold my hand."

Part One: A Difficult Decade, 1934–1944

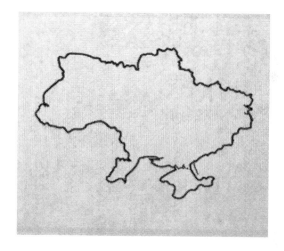

Ukraine

Chapter 1: Peasant Farmers, 1934

"Here, Nadiya. Dig the ditch over here to divert water from the pond," Anton called out through the sheet of rain pelting his face.

"Then the road will wash out," she yelled back, soaking wet in the shapeless brown overcoat of a peasant woman.

"We rebuild the road every year." Pointing to the fast-running water, he persisted. "This rain is worse. If we don't dig here, the dam at the pond will collapse and flood the low land and barn. Ask Aunt Alya to bring a shovel."

Nadiya leaned into the harsh wind to rewrap the heavy black scarf that kept rain from trailing down her back. "She is tending Dmytro."

Before he was Luboš, the infant had been named Dmytro, lover of the earth. Dmytro's life began in 1934 at the fringes of the former Soviet Empire in southwestern Ukraine, where fertile fields and smooth terrain proved irresistible to covetous tribes and competing powers. The legacy of nature's richness was a bloodland of shifting frontiers, various languages, rival religions, and countless dead.

Former serfs in Imperial Russia, generations of Dmytro's family had been free tenants since the 1870s cultivating their small allotment within their commune, the Russian social and land-holding system. Decades earlier, the elders of the commune deemed their land unsuitable for re-divisions and granted them perpetual use of their remote plot. Land on either side was unproductive, and their closest neighbor was kilometers away.

After the Bolshevik Revolution, Nadiya and Anton, Dmytro's mother and father, carried on farming as peasant owners, assisted by Nadiya's Uncle Yarik and Aunt Alya. Now they feared their land would be seized to complete the kolkhoz, the local collective.

Snowmelt, spring rains, and a swollen stream that flowed to the Dniester River plagued their rocky patch not far from the borders of Moldova and Romania in the Vinnytsia Oblast. These downpours drowned their crops and blocked the only road to the village.

The deluge didn't threaten the goat shed or chicken coop on high ground adjacent to the farmhouse. The rutted road led to the mire at the barn, which Yarik called "cursed" because it was situated close to the outhouse at a lower elevation than the pond. The barn flooded too often, but neighbors who could have helped frame a new barn were either dead or exiled to Siberia.

Rain was still falling at dusk when they completed the trench. Anton, Nadiya, and her uncle and aunt ducked through the doorframe under the low thatched roof. Inside the cramped hut, they set their muddy boots at the entrance and hooked their wet outer clothing on wooden pegs. Baby Dmytro slept in his box. The foursome sat exhausted on two rough-cut benches at the tiny table.

No one noticed that the typical odors of sweat, long-worn clothing, and manure on their boots were worse than usual after days of soaking rain. The straw roof deadened the sound of heavy rain peppering the house but did little to slow the leaks. They didn't have the energy for conversation. Their sunken eyes stared at the floor.

An unframed photo of Nadiya and Anton at their wedding, clay jars empty of spices, and woven baskets to barter in the village, rested on crude shelves. The base of the ladder to the loft was nailed to boards hiding their hoarded root vegetables and the cross of the Ukrainian Autocephalous Orthodox Church.

Nadiya and Aunt Alya had stuffed fragrant wildflowers, especially lavender, into the rafters in a futile

8

challenge to the smell of the unwashed farmers. The flowers' scent and color had surrendered to the dark, smoky interior. Although the family had lived there for decades, it was barely a home.

Hair matted by the rain, a relieved Anton broke the silence, "The barn will be safe. I'm not sure about the wheat."

"The sun will return," usually pessimistic Uncle Yarik announced. "There is no more water in the sky."

After consuming Aunt Alya's hearty borscht cabbage soup, Uncle Yarik read from the family Bible in flickering firelight. They possessed no resources for candles or an oil lamp. Nadiya asked her husband, "If this rain continues, will we lose the winter wheat crop?"

Nadiya and Anton were born at the turn of the century and descended from a long line of hardy peasants. Experience and adversity had been their teachers. Nadiya had been attractive in her youth, with a pleasing round face, full lips, and a husky voice. Her tapered nose, high hairline, thin eyebrows, and chocolate brown eyes were reminders of why Anton had been drawn to her.

Now with gray threads of hair, she was stout and weathered from relentless farm work yet still attractive. Nadiya heaved a hoe with her calloused hands and powerful arms better than Anton, whose war wounds hampered his work in the field. In their peasant society, she was an assertive woman.

Nadiya's simple practicality prompted her to ask worrisome questions, forcing her more complaisant husband to think ahead. He was self-conscious about his thin mustache and narrow mouth, and he conversed in soft tones. His lackluster eyes hid behind the river of wrinkles wandering his face. Terror from war, limits on physical strength, and an energetic wife led Anton to be a listener.

"If the rain stops tonight and we have sunny weather," Anton said quietly, "the seeds in the upper field will germinate. Then we can harvest the winter crop near the barn."

Nadiya, Anton, and Uncle Yarik resumed their seasonal grousing about too much or too little rain and the quality of the seeds. Even if they delivered a plentiful spring harvest, they would barely meet quota.

Yarik was a tireless peasant born after serfdom had been abolished. With Aunt Alya, he had farmed his communal plot close to the village for 40 years. His white beard grew high on his cheeks and swept down to his sternum. His broad nostrils flared, and his brown eyes glistened when he let loose his anger at Communism. He ran his fingers through his wavy gray locks until Alya bumped him with her elbow.

He was traditional in his ways, the first to rise in the morning, and the best reaper despite his age. And he was bitter. He snapped off a piece of stale bread and chimed in with comments he voiced all too often. "Taxes. That's why we were forced off our land."

Komnezamy activists, fellow peasants, had legally seized his land to force him to the Collective system where peasants worked, attached to what had been their land. But Nadiya's aunt and uncle had refused and moved into Anton's cramped hut to help work the farm.

Yarik said firmly, "First we were peasant serfs, then peasants under the thumb of the landowners, then came the communes. Now the collectives want to control us. Your Aunt Alya and I go to the city and beg in the streets before going to the Collective. And what about the baby in these times?"

Alya was a head shorter than her husband, with white curls that refused to stay put and dark shadows under her old brown eyes. She was a feisty companion who tried to temper his passionate opinions. The two sixty-year-olds preferred the Tsar to the Communists.

"They wanted the horse and land more than you and the taxes," Anton chided him. "Tomorrow, they can say Nadiya and I are class enemies or kulaks or bourgeois profiting from your labor, and we all go to Siberia. They can do that or anything." Anton spoke with the resignation of a man without power or recourse.

Not known for plentiful harvests, their plot yielded little. After the sun shone for several days, the peasant family cut and tied the wheat into stacked sheaves to dry. Alya spread their damp clothing on a rope strung between a post on the chicken coop and a hook on the hut. They cut tree branches to mend the stick fence of the goat corral, repacked mud into gaps in the hut walls, and repaired the road. Nadiya, Yarik, and Alya threshed and winnowed the wheat onto the tarpaulins while Anton busied himself in the barn.

Anton's bowed legs pained him to walk and limited his ability to move heavy sacks of grain. Conscripted in 1915 into the Imperial Russian Army to fight the Germans, he had suffered leg wounds and had been evacuated before the onset of winter, when the healthy soldiers froze. He considered himself blessed to have survived with only a painful limp. His mild temperament and agreeable disposition carried him through adversity.

Even though Anton had limited strength, Nadiya encouraged him any way she could. While nursing Dmytro after a satisfying day in the field, she found ways to compliment him. "You were the best dancer at our church festivals."

"My friends and I practiced showing off for the girls," he joked, rising from the short stool and raised his crippled leg in the air as if to dance.

"My father recommended you. I had his blessing," Nadiya affectionately added.

"With two good legs, I would be the best dancer. Then the war. Now the festivals are banned."

"We have our baby. He will dance."

The harvest was ample, and the couple prepared to deliver wheat to the village to acquire seeds and trade for a second horse. Nadiya would face the unscrupulous weighmaster who always complained about the grain quality and shorted them ration coupons. No peasant dared argue with the pudgy Communist who refused to speak Ukrainian.

"I will load the wagon," Yarik said while bouncing the baby on his knee. "If they give you enough coupons, bring home salt for the fish."

"First, we need another horse," answered Anton, ever mindful of taxes. The Tsar's army had confiscated the healthy horses in the world war, and the Communists did the same during induced famines that targeted Ukrainian peasants. The horse and plow would replace the rakes and crude hoes Anton had fashioned from the skeletons of vehicles destroyed in battles for Ukrainian independence. "Then, I will look for foot wrappings."

Intemperate Yarik complained about the twenty years of Bolshevik policies: The New Economic Plan, purges in the village, General Secretary of the Communist Party of the Soviet Union Joseph Stalin's Collectivization, exiled Kulaks, Five-Year Plans, and more. Yarik pressed on. "What do we have? Not much. They stole our grinding stone to prevent us from making flour. Look to the east. A cloud of smoke on the horizon means a peasant is burning his crop before it is confiscated. Except for Moscow, people starve in the city. People starve on the farm. How can a farmer in Ukraine die of hunger?"

"Quiet. You will upset the baby," Alya scolded her husband.

Anton called for him to calm down and chided, "You and Alya watched me go to war and the tragedies that have chased us. Say that in the village and the Communist leaders won't waste space on the 6,000-kilometer cattle-car train ride to Siberia. It will be a bullet for each of us."

Yarik didn't stop his rant. "The new representatives who have no hair on their face and soft hands control us. They don't speak Ukrainian. They are the ones who are fat and shoot us. And we have to beg for seed."

"Enough, Yarik," Nadiya declared. "Give me the baby. He needs to hear pleasant words."

Chapter 2: Little Dmytro

Dmytro was born into a police state of a flawed economy, a fractured society, and the vengeful depopulation of the peasant class. The famine of the early 1930s was the last straw designed to complete the collapse of the Ukrainian resistance. Oblivious of this, the baby wiggled and slept in his blanket wrapped tight to his mother or Alya as they worked in the field.

"He is hungry," Aunt Alya announced, walking across the uneven furrows to deliver the baby to Nadiya. During the planting season, the two women sang in unison with the swing of their hoes, making their work seem more tolerable. During harvest, the sweep of the scythe was smoother, and the rhythmic motions kept Dmytro sleepy, bundled in the shawl. To nurse, he cried out in sync with the sweep.

"The baby gets a midday meal, and we don't," Yarik griped. "Before the so-called October Revolution, Alya brought us our meal in the field. We had plenty to eat. It isn't Nadiya's fault, but we haven't eaten those meals in years."

"Yarik," Nadiya insisted. "Stop."

The four adults played with the baby and discussed the weather, the condition of the barn, and Dmytro's rapid growth. The baby reveled in the attention. His great uncle carved horses or fish while Aunt Alya wove figures from straw for him. Yarik strummed the round-bodied five-string kobza that he had constructed when he courted Alya. She hummed or sang psalms to bolster her spirits. Her clear voice resounded inside the home and when outside, across the field. Yarik, Anton, and Nadiya chimed in to lift their minds from the toil. The humming was soothing to Dmytro whenever Alya carried him.

13

For twenty years, either Anton or Nadiya had delivered their grain to a nearby small village. It was now deserted. Large plots of burial grounds and buildings stripped of wood reflected the heavy hand of Collectivism. When Nadiya drove, either Yarik or Anton rode along to protect her from marauding gangs of starving peasants.

Sitting beside Nadiya on the wagon's bench was one of Yarik's long-haired, mongrel dogs; the other dog guarded the farmhouse. Baby Dmytro slept in a basket until a pothole in the dirt road jolted him awake. Nadiya tapped her breast where her cross had once hung and sarcastically mocked the large Stalin poster, "Thank you, Comrade Stalin," that she would pass in the slow-moving queue at the government store.

Their now-longer trips on the slab-sided wagon or the sleigh to the village west of Kamianets-Podilskyi lasted the entire day. The unpaved road was rough, and their mare, Blackie, pulled the double-axle cart down rolling hills. The less familiar countryside was brown and lifeless as they passed tree stumps of old orchards and foundations of abandoned farmhouses. Anton had scavenged one for glass for their only window.

Songbirds did not return from southern migrations, and there were no neighbors to hail. Squeaking wheels interrupted the silence until they heard Radio Moscow blaring propaganda from loudspeakers at the town square. The atmosphere in the village was glum. The granary, reconfigured by the Communists, filled a once beautiful church where Nadiya's aunt and uncle had once worshiped. Lumber taken from its steeple built the gallows at the town's entrance.

When he was old enough to sit on the wagon bench, Nadiya distracted her son from noticing the bones of starved peasants along the roadside. His earliest memories at age four were electric lights in the stark concrete government provision store and scrawny peasants in ragged clothing. Dmytro's parents tensed up and spoke Russian in the village.

Years later, he remembered the fear in his mother's eyes and the watchful gaze of his father. Nadiya complained to anyone they met about their poor land so no one would deem it worth seizing.

Nadiya maneuvered Blackie through the village past the scrutiny of officials and fellow peasants. "How is your little boy?" one of the dreaded prodrazvyorstka confiscation squad members remarked. "He is chubby. I will check when we last inspected your farm."

Peasant neighbors in their district had starved in the famines or continued to disappear if they did not adhere to Communist directives. Stalin's Great Terror was underway. Nadiya briefed her son. "Don't talk in the village except to the doctor. I'll hold your hand, and if I squeeze it, hush up." He rarely heard harsh words from her and scowled, trying to understand. The family couldn't risk an innocent slip of the tongue to an informant about the hidden root cellar by the goat corral or the apples from their remote orchard.

As Dmytro grew, his mother taught him to churn goat milk for butter and, if there was vinegar in the jar, to make tvorog farmer's cheese. He would keep the chickens away from the precious planting seed, helped slaughter chickens, collected eggs, and weeded the remote vegetable garden.

"You squirt more milk to the cats than to the bucket," Nadiya complained to her son.

"They are thirsty."

"We are thirsty. Fill the urn, clean the horse stall, and draw water from the well," she said impatiently.

"Yes, Mama." Dmytro was an obedient child with a playful streak. He signaled to the dogs to come for a squirt and addressed them: "Shhh, don't tell."

"Why did they assign you a horse?" Nadiya asked her husband upon his return from the village.

"The Collective was below quota. They sent the peasants to Siberia and took their horses. I overheard gossip

15

in the village that their tractors were broken. They complained about the lack of spare parts. Instead of punishing the tractor makers, they convicted the peasants."

"Anton, did you enter the conversation?"

"No. My back was turned. I adjusted the halter while listening."

"Thank goodness. That was smart," Nadiya exhaled.

"I see her ribs," Yarik chimed in. "That horse is scrawnier than the peasants in the village."

"They gave us this plow and expect us to till additional land. The seed is for rye, and they raised our quota."

"Rye will do poorly in our soil," Uncle Yarik said. "Why rye this year?"

"They require black bread to feed prisoners and didn't give me a choice. Glad I had two horses to pull the extra weight uphill. They don't quarrel and are a good team. Dmytro and I will take her to graze in the hills tomorrow and fill her stomach."

"Tato," Dmytro eagerly interrupted his father, "can we name her Brownie? Can she be mine?" The horse's gaunt frame did not dampen the boy's enthusiasm.

"Brownie is an appropriate name," Anton said approvingly. He patted the boy on the head. "Treat her well, and you and the Communists will own her."

Each draft horse had plowed the earth for years in a Collective and was docile enough for a five-year-old to ride. In short order, Dmytro, wearing his bast shoes, was behind the plow beside his uncle, learning to keep his furrows straight. He was full of energy and eager to please.

"Tell me the *Pea-Roll Along* tale again," Dmytro encouraged Alya, even though he could recite the entire story. He loved her folk songs, stories, and legends.

"Little one," Alya replied, sipping hot tea brewed from tree bark and herbs, "do you enjoy that tale for the dragon or the princess?"

"The dragon. The evil dragon is slain. I don't know a princess."

"Well, someday a princess will find you," Alya replied optimistically. He listened to stories about his grandparents and visualized the beautiful dresses, sashes, and embroidered tunics they wore for Orthodox Church festivals. The Communist atheists had executed bishops and confiscated churches before his birth. His only religious connections were pictures of those festivals and the illegal costumes worn secretly on holidays and hidden from inspectors.

"Life was better when we believed in God," Anton reminisced. Each night Yarik read from their tattered Bible. At a word of God or church, Alya raised her voice in one of her favorite hymns to take herself to the promise of God's strength over evil.

When one of them spoke in a subdued voice too softly for Dmytro to hear, the topic was usually the village, Collectivism, famine, or something else out of their control. The mandate to grow more grain on their plot of land drove their lives. Fear dominated their life outside the farm.

Peasants, Communist activist ideologues, and informants threatened their lives, and the isolated family trusted no one. What they had witnessed about Communism drove them to despise it. By the mid-1930s, most farms had been collectivized. The specter of seizure and displacement haunted Anton.

"Over here, Dmytro." Nadiya implored the boy to stand at the ladder over the illegal storage space. He felt his parents' fear and watched investigators poke their iron rods, searching for hidden voids or false walls to hide valuables or grain. If caught hoarding, they would be sent to Siberia. They purposely let their mud hut appear shabby and the barn unsafe to discourage thorough searches where the inspectors might find the potatoes and beets.

To keep his family safe, Anton was coerced into a bargain with certain Communist officials. Anton was given

17

extra ration coupons if he provided vegetables from Nadiya's distant garden. Arrangements were delicate.

"Comrade Anton, the inspection is complete. You met your quota," the apparatchik complimented, "and we are pleased you support our socialist goals. How old is your boy?'

"He is six."

"He is healthy. My wife has a new baby. If you have extra potatoes, I will remember." Anton never initiated an offer, but he responded to requests from an official he hoped to trust. However dedicated they were to the principles of socialism, an official's need for food overrode doctrine.

Uncle Yarik began to teach the boy Ukrainian Cyrillic letters and numbers by playing the card game Durak, where the loser is the last one holding cards. His great aunt and uncle were much older and had saved colorful Lubok prints of their youth and kopeck newspapers, named for the coin of the realm. Dmytro relished looking at the tattered pages, and his often-ornery uncle did his best to coach him to read and write a handful of phrases of Ukrainian and Russian.

Though Anton and Yarik read and wrote limited Ukrainian and Russian, the women were illiterate. Nadiya said to her husband, "A detachment of Young Pioneers in the village teaches children, even girls. I want to send Dmytro."

"They may teach writing and reading, but mainly they teach Lenin and Stalin. We live too far from the school."

"Dmytro should write proper," Nadiya insisted, leaning over her unresponsive husband.

Chapter 3: Fishing Together

Anton's sole respite was fishing with his son in streams or at their pond. Aunt Alya had unwound thread from grain sacks to make crude fishing lines to attach to the hooks that Anton bent from scrap wire. He taught Dmytro how to cast the long pole and where to send the hook and bobber. Water at the pond was smoother than the flowing stream, and Dmytro learned the difference between a nibble and a bite on the hook. The boy followed the line weaving left and right, flicking beads of water off the tense line as the fish swam to break free.

Sitting under the shade of the willow tree, Dmytro complained. "I don't want to dig for worms. They are squishy and squirm around. Why do the fish eat them?"

"When I put them on the hook, they wiggle. Fish chase the movement."

"I don't like taking the hook out while the fish flops."

"You are learning about nature—it's your name. You have caught a good size trout. You have watched me clean and gut the fish. Now it is your turn."

"Your knife is too big for me. Will you make one for me?"

"Ah, tomorrow will be a fine day to pick apples at the orchard. We will pass the old trucks in the gully and find metal for your knife."

"Pick herbs and mushrooms in the forest," Nadiya mentioned to her husband that evening. "Show Dmytro which ones are non-poisonous and bring back all you can carry."

Anton and his son rode Brownie far into the hills and forest to their hidden orchard. They kept alert for signs of wild boar to shoot. Generations earlier, his grandparents

19

had cut down a remote stand of pine trees to plant apple seedlings. Ever since, the family had cut straight saplings or long watersprouts in the spring to replace fishing poles, rake handles, and tines. In the fall, they picked and dried apples.

"Help me bend this metal strip." Anton was unable to tell which vehicles were Bolshevik or White Russian or Nationalist from that decade of conflict. Their saw was for cutting wood, not metal. They rocked a beam of the roof back and forth until the metal weakened and broke off. Anton said, "This long piece will make a scythe blade, a heavy cleaver for clearing brush, and your knife."

"I'll have a sword and slay dragons," Dmytro declared, making imaginary sword thrusts in the air.

"Well, there are dragons."

"Look, Tato. The dogs are barking at a man on a covered cart," Dmytro said excitedly as he stood up and dropped his pole at the edge of their pond.

"He must be lost," replied Anton. He turned around half-asleep, waiting for a fish to strike.

"He stopped. The dogs frighten him."

"He doesn't seem dangerous."

The slumping horse and the frightened, bedraggled man waited for Anton and Dmytro, who were trailed by Nadiya, Yarik, and Alya. To the stranger's relief, Yarik whistled his dogs quiet. The man submissively approached a few steps at a time and asked for directions to Kamianets-Podilskyi, adding, "It is a beautiful city. I ought to go before I die."

Anton pointed the way. "It has a large fortress. We deliver our grain in a different direction and haven't been there."

"I'm trying to stay off the main roads." The stick-thin man paused and asked, "Do you want a picture of your family?"

"Same as the ones of Lenin and Stalin?" Yarik quizzed.

"A picture, yes, but of your family. I print them in my cart."

"Pictures were once taken at the church festivals." Laughing, Yarik said, "Ha, today, the camera comes to us."

"We don't have ration coupons," Nadiya interjected. "We don't have kopecks."

"Owning a camera and taking your money is illegal," the man confessed. "I'm hungry and have to trust you. Will you give me a good meal?"

"How do you have that camera?" Anton asked. "You can be shot."

"I was a storekeeper. The young agitators from Moscow descended on us and closed independent shops. They found several of my cameras. I have been hiding the rest of my equipment since 1928. It's a miracle the chemicals survived."

"And a miracle you are alive. Informants are everywhere."

"I don't have much time remaining. I take pictures of what the Communists have done to us. Someone has to."

"Yarik is correct," Nadiya broke in. "We will have pictures. What do we do?"

"I'll position my camera. You line up in front of the farmhouse."

Yarik and Alya stood behind Anton, Nadiya, and Dmytro, and the itinerant photographer shot several pictures. "Can we have a picture at the pond?" Dmytro requested, jumping up and down.

Later, the photographer squeezed into their hut and delivered the mostly pocket-sized pictures. Stiffly erect, side-by-side in front of the hut and at the pond, they wore no smiles.

"That's me?" an amazed Dmytro declared. The meal was the best Nadiya could offer and the peddler's best in weeks.

"We will hide your pictures and say you passed in the night," Anton said to conclude the visit. "Please don't keep one for yourself."

Uncle Yarik was pleased the boy now had a memento of his youth. Confidently, Uncle said, "These pictures at the pond will last longer than Stalin."

Chapter 4: The Germans, 1941

Relations between Anton and Party officials remained strained. The trip to the village became more dangerous when the Red Army moved west to invade and occupy much of Poland per the undisclosed Molotov-Ribbentrop Pact of 1939. The two leaders—Chancellor Adolf Hitler of Germany and Soviet Union leader Joseph Stalin—had agreed to spheres to divide Europe from Finland to Romania. The family worried that Anton would be conscripted for his second war against the Germans.

"What is conscripted?" Dmytro asked.

"An oblast has a quota to send men to fight. If young men are already at war, older men my age will be next. The army is supposed to defend the Motherland, but no mother steals our food and gives us famine the way these Communists do." Nevertheless, Anton did not consider fleeing to the hills to join nationalist partisans.

Though Anton was too pained to walk behind the plow, he was deemed healthy enough to fight again in 1940, this time for the Soviet Empire. His wife and six-year-old son drove the cart to the village, where Anton stiffly climbed aboard a canvas-covered military truck packed with older, infirm peasants.

"Tato, when will you come back?" a forlorn Dmytro asked, peering up from the dirt road.

"They won't tell us. When I return, you will be a man." He carried one of the new family pictures, unsure he would live to see his wife and son again.

At the farmhouse, Nadiya was silent, Alya prayed out loud, and Dmytro ignored his fishing pole. They were somber and grew accustomed to Anton's absence. Meals lacked the typical comments about the weather or growth of the rye seedlings.

Yarik, tired of playing mournful music on his maple kobza, changed the mood by pointing out overdue farm work. Nadiya gathered her strength and announced, "Tomorrow, we will prepare the field near the barn and then weed the northwest corner. Dmytro, clean the stalls. Yesterday's rain softened the earth. It will be a good day."

After the seeds were in the ground, the family awaited a balance of rain and sun. They set out to repair the leaking roof, move the privy past the pond, and raise the chicken coop. Uncle Yarik was too unsteady to repair the thatched roof. He taught his grandnephew his technique of bending the straw ends into a knot and stuffing them into the hole.

"Your father will be proud of you. These months you do the work of two men," Yarik proudly exclaimed.

A soldier more literate than Anton wrote letters for him. They described his tasks to dismantle factories for shipment east and his deployment to the new German-Soviet border in former Poland.

On June 22, 1941, a year after Anton reentered the army, the Germans breached the Molotov-Ribbentrop Pact. They launched a massive invasion, Operation Barbarossa, into the Soviet Union along a front from the Baltics to the Black Sea. Stalin's Great Terror had decimated the ranks of Russian Empire officers and intelligence service. He had ignored evidence of German war preparations and missed the opportunity to mobilize his forces to defend his country.

Just as Nadiya's plot of land held little value as a farm, the immediate area in their oblast was of limited military importance. The Red Army was deployed north and south of them for strategic defense, and the family watched and listened to battles from a safe distance.

The attacking German aircraft indicated the progress of the German Wehrmacht, the combined forces of the army, Heer, and the air force, Luftwaffe. Control of the sky by the

Luftwaffe enabled their army to advance. Black smoke from burning Russian or German airplanes in a slow-motion death spiral painted the sky. In the distance, nightlong artillery barrages electrified the darkness; the explosions flickered as shells found their targets. They felt the earth tremble, and Nadiya imagined her husband wounded and limping among the bomb craters.

German ground forces quickly overran Soviet defenses in well-planned attacks. The family did not sleep for days until quiet dawned after the Wehrmacht swept past them deep into Ukraine. Chaotically, Soviet forces had abandoned positions.

Desperate refugees fleeing the carnage told of murdered village leaders and Jews massacred in Kamianets-Podilskyi by the Nazis.

"We are farmers. What can we do?" Nadiya asked Yarik.

"Why do we have an army if they don't fight? I bet the Communist village leaders are safe in Moscow. Poor Anton."

"Poor us. Only German airplanes fly over the countryside. Best we dig the spring beets and hide them."

Ukrainians were ordered to report to the town square. En route, Nadiya passed dead men and women hanging from trees and fresh dirt above burial pits. Birds pecked at the decaying corpses and flies swarmed in the summer heat. Massive flags of red, white, and black swastikas swung from the tallest buildings.

"What did they do wrong?" the boy wanted to know as they passed beneath the dead.

"Maybe nothing. Yarik, you put us at risk when you speak your mind," replied Nadiya. She was aware of the organized extermination of any dissenters and the Jewish population.

"I will be silent."

Once the peasants assembled, the blond Reichskommissariat commander entered on his 16-hand horse and, with the morning sun behind, stopped. The frightened, shabbily dressed peasants squinted at him in silence. He eyed them for two minutes from his imperious position. The silence was penetrating—even the crows stopped squawking.

He took the microphone and ranted for five minutes over the loudspeakers that formerly had broadcast Radio Moscow. "Russians, Ukrainians ... Your army deserted you ... I demand your adherence to our laws ... saboteurs hang from the trees at the entrance to your town... Germans advance easily to Stalingrad... an act of defiance will be dealt with immediately... keep your crops under cultivation... hoarders will be shot... carry your identification papers... Heil Hitler!" The new master was even more brutal than the last.

"You, why are you head of the family?" challenged a German officer in broken Ukrainian at the registration table. Nadiya's farm plot was circled on a map.

"My husband is in the army," she replied in her new, broken German.

"What about these two?" he asked, aiming his pen at Alya and Yarik.

"They are my uncle and aunt."

"How old are they?"

"Sixty-five."

"They will go to the area to the right. You and the boy finish registration."

"Why are we separated?" Nadiya asked deferentially, squeezing Dmytro's arm to avoid erupting in tears. "Where are they going?"

"Away."

"Herr Oberscharfuher, you see our land on the map and our quotas. I cannot meet the quota unless they stay." Nadiya did not beg or reveal weakness. "Our farm has met Communist quotas because my aunt and uncle do most of the work."

The officer looked for a minute at Nadiya, the boy, Yarik, and Alya. "Okay. Register them, and we will raise your quota."

"Danke," Nadiya replied, and she relaxed her grip—the foursome intact.

"My arm hurts," Dmytro said after the identity papers were issued.

"I was worried. I'm sorry. They almost sent Uncle Yarik and Aunt Alya to labor camps in Germany."

"You saved our lives," Alya cried, and she and Yarik hugged Nadiya after they boarded their wagon to retreat to their farm.

"Thank God he changed his mind."

The Nazi administrators inspected the formerly productive Ukrainian farmland to resettle Germans into what they called Lebensraum, the "living space" to efficiently grow crops for the Third Reich. The German populace was under food rationing, and the Nazis demanded grain to ship home.

Half a year after registration, Dmytro pointed to a trail of dust. "A car is coming. We never see cars."

"Tell Alya to hide the Bible," Nadiya directed. The fast-moving German auto bumping and bouncing on the dirt road meant trouble. It skidded to a stop, and a young Volksdeutsche family poured out. Two yellow-headed children rushed to the pond. Their father walked to the barn. The dogs barked at the car's driver as he unpacked luggage. Nadiya called to Yarik. "Calm the dogs."

The mother pushed in to survey her new home. Nadiya, powerless, followed her. The visitor put her hands on her hips, kicked the bench, and yelled into Nadiya's face. Nadiya trembled and appealed to Uncle Yarik. "Your German is better than mine. Talk to her."

Yarik answered the woman. "Nein. Nein. Nein."

"What is she saying?"

"They have been assigned to our farm and are ready to move into our hut. She asked questions. I told her the road washes out after light rain, and we don't meet quota.

"Tell them the roof leaks over my head and the well runs dry in summer."

The woman stalked outside, yelling at the driver until he reloaded the auto. The Germans piled in, less than ten minutes after their arrival, and stormed off beneath the same trail of dust.

As terrible as the Nazis were, unless you were Jewish, numerous Ukrainians viewed the conquerors better than Stalin. Co-opted Ukrainians joined the Organization of Ukrainian Nationalists to form army divisions to fight the Soviets, promised that Ukrainian independence would follow. Ukrainians of a different mindset linked with the Ukrainian Auxiliary Police under the German Reichskommissariat to administratively govern under the supervision of the Gestapo. Nazis or Communists eventually killed members of both factions.

A young Ukrainian fleeing to the partisans told of the Red Army falling back. "Trains make their way to forced labor camps in Germany jammed with Russian prisoners. The dead are pushed out when they unlock the doors to throw food in. We are in disarray in Stalingrad."

"Oh no," sighed Nadiya. Anton had survived war, the Communists, and the famines. Could he survive the Germans a second time?

"Is Tato on a train? Is he in Stalingrad?"

Holding her son's shoulders, she admitted frankly, "Dear, I don't know. We haven't heard from your father in two years." Nadiya struggled to believe her husband was alive. She was thankful that Dmytro was strong enough at age eight to keep pace in the field with aging Alya and Yarik.

During this new foreign conquest, the family walked a fine line to avoid offending any authorities. They avoided interaction with possible Ukrainian informants, stayed apart from German colonists, met the harvest quota, and hid their vegetables.

Dmytro's mother tightened her scarf over her head and around her neck whenever she approached the colorless village to deliver grain. She reckoned she was safer with her son because the soldiers played football with Dmytro. The Germans were lucky to be stationed in this unimportant village instead of on the front lines to the east. They were confident and cheerful. They played strange musical instruments and sang lively German ballads in a rustic beer hall. Nadiya wondered at the clean-shaven men in their neat uniforms who contrasted with the haggard, bearded peasants. She worried that Dmytro would admire these cheerful Germans.

Nadiya rotated the farm's crops and delivered grain regularly. While she didn't show it, she welcomed the sight of an older silver-headed Heer Unteroffizer. He was polite and adjusted the weight of the grain in their favor to give them extra ration stamps and Karbovanets, the currency introduced by the Germans. She did not ask why but offered a slight smile. He was attentive to her and quick to smile back. In his mixed Ukrainian, he said, "I have a grandson the boy's age. Please give him these treats on your way home. Where is your farm?"

"To the west." Changing the subject, she said, "We need Karbovanets for salt and shoes. We have woven baskets and carved animals to barter."

"I will buy them to send back to my home," he enthusiastically replied. "May I come to your farm?"

"No, no. Don't come," she quickly responded. "I will bring them next time."

"My name is Jan."

Nadiya acknowledged him with a dip of her head.

After the weighing, Jan lifted Dmytro onto a bicycle seat and pushed him on the dirt street, smiling at the boy's cries of joy. He gave football advice in the former churchyard, coaching, "Bend your knees to change direction. Dribble with the side of your boot."

"Mutter, I'm learning some German words," he said enthusiastically.

"Ja, a good idea," she admitted, as she walked on one of the streets renamed in German.

29

Sabotage was one way to thwart the Nazis, and rail lines were frequent targets of Communist or Ukrainian Nationalist irregular partisans. Harboring or aiding them meant torture until death. When the partisans of the UPA— the Ukrainian Insurgent Army—found Nadiya's uncle harvesting apples from the orchard, they threatened the family. Nadiya was compelled to relay UPA messages back and forth to supporters in the village. The family was now in danger from both the Germans and partisans.

❖ ❖ ❖ ❖ ❖

The Red Army had defended Stalingrad two years earlier, and Dmytro, age nine and in his third year of German occupation, sensed increased tension among the invaders. He and Nadiya drove to the granary past swastika flags, faded pink.

"They don't play football anymore," the boy said, dragging his mother to the yard. Large German Luftwaffe transport planes had flown unopposed high overhead, but the dominance had shifted, Russian aircraft on the offensive bombed German targets. Dmytro was glad, once again, that their farm was far from rail depots. Smaller fighters met high in the sky, threading thin white lines, until one of them— maybe Russian, maybe German—was shot down.

As the battles continued to go against them, German support troops were sent east to fight with the Ostheer at the front. To the west, the Slovak National Uprising of August 1944 forced the Nazis to become more brutal defenders of their conquered lands. Airplanes fought daily in the skies as the battle lines of the retreating Germans drew closer.

The family knew that at any time, a Ukrainian partisan, a Nazi official, or a drunken soldier might take their lives. And they knew the godless Communists would be even more savage upon their return from the east.

"Men flee to the mountains, sometimes stealing from our barn," Nadiya remarked. "There must be more we don't see."

"What can four of us do?" Aunt Alya asked as Dmytro's family deliberated whether to quit their sanctuary of generations.

"We can run to the hills with our vegetables and die," Yarik answered.

"Yarik, such talk is not helpful."

After three years of Nazi subjugation, Nadiya didn't expect her husband would return. Staying and hoping was not enough. However, they had no plan.

Chapter 5: The Deserter, 1944

Before the first rooster crowed, the dogs barked and growled, holding their ground at the entrance to the barn. From the darkness, a terrified Dmytro shouted, "Mama, a German is in the barn!"

Nadiya was first out the door, pointing the hunting rifle. The aunt and uncle collected their butcher knives and followed. The fur on the backs of the dogs stood straight up, waiting for Yarik's approval to kill. The soldier cautiously stepped out, laid his rifle on the ground, and slowly raised his arms. He was more frightened than the farmers.

With her rifle aimed at his heart, Nadiya commanded, "On the ground!" surprising herself and her uncle. "Yarik, take his weapons."

In the dim pre-dawn light, Nadiya challenged, "Who are you?"

"My name is Jan." Immediately, Dmytro and Nadiya recognized the voice of the soldier who weighed their grain in the village.

Nadiya signaled her uncle to whistle his dogs quiet. She moved her finger from the trigger and demanded, "How did you find our farm?"

"The boy gave me some landmarks." She frowned at her son.

"Why did you give us extra kilos on the scale?"

"In you, I saw my family. I tried to be generous."

"Why are you here?"

"I am a deserter."

In his desperate mixture of Ukrainian, Russian, and German, he explained, "I was happy to do a favor. I'm a

32

farmer from the Sudetenland at the Czechoslovak and German border. I was conscripted into the army before the invasion of Poland. I'm not a Nazi. They don't trust me on the front lines."

Nadiya considered killing the deserter to claim the bounty. Reluctant to believe him, she kept her rifle leveled at him and directed, "Sit up. Keep talking,"

Jan sat cross-legged on the dirt, yielding to Nadiya, and presented his observations—and his proposal. "I'm Czech. German colonists displaced my family the same as here. To resist conscription in 1939 meant death or a labor camp."

Jan had to convince them, mainly Nadiya, quickly.

"I have been pulled into my second war and am simply a grandfather trying to return home. This is a crazy man's war about Jews and the dominance of the German master race. I had a little protection from these madmen because I had married a German. I kept my anguish inside and avoided the major battles of the Wehrmacht push into Russia."

The goat bleated and chickens milled about, ignoring the tense dialogue. "Hitler's Eastern Front headquarters, Werwolf, was 150 kilometers away, north of the city of Vinnytsia. When he withdrew from his fortress, it was clear we, I mean the Nazis, were losing the war. Fraternization with Ukrainians is prohibited, not even sports with children. The soldiers are tense."

If either the Germans or the partisans had found the deserter at the farm, they would be doomed. He laid bare everything. Thousands of tanks and millions of soldiers were fighting. Their farm had been spared in 1941, but soon the retreating Germans and advancing Russians would destroy everything in their path.

Jan was the first person to offer the family a chance to survive. "Travel the main roads and valleys and you will be arrested for slave labor. I have studied these maps. The mountains will be our best protection."

Nadiya counseled with Yarik and Alya. The deserter spoke Czech, German, some Slovak, and Ukrainian, and he was a farmer. He was army trained, familiar with the land to the west, and offered—pleaded—to lead them. Her husband had been conscripted in two wars, and she understood Jan's plight. Best of all, he carried a powerful Mauser rifle, a Lugar handgun, and a Fuess marching compass. He had been planning to desert since the day he was sent to Ukraine.

Jan had noticed Nadiya's strength and confidence and had gleaned enough information at the granary to guess the family possessed the means and desperation for a long journey. He persisted. "Your farm is a night's travel from a shallow fording site on the Dniester River. The summer drought has lowered the river level. We have no moon."

Yarik had a limited sense of geography and asked, "Why not go north to Belarus?"

"Belarus and the Balkans will bleed until there is no more blood. And they are too far away. The mountains. We must go into the Carpathians."

He entreated passionately, "The Red Army is coming. If you commit, know that we will have a long and dangerous journey."

"How long?" Yarik asked, positioned behind Nadiya.

"To reach my family north of Prague, about six months." Jan was aware that 1300 kilometers might take much longer.

"Mama, I don't want to go back to the village." She swiveled to her son but didn't respond.

Yarik, age seventy, eyed Alya with an expression that suggested they wouldn't live long enough to see Prague. Minutes earlier, he had pulled Alya aside and asked, "Stay a family or remain here?"

"She saved us from a labor camp three years ago," was Alya's non-answer.

Jan broke the silence. "We move faster than armies. The first days hold the greatest peril from German patrols, two rivers to ford, and hiding during the day. Next, we reach the foothills about forty kilometers west."

34

Nadiya realized they could not stay to harvest the spring crops, or go southwest to the savage Balkans, or wait for the carnage of Russians killing Germans and collaborators. They must go west into and along the Carpathian Mountains ahead of the battle lines. With Jan leading, their chances improved.

Nadiya decided for Dmytro and her aunt and uncle. "For sixty years our family has survived on our farm by avoiding our rulers. My husband was sent away to die. We will go west to live. This is my decision. It is time."

Nadiya didn't know whether her husband was a prisoner or dead. She had given up on him.

"Thank you for your confidence. I have something important. Dmytro's boots are worn. These high boots will keep the snow out."

"Snow!" she exclaimed.

"We will negotiate high elevations in winter."

"Oh," a startled Nadiya said. Winter was a passing concern until now. Boots were scarce, yet she forgot to thank him. "Dmytro, put these on."

"How do I address you?" asked the soldier.

"Call me Nadiya. This is my Uncle Yarik and Aunt Alya, both strong in the field, and Dmytro. Alya, pack our warm clothing. Yarik, feed the animals."

Nadiya had prepared to leave the farm, and along with clothing, dried vegetables, and fruit, she had set aside some tools. What they did not have were rubles, kopeks, marks, gold, or silver.

The family rushed to finish their preparations. To appear more Ukrainian, Jan squeezed into Anton's clothes and burned his German uniform. They stowed their few treasures in trunks on the floor of the wagon and were ready at dusk. Their goal was to travel faster than the Russians and apart from the Nazis. Every kilometer west would take them farther from her husband and their farm.

Just fourteen hours after the deserter shocked them, Nadiya ordered, "Let's go."

Chapter 6: Westward Flight at the Summer Solstice

"Hush. Quiet." Jan whispered, once again holding his arm high in the air to signal for silence. He stopped periodically to listen for a patrol or check an open meadow or just follow his instinct. Nadiya knew the way; Jan knew the army. Go, stop, listen, go, stop, listen. He walked ahead with Dmytro while she reflected: two days ago he was an enemy, yesterday he was a deserter, and tonight he is our leader.

"Dmytro learns from our new German friend," Alya said optimistically to Nadiya while resting aboard the wobbling wagon.

"Yes, they are a special pair."

Fate gave them the shortest night of the year for their flight. Nadiya drove the horses as fast as she dared. The first night might be the most dangerous of their escape, but the hot axles did not care and cried high pitches to shout their presence.

Jan expected his superiors had mobilized to find him. After another pause, he walked back a short distance, alert for a German Dingo scout vehicle that could follow their night's progress in less than an hour. The tracks of their wheels awaited discovery. The Dniester River was not far from the farm, but their short trip over mild, rolling hills by day was an all-night effort under the threat of patrols.

A fast-moving storm was a mixed blessing. Rolling thunder masked the squeaky axles while periodic lightning flashes exposed them.

Twisted lightning bolts etched the sky and marched toward the new partnership. Jan and Yarik wrapped their arms around the horse's necks and stroked their heads, offering comfort to keep them from bolting. Within minutes, the deluge above and the puddles below soaked them. In the storm's center, thunder and lightning struck at the same time. Luckily, the storm moved on quickly.

Cloying mud sucked at their boots and the wheels as they pushed the laden wagon up an incline. At the top, the deserter called for rest.

"You are unafraid," Jan said to Dmytro, watching the water drain from the sloppy road. "Most kids would have hidden under the bench. Good that you have new boots."

Dmytro accepted the compliment and replied gratefully, "The old ones would have filled with mud. Will we have more rain? My feet hurt."

"The stars have returned, so no more rain. New boots hurt until broken in," Jan explained, lifting the boy onto the wagon next to their trunks. "Rest and change back to your old pair."

"Are these high boots for snow?" asked the boy, apprehensively.

"It is possible," the former soldier said, knowing that a harsh winter was inevitable. Nadiya looked away, choosing not to believe what she overheard. She gave her son a prolonged embrace, more to comfort herself than Dmytro. Aunt Alya and Uncle Yarik walked until they tired, then rode, relying on Nadiya to lead them to ford the river.

"Will you carry your rifle home?" Dmytro asked the deserter at one of the rests.

"I will carry it until I run out of ammunition. How are your feet?"

"They are dry. The dogs were ready to attack you. I was scared at the barn."

"Me too, by the dogs and your mother and her rifle."

"Uncle Yarik will teach me to whistle to control the dogs."

Although Dmytro and his father had fished and harvested apples to the south toward Moldova, the boy was not familiar with the path to the Dniester. He kept his young eyes roving in the pitch-black night to point out rough spots for Nadiya to navigate around.

Jan looked east to the black sky beginning to turn cobalt blue.

"A few more rises," whispered Nadiya in the predawn light at a stop to help Alya onto the wagon. To whisper was absurd given the racket from their axles, but they listened. The only sounds were the horses shaking their bridles and the frogs croaking for mates after the downpour. On they went.

Nadiya pulled in the reins at the top of a rise and announced, "The Dniester is there."

Jan slogged upriver to scout and disappeared for fifteen minutes. He returned and said, "I found an easy rise on the far side. Keep twenty meters behind."

Starlight revealed Jan's shape ahead wading cautiously forward, sometimes backtracking and redirecting Nadiya. The songs of the river's early-rising birds were interrupted by the bleats of their cantankerous goat. Jan was tempted to drown it. The wagon couldn't hide in the river, but at least the axles quieted.

Jan found a stand of birch trees and thick bushes for their first day in hiding. The location wasn't perfect—the ground was wet from the storm—but the partial light, already orange before daybreak, forced their choice. Jan complimented Nadiya. "You drove the entire night. You must be exhausted."

"I'll be ready for sleep. Yarik and Alya were able to ride and rest. Look at Dmytro. He is already asleep. You feared patrols?"

"The storm protected us, and the patrols are reduced after the battles in the east. After tomorrow night, we will move in daylight."

Nadiya had entrusted the family's fate to the deserter, a man of medium height, trim and square-faced, whom they

38

barely knew. Nadiya was amazed that he was so generous to Dmytro and kind to her and even the cranky Yarik. They ate an apple and fell asleep next to each other, cooled by a hint of a breeze. Jan didn't set a guard.

The passivity born of years of threats was released the instant Nadiya said, "We will go west," just hours earlier. Her family wasn't waiting for someone else to control their fate. Now her uncertainty about remaining on the farm was replaced by the unknowns of the westward journey.

On the second night, they would ford the Prut River, close to the irrelevant former border between Soviet Ukraine and Southern Poland, demarked by the 1921 Treaty of Riga. The Germans had subdued the lands in 1941 except for hit and run partisan attacks.

"Nadiya," a tormented Yarik said, "The sideboards broke, and one of the trunks bounced off the cart. I can repair it, but we carry too much."

"We brought only what we needed," she pleaded.

"Alya and I will give up our tunics and Cossack trousers—more if you ask. We have to lighten our load."

Nadiya rummaged through their possessions spread on the ground. Downcast, she said to Jan, "I can't do it. You choose what to leave." The winnowing was too emotional for her, and Jan was unsentimental.

Reluctantly, he agreed and removed festive attire and trinkets—the small residue of their life. Yarik didn't let him dispose of his kobza, the last treasure from his youth so that he could teach Dmytro more songs. Dictated by Jan, they dumped their nonessentials in a heap.

Nadiya stared at Jan's muscular arms and the way he fluidly moved his body. She sat upright, unsettled, recognizing that she was attracted to this healthy man dressed in her husband's clothing. She was confused and troubled.

Dmytro slept while Jan outlined the next night's movement. "The river we ford tonight is shallower than the Dniester. We can cross ten kilometers south of Chernivtsi. Europeans called the city a 'Little Vienna.' No more. It was

Romanian, then Soviet, now German, and who knows what's next. The Romanians fled south, the poles north, and Jews died in ghettos or were deported. The city was heavily damaged when the Germans overran it."

"Was the city reconstructed?" Yarik asked.

"They repaired only the rails and roads for German families to farm. The soil is fertile, and the new farmers sent grain home for three years. I overheard officers discuss a coded message that ordered the emergency evacuation of these same colonists. We will walk past those farms after dark and pray they are empty. A farmer will hear us before we see him. If they are Ukrainians who didn't leave after the Great War, they won't bother us. If we meet soldiers, we will be shot."

The horses were restless, waking Dmytro, who mumbled, "I'm hungry."

"So are the horses. Eat this apple," Nadiya said, cuddling the boy. "Jan, only the goat grazes here."

"Okay, we will stop for grasses for the horses. I will walk ahead to determine if we will be safe to move at dusk. Pray for an uneventful passage to put us in the rise of the Carpathians."

Jan returned an hour later, confident they could resume shortly after sunset. Yarik readied the team and they set off. Jan and Dmytro walked ahead on existing trails or made their own. Nadiya was pleased the two of them were close together. The wagon bumped high and hard on the uneven ground, and with the sky darkened, they were forced to slow down.

"This cart creaks and groans. We won't surprise anyone in that farmhouse," Jan noted. "They will watch us while holding their loaded guns. They pray we will keep going."

"Yes, I remember seeing those people pass our farm. Now we are them."

The Prut River was shallower than the Dniester, and the axles squawked until Jan splashed water on them. Under the black sky, Jan selected a spot on the far side that was too steep. "The horses will break their harnesses and break a leg. I will check upriver. Yarik, you check downriver."

Jan returned to say he found a suitable cut. They filled their water jugs, and the horses and goat drank until gorged. They sat on the half-submerged wagon waiting too long for Yarik—far too long.

"We haven't heard gunshots," Alya sighed. Finally, they heard splashes in the water and caught sight of Yarik. Relieved, they slogged upriver, hugging the shore until the horses pulled their burden up the embankment. Moving from Chernivtsi, they followed a tight passage through the dark canopied forest. Without illumination to read his compass, Jan followed the trail, hoping it led a westward course.

He chose a farmhouse abandoned by German farmers. A fractured picture of Adolf Hitler lay on the floor. He checked for booby traps and hid the horses and wagon in the barn.

"Touch it. The fireplace hearth is warm," Nadiya announced after she set kindling and already split wood on top of the remaining embers. She prepared a heavy soup from unharvested spring vegetables, pleased that produce was plentiful.

"The Hungarians were forced out in 1920, the Poles in 1939, and the Germans this month. After the war, a different country will resettle it." They had not traveled far, but far enough to feel safer. The rivers, the one city, and army patrols were behind them.

"On the occasion of our first hot meal," Jan continued with a knowing smile, "we will celebrate our progress to freedom. Tomorrow we will leave at daybreak. First, give me your German identity papers. They are useless, and I will destroy them. Next, Dmytro, your mother said that you and the Communists owned Brownie. Now, you own Brownie. No Communists or Nazis will take her."

"Really?" The boy cried and ran to the barn to hug Brownie. Yarik, Nadiya, and Alya laughed and congratulated him on his capitalist achievement.

41

"We have more to celebrate. I saved something special for you and your mother. Have you seen a Matryoshka doll?" Jan asked Dmytro.

"Aunt Alya described them to me."

"I held one at a shopkeeper's. I opened it," Nadiya said, curious what was next.

"I bought these for you and Dmytro."

Jan placed the wooden nesting doll in Nadiya's open hand. Nadiya slowly spun it round and round to study the colorful design. She opened it to find a smaller one, which she gave to Dmytro. She hugged her doll and cried. Dmytro was about to blurt out his pleasure until Uncle Yarik shushed him.

Mother and son opened and closed the tops and bottoms repeatedly, in a daze over the precise fit of the dolls, vibrant colors, identical design, and oversized eyes of the girl.

Nadiya couldn't fathom how in a few days, Jan had stolen her heart and Dmytro's. The doll was vivid and cute for Dmytro, and for Nadiya, it was a priceless recognition of her role and his thanks.

"How may we thank you?" Nadiya asked. "This is the best gift either of us has ever received."

"Seeing your pleasure is enough."

Dmytro was spellbound and repeatedly set his doll in and out of his mother's. He understood that Jan was leading him away from the farm, the pond, and his father.

Nadiya viewed Jan through a new lens. Even more than the previous day, she saw a handsome, smart, skilled leader who was compassionate. He was about her age, and she couldn't deny that he was more capable than her husband. At the same time, she reassessed herself. She noticed him sneaking glances at her. The next day she purposely loosened her shawl to allow a peek at her breasts. He was drawn to her, and she was flattered.

At sunrise, Jan underhandedly hid their registration papers in the rafters of the barn. In case they didn't survive, those documents would mark the existence of one family.

Chapter 7: Pleasure and Guilt at the Carpathians

The first days of cautious movement established their routine. After sunrise Nadiya prepared soup, Yarik checked the cart and harnesses, Jan scouted, and Dmytro folded the tarpaulins. Yarik and Alya foraged for cabbage, beets, and potatoes from the fields they passed. The bounty lasted the first months. Along with the goat milk, they were well nourished.

They followed trails between farms and later smuggler routes to zigzag west until the forest finally swallowed them. Fir and aspen saplings that hid them from German patrols became their nemesis and were hacked down by Anton's machete-like blades. The summer heat and humidity were worst late in the day. Jan preferred to set up camp at streams. They washed dried sweat and accumulated dirt and scrubbed their clothing for temporary relief from the swarming black flies. Nadiya cooked their meal, and they sang or told a story before falling asleep, exhausted.

Privacy was limited and they huddled around a fire or under the tarpaulin-covered wagon—but not impossible. Nudging her affectionately, Jan quietly asked, "Do you remember the first night after we crossed the river?"

"Yes, of course. We dried our boots and socks and slept until the goat stirred."

"I woke early and found you leaning on me."

"I fell asleep quickly," Nadiya said, turning away from him. "What are you saying?"

"I didn't wake you in the middle of the day because it was a precious time for me. You were asleep, and I wanted to rest at your side."

"It isn't fair to say only, 'I fell asleep quickly.' I fell asleep thinking all about you. Nadiya playfully tugged at his salt-colored whiskers. She was tempted to pull his face to hers.

"Me too."

Jan kept to the plan at the beginning of the trek. "Keep the sun on your back at sunrise and in your face at sundown. Motion is progress," he said each morning, regardless of the weather.

"They came out of nowhere," Alya called out to Jan, still distressed by her encounter. New hazards replaced the threat of German patrols. Displaced Poles returning north to their country had frightened Nadiya, Yarik, and Alya. "Yarik's loud whistling kept the Poles away. Are you too far ahead of us with both dogs?"

"You're right. I'll stay closer with one dog, and the other will stay with the wagon."

"When you and Dmytro came in sight carrying your rifles," Nadiya said approvingly to Jan, "they moved on."

"We will see more dislocated people competing for shelter or sustenance. The last days of the Polish government in 1939 were in these foothills in the village of Kuty, about fifteen kilometers from here. It is a straight route for Poles to return home."

Their escape west to safety would expose them to all seasons. The summer and fall weather was benevolent, and Jan was pleased by their progress. Ukrainians, Poles, Jews, Hungarians, collaborators, Wehrmacht deserters, criminals, and Roma were fleeing in different directions, searching for a place to survive free of political, religious, or ethnic conflict. Groups were wary, and Jan preferred his charges travel alone. A healthy man dressed in borrowed peasant clothing, he was the toughest, his German rifle was feared, and he asserted his leadership.

Refugees shared their knowledge of the war in Europe and especially the armies fighting in Northern Italy. Jan learned that American armies were progressing towards Austria. It was their best chance for sanctuary. Surprisingly, he decided the destination of Austria was safer than his home in Sudetenland.

Seasoned wood was plentiful, but they were cautious about telltale smoke and let the fires diminish before sunrise. The boy was an excellent shot. He and Jan led, sometimes far ahead, to search for the best path and to hunt. Dmytro kept a keen eye for game and prudently managed his limited supply of ammunition.

The tarpaulins and rifles were equally crucial. At dusk, Dmytro placed the canvas on a ground cover of pine boughs and around the cart to shield the family from the elements. Dmytro would announce to Jan, who the ten-year-old called Uncle Jan, "We have tonight's castle set up."

"Another good shelter. We will warm up soon," Jan would say, quick to compliment. Jan feigned optimism despite his worry over their progress. Fire was critical to their limited comfort, and their enemy. They curled up downwind of the flames to seek mutual warmth. More than once, the wind shifted the flames, singeing the tarps and their boots.

"Germans who didn't know a cow from a goat," Jan said to the boy as they ranged over the hillside, "displaced my family from our farm in Czechoslovakia. You are a better farmer, and the horses pay attention to you. You will like our farm."

"Will there be quotas and people with guns?"

"I am not sure what we will have."

"We will have better soil, I think. I steer the team well," Dmytro proudly exaggerated while sitting on the bench next to his mother. Guiding them was tiring, and Yarik, Nadiya, and Dmytro alternated steering the cart.

"Driving in this terrain is dangerous, but you are following Jan carefully. On our flight from Ukraine, you will have plenty of surprises," Yarik said, fully aware of the peril and preparing Dmytro for it.

"I set up the camp, direct the horses, and shoot rabbits. What else?"

Yarik did not answer.

"Do you see the way they brush against each other?" Yarik said to his wife as they walked behind the wagon and the pesky goat.

"Yes, whenever they can. And they gaze with, you know, those eyes."

"The eyes speak."

"Are you looking at me with those eyes?" Alya asked sweetly.

"Maybe. First, we will encourage them." Yarik accepted that war might bring strange bedfellows.

For the first time in a week they were dry in a farmhouse. Jan rummaged through the one room, its windows broken and the stove upended.

"Dmytro, the dogs picked up a scent. Let's track the deer." Yarik nodded to Nadiya—she would be unhampered by her family.

Jan pretended to search for supplies, and once Yarik and Dmytro were out of sight, Alya wandered off. Nadiya rushed to the soldier. Words or caresses were unnecessary. Both had anticipated the possibility, and when the opportunity came, they shed enough of their clothing. He took her. And she took him.

"At last, a farmhouse. I've been bursting to hold you."

"Yarik is a sensitive man to encourage us."

"My aunt and uncle view me in a new light. Our past is over."

"You hid behind your scarf the first time at the granary," Jan said, resting next to her. "I imagined this moment. For more than a year, I have desired you."

"This is a confusing situation. I feared you, I smiled at you, I almost killed you, and here we love. I haven't felt this way, ever.

"Jan, again. Now!" she said to her amazement.

Slowly this time, Jan removed her remaining layers of clothing while she undid Jan's in a manner she had never done with her husband. They groped until they fell onto their clothing, she trying to quiet her moans.

As the hunters returned after their prolonged search, Alya walked to the farmhouse, loudly singing a hymn.

Nadiya and Jan were sweet and tender the next morning. Her aunt and uncle winked, pleased that their niece was happy and satisfied for a moment.

At midday, they stopped to graze the horses, and Nadiya and Jan sat on a downed tree trunk. She covered her face with her hands and began to cry. "What is it?" Jan asked.

"You have a long scar on your back, and you froze when I ran my hand along it."

"I can't hide the scar." He turned his head. "It hurts."

"Is it recent?"

"Before I came to your village."

"In the army?"

"Yes."

"You are still in pain," Nadiya persisted. "Do you want to talk about it?"

"No, but now I must."

"I am tormented. I told you I avoided battles in Poland in 1939 and Russia in 1941. I lied. I fought in all the battles. I was injured by a Russian landmine that exploded under the tank I was riding on. I was the lucky one. I recuperated for a year at home in Bohemia and was sent to your village for easy duty. I want to forget the war and believe my lies."

"Your recovery is complete. You are sturdy."

"Sturdy enough. Some of me will never recover. Ahead of an offensive, we took tablets to keep us fighting for days and days. They drugged us, and we craved the pills. That's how we crushed the Soviet armies.

47

"Drugs do that?"

"The Nazis distributed millions of pills called Pervitin. You concentrate, stay awake, and lose your fear. Coffee lasts hours, Pervitin lasts days. The doctors where I recuperated told me they are methamphetamines. You are euphoric, you are invincible, you drive a tank or fly an airplane forever. And you are mean. You chew tablets and keep going. You are addicted, and you lose your soul. You have heard of the atrocities against Ukrainians and Jews?"

"Refugees told us of massacres."

"My first war was horrific. This war is barbaric. I believed we were required to annihilate the enemy, anyone in our way. Pervitin encouraged me to commit terrible acts without conscience—until later. I killed and killed for no reason. I am ashamed, and I can't run from purgatory. You should hate me."

"You wake up frightened."

"My nightmares."

"I see a principled man," Nadiya said, trying to support him.

"I deceived you. I'm trying to compensate for my crimes."

Yarik rustled the bridles to signal that the horses were ready. Jan took his rifle and one of the dogs, opened his compass, and looked west.

After Nadiya occupied her place on the wagon, Yarik walked to her and asked how to help. "He is carrying a dreadful burden," was her response.

Nadiya loved Jan. Rather than condemn him for his past, she empathized with him, and they stole away at any opportunity. At Nadiya's suggestion, they agreed to maintain his narrative far from battles. She had been a person sweeping a scythe for too long. Now she counted herself desirable and was pleased he renewed her as a whole woman.

Jan couldn't erase his guilt, although he endeavored to atone for his actions. Deserting gave him the possibility of seeing his grandson. Escorting his new family through danger might provide him salvation.

"He has more energy than any of us," Jan said, snuggled next to Nadiya, "and he is a keen lookout."

"He walks proudly next to you carrying his rifle." Not knowing that Dmytro was listening, she said, "I want you, closer."

"I'm close now," Jan breathed. Their bond, forged so quickly, was intense. Dmytro was grateful she was well cared for. In the farmhouse, young Dmytro had heard the sounds of lovemaking. When fortune provided shelter for Nadiya and Jan, the boy recognized it and approved.

Chapter 8: Winter Takes its Toll

A cracked wheel forced Jan and Yarik to cut the wagon to a single axle. Though they moved faster on the shortened rig, the ride was harsh and offered less protection from the elements after they set camp.

Alya, who had been sitting next to Nadiya for days, was too weak to hold on to the seat. Yarik watched his wife's decline and attempted to cheer her by singing hymns from their safer years before 1917. Snow flurries announced colder weather, and Aunt Alya developed a fever.

"Aunt Alya, please sing me that hymn when I was little in the fields?" Dmytro asked her nightly for a song or story.

"Let's sing together," Alya said weakly. Surprisingly, Jan hummed the tune.

Sparks crackled and yellow light danced on their faces while Yarik apathetically plucked his off-sounding kobza, now missing a string. He didn't sing. The previous night he had said goodbye to his wife of fifty years.

"My favorite story is *The Old Dog*. Please tell it."

"Ah, a short one," Alya said to please her grandnephew. She narrated it, frequently pausing to catch her breath and glance at her husband.

"Aunt Alya, tell me another fairy tale, *The Golden Slipper*, please. Please."

"Too long. Perhaps tomorrow."

Yarik was amazed Alya had the strength to complete the story. It was her farewell gift to Dmytro.

Unable to sit next to Nadiya on the jolting and rocking bench, Alya lay sweating in misery on the cold boards, her head steadied by Yarik walking at her side.

Nadiya traversed the snow-dappled hills until the left horse harness broke and then the right.

She screamed, pulled on the reins, and scrambled forward onto Brownie. She was almost trapped in Blackie's leather straps as Blackie and the cart slid backward, tumbling down the hillside. The trail of their possessions led to the bottom of the gully where Alya lay, arms and legs askew.

Jan ran to steady Brownie and asked Nadiya, who would not relinquish her two-handed death grip on the horse's mane, "Are you okay?"

"I'm okay. See Yarik."

Jan went to Yarik's side and said, "I'll go check." Yarik, transfixed, stared at his motionless wife at the bottom of the gully.

"There is nothing to check," Yarik said in defeat. "The bridle's leather was cracked and about to break. It is my fault."

"We had no more leather. It's not your fault."

Alya was pitifully light. Jan carried her back to the trail while Yarik grieved, crouched among his dogs. Out of sight of Yarik, but with his consent, Nadiya removed Alya's outer garments and boots. A cross of two branches wrapped by a vine marked the shallow grave. He did his best to read a passage from their Bible.

"Was Aunt Alya old?" Dmytro asked after a minute.

Nadiya searched for an answer. "She wasn't young, and her life was difficult these last years. My God, she loved singing to you."

"She was my life's steady companion." The loss of Alya devastated Yarik, and he went to uncharacteristic silence. He and Jan gathered boards from the shattered cart and built a sizeable Finnish design sledge for Brownie to drag over the mushy ground and snow patches.

Jan retrieved the few unbroken bowls and the cooking pot and repacked their diminishing stores onto the makeshift toboggan. Except for photographs stuffed in their pockets and the Matryoshka dolls, they discarded their remaining cherished mementos. Weak from hunger, Dmytro did not have the strength to heft his rifle. The boy's weapon, the Bible, and Yarik's broken kobza were laid at Alya's gravesite.

Pleasant fall weather and the daily fly invasion gave way to weekly frontal passages. Dry leaves crackling in gusty winds disturbed the family's sleep, and once fallen, the leaves froze, turning the forest floor slippery. Bitter storms forced the family to hide for days from the fury while rain, wet snow, or sleet hit their tarps. Unable to sustain a fire, they were miserable. Jan was frustrated by their lack of progress.

Brownie, her nostrils blowing plumes of fog, pulled the sledge to higher elevations as they continued to meet other refugees seeking their homeland before winter arrived. Unburied frozen corpses exposed by fierce winds evidenced the dangers. Without hesitation, Jan and Yarik salvaged clothing and boots to replace garments to appear less Ukrainian.

The family struggled against the sadness of Alya's death, the weather, and the terrain. Nadiya replaced folksongs with stories about Ukraine before the Communists and how fishing with Dmytro had given his father joy. The ritual repetition reassured Dmytro and herself. They studied the damp pictures they carried of the pond and of Anton in his festive Ukrainian Easter garb and then pressed next to the dogs' fur.

"We move more quickly pulling the sled, even when you or Yarik ride on Brownie. Still, each step is hard for her." Despite the snow squalls, their progress was satisfactory to Jan.

Dmytro overheard Jan discuss the horse's condition and searched more fervently for grasses to feed his animal.

Brownie's ribs were more visible than the day she arrived at the farm.

From the onset, the horses were working animals and a future meat source. When the terrain became too rough and deep snow covered the grasses, Jan accepted that their last famished horse would not survive much longer.

Jan chanced upon shelter in a hunter's cabin and told Dmytro, "I am sorry, but Brownie is starving."

"She pulled the plow wherever I directed her." Dmytro wasn't surprised and gave his horse a last kiss. "I won't watch you shoot Brownie."

"You have butchered chickens," Jan said after the gunshot. "Your father made a knife for you. Come, help me."

To distract the boy, Jan withdrew his whetstone from its leather sheath and sharpened both knives.

Dmytro didn't voluntarily butcher Brownie but did what was asked. While he longed for the relative security of his young life on the farm, he kept those thoughts to himself.

Sad meals of stringy horsemeat lasted several days, and Jan, Nadiya, Yarik, Dmytro, and the dogs regained some strength in the warmth of the cabin. Jan, trained in survival skills, and the boy, who had learned from his father, searched for herbs and bark to supplement the stew. They froze meat and cooked jerky, knowing they would be hungry within a week.

Jan and Yarik rebuilt a smaller sledge for one man to pull. They cut walking sticks to steady them on the slippery ground. Jan took the first turn, his body leaning precariously forward into a harness tied from the remaining leather of the horse bridle. His boots punched the crusty snow with a crunch, and the sled lurched ahead. Nadiya, followed by Dmytro, who was comfortable in his mid-calf boots, stepped onto Jan's footprints. Jan set a painfully slow pace, yet he swelled with pride at the resilience of his charges.

Chapter 9: Uncle Yarik Disappears

The Carpathian Mountains lead west-northwest, away from Ukraine. Jan's maps dictated an average 280-degree course, which was a challenge across the deep ravines and streambeds. They traveled along the southern slope at a high elevation along the tree line, the high boundary between granite and the spruce forest where the wind howled, and German patrols did not venture.

Buoyed by a bright sunrise, Jan would stir the fire for Nadiya's reheated soup and then scout ahead. The sledge slid easily until the midday sun warmed the snow, sinking it deeper.

"Mama, can we stop?"

"Even though he walks in our footsteps, it is hard for him," Nadiya said to her lover.

"The dogs are tired jumping in the deep snow. Soon we must send off our faithful partners."

"Dmytro and Yarik will be brokenhearted."

"Look to the west," Jan said to Dmytro while he rested against a large stone outcropping warmed by the sun. "We have seen and avoided castles and ski lodges. A time may come in your life when you return and appreciate such a view."

"Like in a fairy tale?" the boy suggested, unconvinced. He found those vistas hard to imagine while frigid and hungry.

"Blue sky, full sun, and no wind," Nadiya said discreetly to Jan. "Today is perfect, yet I shiver. I couldn't

54

have imagined how punishing each day is. Nine hundred kilometers is a long way along these mean mountains and so are the five kilometers to that ridge. One more kilometer to tonight's camp is too long."

"Not in front of Dmytro, please." Jan's mitten was poised at his lips.

"Jan is correct." She spoke louder to reassure her son, "I bet someday you will ski down the slopes to a lodge and dine at a castle."

Even though Jan was often struck with doubt, he never showed weakness. Jan's assessments of distance, available food, and condition of his charges and weather were grim, but he was glad to see Nadiya and Dmytro keeping up and marginally healthy. Yarik remained vigorous but subdued.

"Dmytro is learning to make the stews, the safest routes to take, and how to evaluate the people we meet."

"Ja, he is a good boy. He asks questions, and I reply in Czech. How are you?"

"I put my foot forward into the depression where you stepped. You and Yarik drag the sledge. That is the hardest. You go. I go. I don't dwell on the cold. I just go."

"Ja. You are brave."

Nadiya held a determined face to Jan as she silently questioned her decision: is it better to die in Ukraine in your farmhouse or freeze to death far away? We have too much to eat or not enough. Alya is gone. What's next?

❖ ❖ ❖ ❖ ❖

"Will you search for him?" Nadiya asked Jan. Yarik had unwisely set off at dusk to follow a deer track.

"It's too dark for him to retrace his footsteps. I'll shoot a round. Listen." The muzzle flash illuminated the snow at their feet and was answered only by an echo. "His rifle might be frozen. I will build a brighter fire." Nadiya dropped her head, fearing the worst. The trio joylessly sipped their thin soup and spooned tightly for the night.

Jan set off at first light and returned an hour later to report, "I could tell the way he dragged his feet through the snow that he was tired. His footprints turned into a long line over a ledge. He slipped and couldn't have survived the night."

"My aunt and today, my uncle. We can't go back. Who knows what going forward will bring? It's hard to rise and face the day."

"We have no choice. If we stop, we will turn into the frozen statues we saw last week."

The confidence Nadiya felt in summer was forgotten. The ardor she and Jan had savored diminished with the colder weather, adversity, and recognition that the Americans were far away. She pressed on for Dmytro's sake.

"We can't bury Yarik properly," Nadiya announced to no one. "We can't even find him. I pray for forgiveness."

Chapter 10: Tested by Partisans

"Freeze! Drop your rifle!" a man shouted as a dozen men and women surrounded and trained their weapons on the trio. "Where did you get the Mauser?"

Arms held high above his head, Jan spoke in Czech, "Please don't shoot. I'm helping this family. I am Czech from Sudetenland, a conscript who deserted."

The snow-covered mountains belonged to the Slovak partisans, and any intruders were suspect. They harassed the German armies, especially during the Slovak National Uprising against the Nazis in the summer of 1944. Deserting German soldiers were striving to return to their homes. The decision of a Communist or Nationalist partisan to kill a German was easy.

"How many Russians did you kill? How many Czechs and Slovaks?" demanded the unit leader, the zampolit.

"None. I was far from the front lines."

"That's hard to believe."

"It's true," beseeched Nadiya in Ukrainian. She didn't understand the words, but she caught the tone of the zampolit. "He was in our village for two years and treated us properly. He has led us through terrible hardships."

"He taught me to play football and gave us extra ration stamps," Dmytro defended in his mixed Ukrainian and Czech. The rifles turned towards him.

"We aren't a threat. We are just trying to go west," Jan said.

"We have tracked you for hours. You have a rifle, a Lugar, and a Fuess compass. Did you kill for them?" the leader challenged.

"To have a chance to return to my home, I stole an infantryman's compass, studied maps, and schemed to steal these weapons in the middle of the night. I gambled this family would leave Ukraine and ran to their farm."

The leader lowered his rifle and replied, "Okay. You are smart to travel high in the mountains. The Nazis abandoned the labor camps and prisoner of war camps. Refugees wander, doomed in the hills. They hear the Russians are undisciplined and rape and kill. We partisans stay hidden to avoid ambush."

"We don't trust anyone. Our family travels alone to Austria. We are going to Austria and the Americans."

"First, you have to go the length of Slovakia. From a distance, you have seen the defensive preparations in the valleys and the passes. Look at this map. The best way west is between Prešov and Košice. A monumental battle between the Russians and Germans at Dukla Pass is inevitable. You will meet these major roads that are filled with German vehicles. How have you avoided the minefields?"

"We avoided the tank traps beside the roads and haven't seen minefields."

"You are lucky. The mines are waiting for the Russians or anyone."

"If we are lucky, I can't imagine what unlucky is. We have lost track of time." Jan followed the moon cycles and was unsure of the precise date. He asked, "What day is this?"

"Today is the fifth of December 1944."

The zampolit directed Jan and his family toward the best route through the Low Tatras Mountains. They returned the weapons and vanished into the forest, leaving the threesome to face terrain even harsher than the Carpathians.

At high ground, they scanned the horizon to avoid blundering into Germans or refugees. A church spire sighted in the lower elevations would draw them cautiously to seek shelter and concealed food. Burned homes evidenced the wrath of the Nazis, and some houses held murdered German families who waited too long to leave. Partisans or refugees had already ransacked those homes. Sometimes they sheltered in vacant ski chalets that had provided luxurious recreation for the German occupiers.

"I miss Uncle Yarik strumming his kobza and Aunt Alya singing." Dmytro asked, "Can we stay one more night? My boots are dry, and my feet are warm."

"We will wait until the morning. If the sun shines, we go."

Winter solstice darkness, cold, and deep snow stalked them before Christmas Eve. Dmytro dug in the snow to find branches and pine straw to build a robust fire and set the canvas to protect them from snow showers. They awoke to a sunny, windless Christmas day. Half a year after their departure, they were halfway to their destination.

Nadiya didn't mention last year's Christmas when they danced wearing the colorful Ukrainian folk scarves, sashes, and long skirts—discarded the first night. Dmytro longed for the missing vanacka Christmas cake of previous years. Christmas was just another dismal day. They shared a watery horsemeat soup, Nadiya prayed and simply said, "God bless us."

The mountains were unforgiving, but flat terrain in the valleys where major roads carried the machinery of war was equally perilous: open spaces exposed the trio to aircraft or army patrols.

Narrow passes where armies had advanced or retreated over the centuries also required extra caution. They hid for days waiting for poor visibility in a snowstorm to hustle across such treacherous sectors.

Limited daylight, snowstorms, and an unhappy holiday invited melancholy. Jan wrestled with memories under the influence of Pervitin, and now he worried about taking this family to their demise. Although Jan's shame accompanied him, he held fast to the vision of his daughter and grandson, with whom he had celebrated Christmas on medical leave three years before. He did not give up for them, or Dmytro and Nadiya.

Chapter 11: More Sadness

Jan strapped into the harness and dragged his burden. His boots sank deep despite the makeshift pine-bough snowshoes. Nadiya and Dmytro looked down, stepping onto his footprints. Only Jan looked ahead.

The trio pushed forward at too slow a clip for Jan, who confided to Nadiya, "Pray this miserable weather slows the Russians more than us."

"Are you troubled about our progress?"

"I can't tell, and we won't know until the spring thaw."

"Spring is far from today. Little Dmytro doesn't complain, and I'm slow. The flames melt the snow to the earth. I look like the drowned leaves."

"Nadiya, you are pretty."

"I don't feel pretty."

"You will, when we find an empty cabin."

"That will be nice," Nadiya twinkled. "I lived day to day and harvest to harvest. I have a responsibility here. I want Dmytro to live free of tyrants."

"The Americans are free of tyrants. You, Dmytro, and I will find them."

Dmytro grew up observing the will and strength of his mother who dealt with the farm, the Germans, the partisans, and now, plodding step for step behind Jan.

She was the backbone of the family until two weeks after the New Year, when she faltered. Her decline commenced with a cough and requests for more rest. Jan set camp for her earlier each day, and they detoured to dry

61

shelter and lingered longer for her to regain strength. He could only try to keep her warm and cook soup for her. He fretted about the lack of progress.

Dmytro comforted her and repeated her prayers. "I say these words, but I don't know about religion."

"We prayed at our church where God was," Nadiya explained without conviction, searching for her cross under her coats and sweaters. "Uncle Yarik and the bishop read from the Bible."

Between coughs, she continued, "We stood or knelt. Tonight, I might pray under your tarp. I close my eyes and visualize God's spirit, clasp my hands, lower my head and begin, 'Glory to Thee, our God, glory to thee.' At the farm, I prayed for a full harvest and safety from the Communists. I prayed for your father to return from war. I...."

Nadiya stopped. She didn't share her feelings with her young boy. Praying was a habit. She did not presume God was listening.

"We are tired at night, and I forget to pray or encourage you. Let us pray." Her prayers seemed futile. Nadiya wondered, did I forget God, or did God forget me?

Dmytro crossed himself, not knowing the proper way.

❖ ❖ ❖ ❖ ❖

Jan was concerned about Nadiya's health, but they had to move west regardless of her cough. He was pleased that she maintained his modest rate. Several sunny days allowed slight progress.

Nadiya's coughing persisted and turned to labored breathing. While Dmytro set camp, she struggled to tell Jan, "A horse has no choices while cold and starving; it keeps going until it falls. A human can decide to stop walking or eating or simply jump into the ravine to stop the misery. Jan, my weakness will kill you and the boy."

"What do you mean?"

"I'm sick, and you can't carry me through the winter. I give up."

"Nonsense. We will go back to the hunter's cabin." Retracing a day's travel pained Jan, and he recalibrated his mythical date to reach Austria.

Dmytro dug for brushwood to burn in the hearth while Jan tended to his Nadiya. She was too weak to mumble the folk songs or hymns. Dmytro and Jan sang or hummed the songs to her.

"Where are we?" Nadiya asked deliriously. "My feet are cold."

"We have passed Košice and are in the Low Tatras Mountains. We are more than halfway to the Americans in Austria." Really, he thought they were nowhere: nowhere for her to die. He had seen death, and her turn was at hand.

"Where is Aunt Alya, where is Uncle Yarik, where is Dmytro? Oh, there you are, Dmytro."

"I'm here," her son said, wincing.

"I see you dancing with your princess."

Her wide-open eyes did not focus. She peered through Dmytro, knowing he would be the last in their family. Her hacking cough worsened, and she forced out haltingly, "I will miss meeting your wife. I am tired. Hold me."

"I will pray for you. Mama? Mama?"

All they could do was hold her.

Dmytro cried himself to sleep, holding onto his mother until he awoke at dawn to see a frozen tear on her cheek. Jan was awake, embracing Nadiya. The boy was prepared for the worst but asked, "Is Mama alive?"

"No, Dmytro."

"She is holding the Matryoshka doll in her mitten."

"She cherished it. Take it. The dolls belong together."

Dmytro unrolled her fingers, placed his doll inside hers, and tucked them into his coat pocket.

He stood up and pounded his fist on the doorway.

Jan hugged the boy tightly and, in his softest voice, said, "Your mother was courageous. We will finish her journey." He carried Dmytro to the fire's radiance and said, "Stay warm while I do the best I can for your mother."

Nadiya's death was a blur to Dmytro. He wept next to her resting place, a slight mound covered by pine branches and snow. Jan preached words he did not believe—not for the Lord, not for Nadiya, not for himself, but for Dmytro, to mark her demise in the same way as Aunt Alya and Uncle Yarik.

"Dmytro, this is the worst day of our lives. We left the farm, knowing our journey would be arduous, and you have seen too much sadness for your years. I loved your fearless mother. Now, you and I are the family. I will do my best to keep my promises. Coming days will be better."

Jan did not know whether his pronouncement was true. He judged the deaths were his failing. Nevertheless, he was obliged to honor his love and pretend confidence for the boy.

"I don't want to go on. All I see is snow and ice,"

"Yes, I see that, but I promised Nadiya to protect you and bring you to safety. Your family would be proud you met my grandson. Can we keep going?"

Dmytro didn't answer. Before the sun reached its zenith, he picked up his stick and walked away from his sadness.

Chapter 12: Dmytro Becomes a Czech Named
Luboš

Orphan Dmytro depended on the deserter, this new
uncle, his only family, to lead him west to a place and an
idea named freedom that he didn't comprehend. Huddled
around a fading fire two days and eight kilometers from
Nadiya, Jan began a sad conversation. "Dmytro, look at the
picture of your family at the pond."

"I try to every night."

"This night is different. In the last war, chaos was
everywhere when people fled in all directions. Whoever
wins will set the rules, and your name sounds Ukrainian or
Russian. We need to prepare you for intense questioning. To
survive in the west, you must forget your name. Forget your
language and continue to learn Czech. You are Luboš. It was
my father's name, which means 'love.' You must burn the
picture of your father."

"Burn the picture? Become a Czech?" he asked,
turning his back to Jan.

"Yes, burn the picture. And the Matryoshka dolls.
They are too Russian. We have plenty of time and hundreds
of kilometers to make you Czech."

Dmytro was silent. He paused, appraising the further
loss of his identity.

"No."

"We will talk tomorrow, and we will burn tomorrow
night," Jan said firmly, yielding one more day.

Jan called him Luboš during the six-kilometer slog
until sunset. Dmytro was tight-lipped as he brooded and

65

absorbed his life change. Jan set camp and built a fire in an unnamed forest in Slovakia.

"Luboš, it is time."

"My father was proud to name me Dmytro to honor the earth. Nature is too cruel. I'm ready to be Czech with a new name."

Sobbing, the boy laid the top of his mother's doll on the burning branches and watched the flames dance and pop to engulf a piece of his past. The fire subsided, and he reluctantly repeated the placement with the remaining doll halves. He removed the wrinkled photograph from his coat. He kissed his father's image for the last time.

The boy slowly moved the picture closer and closer to the flame's edge until it shrank, singed, and finally ignited. He held it too long and burned his thumb and finger. The ashes floated away. Luboš and Jan tried to fall asleep back-to-back.

"Uncle Yarik would be disappointed that the picture is gone, and Stalin is alive," the boy said the next morning to the still-warm ashes of last night's fire.

"Borders of countries in Europe will be re-drawn, and the losers will feel pain. That's why you learn Czech—or the Americans will send you back to Stalin."

"Will the Czechs win the war?"

"The Czechs won't win the war. The partisans told us of the war's progress. We are going to Austria, to the Americans."

"Will the Americans win the war?"

"The Russians are winning in Ukraine. The partisans said the Americans are pushing the Germans out of Italy. For sure, Germany is losing."

"Why are the Americans better?"

"Because they aren't Russian or German."

Continuing was taxing. Their strength waned, their decision-making was suspect, and their emotions were at rock bottom. In a trance, numbed by fatigue and cold for days, they might commit mistakes with an enemy or misjudge the slope of a hill.

The cold was more intimidating to Jan than an army, but he did not let on. "We can do this. The sun is shining. Today will be better. Luboš, you guided us correctly by the compass yesterday. Today I will follow you."

He taught Luboš as if they were father and son. "My grandson is your age, and I hope he is shielded in the same way I protect you."

Late one overcast afternoon, snow crust reformed, and the sled found a life of its own, threatening to pull Jan down the fall line of the slope. Jan misjudged his steps, and he and the sledge tumbled down a steep incline until he slammed into a tree. In the seconds of his slide, he wondered if Yarik had died in the same way.

Fatigue and cold were constant, and now he was in pain. Winter was on the cusp of defeating the pair. They needed a reason for optimism.

The next morning from high ground, Jan pointed to diffused smoke rising from the edge of the pine forest.

"The compass reads 240 degrees. Notice the trees and terrain near the smoke," Jan said, elated but apprehensive. They plodded an irregular track down the slope and around gullies, hoping their average course was southwest.

Good instincts and luck guided them to the log house protected from snow and wind by pine trees to the north. Snow-covered furrows of the winter crop surrounded the rest of the farmhouse.

Do or die. They eased from the protection of the tree line toward a man repairing a fence.

The farmer froze in place, knowing his rifle was out of reach. Jan laid down his rifle, which sank into the knee-deep snow. The newcomers appeared threatening—the man wrapped in torn clothing carrying a gun, the boy a round shape. Head wrappings obscured their faces and they raised their arms in surrender. From a safe distance, Jan offered, first in garbled Slovak and then in Czech and again in Slovak, "I can hammer the nails. I'm a farmer and can repair the fence."

The aged farmer dropped his tools and bag of nails and backed away.

"I built fences and repaired houses," Jan said and dug up the hammer. He pounded nails into the fencepost and asked, "Is that the next post?"

The cold wind sang through the pine trees, and last night's snow swirled. The three of them stood statue-like, casting long shadows on the field.

When the hammering stopped, the farmer's wife looked outside to see an unknown man and a child. She grabbed their loaded rifle, opened the door, and yelled to her husband, "Jozef, move to your left!" She strode from the farmhouse wearing only a lightweight dress. "Who are they?"

"I don't know," the farmer responded.

"I asked you to move to give me a clear shot at the man."

She stood next to her husband, aiming the rifle at Jan, her finger on the trigger. Jan spoke slowly and softly, hoping to gain their confidence before she killed him. "This boy, his family, and I began our escape from Ukraine six months ago. Two of us remain. We met partisans who gave us advice and let us pass. We are trying to reach American soldiers in Austria."

"Why did you come out of the mountains?"

"We are almost broken. I injured myself in a fall and can't pull the sledge farther. It is too much for us. We saw the smoke from your chimney. You are our last chance."

"We were stupid to add more logs last night," the woman angrily said to her husband.

Silence, interrupted by the rush of exhaled breaths, dominated the scene.

The farmer asked, "Which partisans did you meet?"

"The M.R. Stefanik Brigade."

"Who was the leader?"

"Viliam Zinger. He has one arm."

The husband and wife quietly conversed back and forth. The exchange ended after the woman asked her husband, "Can we trust them?"

"Zinger didn't kill them. They should be okay."

She nodded, and the farmer told the intruders not to move. He retrieved the stranger's rifle, then the wife directed, "Walk to the house." The husband and wife kept the weapons trained on the man. Her hands shook, and her body trembled. Jan feared she might pull the trigger by mistake.

Jan ducked his head below the low doorframe. He and Luboš stepped into a warm, dry room that held cooking utensils, a table, and four chairs. Decorative carvings above the doors to the two bedrooms reflected pride in the home. Jan inhaled the pleasant aromas from the cook pot on the warm stove. His mouth watered. The woman pointed her rifle to a corner for the interlopers to sit and said, "I wanted to shoot you, but my husband was in the way."

Jan studied pictures of the peasant family and crucifix on the wall behind the woman. "We are fortunate to have traveled this far. Our luck was about to run out. The M.R. Stefanik Brigade was kind to us, although they almost killed us. We were able to show we were harmless and not their enemy."

"What do you want from us? "

"To stay alive," Jan said, flexing his toes in his thawing boots.

"That's what we are trying to do."

The husband and wife parleyed again until the husband told Jan, "The boy stays here. Bring the sledge to the door."

Jan padded through the snow, knowing that if the farmers chose to kill them, they would have shot them at the fence and not in the home. It was time for his first smile in a month.

"What is your name," the old lady asked, "and where did you grow up?"

He should have been ready for the question, but he was bone-tired and unprepared. Perplexed, was he Dmytro or Luboš?

He searched for Jan for advice. Hesitating, he said he was Dmytro from a farm at the Moldova-Ukraine border.

Jan returned to hear the farmer's wife ask, "Dmytro, did you have brothers and sisters?" Jan stiffened his entire body, and the boy realized he had violated his commitment.

He broke out wailing, "I'm Luboš, Luboš, Luboš!"

The memories suddenly enveloped him: the violence, the deaths, the fatigue, the cold, the starvation, and the sadness. His first chance to release his grief erupted in the farmhouse.

The woman set her rifle against the wall and said, "My name is Petra, and this is my husband, Jozef Babiak." She held the child's boney frame and gave a long hug.

Jan knelt in front of the boy, saying, "You will feel better soon."

"Luboš, drink this hot soup," she said, somewhat confused by the name change. "Jan, your coat is falling apart. You will sleep in our son's room." Exhausted, the trekkers collapsed on the bed.

Jozef slumped on a chair. "They didn't have another day in them. On the sled are a torn tarpaulin and a can of sausage. What will we do?"

"We have space for them. The man can patch the barn. We will treat them as family."

The quilt lay on the floor. Petra tiptoed past Jan to cover the youngster. She said to her husband, "Now we will fill four chairs."

Chapter 13: Guests in Slovakia, January 1945

"The frostbite sends lightning to my feet," Luboš groaned at the room's doorway.

"The pain is terrible, I'm sure. Let me massage your feet," Petra said after she set the boy on her chair. "Our son experienced frostbite, and the pain lasted weeks. I will knit socks for both of you. Jan, when was the last time you slept under a roof?"

Jan sipped hot cider, and Luboš snoozed on Petra's lap while he glumly narrated the family's trek and his false story serving in the Wehrmacht.

Petra lowered her head and said, "Our son was a partisan killed by the Nazis. After Slovak leaders sold out to the Nazis, our son was conscripted into the Slovak army in 1939. He fought for the Germans during their invasion of Poland and battled the Soviets in Ukraine until 1943. Back in his country, he realized he was tired of fighting on behalf of the Nazis."

"He yearned to preserve our nation's independence," Jozef added. "When the Gestapo deported Jews, he deserted. He joined the national resistance, the M.R. Stefanik Brigade you met. Our National Uprising of last summer brought them out of the hills to fight, and the Nazis killed our son. These lands are bloody."

Jan listened and held back the ideas whirling inside him. Jan's war experiences were like their son's—except Jan was alive. He wept for the first time. "I shed tears for you and your son. You have saved our lives. Thank you."

"You and the boy rest. You may stay here."

71

Writhing in his nightmare, Luboš fell off the bed and called out, "Mama, Mama! Uncle Jan!"

Jan whispered, "They are our friends."

"I had a terrible dream. I was walking without legs," the boy said, pushing his head against Jan's chest.

"Here, feel your feet. The dream will go away."

Jozef and Petra Babiak had built their farmhouse after the defeat of the Austro-Hungarian Empire and were accustomed to fieldwork. Jozef was gruff, and the two haggled amicably over which herbs to put in the stew or how much wood to put in the stove. Seventy-five years old, Jozef appeared even older in his loose-fitting embroidered shirt and heavy pants. His snow-white beard was trimmed short, and his white mane flopped down when freed from his cap. He acted cautiously, as if he was calculating each step, each sip of soup, and each word.

A lightweight scarf over Petra's gray mop pushed her ears forward unnaturally. Her eyelids were so droopy it was a marvel she could see to hit a target. Her wrinkled face wasn't appealing, but she was a levelheaded, cheerful person who held her turn at the hoe.

Petra was thrilled to have a child in the home again and thought he was a gift from God. Luboš was new to the Czech and Slovak languages, and he wanted to understand dialogue and be active. He said, "I can milk the goat and roll pastries."

"Did you churn butter?" Petra inquired. "Did you have a garden?"

"I love butter," Luboš said with the sunny excitement of youth. "I tended our garden. I steer the horse and plow. My Uncle Yarik said the furrows were straight."

Luboš accomplished chores assigned by Jozef and was ready for the next task. He learned and sang the Slovak folk songs and hymns that Petra sang to her son. The recitations were eerily similar to those of Aunt Alya.

Jozef's winter task was to select the best seeds to plant wheat in the spring and pray for a full harvest. Typically, they drove their wagon to acquire new clothes and to sell or trade straw baskets Petra had weaved. This year's heavy January snows blocked outdoor work and their ability to go to the distant village, Smižany.

The white, damaged skin from frostbite on Jan and Luboš's feet and fingers slowly healed, and they rebuilt their strength. Jozef read to Luboš from the books in the son's room, and they chatted amiably. Jan talked a bit, but he was unwilling to fully mention his Wehrmacht service.

"We are far up this valley that runs north to the mountains," Jozef said. "No Germans came except the Messerschmitt fighter planes strafing the barn. Army patrols came only after the National Uprising last August."

Luboš interjected, "Uncle Jan taught me to play football. We raised goats and dogs. I fished at our pond."

"We fish too, even in the winter," Jozef said, taken aback. "We hid treasures in the forest to avoid confiscation. We lied to the soldiers. We showed our son's army records and said he died in Ukraine fighting Soviet forces. They pitied us, and now we are guilty before God. Weeks later, he was killed in the failed National Uprising. We caused his death."

Jan shook his head, remembering scavenging clothing from dead people. "We do what we must each day. We have regrets."

When the weather permitted, Jan repaired the barn while restless Luboš climbed high in the scaffolding to play. The neglected thatched roof leaked, and Jozef was too old to fix it. After several days of sun, the south side of the roof was free of snow. The boy watched Jan fold and tie the straw, insert it tightly into the roof, and beat it down flush. "Uncle Jan, I repaired our roof. Let me climb up."

Jozef noticed Luboš's scruffy boots and remarked, "Do you need new boots?"

"Yes, Uncle Jozef, this is my second pair, and they are tight. Will we go to the village?" Jan was pleased that Jozef was also called uncle in Luboš's family.

"Petra's porridge is going to your feet. We won't go to the village until spring. We will find leather in the barn. I worked for a boot maker."

They searched the barn until they found rusted needles and leather pieces for the sole and upper parts. For Jozef, this was a fatherly task essential for the continuation of the trek. He was the teacher and patiently explained the foot measuring, left and right template, cutting of layers of leather, stitching, and hole punching. Over two days, Jozef stitched the first boot.

"It fits. May I make the next boot?"

"I am sorry. I don't have enough leather. We cannot afford a mistake."

Winter at a snowbound farm might be slow-paced, but not for Luboš. At age eleven, he milked the goat, worked on the barn, and sawed, split, and stacked wood by the entrance. He trailed Jozef and Jan, assisting in chores. Jozef mentioned ice fishing with his son at a nearby lake.

"How do you ice fish?" asked Luboš.

"First, don't go on a lake in good visibility, or you will be target practice for the Germans. My son dug for worms for bait under the woodshed. After the ground froze, he used a polished scrap of metal to attract the fish. We hefted sticks, a shovel, and heavy clothing and lit a small fire on the thick ice to stay warm."

On the next dreary day, they put on Jozef's proper snowshoes of bent wood and leather thongs and set off carrying their shiny lure and hooks fashioned from wire. Jozef cleared snow where he and his son had cut holes. Jozef and Jan hacked in the thick ice while Luboš scooped out the ice chunks and slush. Jozef dropped the weighted fishhook in the water until he found the bottom and raised it a bit. They rigged a post to help detect the slightest movement of the frozen twine. Jan set the string and waited—and waited.

"I'll clear more snow, and we will jump up and down to bring the fish to us." That is what Jozef believed since the tactic had been fruitful in the past. He muttered kind words into the hole and encouraged Luboš to communicate to the fish. They waited for the string to move, but nothing happened.

"Uncle, no wonder. The line is frozen. We won't know if the fish bites."

Jan pulled the string in. "Let's add a second hook and line at a different depth and jiggle the lines to mimic a minnow."

It was cold, and Jozef was about to leave in frustration, but he agreed to keep trying. He fell asleep sitting on the stool, which Luboš considered a favorable sign.

Luboš and Jan jiggled each line until one of the strings tugged. Luboš jerked the line and yelled at the resistance. Jozef fell off his stool, and Jan reached out to keep him from slipping into the hole.

Jozef, wide-awake, coached the boy to pull the line slowly and steadily until a nice sized trout flopped on the ice. After Jozef removed the hook, Luboš dropped the line back into the hole. The boy rubbed his freezing hands near the fire and rocked back and forth to warm up. Fish continued to bite, pleasing Luboš.

"Can we come back tomorrow? We speak their language."

"This is a good beginning with enough for two meals, "Jan said as the winter sun set. "Depending on the visibility, we will come back often."

Luboš pushed a stick through the mouths of the frozen fish and carried them to the barn to gut.

Jozef and Petra were thankful for their winter companions. The farmers were pleased to have rescued the two starving foreigners who eased their own grief. It was a relatively happy time, especially since patrolling Messerschmitts had been diverted to the eastern front.

"How is my accent?" Luboš asked Petra. "I can understand you and Uncle Jan and Uncle Jozef."

"For two months speaking a Slovak, your accent is good."

Though the farmer didn't suggest it, he wished their guests would stay long enough to harvest the winter wheat.

"You are a good fisherman and roof maker," Jozef said to Luboš. "You will find peace in Austria. The mountains will protect you and improving weather will speed you onward. You are healthy, and your high spirits will send you a long way."

"The sun will be our friend," Jan said, trying to hold back his emotions. "You have saved our lives, and we are beholden for your friendship."

Luboš held Petra until Jan gently pulled him to the door. "Uncle Jozef and Aunt Petra, I have a full stomach and new boots. Thank you." With mutual gratitude and eternal thanks, the aged farmers sent the visitors on their renewed quest, towing the sledge loaded with dried and smoked trout.

Chapter 14: The Trek Resumes

Winter gave way to early spring. The boy and the deserter had miraculously survived, finding their daily rhythm in a diminished family. Crocuses pushed through the snow. The warmer nights and longer days invigorated them. Glittering morning dew replaced the frost on the icy rocks. Once again, the sun was in their faces at sunset as they traveled west as quickly as Jan could pull the sled.

Walking side by side, Luboš was curious about everything. Jan spoke Czech to explain the natural sciences of the green buds on branches, wildflowers breaking out, rock formations, and the several calls of birds returning to nest. Luboš answered in ever-improving Czech and a smattering of Slovak.

Although their handful of kilometers a day over the jagged rock formations were punishing, they moved steadily. Jan was pleased to see Luboš's maturity and that the war machines of the two countries seemed stalled behind them.

They grumbled about the monotonous smoked fish Jozef had packed. When it was gone, they longed for more. When dragging the sledge over the snow and mushy ground became too difficult, they left it and slung tarpaulins across their backs to carry their scant possessions.

The boy took naturally to using the Fuess compass, and Jan entrusted him with navigation. They took turns leading, and one morning, Luboš lagged. He removed his mittens and dug again and again into his pockets. Jan stopped to rest and asked, "Am I walking too fast?"

"I lost the compass," the eleven-year-old whispered. He slumped on the snow and didn't make eye contact. "I checked our heading at the last ridgeline and put it in this pocket. I want to go back and look for it."

"Two kilometers, and in the snow, we won't find it."

"You trusted me with the compass. Now we are lost."

"Not lost. Our navigation will be harder," Jan replied, careful to limit the boy's anguish and support him. "We have the sun and night stars, the same as ancient sailors. I will teach you dead reckoning navigation.

"We have traveled far in these weeks, about 150 kilometers since we left Jozef and Petra, and we might reach the Nitra Valley in two weeks. At night we will follow Venus as it passes the stars of the Seven Sisters. The planet is brightest this time of year and will steer us north of Bratislava to avoid the battle for the Slovak capital. We will be okay. Don't worry."

Luboš didn't worry. He trusted Jan as a father.

The mountain range veered to the south, leading them where battles would inevitably rage. The terrain in the lower altitudes was smoother and faster; however, Jan had concluded that the possibility of detection was too high. Jan chose his higher route, ignorant of the progress of the Red Army spring offensive.

Dogfights in the sky between German and Russian fighter planes were the first indication that retreating Germans were pushed farther west than Jan had anticipated.

A week later, he calculated from the movement of the air battles that the Russians were advancing rapidly toward Bratislava on the Danube River.

Jan was troubled that they would be on the Soviet side at the inevitable surrender and assumed more risk. They didn't detour far from villages, and he descended well below the tree line to travel faster. They and the withdrawing Germans rushed west—separated by the first rise of the foothills.

T-34 tanks of the mechanized Red Army pushed through the broad valleys south of the Low Tatras at a rate that rivaled the German advance into Russia in 1941. The duo warily converged to tank battles at the flank. Airplanes fought in the sky and crashed in a fireball. Seconds later, they heard the *crumpfh*.

During the day, clouds of smoke from burning instruments of war darkened the sky. The south wind sent them the sulfurous smell of exploded munitions and the thunder of combat. They witnessed the night sky illuminated by fingers of jet flames from thousands of Soviet Katyusha rockets launched to kill and terrorize Germans. They heard the distinctive whine of the missiles and saw the flashes of their impact. Brilliant white parachute flares launched by Soviet army artillery floated for minutes until they expired. They turned the night battlefield into day. Luboš was spellbound watching the display.

Jan held no sympathy for the Germans; he wasn't a religious man, but he prayed for the Soviets to bog down. He regretted leaving their winter haven so late.

Day and night Jan pulled Luboš onward in a race against time. The waning quarter moon provided little light. They couldn't see where their boots landed. They fell together. They got to their feet, and Jan pulled the boy until they fell again. They only stopped in a clearing long enough for Jan to check the polar star for navigation, or to drink from a stream, or if they were spent.

"We are running, and the branches are cutting me," complained Luboš, who lay collapsed on the ground.

"You are right," said Jan, who realized a fall would jeopardize them more than the enemy. "Go to sleep. At sunrise, I will re-cook the meat."

"It was a baby deer."

"It saved us."

No matter how hard they pushed, they couldn't move fast enough. Over several days Luboš lost count of Luftwaffe aircraft plummeting to the ground. Russian fighter planes supporting their army's advance controlled the skies.

Katyusha rockets, parachute flares, and the smell of sulfur were gone. There was no rumble of tank machinery. The battle lines of the Red Army were farther west, between them and Austria.

"We have rehearsed our story when the fighting ends."

"You are my uncle. After the Germans confiscated our farm in Kadan in Sudetenland, my Czech mother, your sister, and I followed you to the forced labor camp in Slovakia, where she found work at a farm. You sneaked away from the camp, and we attempted to return to Bohemia. Must I say my mother died?"

"Yes."

Chapter 15: The Red Army, April 1945

"Get down!" Jan said, pushing Luboš to the wet ground. He recognized the whine of German Zundapp motorcycles and thought a patrol was searching for partisans. Peering from a cluster of bushes, they followed two men on motorcycles spinning their wheels in clouds of mud and grass, weaving around trees in the field. They were not wearing uniforms and howled as loud as the engines. The bikers zoomed out of sight below their hide. The motors revved high and low until the bikes burst into view, roaring straight at them.

Jan readied his rifle, his last three cartridges, and aimed at the closest joyrider. The driver weaved and careened out of control, falling in a heap onto the ground. Jan's finger eased off the trigger. The men were drunk, and it was clear they were jubilant astride abandoned military motorcycles.

Jan presumed a significant event had occurred. He hid his weapon, not sure he would pull the trigger again. He shed his filthy outer garments and nervously walked into the open to the bikers, who exclaimed, "The Red Army defeated the Germans at Bratislava two days ago. We are celebrating!"

The motorcycles sped down the hill out of sight, yielding silence. Jan flopped on the ground, his rifle at his side, and swept the silent sky.

"One last time, check your pockets for anything that might betray us." Jan emptied his pockets of the remaining ammunition and disgustedly said, "I won't need my rifle."

Luboš tightened his eyes and asked, "Why not? You said we are just days from Austria."

"The Russians will shoot a man holding a rifle. It's simpler for them to kill than ask a question."

"We aren't going to Austria?"

"Uncertainty was our friend when the two armies were fighting. However dangerous the partisans or the Germans were, we were able to move west. Now we know. The Russians rule Slovakia and will clamp down, hunting for any opposition. Better in a refugee camp than shot in a field."

"We aren't running?"

"This will be our last night."

"We might be separated tomorrow?" Luboš desperately queried.

"We will stay together. We will meet refugees tomorrow—that's why you speak Czech and Slovak. You are Slavic, a Northern Slav."

They cut each other's shock of hair with Jan's now dulled knife, its whetstone lost in snow. One sleeve of Luboš's coat dangled. Jan had lost so much weight that he seemed to hide inside his coat. It had fit him in Smižany.

The end of World War II, the Great Patriotic War, was close at hand. For two bloody years, the Red Army had pushed the Germans west through Ukraine, Poland, and Slovakia. The pair had traveled 850 kilometers along mountain ranges that protected and tortured them, but it was not far enough.

Their long flight from Ukraine ended in Soviet-controlled territories, short of the American army. Czechoslovakia was a broken country. Hitler had annexed Czech lands of Bohemia and Moravia in 1938. Slovakia, subordinated to Germany, had declared its independence in 1939. Jan anticipated confusion would reign until a new hierarchy was established.

Jan had endeavored to fulfill his promise to Nadiya, to lead her son to freedom. He had failed, but he kept his dismay from the boy. Before they set off the next morning, the deserter drew his army knife from its sheath for the last time. He ran his finger along its ragged beveled edge and angrily stabbed deep in the soil to its crossguard. He ditched it, erect, next to the sheath and their last tarpaulin, damp from the overnight rain.

Jan did not tell his charge that he was ashamed to have surrendered to winter and would soon to the Russians.

"We must be vigilant," Jan instructed. They descended from the protection of the mountains and entered the broad Nitra Valley. "Now, we keep quiet and listen."

Jan and Luboš joined a stream of scores, then hundreds, of impoverished men, women, and children. They, too, had conceded and plodded sluggishly, unknowingly, to the new system.

Luboš and Jan were wretched, and their odors challenged their surroundings. The muddy highway was littered with destroyed vehicles and reeked of oil, stale smoke, and rotting flesh of humans and horses. The miserable mix of refugees walked south, anxiety troubling Jan more than young Luboš.

They were unsure where they were going. By midday, the growing multitude approached a sloppily painted sign, "Nováky," in Russian Cyrillic script. The sick and malnourished fell along the way for the last time, moaning weakly. Women sang solemn hymns, perhaps expecting salvation. Jan processed the rumors spread in various languages.

One man drew Jan's attention to a slave labor camp they passed. He said to Jan in Slovak, "I worked in that coal mining camp. I slipped away last year. From that loading dock, we sent coal to Germany. Priorities changed, and then the trains took Jews to a place called Auschwitz. It is in Poland."

Since 1943 Jan had seen German army message traffic about the urgent deportation of Jews to Poland. And he knew why.

"Were you hiding or trying to go somewhere?"

"Hiding. We gave up trying to reach Austria or Switzerland," the former slave miner said dejectedly.

"Oh."

Jan never mentioned the Jewish plight, and Luboš did not fully understand. "Why were Jews sent to Poland?"

"Hitler and the Nazis hated them." Jan was pained to have been associated with such an evil country.

"We met Jews last fall."

"We did, and I hope they are safe."

"I can't tell the difference between the people we see. We are the same: tired, hungry, and ragged."

"Yes, but we have different tongues. You have been learning Czech for seven months and Slovak for three months. The languages are similar, and you think in Czech. You think in Slovak."

Later, the miner nudged Jan and raised and turned his head to the side of the road. Through the few trees not mown down by artillery explosions, Jan viewed lined up bodies of murdered Wehrmacht soldiers. Jan was grateful Luboš didn't notice.

Jan tramped on, hoping their well-rehearsed story would be accepted.

Czechoslovakian President Beneš, in exile in London and under guidance from Czechoslovak Communists in Moscow, had issued cruel exportation decrees that resulted in murderous repatriation policies. Russian and Slovak political officers of the NKVD and Povereníctvom Welfare wielded unlimited authority to filter the subjugated population and deport intellectuals, German collaborators, Hungarians, Ukrainians, Poles—indeed, any non-Czechoslovak.

One step at a time, the dirty brown mass followed the signs. In sight of the church steeples of Nováky, they stopped. Red Army soldiers guided the war-weary refugees to a stadium for processing. The Russians were the winners, and they deemed the filthy mortals in line, losers. The losers were searched for weapons, and the winners stole their valuables. A soldier wearing three watches on his wrist was common. The butt of a rifle met any protest.

The twosome moved at a snail's pace until they saw officers ahead conducting quick examinations of individuals and entire families. Getting closer, Jan heard officers utter snap judgments and motion right or left. Refugees guided to the left were registered and accepted the officer's decision. Refugees conducted to the right raised their voices and wretchedly asked for reconsideration. Bayonets fixed, soldiers forcibly prodded the complainers. Jan soon understood why. The hapless sent to the right walked between barbed wire fences leading out of the stadium to railway loading docks. Jan's story must convince the authorities, or they would be pushed to the waiting train.

Jan clenched Luboš's hand and stepped forward when called. "Where are your papers?" demanded the Russian officer.

"We, we have no papers," stuttered a tense Jan in front of the table.

"That is a complication. Where are you from?"

"We are Novák from Kadan, Bohemia."

"Let me question him," said the Slovak officer assisting the Russian. "I'm familiar with that area. You, why are you in this line?"

Jan recited their account of dislocation.

The Slovak officer asked question after question until the Russian interrupted and curtly declared, "Hurry up, left or right?"

"Left."

Their names were registered and noted as boy and uncle. Their possessions were written as "none."

Clear of the officers, Jan exhaled and said, "Thus far, we are okay."

"Our last name is Novák?"

"Yes, you are Luboš Novák. I can't use my real name, and Novák is a respected Czech name for you to commence your new life."

"What is your real name?"

"Czernek, but forget that name."

Late in the unseasonably hot spring day, they were directed to a fenced-in field. Luboš and his uncle gulped their first water in two days and splashed water from a bucket on their heads to cool off. They took off their sodden boots to dry their sore feet. There was nowhere to run.

Jan found that only Czechs and Slovaks were in their segregated corner of the field and did not know if the separation was good or bad. Jan and Luboš spent one more night under the sky.

Those not selected for registration faced a dark fate at the railroad tracks. Slatted freight cars stamped CCCP and Lviv were destined for the Lviv Transit Prison in Ukraine for transfer to labor camps of the Gulag in Siberia.

The din of war was far to the west. The loudest sounds in Nováky were the slamming of cargo doors, the chugging of the steam locomotives, and broadcasts in Russian from Moscow Radio paying homage to the Workers' and Peasants' Red Army.

Optimism gave way to the reality that the war's end began a new struggle for survival, except without tanks and airplanes. Soviet-controlled countries in Europe were ridding themselves of their diverse Ottoman and Austro-Hungarian heritage through elimination and expulsion. In Czechoslovakia, they called it Reslovakization. "Cleansing" of the refugee population meant murder, forced labor, or unwilling repatriation to the country from which they had fled.

Russian counter-intelligence officers conducted a more rigorous filtration in a second round of interviews to ferret out Czechoslovaks who had been in contact with Westerners. Even prisoners of war were prejudged traitors and dispatched to the trains.

"Hand over your papers," ordered the officer, waving his Tokarev TT 33 pistol. "This boy is your nephew? He doesn't look to be in your family. Where are you from again?"

"Here is our registration from yesterday. We will look alike after I shave my beard."

"Don't be smart," the Russian threatened.

"I'm sorry, I didn't mean it that way. I was slave labor to the east. I told my family to stay in Bohemia, but they traveled to Smižany in 1942. We escaped last summer, and he is the last to survive."

"You are Czech or German?"

"I am Czech, I am Bohemian," declared both Jan and Luboš.

"Boy, your accent is wrong. Where are you from?"

"I grew up on a Czech farm. My mother brought me to Slovakia. I mix the languages."

"Get going." Jan's account was holding up under intense scrutiny, and they returned to the Czechoslovak corner.

Later, Jan put his hand on Luboš's shoulder and said quietly, "We can trust no one here." Everyone owned a survival story, and few dared share it. "And don't forget."

"Yes, uncle. I am Czech."

"I'm amazed at the efficiency of the interrogation and immediate distribution of refugees to the trains," Jan remarked later that day. "I was expecting confusion."

Luboš gripped Jan's hand throughout the first days. He was in a daze gawking at the already defeated people enduring more humiliation. The possibility that his father died a prisoner on a train tormented him.

The displaced Czechs and Slovaks marched to a recently vacated barracks of a forced labor factory. On their second day in detention, their heads were shaved, and all were sprayed for lice. Jan saw a scrawny, hollow-eyed child. Luboš saw an emaciated man with a long scar on his back. The boy did not inquire. They were given ill-fitting clothing leftover from the labor camp and ravenously drank the gruel, their first nourishment in days.

Captives though they were, the novelty of regular meals and a stable roof over their heads gave them a sense of stability in their tenuous world. The barracks disclosed a dark, recent past. Names of Jews etched on the walls marked a footnote of their existence.

"Should you scratch our names on the wall?" Luboš knew how to write Dmytro in Ukrainian, but not Luboš Novák or the current date in Czech.

"No. You and I will not be forgotten," Jan said, shuddering as he recalled his deception when he hid the family's registration papers in the empty barn.

Luboš pointed to the barbed wire fence adjacent to the rail siding. The sign "Juden" lay askew at the entrance.

Jan struggled to inform Luboš. "In the Nazi-occupied countries, Jews were arrested... they were sent ..." Jan fumbled his words and gave up trying to explain the unexplainable.

"The camp is empty."

"The Germans in Slovakia surrendered a few days ago," Jan said, looking aside.

Instinctively, Luboš avoided the topic.

Were they refugees, prisoners, internees, or detainees? Thus far, they had survived the arbitrary decisions of the officials and the boy's repatriation to Ukraine.

Luboš had departed the farm a playful youngster anticipating a long walk with a good-natured German. His wiry frame was now dangerously thin, and blank stares revealed what words could not describe. Every child in the camp had faced danger, Luboš especially.

The Czechoslovaks passed the empty days awaiting their disposition in what they were told was a resettlement camp. The weeks were colorless and filled with anxiety, interrupted twice by drunken Slovak and Red Army soldiers who roamed the camp, shooting their weapons into the sky. The victors celebrated the 30 April suicide of Adolf Hitler and Germany's unconditional surrender on 7 May. The refugees did not celebrate as enthusiastically.

Idle time forced Jan to question his motives. He justified his desire to avoid more combat by leading himself and a family to freedom. Selfishly, he had convinced Nadiya to leave Ukraine. The love that developed between them was real, although he had led most of them to their death. He was unable to reconcile his defeat. All he could do was protect Luboš.

"I told you that our situation would improve. The Russians are well organized, and I'm certain they will send us to Bohemia soon. They won't feed us forever."

Regrettably, Jan misjudged the chaos in Europe. The Communists were reluctant to release men while labor was required to repair war damage. The new routine in the temporary transit camp was to rise early, eat the gruel, and work wherever the guards dictated. Adult internees marched to former battlefields to bury the dead in mass graves, dig out buried trucks, and clear minefields.

Several in Jan's work brigade were killed after stepping on landmines until he explained on the morning march his technique to dig and disarm them. He kept to himself his knowledge of the mines he had placed in 1940 to protect German defenses before Operation Barbarossa. A few months earlier, he had passed blindly through German minefields north of Košice, and here he was near Bratislava digging up the identical type mines he had placed five years earlier. He was more terrified digging for mines with his makeshift trowel than in combat against the Poles or Russians.

For Luboš, the days were idle, but he and Jan slept side by side at night. After a month of modest nourishment, Luboš, a head shorter than his adopted uncle, gained weight and developed a stringy rugged build. Minimal camp sanitation attracted more biting flies than their worst day on the trek. Sickness was pervasive.

By summer, work slackened. Manual labor was called for less and less. Half of their Czechoslovak assembly had died of disease or been transferred. Jan trembled at each broadcast of names to report to administration.

Three months after their arrival in Nováky, Jan and Luboš were called for distribution to different transit camps. Luboš cried out a step behind as Jan ran to the office of the camp superintendent to ask for a review. Jan's lips quivered and he appealed, "There is a mistake. They did not mean to split us. Can we stay together until a review is complete?"

"There is no error. It's final," the Slovak officer gruffly declared.

"Can't you see my boy should stay with his family?" Jan pleaded as Luboš hugged his leg.

"If you miss your truck and he misses the train, both of you will be on your way to Lviv on one of those railcars marked CCCP."

Luboš held onto Jan and cried out, "Uncle Jan, don't let them separate us! I'm afraid."

"Both of us are afraid. We must collect your clothing. Hurry."

"Uncle, where am I going?"

"I don't know where either of us will go."

"I want to go with you."

"Luboš," Jan said as he steeled himself to avoid tears, "you have learned how to survive."

Jan stopped outside the barracks entrance and knelt. "We held on through the winter. It is our strength. We will cherish the memory of your mother, your family. We will meet again."

"I have no one."

"You are no longer a boy. You are stronger than you think. I will find you." Jan stood up and rushed Luboš to the rail siding. It was the same siding that had sent Jews to Auschwitz and unfortunates to Lviv.

Jan stopped and repeated his words of encouragement. "Look at me. Remember this, Luboš; you are stronger than you think."

"I'm scared," was all Luboš could say before Jan ran to his canvas-covered truck. His eyes locked onto the back of his mentor as the distance between them grew.

I led them to their death, Jan thought, while running away from Luboš. Jan was as unsure of his future as the day he was blown off the tank. The boy is torn from me. I may jump under the wheels of the train. Then Jan's inner strength reasserted itself.

He turned and called out, "I will find you."

Part Two: Luboš Becomes a Man, 1946-1955

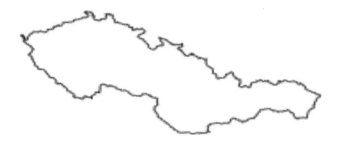

Czechoslovakia

Escape From Ukraine

Chapter 16: Luboš Alone

Luboš lowered his head in defeat and pushed through the railcar entrance. Soldiers swore at the occupants to make room for more boys, then slammed the door and pounded a spike into the staple of the hasp. Steam whistles sounded, the locomotive lurched, and couplings clanged until the freight cars stretched out.

His oppressively hot box rolled and rocked on uneven tracks. Luboš hallucinated about trains marked Lviv, jam-packed with frightened refugees. He worried he was deceived and riding east on the wrong train towards Russia. To his relief, sunlight shining through cracks eventually convinced him that he was traveling northwest.

While some of the boys were thrilled to leave the unpleasant camp, he barely breathed. The same numbness that had descended upon him after his mother died reappeared. Then, an adult had protected him. Luboš was alone, and Uncle Jan's reassuring hand was missing. The stop and go train traveled day and night and brought whimpers from the cast of young boys.

I have to be stronger than I think, Luboš repeated to himself. Memories of Jan's confidence carried him through the first days of separation, tempered by his father's final advice, "When I return, you will be a man." He must be manly enough to locate food, find a blanket, and defend himself.

He was fortunate to have been categorized as Jan's nephew at registration the first day. It distinguished him from "unaccompanied child" or a waif stealing on the streets. Luboš departed Nováky with new identity papers, a few garments, and Jan's advice to be wise to your surroundings and be invisible.

The boys disembarked at a youth transit camp between Bratislava and Prague. It was a former prisoner of war camp and little improved. If this was peace, Luboš reckoned, it was awful. The lightly supervised facility provided minimal nourishment, unheated shelter, no medical care, and no protection from bullying. He listened and stayed out of the way or fought fiercely when necessary.

The transfer or release of youths orphaned by war was random. Unsure how long his assignment would be at the camp, Luboš found friends for self-protection. He observed how new arrivals fit in and befriended any he might trust. He would initiate a chat in the afternoon before meal call and say, "When I first arrived, I rushed to the head of the line for bread and a full cup of watery soup."

"Is it always soup?"

"Millet soup, sometimes with carrots and potatoes. Rarely pork. The man holding the ladle does not dip to the bottom of the cook pot. Then I went to the end of the line. That was worse."

"Why not the end? The best is at the bottom."

"At the end of the line, they might run out of both bread and soup. The men in the kitchen are the only people in Czechoslovakia who have a belly over their pants. They take the first sip of the soup and finish the last bites of meat. I position myself in the middle of the line and maybe get a bite of pork."

"Is this a good place?"

"It should be," replied Luboš as he expanded his cluster of friends.

Russian and Czechoslovak Communist leaders controlled critical levers of government and the daily camp regimen. In the streets, factories, and city offices, the contest for the future was between democratic principles and Communist doctrine. Luboš knew nothing of the political fight that would influence his life for forty more years.

While foreign relief agencies sent flour, grains, and necessities to needy organizations, proper distribution fell victim to black-market thieves, greedy officials, and the guards.

On rare occasions, Luboš saw inspectors of the United Nations Relief and Rehabilitation Agency escorted through his camp. The internees were warned to expect punishment if they accurately described camp conditions.

One day, Luboš heard a Russian and American arguing in Czech about poor camp conditions, in particular the American's insistence that a refugee should consume 1500 calories daily. The American pointed out the well-fed guards while children remained gaunt, long after the fighting ceased.

"You. Hey, you." Luboš turned around to see the Russian calling him.

"Me?"

Boring deeply into Luboš's eyes, the Russian asked, "The American will ask what you eat. Go ahead, Captain."

"I'm here to learn about your camp. How long have you been here?" the crisply uniformed American asked with a smile, clipboard poised.

"Uh, about two months."

"Tell me about your meals yesterday."

"I ate bread and soup."

"How often do you have bread and soup?" the U.S. Army officer continued.

"Twice a day."

"Are you hungry now...?" He started to ask more questions but was cut off by the Russian.

"See, they have sufficient food. Everyone in Europe is hungry except you Americans. Your inspection is complete." The boy followed the pleasant American as he was ushered out. Luboš thought, no wonder we were trying to reach them.

Luboš did not know what a calorie was. However, he knew hunger around him. He knew it when they butchered the animals, including the goat and dogs. Hope turned to disillusion, and suicide was common.

The smarter youths were sent for indoctrination and admission to gymnasia schools to become future acolytes of the Communist system. Luboš spoke Russian poorly and was not rated smart enough for that select circle.

Overwhelmed government camps gladly sent children to orphanages funded by international religious and relief organizations. The next step for Luboš in the post-war relocation process was assignment to a Young Men's Christian Association International orphanage in Prague. Though it was a dismal place, it was far better than the forest or transit camps.

At the farm and in the village, Luboš had no friends or formal education. The YMCA staff introduced him to hygiene, manners, the use of cutlery, and flush toilets. They gave him a basic education and his sole structured religious instruction. Though he admired the morals of the staff, he did not accept God.

Luboš glimpsed from the classroom window the oppressive Russian occupiers and daydreamed during Russian language instruction. Luboš diligently studied to improve his Czech reading and writing.

Beyond the orphanage, aspirations for a free society were dashed in 1948. Communists grabbed total control of the government in a coup d'état in a fraudulent election. Wary families fled to the United States Allied Occupation Zone in Austria. This time, no adult said, "Let's go."

Chapter 17: Young Worker, 1948–1955

The Czechoslovak Interior Ministry, alarmed that outside organizations might adversely steer youth to Western values, starved the YMCA of necessities. The era called for young refugees to mature quickly, and after three years of gloom, Luboš was thrust into a slot in the industrialized country to fill the workforce shortage. The director of the YMCA found the boy an apprentice position at a truck maintenance enterprise where he was assigned menial and dirty work. He cleaned the premises, changed oil, and slept in the basement by the coal chute. Luboš was a fourteen-year-old toiler in Czechoslovakia's first Five-Year Plan.

For Luboš, the tallest building in Ukraine was the former church that held the granary. Nováky's largest were three stories, and from a distance, he had spotted the magnificent castles high on the hills of Bratislava. The newly freed young man transported to the middle of congested Prague was overwhelmed, and he hesitated to venture out.

Luboš was shy and cautious in the new setting. Neither a boy nor a man, he was lean and handsome with a well-shaped chin, broad nose, and peach fuzz on his cheeks. His serious face gave no hint of a smile or frown. His days of curiosity and adventure at his farm and in Smižany were over. His world expected him to submit. He adapted quickly to those confines. Following Jan's guidance that it is best to listen, Luboš responded in conversation but seldom initiated one.

The Germans and the Communists had confiscated tools and machines, making business recovery difficult. The owner of the truck garage criticized government policies and relied on the black market for equipment. Luboš was content to hide in the shadow economy.

Luboš was a loner, but he wasn't lonely. He worked and then whiled his spare time at the muddy-brown Vltava River, watching tugboats pushing or pulling barges. Brief chats with fishermen on a bridge or the beach at Zlute Lazne beneath the hills of Prague revived his interest in fishing. Five years had passed since his ice-fishing adventures with Jozef and Jan.

And where was Jan? Every transfer had reduced the chance for Jan to track Luboš through the bureaucracy.

Luboš's father had pushed either crickets or worms onto homemade hooks and floated chips of wood for bobbers at their pond. Luboš asked one man, "The Vltava flows rapidly. Do you drop your hook to the bottom? What kind of fish is that?"

"Are you new here? Are you from here?" the man asked without turning his head.

"I fished in the lakes of the Low Tatras Mountains."

"Your accent is not Prague."

"I am from Slovakia. I change oil in trucks." To strangers, it was simpler for him to be a Slovak from Smižany. To an authority, continuity required Luboš to be from Bohemia.

"It is barbel, and it tastes good cooked in lard." The response was the best one could expect.

The fast-moving river water was far different from his pond and stream. Luboš appreciated the tips he gleaned from fellow fishermen about the proper poles, hooks, bait, and technique. He developed his skills and cooked his catch with lard on top of the shop furnace. Luboš thought wistfully of the fish his mother and Petra had cooked with butter that he had churned.

His mind ran free at the water's edge, where he swept through memories of his parents, the trek, Jan, or Aunt

Alya. Luboš understood Uncle Yarik's hatred of Communism better after hearing his co-workers complain. His mother was a woman of great fortitude, which he appreciated in hindsight more than at the moment. He followed the tugboat's frothy waves until they crashed into the embankment wall and bounced back—echoing his first seventeen years.

Luboš was quiet and polite, and he fit in at work tuning engines and repairing damaged vehicles. He spent a little extra money on a change of clothes and avoided political discussions, in part due to his accented and limited Czech. He listened and learned about the trials and purges from the Communist takeover.

As Communist central planning expanded and industry revived, Luboš's garage was nationalized in 1952, and he moved from his semi-indentured status.

"Hey, Luboš," the owner hailed. "My business is no more. It is true; everyone has a job in socialism, ha, ha. We won't have to steal or rely on the black market. We will be state employees of the Prague Transport Enterprise and repair trucks and buses."

"All right, I guess," Luboš replied while lying under a truck, turning an oil filter. "Will we receive more ration coupons?"

"It's better than that," the owner yelled. "You will be assigned housing for single men. We might have a cafeteria here."

"Will all of us work there?" Luboš asked after emerging with oil splashed on his coveralls. He wanted his amiable friend Bohdan, a marginal worker, included. Although Bohdan lacked a diligent work ethic, he was a constant companion with a cheerful face, tubby pretense, and fun-loving nature.

"Yes, all of us. You will do the same work, and they will give coupons regularly." The new system was as the owner described. Luboš claimed a bed in an ancient dormitory for those struggling at the bottom rung of society.

The countries of Eastern Europe were reconstructed in Russia's oppressive image between 1945 and 1953. Although not all citizens agreed, Luboš welcomed Stalin's death in 1953. The famines, the purges, the Gulag dictated by Stalin, were reassessed, and the government-initiated improvements.

The Czechoslovak Communist Party, the KSC, called for the removal of bronze and granite statues of Stalin. Luboš was on the Prague Transport truck crew that relocated them to a remote field on the city's outskirts. Unceremoniously, the former icons were pushed off the flatbed. Luboš took great pleasure banging Stalin's head with his crowbar.

"This one is from Uncle Yarik." At each swing, he added, "This is from my father. This is from my mother, this is from my aunt," until he stopped to rest.

"My turn, my turn," Bohdan passionately demanded. "Give me the crowbar!"

Chapter 18: Private Luboš Novák, 1955–1956

Luboš expected his conscription at age twenty-one into the Czechoslovak People's Army. Unlike the years when his father and Jan were sent into combat, his new country was not in a hot war. They were a buffer on the world stage between east and west and in a constant state of tension. Although he was older than fellow recruits, he was less educated. He was mentally prepared for the demeaning indoctrination and hazing in the Soviet military template. Ramrod straight for inspections, he thrived on the challenges and gained strength from his improved diet.

After boot camp, he began his infantry training to be a foot soldier—a grunt. He was naturally intrigued by the disciplines of map reading and ground navigation. During meal breaks, he went to maps of Slovakia and neighboring countries and retraced his route to Nováky as best he could. Jan would have traced the route precisely. He daydreamed. Nováky to Austria, 150 kilometers and two weeks would have meant safety. For him, that was infinity.

Brought from his daze, he heard, "Congratulations, Luboš, for winning the award for best in our company for field skills," said an admirer. "How did you find the target during our night navigation test?"

"We started at dusk, and after the sky darkened I referenced Venus and the polar star. The exercise was to the west, and those stars were familiar. If the night was cloudy, or the direction was not west," he joked, "I would still be lost." The recruits did not know how hard-won his skills were.

Luboš paid strict attention in basic training, where he learned how to arm and disarm landmines. One day the men loaded sixty-six-kilogram projectiles into tubes of a massive Katyusha rocket launcher. Luboš was selected to arm the system and trigger the entire salvo of forty-eight rockets.

"That howling sound is amazing," a soldier stated. "No wonder the Germans feared the Katyusha."

"At night, they are devilish," Luboš replied. "If they were aimed at me, I would be scared shitless."

Ice hockey was the most popular sport in Czechoslovakia. Stars on city hockey clubs were drafted into the army. Several were selected to represent the country in the 1956 Olympics, and the base commander allowed radio broadcasts of the games in the mess hall.

Luboš's enduring devotion to the sport began with his military pals passionately following the Olympics. One asked him, "Which is your favorite team in Prague?"

"At work, they say Sparta is the best."

"Sparta. They are the best in Czechoslovakia," declared an avid hockey friend. "The center on the second line, Slavomir Barton, plays at Sparta. He played on the army hockey team last year and scored in yesterday's game."

"Well, I will root for Sparta, and tomorrow, I will cheer for Barton." He found common ground as a Czech. When the Czechoslovak team finished in fifth place, Luboš was disappointed. The outcome was even harder to tolerate because Russia won the gold medal.

Luboš was proficient in firing his weapons and identified as the top recruit. He was confident in his duties in support of the Czechoslovak Socialist Republic (CSSR), which included patrolling southeastern Slovak regions densely populated by Hungarians.

Infrequent trips to the Hornad River to fish broke the monotony. "Okay, fish, I'm tired of waiting. Uncle Jozef jumped up and down on the ice. Here, I give you fresh grubs." Luboš brought back bream and carp to supplement the meals prepared for the conscripts.

Luboš remembered the bitter wind and blinding snow at age eleven when he had crossed the frozen river on his way, seeking the Americans. He was unnerved stationed not far from Smižany in the mountains, passes, and valleys painfully tramped. At least in the army, he wore warm clothing, ate three meals a day, and slept under a roof or a massive canvas tent.

He scrutinized detailed topographic maps and contemplated. Hmmm, we started in June and ended in April in Nováky. Ahh, Luboš tapped the map, this might be Jozef's icy lake. We passed south of Prešov and waited for days at this major highway. His eyes welled as his finger passed over where his mother, Uncle Yarik, and Aunt Alya met their fate—ill-defined areas on the map.

Autumn 1956 placed Private Novák at an army camp south of Košice off Highway 17, not far from the Hungarian border. His company was hastily issued live ammunition in a full force mobilization and marched south past Kechnec at double time. Czechoslovak T-34 tanks and Katyusha rocket launchers sped past them to defend the border—or to initiate an assault into Hungary. The vehicles drove into the edges of the forest and aimed their weapons south. Luboš, already exhausted, dug his foxhole between the border and the tanks. The exhilaration of impending battle was balanced by the memory of his father's wartime injuries.

The following day trucks brought mines for the infantrymen to conceal near the major highway. The officer gave strict instructions: "Follow the proscribed grid. If the Hungarians don't attack, you will dig up these mines." Luboš had been attentive when Jan described clearing mines near Nováky. He ensured his fellow soldiers were precise.

The Russian political officers were unwilling to disclose the mission. Still, rumors alluded to Hungarians rising against the Communist Party. Vaguely trained in the alliances of the Warsaw Pact, he was unsure of the reason to fight. His family mistrust of Communism in Ukraine and his experiences in Prague led him to question whether any cause was just.

The soldier next to him peered south, holding his rifle at the ready. Luboš asked, "Why are we in a foxhole for two days?"

"Just what they tell us."

"I mean, more than what the Russian told us about the Hungarian deviation from Soviet ideology?"

"I was born not far from here," the soldier replied, more interested in his situation than Luboš's question, "and I have Hungarian relatives. At the personnel shift of last spring, Hungarian conscripts were sent north to Prague and Czechs like you replaced them here. Our generals feared that in a conflict against Hungary, there was a chance of mutiny. Don't you remember the short war between Hungary and Slovakia in 1939?"

"No. I came to Smižany in 1942.

"That was a strange time, you know, with the war."

"I was young and followed my family.

"Were they German?"

"Czech, slave labor." Luboš ended the thread and asked, "You are Hungarian. Why are you here?"

"The records don't show it," he said in a matter-of-fact tone. "I was in a camp after the war, and we marched to clean up the battlefields. Step out of line and a Russian sergeant hits you."

"Maybe Hungary stepped out of line," Luboš suggested.

"That makes sense. What will you do if the Hungarians cross the border?"

"Shoot. What will you do if we attack Hungary?"

"I don't know," replied the puzzled Hungarian conscript.

Luboš didn't share his Ukrainian heritage or tell his buddy what he was thinking. Jan wore his uniform and reluctantly did what he was told. His father fired his weapon for a system he despised. Both fought in two wars, first a young man, later an old man. Is this my first war, he mused?

Luboš shivered under his poncho in early snowstorms, evoking his slog twelve years earlier. The adrenalin rush anticipating combat quickly wore off. Luboš ate cold food and longed to light a fire to ward off the cold.

After sixty days, the Hungarian insurrection was declared crushed, and the alert was rescinded. The soldiers set about the most hazardous aspect of the Russian invasion: find and disarm each mine. The officers were relieved the mines were safely returned to storage and commended the soldiers for their diligence.

Czechoslovak army presence returned to normal, and Luboš's two-year obligation was complete. He mustered out a confident man.

Chapter 19: Elite Bus Assignment, 1957–1967

The army had been a success for Luboš. Now broad-shouldered from his improved nutrition and exercise, he walked with a lively step. He was self-assured with his commendations and confirmation as a Czech. His confidence was short-lived.

He returned to Prague on a mission to search for Jan, whom he last heard from at their climactic separation when he asserted, "I will find you."

Luboš traveled by bus to Kadan and inquired at the office of the collective farm for information about Jan Novák, hoping Jan had kept that name. Luboš described the uncle and all the information he could remember. Each official rudely rebuffed him.

He was tempted to ask for Jan Czernek, but Jan had said, "Forget that name." Luboš had lost his birth name, Dmytro, and Jan had reason to forget Czernek. Unsettled by his poor reception in Kadan, Luboš did not inquire.

At the Interior Ministry in Prague, he asked for assistance to research 1945 records of the Nováky internment camp. The supervisor overheard and detained him in his office to ask detailed questions from his birth onward, as though Luboš were a threat to the state. He gave up, upset that he might be under suspicion for his curiosity. He still feared displacement to Ukraine.

Upon his return to work at the transportation facility, Luboš resumed the passive spirit of the Czech citizenry. He rushed each evening to a state store to queue for bread, finding only empty shelves. The next day he waited at a different store for vegetables to buy a soft potato. The twenty-four-year-old did not complain. There was no one to complain to.

The loss of men in the war enabled quick advancement for those who remained. In recognition of his army skills, Luboš was reassigned to a unique motor pool within Prague Transport. He worked on modern air-conditioned buses that transported elite Communist dignitaries and delegations to official guesthouses and Party functions in Czechoslovakia. The large coaches, equipped with toilets and a petite galley, also traveled to Warsaw Pact allies and the western countries of Austria and West Germany.

"I didn't ask for a new situation," Luboš said to Bohdan, his longtime friend, "but I'm glad the boss picked us. Our schedule is easier, and we get leftovers." Bohdan was the chubby, happy one in the tight-knit clique of ardent hockey fans. He was the liveliest, pranking whenever he could.

For Luboš, life was okay. A trusted worker, he repaired, cleaned, and positioned the buses for maintenance. His work at the motor pool wasn't challenging, he was never sick, and his boss counted on him to be sober for inspections. One week a month, he was assigned night shift, and he valued the change of routine and its benefits: reviewing with Bohdan the latest Sparta hockey game and playing the card game Durak with whoever was awake. Uncle Yarik had taught him the game, which he had played endlessly in the army. He could snooze at midnight next to the diesel engine case and stay warm. His responsibility was to wake his comrades before the boss arrived.

Prague had been spared aerial bombing in the war, leaving ancient city landmarks intact. However, the years of Communist oppression stole the vitality of Czech citizens. The unstated bargain was that the populace had a semblance of comfort if they accepted domination.

To carry on under the menacing system, most fell to the attitude of a "Švejkism compromise," complying and not believing. Named after the fictitious Austro-Hungarian soldier Švejk in *The Good Soldier Švejk,* the satirical book by Czech author Jaroslav Hašek about the Great War, Švejkism was passive resistance.

Czechs listened but did not hear and submitted but did not approve. Unknowingly, Luboš had been acting in the Švejk character since 1945. Fishing, following ice hockey, and work fulfilled him.

Švejkism was the realpolitik response to the fear of Communism.

Luboš attended mandatory political education meetings promoting the latest Five-Year Plan heralding model comrades, udarniks, who increased their production by hundreds of percent in factories and mines. Luboš was pleased no quotas or competitions existed at Prague Transport Enterprise. He knew nothing about Marx, a little about Lenin, and too much about Stalin.

It was easy to be a nobody in the society of expressionless stares. Except for his growing ardor for hockey, the years were barely distinguishable.

Luboš read old newspapers left on the buses to keep track of hockey league standings and the best players on Sparta. They had been the national champions of the early 1950s, and lately, they were attempting to regain lost glory. Luboš, Bohdan, and fellow transport workers attended the games, where they drank beer and cheered and jeered as staunch fans will. At their animated game reviews the next day, they offered their versions of advice for players and coaches.

The maintenance crew appealed to the boss to watch the 1960 Winter Olympic Games contested in America at Lake Placid. "There is a nine-hour time difference, and games are played before work. May we put a television in the conference room?"

"No," the boss replied, pointing to a room deeper in the maintenance area. That was tacit approval for a TV—just don't tell him and don't let it interfere in the maintenance of the buses.

The workers were confident in their hockey team. The day and night shifts crowded together, their eyes glued to the too-small Russian-manufactured Junost black and white television. The Soviet Union beat Czechoslovakia in the first game of the medal round, and six days later, the Czechoslovaks had the opportunity to win the bronze medal if they beat team USA.

"The Americans are lazy, they are fat," yelled the chorus. "The referees call penalties against us and not the Americans. Our goalie is hot. We are ahead 4-3 in the second period. We finish strong." The non-stop happy banter swelled until the final twenty minutes when the Americans scored six goals to win 9-4 and the gold medal. "How did they blow that? We owned them. We should have won the bronze. Get rid of the coach. The team is too old. Fourth place stinks." Czechoslovaks were despondent.

After hockey season, Bohdan, the ringleader directed the enthusiasts to the sport of bowling, recently introduced to Czechoslovakia. The evenings of boisterous drinking were social, with more passion for the women bowlers than the game. Although Luboš's calm temperament drew friends easily, his friends in the troop were savvier with women. He had witnessed affection and peeked at lovemaking in the farmhouse, but he didn't have the confidence to compete for a woman. He attributed his lack of interest to his shyness and accented second language.

Luboš moved to new communal rooms for displaced single men after his old dormitory was declared unsafe. Conversation penetrated the walls of the hastily built five-story Stalinist panelák towers, known for their prefabricated concrete structure. Four beds, a tiny kitchen, and two chairs filled the space. The window leaked, the ceiling light fixture dangled loosely, and the small refrigerator rattled. The common toilet was down the hall. Luboš washed his clothes in the basement and hung them to dry wherever he could. At an illegal open-air market, he bought a cardboard closet to store a change of clothes, an extra pair of boots, and his army private pin. The crowded space offered nominal privacy and no dignity. Roommates maintained a solitary routine. The courtyard was for mothers to rock their babies and informants to eavesdrop.

The anonymous structures were identical in their formulaic neighborhood, anchored by a statue of Lenin. The streets were bare of trees, and the few operative lights cast long shadows. On several occasions after his multi-tram commute from work, Luboš walked obliviously through the maze and up sterile concrete stairwells to find that the key to his door did not work. Numbly, he had turned at the wrong corner, the wrong street, and entered the wrong building.

Luboš's boss called him aside one day and, in a low tone, explained that an important person would meet him the next morning. Luboš asked, "Who is it, have I done something wrong? I'm on time and don't break equipment. Does anyone else know?"

"You haven't done anything wrong. You are reliable. Don't lose sleep tonight." The boss walked off, leaving Luboš bewildered by his positive tone and worried that bad news was coming.

He reported early to work in his best clothes. His friends teased him for wearing dirty coveralls over a new shirt. Waiting at the parts department, a stranger said, "Follow me."

Luboš trailed a stocky, thick-necked man to the East German-made Trabant in the parking lot. Directed to the open car door, Luboš slumped onto the cramped back seat. His knees pressed against the front seat, slid far back.

The man walked to the opposite side and settled in the back seat. His suit was a size too small and his tie crooked on his unbuttoned collar. He placed his red and raw knuckles on his knees.

"My name is Comrade Černy. I am your case officer."

Case officer? Holy shit!

"Good morning, Comrade," Luboš answered, looking up to piercing, tight-set eyes topped by broad eyebrows that met. Three deep furrows on his forehead rose and fell when he opened his eyes wide.

"Your supervisor tells me you have been a loyal Soviet for ten years. You are the worker to emulate. You are not a slacker. You are the man who makes our Socialism succeed, and we will reward you."

"Thank you, Comrade Černy," he replied submissively.

"You might ask how the state will reward you, eh?"

"I am pleased in my position."

"Your position is honesty, which the state recognizes. We demand more honesty in our country, our city, and our work—in particular, this state-owned enterprise. Do you know what I am saying?" Černy held his cigarette pack and jiggled it, offering him one. Luboš shook his head. Černy struck a match to light his cigarette and exhaled onto Luboš.

"I don't. I agree about honesty."

Černy referenced a notecard filled with typed phrases and recent pictures at the bowling alley and ice arena.

"Now, Comrade, did you find your uncle, Jan Novák? You were searching for him after your military training."

Case officer, this notecard, searching for Jan, what else do they know? Do they have a record of my ticket to Kadan in Bohemia, or some hint of my birth in Ukraine? What has my face given away? Luboš thought: I'm fucked.

"We were separated after the war," Luboš answered, trying to act normal.

"Did you find him?"

"No."

Černy had proven his point: I have a grip on you.

"Well, Comrade Novák, engine components have been pilfered from the stockroom, and illegal materials have been smuggled on buses returning from the West. The parts are resold for profit in the black market. The propaganda from the gangsters in America is a direct threat to us. These acts reflect anti-socialism, and the perpetrators against the state will be imprisoned. Heroes weed them from society. Are you a hero?"

"Comrade, I don't know about stolen parts or smuggling." Černy's eyes were recessed deep in his skull, unnerving Luboš.

"I believe you. You are an exemplary worker, and we have confidence in you. Do you prefer a comfortable apartment or a holiday in Bulgaria?"

"I am not a complainer."

"Comrade, the Party needs you to find these wreckers who undermine us. We are on the gateway to an ideal society. We work together. Sickness is contagious and must be eliminated immediately. Will you be of service to your party?"

If Luboš asked to postpone the decision and later said "No," he would be marked uncooperative. If he bluntly said, "No," he would be worse off. Was it possible to leave the Trabant and not be under suspicion? If he was tentative and offered to assist in a partial capacity, he was hooked. If he was a snitch, his co-workers might hurt him in a supposed accident.

Luboš processed these conditions in seconds and responded, "Are you asking me to be an informant?"

"We don't use that word. We expect you to be patriotic and give information about the enemies of the people."

"Comrade Černy, I am an honest worker of the proletariat."

"If you observe criminal activities in the future, are you willing to report them to us? Providing discreet surveillance might be a better way to describe your dedication—keeping your eyes and ears open."

"I must report criminal activities."

"That's correct. The Party will salute you as a member."

"Thank you, Comrade."

"Your boss knows how to contact us. If you discover that he is involved in these crimes, I will be on the top floor of our State Security headquarters. Do you know we are on Bartolomějská Ulice?"

"Yes." Like all Prague citizens Luboš was conscious of the dreaded Czechoslovak State Security headquarters, the StB, at No. 4 Bartolomějská Ulice.

"Come to the front door. You are dismissed."

"Thank you, Comrade." Luboš shut the car door, hoping he was midway between a solid "No" and a solid "Yes" in the menacing interview. He walked past the parts department and suspected every eye marked him. My friends, my boss, and the thieves know I was in the car. They will expect me to snitch. They won't trust me. I must be alert for accidents. "I'm doomed," he breathed.

When the upcoming month's schedule was posted, Luboš was the only mechanic put on the night shift for the entire month. Shunned, he worked by himself, ate alone, and no one answered when he asked to play Durak. He gave asides to friends in the depot. He simply claimed, "I'm not a snitch."

Jan's advice at their separation was Luboš's guidepost in the cattle car, in the internment camp, and at the orphanage. He had managed adversity because Jan told him he was strong enough. Černy was the newest challenge.

Few would be shocked to find a friend or a neighbor was an informant, but not Bohdan. He and Luboš purposely never discussed their bashing of Stalin's statue—it was their shared secret. Bohdan would have already been jailed were Luboš a snitch. He regularly delivered comments and suggestions at work that supported his friend.

Over time, Luboš returned to day shifts, playing cards and attending Sparta hockey games with his friends. He had learned his lesson. Lay low and believe in something. He believed in another decade of Švejkism.

Chapter 20: Marcela, Fall 1967

Comrade Černy's query was the single exception to the pattern of previous years until, at age thirty-three, a dramatic change swept over Luboš.

Holding his place in a slow-moving line outside a stark government produce store, he noticed an attractive woman behind him dressed in a gray and white checked wool coat. She was a bit shorter than he and wore a knit scarf around her neck. He had seen her several times in lines at government stores and on trams. Luboš presumed she lived or worked nearby.

The boldness to speak more than a few words to an attractive woman had eluded him. Invariably, those words were wrong. Luboš smiled and turned slightly left and right to make eye contact. She did not turn away from him. Although informants made speaking to strangers dangerous, he cleared his throat and forged ahead.

Inspired by momentary eye contact, Luboš blurted to her, "I'm looking for lard. To cook fish." She acknowledged blankly by nodding her head. Minutes later, he turned toward her, shifting from foot to foot, and awkwardly said, "My name is Luboš." They nodded their heads one time. What does her nod mean? What does my nod mean? Lacking encouragement, he gave up and faced the front of the line. He wore the face of a man who worked outdoors; his drab clothes were forgettable. Unsurprised, his attempt at communication ended quickly.

She was curious about the man ahead of her who had enough nerve to introduce himself. She tugged at his sleeve. He turned around and she said, "My name is Marcela.

115

Marcela Burešová." Her stunning blue eyes trapped him, and he stared a little too long. Her cheeks were ruddy from the cold breeze. While looking at him, she tightened her scarf with her gloved hands. On unfamiliar grounds, he repeated his name.

Following a pause, she broke the ice. "I'm not fond of fish, at least not the fish I get."

Luboš was almost speechless that she responded. He eventually replied, "I catch fish at the river, fresh fish." Their subdued exchange continued awkwardly. In the long line, they spoke about the weather. He asked, with a rise in his voice, "May I wait for you?"

"Yes," Marcela responded and he too with a broad smile.

Both departed the store in a cheerful mood, she carrying almost fresh vegetables and he lard in their mesh bags. They agreed to meet the next week.

Luboš was stunned to initiate a dialogue with a woman. He had no idea how he had the courage.

He waited outside Cukrárna Katka, a cafe Marcela had recommended. He wondered if he would recognize her. He tried to visualize the precise color of her hair and the shape of her figure. Her blue eyes were unforgettable. They lit up when she saw him. Saved from embarrassment, Luboš greeted her and said, "Your hair is parted on the side. You look different."

"Thank you for noticing. You are observant," she said in her confident and unhurried voice. "I draw it back for school and government lines."

She repeatedly brushed aside honey-brown strands dancing across her face. He wished to tuck them behind her ear. Her dark paisley scarf around the collar of a lighter weight green overcoat kept the mystery of her appearance. Her scarf was coordinated for image and not warmth. Once inside, Marcela ordered káva and a cheese-filled kolache. He asked for the same.

He took a table in the high-ceiling, smoke-filled room, and, holding her coat, he followed her slender frame

116

and the graceful way she moved to her seat. She tipped her head and threw her hair behind her neck to glance at him. Marcela suspected Luboš was gauging her. Why not assess him? She made her observations: nice looking but not a movie star, about her age, full head of hair, pleasant smile atop a firm chin, polite, hesitant, awkward man from the country, perhaps not a Czech, a worker with ration coupons, apprehensive—possibly an appealing man.

Despite the encouragement of his hockey friends, Luboš had been reluctant to meet women at the bars and bowling alley. He had simply acknowledged that women were off-limits—until now.

Sporting a new red turtleneck for his first real date, Luboš was excited to sit facing her. Her long eyelashes, light mascara, and thin eyebrows held their place above her narrow nose. A long necklace dangled a watch that accentuated her breasts under her thin blouse. He kept his eyes moving. Her lips held an agreeable upturn, and he admired her clear skin and swan-like neck. She wanted to give a good impression, and she did.

Luboš was smart enough to learn from the cues of this beautiful woman. He waited until she put a petite spoonful of sugar in her cup, then he added that amount to his and repeated with the milk. He took the same size bite from his pastry to act civilized. He was entering a new zone to a sincere friendship—and longing for more.

Although he was generally restrained, he uncharacteristically began, "Please excuse me. Your eyes are different, bright, same as the sky. The blue is crisp and the edges distinct from the white and the black center. I am sorry to stare."

"That's okay. Cerulean is the color. Do you see some amber color at the edges? For my unruly students, I scrunch up my eyes, and they call it the 'evil eye.' "

"They are not evil to me. I didn't learn the names of the parts of the eye. What's the blue part?"

"The blue is called the iris," she answered, aware of the limited education of men his age. "An iris is also a flower."

"My iris is brown."

"I see. They are clear."

"Your earrings are cute. Are you a skier?" Luboš asked as he inelegantly shifted his focus. He spoke in an uneven voice; with several languages to choose from, he might select the wrong words.

"Oh, these," Marcela replied, fidgeting with the earrings of a pair of skis. "Before the war, we rode the bus to ski several times a month on the Krkonoše Mountains. My mother gave me these when I was six. They're not fancy, but they are my dearest. We ski, Máma more than me. Do you ski?"

"I despise the cold and the mountains. Do you play ice hockey?"

"No," she responded in surprise. "Do you?"

"I played a little, but bigger boys started much younger. I was falling on the ice more than skating."

"I enjoyed figure skating on the ponds. I'm not acquainted with girls who play ice hockey. Why do you ask?"

"Ask you what?"

"You asked me if I played ice hockey." Marcela conversed in a deliberate cadence in contrast to Luboš's abrupt surge of words.

Distressed and red in the face, he said, "I meant to ask whether you enjoyed ice hockey games." Subdued, he stared at his plate.

Marcela placed her last piece of pastry on her new friend's plate and opened her hand to signal he was forgiven. Her long fingers were gentle. She wasn't a laborer in a factory. His large hands and fingers were meaty. After Luboš finally raised his head, she asked, "Do you watch hockey games, ice hockey games?"

"Yes."

"My mother watches if it's the only channel on television."

118

"Sparta is the best team in Prague." Revived by her vote of encouragement, Luboš continued, "I go when I can. They are exciting. Would you go to a game? I mean, will you go to an ice hockey game with me in the winter? The arena Sportovní hala is a tram ride away."

They spoke about nothing consequential at their first meeting and, although his Czech speech was clumsy, she was eager to spend more time with him. At the next Cukrárna Katka date, they ventured to share bits of their past.

Marcela inspected the room and picked a table for two in a corner. "I first taught in 1950. After seventeen years, I teach the same grades at the same school. If I became a member of the Party, my life would be improved, and I would have more time to paint. My mother and I live in the same apartment the Nazis put us in," Marcela said, slightly embarrassed. "The Communists keep us there. I instruct the normal courses and, of course, our students study Marxism-Leninism and the Bolshevik Revolution."

"My Czech was poor, and I missed the normal courses. In the orphanage, they selected smarter boys for the gymnasia schools. They didn't care what I learned, and neither did I."

"You learned enough to pass the tests, fix the engines, and satisfy your boss. Men were needed after the war; many simply walked over the border. You learned to survive during a difficult time."

Luboš, socially out of sync, missed the nice cue and shifted to his next idea. "Have you ever caught a fish?"

"No, and rarely have I found fish in the market," Marcela replied, startled at his change of subject.

"The fish in the market aren't worth eating. I will teach you how to catch a fish."

"I'm not persuaded I want to. You told me about pulling the hook out and cutting the fish open. And the scales. That's a mess."

"Next week we will go, and I'll clean the fish. I will teach the fish to bite your hook."

❖ ❖ ❖ ❖ ❖

The following weekend Luboš brought Marcela, dressed for late autumn, to a pleasant spot at the Legion Bridge to demonstrate his skills. He set the bait bucket between his legs, picked a worm from the ones dug that morning, and baited the hook. She looked away. He held his crude, slightly crooked pole cut from a tree in a park, dropped the baited hook and bobber into the Vltava, and waited for the pole to bend.

While he described in detail his technique, Marcela, her arms tight across her chest to stay warm, paid little attention while she counted church spires in the center of the city and searched in vain for the Orloj, Prague's Astronomical Clock. The fish weren't cooperating, and she was bored.

Usually quiet, Luboš realized he had filled the windy morning with fish chatter. About the same age, he asked about her upbringing during the war. Marcela grew comfortable with this new man in her life and spoke openly about her family.

"My father taught us to ski, and at age five, I raced him down the slopes. His job at a factory making trucks lasted until the Nazis. Then he built tanks for the Germans and was paid in ration coupons. They put him in the army so quickly we did not get a picture of him in uniform. Hitler invaded Russia in 1941, and our father was killed." Marcela dried her tears and continued. "We found out a year later."

Luboš listened attentively to his new companion, thinking of his mother, who never received any government notification after her husband was pushed onto the truck.

"German rule was cold, hungry, and dangerous," Marcela continued, elbows on the railing, and her knit cap pulled past her ears. "Máma was forced to work in a clothing factory in nearby Kojetice, the town where she was born, making uniforms for the Wehrmacht. She risked her life, returning each night, bringing home stolen pieces of cloth to stitch vests and short pants for us to wear underneath our clothes."

Marcela described the haphazard supervision at the apartment collective, which motivated Zuzana, her older sister, to intrigue. She was a Communist courier sneaking around Prague. Zuzana's reward after the war was support for her application to Charles University. Zuzana helped her sister gain entry the following year. Zuzana's commitment to Communism had increased while Marcela remained unenthusiastic. The sisters were not at odds, though somewhat distant. Marcela's first years as a schoolteacher were under the grim umbrella of Communism and improved slightly after Stalin died in 1953.

"You have been direct about those years," Luboš said quietly, "I will share a story with you."

"Okay."

"In 1953, I was young and full of hate. Wait, I remain a little hateful. Okay, I will tell you. I pushed statues of Stalin off a truck and hammered his head with a crowbar."

"Too many people revere Stalin, still. Were you caught, someone would've killed you."

"Funny, I was the one who was a revolutionary," Luboš said, laughing off the danger. Not laughing he added, "Too bad our lives didn't improve,"

"Well, I suppose I can safely tell you that our curriculum includes even more progressive instruction and speeches from Party officials. We celebrate the fiftieth anniversary of the great October Revolution and waste time. We have less education in the music and art that I prefer. Meanwhile, university students march for new rights using words like 'freedom.' "

"Softer, please. We don't want anyone to overhear a word of this. No one mentions those protests at the garage. My boss suggested I join a worker's council. I stall him, and then he forgets. I am artificially zealous at the May Day Parade. After all, we Czechs," Luboš said, exaggerating his heritage, "aren't overenthusiastic about our Communist holidays."

She was ready to leave her gripes behind. "We accept little things, like this carp. Congratulations."

"One is not enough. Back you go little one. See you next year."

Both were contemplative as Luboš walked Marcela to her tram stop. He found his new friend was a liberal idealist, which was part of her appeal. But the frankness of their conversation startled him.

Demonstrations for political and economic change were a limited undercurrent in the country. Luboš regretted using the word revolutionary. In his spookily lighted tram ride home, Černy seemed to reappear, and Luboš hid his face.

As the cold and shortened days of winter set in, Marcela borrowed her mother's fur-collared coat, and the two chatted while fishing on the bridges on weekends. One day, after a quiet spell, Luboš remarked, "I have a favor to ask. I'm self-conscious about my Czech speech. Please tell me when I use the wrong word at the wrong time."

"I'm not complaining about your speech," Marcela replied, pleased that he had the ambition to seek self-improvement.

"If you teach me, I will learn."

"You use an economy of words, and you are direct, which is fine. I don't want to be a tutor and you a student, but I will make comments if you wish."

As the relationship progressed, Luboš sought her soft fingers. The touch brought new emotions. He smiled thinking of her.

From her artist friends, Marcela caught the looser atmosphere brewing in the country. New ideas cautiously challenged old ways. At Marcela's recommendation, Luboš grew bushy sideburns to imitate rock and roll stars and let his wavy mane grow in the style of the day. He bought new clothes and washed thoroughly to dispel the oily residue of the maintenance shop.

Luboš shared his hockey passion with his new friend, perhaps a girlfriend. Although the sisters had skated together and viewed pick-up games on frozen ponds, Marcela eagerly anticipated her first indoor ice hockey game. He suggested she wear the burgundy colors of Sparta in the special Sparta cheering section. Luboš greeted her in his faded burgundy jersey. Marcela wore a purple scarf, her favorite color, and the closest she had to burgundy, loosely around her neck.

Marcela marveled at her first sporting event in the 13,000-seat Sportovní hala. They met Bohdan and his pals from the motor pool, and Luboš gave her a quick tour while trying to explain the rules and strategy of the sport. Once the puck dropped to start the game, conversation ceased. Luboš, cheering excitedly for his team, jumped up and down and splashed beer on her. She enjoyed the fast action of the players and the revelry of his friends. Marcela hoped her mother would not complain about the smell of beer on her clothing.

"That is a strange truck cleaning the ice," Marcela noted when the friends returned from intermission carrying a round of pivo. "The back swishes in sharp turns and hits the wall."

"Oh," Bohdan enthusiastically responded. "The ice scraper is new. The old one was made in Poland and was junk. The arena spent big money and imported this monster. It is called a Zamboni, made in America. It doesn't break down. Too bad, the director was canned for importing from the west." Before the game resumed, he said, "Hey, we are going to my pub after the game. You will join us, right?"

"Will it be quieter? Will there be this much smoke?" Marcela asked. She breathed too much smoke at home, and cigarette smoke filled the arena.

"We go to pubs that have soft music, and no one smokes," he joked, puffing away on his Sparta brand cigarette.

After Sparta won the game, Marcela asked at the ticket office about open skating hours and figure skating events. Her arm in his, Marcela said to Luboš, "I will ask

Zuzana to skate with me. I might invite you to a figure skating competition. Ha, watch a figure skating competition with me," she said, nudging him with her elbow as they trailed behind Bohdan.

The next weekend Marcela brought Luboš to her mother's third-floor apartment in the Žižkov district, leaving the fishing gear in the hall. Upon entry, Marcela swiftly took down and hid the dry undergarments. It was neat, with one tiny bedroom and a makeshift closet. A wire strung across the high ceiling held a heavy privacy curtain pushed to the wall. The snug fit for her mother and sister had been even tighter before Zuzana left for university. The pleasant aroma of yesterday's seasoned cabbage and onions challenged the haze of stale cigarette smoke. Heavy brown velvet window drapes dangling tufted balls muffled noise from the street and neighbors. The sideboard hosted pictures of the family skiing and a collection of porcelain figurines. Four chairs competed for space around the small dining table. The rabbit ear antennas on the Junost television on the countertop threatened to poke anyone who squeezed by.

Marcela's mother, Miluše, was not home. Marcela placed her overcoat on a hook and Luboš pondered a romantic advance. Too shy, he watched her boil water for tea. He continued their exchange about the politics of the day.

"Your sister is on the other side of the fence. You don't speak this way to her, and you don't talk to your mother about demonstrations, do you?" Luboš had witnessed protestors beaten and dragged by police and Party thugs. He had been at ease wearing long hair in the political atmosphere and sounding off to her but did little else to challenge authority.

"I'm not this open to Maminka. You met Zuzana last month and know she was a dedicated Communist at age fourteen and a true believer after the election. We have different views and don't analyze the news. We ski and skate together several times a year and are cordial. Since the student rallies, I tell her my new hobby—watching fish leap into your bucket."

1967 was a transition year in Czechoslovakia. Intellectuals, students, and bureaucrats sought liberalized policies for speech and permission to manage local industry. "Let the Czechs and Slovaks decide what to manufacture, not Moscow," Marcela noted. "We waste our time in lines at government stores."

"Get rid of the lines, and we can fish all afternoon."

"Yes, by yourself."

Marcela's mother rattled her keys and opened the apartment's only door. She smiled at her daughter, pleased the laundry was hidden, and at her guest sitting at the table. "Máma, this is Luboš, the man who fishes."

"Mrs. Burešová," he stood up and said in embarrassment, glad he had not kissed Marcela. "A pleasure to meet you."

"You are teaching my youngest to fish?"

"She will learn, and I'll clean them."

"Don't let her fall into the river. She is my baby," Miluše said, patting her on the head. Mother and daughter had discussed the new man in Marcela's life.

Later that night, 5 January 1968, Leonid Brezhnev, General Secretary of the Communist Party of the Soviet Union, disillusioned by the divergent political schemes in Czechoslovakia, installed Alexander Dubček, a Slovak, as the Czechoslovak First Secretary. Unaware of the orchestrated leadership change, Marcela and Luboš watched the skating competition in the hala.

Chapter 21: Friendship Evolves

"Did I tell you about the 1964 Olympics?"

"Yes."

"The Communists use a Five-Year Plan," Luboš reran his stock story, "and I prefer my Four-Year Plan. Most Czech men do. The Czechoslovak ice hockey team is one of the best in the world. Hockey is our way of expressing anger at the Russians. The players play fiercely, and we cheer the same way. In 1964 we won the bronze medal, third place, and next month we will win the gold medal, first place."

"Yes, yes, gold, silver, bronze."

"We have our top players back and a fantastic young goalie. Your school might cancel classes."

"If they cancel classes, I will sleep in."

Two tides were flooding at the start of the year: Alexander Dubček's liberalization reforms and passion for the upcoming winter Olympics in February in Grenoble, France. Bohdan, Luboš, and the entire staff parsed the sports news leading to the games and were glad for the limited bus schedule.

The ten days of the medal round were tense, and on Czechoslovak game days, Luboš wore the bold red and white hockey jersey Marcela gave him for his birthday. They cheered as loudly as the boss in the conference room where the new TV was in full view. A win over Sweden in their final game would earn the gold for Czechoslovakia. Sadly, nationwide support and cheering did not help. The game ended in a 2-2 tie, and Czechoslovakia was awarded the silver medal behind the gold won by the Soviet Union. "How can this be?" they complained in a rage. "We beat the

Ruskies 5-4 last week. The referees called stupid penalties. They play dirty. They bribe the referees. The rules were changed. Why do the Russians win all the time?"

Suddenly mindful where they were, everyone in the room—the boss, Party members, Luboš, and his hockey pals—froze and eyed the floor, speculating that their comments about Russia were too much. The workers hoped this indiscretion would not go outside the room. Did the swelling street rallies and protests give them new liberty to express their anger?

The entire nation was shaken, and the highs and lows of Luboš's emotions during the Olympics confirmed again that he was Czech. He was not a Ukrainian and not a Slovak. He was now a Northern Slav, his mother's preference.

"Which is better? Me, or fishing with me?" Marcela asked, bundled up and leaning on the railing of the Manes Bridge. Although he was excited at each sweep of his net to land a fish, she did not absorb his interest.

Startled, Luboš replied, "Well—you. At the river, we talk about our ambitions. We view the beautiful sights. Am I ignoring you?"

Marcela stared at Prague Castle, trying to figure where this friendship, perhaps a romance, was heading. It was too early to tell if he would be her lover, her husband, or the father of her child. She didn't want to press him, but other men were waiting.

"Am I selfish to fish this often? We developed confidence at the river."

"Here we speak safely, which is okay because I hold forth too much."

"Where else can we talk privately?"

"We can sit on a bench," she proposed firmly. "I don't catch fish, and you net enough for Máma and her friends. You should spend less time on the Vltava."

Once again, Luboš was tone-deaf, and his response was to offer to buy her an imported bamboo pole. Marcela preferred a different result. She wanted to be with him, yes, but not at the river. She insisted they spend time together in the city and guided him to the zoo, the Old Jewish Cemetery, tearooms for the younger set on Wenceslas Square, and the flea market. She introduced him to the city that had overwhelmed him in 1948.

Marcela's preferred place to rest was at the Botanical Garden of Charles University, where the sisters had graduated. They sat on the low patio wall to revel in the buds and fragrances of the flowers, shrubs, and trees of the season.

Sunlight filtering through sycamore leaves revealed a tear. "Here, my father bent down to put his nose in the lilies and breathe deeply. We played noisily. He held his finger to his lips and softly whispered, 'Smell the lilies' and 'Listen to the birds.' "

"The four of us boarded trams or walked on Sunday after church to the beautiful sights of Prague or to visit Máma's relatives in Kojetice," Marcela said wistfully. "We finished at Wenceslas Square, where Zuzana and I sipped hot chocolate at an outdoor table.

"That was until our government gave up. Hitler and the Nazis came in a huge parade with endless airplanes flying overhead to celebrate our loss and their victory. I was seven years old. We never returned to the square because the rude Gestapo filled the cafés. Táta was conscripted the next year, and we were forced out of our apartment," she mused, twirling the stem of a yellow flower she found in Havlicek Gardens.

Luboš listened and realized the months near Smižany were the best of his life. He had been safe and worked and played like a normal farm child. Though the adverse times overwhelmed the pleasant times, with Marcela, the best years lay ahead. Since his release from the orphanage, Luboš had watched and listened—no longer.

❖ ❖ ❖ ❖ ❖

Prague was the cultural focus of Central Europe, toying with a westward view of the world. Luboš brought Marcela to a revival of the 1956 movie comedy, *The Good Soldier Švejk*. He recounted absurdities during his short army stint.

Alexander Dubček inspired a generation by delivering substantial reforms to the country's Communist system. Prague and the couple blossomed. The popular song, "Prayer for Marta," inspired them, and they imagined a promising future. Restrictions on literature, art, and speech were relaxed, and optimism about their national politics filled the spring. Marcela complained about the promised worker's paradise and read renegade newspapers instead of the official Communist Party newspaper, *Rudé právo*.

Luboš watched Miluše hum a tune and cheerfully prepare her late afternoon dinner of fresh vegetables from the illegal market and bream, this time freshly caught by Marcela. She was proud of her mother's culinary skills, perfected despite limited German and Communist rations and poor-quality foodstuffs.

"The fish would taste better if we could see it," Zuzana teased her mother and added in a harsher tone, "Look at these new cigarette burns on the table."

"Zuzana is correct. There is more smoke here than at the bars, and I live here," added Marcela after she fully opened the window.

Except for Zuzana's hair bound tightly in a bun and a more intense face, the sisters were identical. Marcela was grateful for the hand-me-down clothes her older sister gave her, although she had few occasions to dress in the stern suits.

Miluše, plump with a raspy voice, sparse white hair, and early wrinkles from raising children during the war, ignored her daughters. She shuffled about in her cloth slippers, yet she skied at every opportunity. Her quiet spell wasn't anger, only recognition of her addiction to nicotine.

129

Their mother started to ramble on about loud music and young students sporting goatees and unruly hair. She dug her hands into her apron pockets and declared, "If a fire starts in one of those subterranean bars, you will trip over those fancy bell-bottom trousers I made. I will lose a daughter for sure and this nice man. And you young people should go to church!"

Zuzana, well established in the Communist hierarchy, usually kept her opinions to herself but couldn't resist saying, "The foreign influence is making our students, even older people, into hippies."

"We aren't hippies," Marcela slipped in. "The changes are overdue."

"The road of change has curves and may lead nowhere."

Luboš watched Mrs. Burešová to avoid looking at either daughter, hoping the evening would not turn angry.

Máma had heard such friction and took charge. "Enough. Help me finish the strudel."

Glad that her mother calmed the situation, Marcela said to her sister, "We are going to a quiet bar tonight. Will you join us?"

"No, not tonight." After dinner, she returned to her finely appointed accommodations in Old Town, suitable for a rising star in the Communist Party.

"The river is raging," Luboš said to Marcela while on the downstream side of the Legion Bridge. He was distressed watching his sapling bend when he fought to bring a carp up to his net. Although the pole rebounded straight, it was about to break. Luboš was disdainful of costly, modern equipment. Fellow fishermen suggested he cut a new pole from bamboo at a nearby park.

"Tomorrow, we will explore Průhonice Park. I'll bring a saw."

"You are a woodsman too? This will be amusing."

"Yes. My father and I cut wood at an orchard."

"I'll bring sandwiches and a blanket."

The sunny day proceeded as Luboš had expected, and they boarded the tram home smiling and giggling. To be gay in public carrying long bamboo canes would have been unimaginable in 1966. Holding his arm, Marcela asked, "Did you like the park?"

"The trees and grassy fields are pleasant, and I have two new fishing poles."

"I'm not talking about trees."

"Oh? Okay. Bohdan said the park was a good place to pick flowers and smooch."

"Which was better, the bamboo or the kissing?"

"Hmmm, let me guess. The kissing. Bohdan said it is the best place to bring a girlfriend."

"I thought your girlfriend was a fish."

"Not anymore."

"I'm glad I brought a blanket."

Walking Marcela home holding bamboo and a handful of flowers, Luboš realized how blessed he was. His mother rarely glimpsed color in her life except for wildflowers and her months with Jan. *What about me? My hockey friends have girlfriends, and now I do. Will we marry and have children? Wait, not too fast.*

Chapter 22: Prague Spring, 1968

Prague and a growing number of citizens in the country were excited by the thaw in Communist rigor. They anticipated the freest spring in thirty years. Luboš was confident enough to disclose his past. He led Marcela across the Legion Bridge late one spring afternoon down the stairs to Hunter's Island to his favored spot for reflection.

"I haven't told you about some parts of me. I apologize for not trusting you."

"You sound serious."

"I wasn't born in Kadan in Bohemia. Until I was ten, my name was Dmytro, lover of the earth. My family fled Ukraine in 1944, and at age eleven, I became Luboš. I fear discovery and return to Russia."

"You've been hiding your past," Marcela said sympathetically, turning to him on the slatted bench and buttoning her sweater to her neck as the temperature dropped.

"I lied, even to you, and I will keep lying to stay in Prague. I trusted my mother and Jan. Tonight I trust you with my secrets."

He divulged his story without emotion, staring north over the Vltava under what he imagined was a brooding Prague Castle. Her lips quivered until she sobbed. Luboš brushed her hair from the tears. She held his hand so tight it hurt. She rested her head on his neck. Neither was soothed.

"We were an element of the earth at death's door under our tarp and in snow caves. If I knew how to die, I would have. Jan distracted me from those ideas."

"You have a soft soul. How are you levelheaded?"

"My mother and Jan taught me to be a quiet person, and so does our government. I've been submissive because it works for me. They say, 'go along, get along.' "

A tugboat sounded its steam whistle to break the silence. Stars blinking in the sky displaced the golden hour after sunset. Luboš woke Marcela in the frosty night to board the last tram.

Drinking establishments thrived more than ever as young and old were in good spirits. High times and Czech lagers flowed at the Vzorkovna, their favorite below ground pub. Ignoring Marcela's entreaties, Luboš shared his beer with the house-dog staggering along the corridors.

The state tolerated western music, and Marcela favored the local band, Plastic People of the Universe. The music reverberated so loudly that listening was impossible, but who cared; they danced in the tight, smoke-filled passageways. They heard local bands play Beatles and Rolling Stones hits and sang accented choruses of "(I Can't Get No) Satisfaction" or "Back in the U.S.S.R." without comprehending the lyrics.

Marcela favored a pilsner and Luboš a darker lager—too many on occasion. On this night, well into his liter, he called for shots of Becherovka, a Czechoslovak specialty herbal liqueur.

"Not Becherovka. It is too strong. I will get tipsy," Marcela pleaded as she pretend-played bongo drums on their out-of-the-way table in the corner. Luboš sang Elvis's "Love Me Tender" into his beer mug.

"Becherovka heals the stomach and the spirit," he asserted. In a serious tone, he said, "Tonight is special. My mother wished I would meet a princess and see me dance. You are my princess, and she would be happy."

"That is sweet. Does that mean you are my prince?" Marcela said, tears welling in her eyes.

"I am your prince. You have put me at ease. Let's toast. Na zdraví."

"Na zdraví." They touched glass and drained their shot glasses.

Face to face, Luboš swallowed a long pull from his one-liter pivo. He locked eyes with Marcela and softly touched her ear lobe, her lips and her neck with his fingers. Carefully, he moved his fingers down. She placed her hand on his and shut her eyes. Luboš's hand, escorted by Marcela's, rested on her breast. "Uncle Jan picked my name. Luboš means love. Marcela, I love you."

"I love you, too." She opened her eyes to see Luboš gazing at her.

Marcela eased her hand away, and a second later, he did. "I'm a little embarrassed by this, just a little. There will be a time."

That time happened quickly. "Tomorrow, Máma will ski," Marcela made known in a coy manner. They were united in most ways and had waited for the day Miluše took the bus to the slopes. They were eager to make love.

"When I held your coat the first day, I imagined what was hidden. This spring, I knew you by caress, and today I know you with my eyes. You are beautiful."

Marcela's elbows supported her on the narrow bed on top of a peaceful Luboš, her breasts resting on Luboš's broad chest. "I was looking at you, also. We took ages to get here, which is fine."

"We should buy tickets for your mother to ski more."

"She isn't simple-minded on the matter. And we will close the windows next time."

"My weather forecast is snow."

❖ ❖ ❖ ❖ ❖

Marcela's school schedule relaxed in the summer while Luboš worked extra hours while somber delegations traveled more frequently between the capitals of Poland, East Germany, and Hungary. Luboš was surprised that snacks were not prepared. The delegates were curt and vexed.

Thirty-four-year-old Luboš restrained his western imitations after his boss counseled him about his clothing style and sideburns. Nevertheless, his wavy mop flew uncombed on weekends. Marcela's matronly principal would cause trouble at school on Monday if she saw her in her flouncy blouse.

"The protests have expanded to rallies," Luboš was pleased to note, while sitting on the embankment wall in front of the National Theatre. He unbuttoned his shirt to imitate James Dean and act cool. "Prague has more smiles, more impromptu outdoor concerts, and Dubček's proposals for more economic reforms. I was a peasant with a bleak future. Now I'm a worker who speaks proper Czech and who has a beautiful girlfriend."

"You came at the same time as the protests last year. Thank you."

"Thank you for pulling on my jacket sleeve. What is next?"

"Everything is next."

Chapter 23: The Warsaw Pact Invades and Occupies

The growing Czechoslovak freedoms were intolerable to the Kremlin. The potential revolution from within was undone on the 20th of August 1968, when 250,000 soldiers from adjacent Warsaw Pact countries invaded Czechoslovakia. The Czechoslovak army did not fight, and foreign tanks and soldiers quickly overran the country. Schools were shuttered, and the transport workers were ordered to avoid public gatherings.

Luboš destroyed militant pamphlets and peace symbols purchased at flea markets. Marcela promptly trimmed his hair. Then he waited in a long line for a proper haircut.

Party directives did not deter them. Two days after the invasion, they cautiously walked towards Prague's city center. Like the Czechoslovak army, the citizens had not resisted or protested. Not in danger, only a few of the Warsaw Pact armored vehicles ran their engines. The birds understood the gravity of the foreign intrusion and were silent.

On each tank stood an imperious duo of tense infantrymen aiming their Kalashnikovs to the ground and an officer who rested his hand on the holster of his Makarov pistol. They weren't threatening or threatened, and a safety perimeter was not enforced.

Marcela clutched Luboš's arm with both hands as they stood beside the vehicles in a surreal situation. They peered up at the uniformed Polish, Hungarian, or Russian soldiers on their tanks, convinced the happy spring and summer days were finished.

"In the valleys at the end of the war these T-34 tanks ran past Jan and I," Luboš said, breaking their prolonged silence. "They kept us from reaching Austria. During the Hungarian Uprising, T-34s protected me at the border. Now this Polish T-34 wrecks our future.

"Our army mobilized in 1956, but our Czechoslovak tanks didn't go into Hungary. We waited, ate cold rations for two months, and returned to our post."

"Did Warsaw Pact armies cross the border?"

"No, only the Russians invaded Hungary." The year of openness had provided Luboš information about the thousands of students and demonstrators killed during the Hungarian Revolution. "It was a bloody crushing of the Uprising."

"I was seven years old when the Germans filled this square. I wonder if these soldiers will again kick us out of our apartment. Are we safe?"

"Maybe. Prague is different—tanks from the Warsaw Pact and no bloodshed. Our government functions."

They drifted around the tanks as if they were in a military museum. "Our Prague Spring did not survive the summer heat. What should we do?" Marcela asked.

"I can't guess."

❖ ❖ ❖ ❖ ❖

Restrictions on Party travel reduced work at the motor pool. Luboš, Bohdan, the boss, all the workers tried to look busy.

Though the citizens were distressed at the reversal of the Prague Spring, the couple's relationship strengthened as they evaluated their next course. Their relationship had progressed slowly with marriage in the background. They focused on the present and made love whenever possible. Luboš repeated a phrase from a counterculture magazine about the "Summer of Love" in the United States: "If you can make love, you should make love."

137

Marcela was cautious in her observations of the dismal changes. Zuzana had opposed Dubček's progressive approach, and her star ascended within the Party. To keep harmony at Miluše's weekly dinners, Zuzana avoided politics. The philosophical divergence between the sisters grew and was safely debated only when they skated together. Those occasions were fewer and fewer since the Communist persisted that her ideas were superior.

The sisters had their differences and similarities. Zuzana supported Marcela's love for Luboš, and she revealed her love for a man, a prominent official in the Party who loved Zuzana. She embraced his love—as his mistress. Marcela learned that he was instrumental in assigning her the large apartment. Marcela was happy for her sister and concerned by the insecurity of the liaison.

Foreign armies had entered Czechoslovakia in the summer prepared for battle, not for passive resistance. The civil atmosphere in Prague chilled and returned to sadness, where one rarely spoke, averted one's eyes, and hoped everyone forgot the summer of zeal. Fall came and went. Tanks belching blue diesel exhaust at every intersection rang in the New Year. The self-immolation of martyr Jan Palach in January 1969 reminded the nation of their subjugation.

Dubček remained a weakened titular leader, and Government bodies convened in a political holding period. Six months after the tanks rumbled in, Luboš and countless Czechoslovak men and women held high hopes for the 1969 World Ice Hockey Championships. They wanted revenge for the 1968 Olympic defeat and especially to display indignation for the invasion and continuing occupation.

The gridlock between the Kremlin and angry Czechoslovaks finally broke in March, when the Czechoslovak national team soundly defeated the Soviet Union team. Czechoslovaks throughout the country were ecstatic. Riots broke out, especially targeting the offices of the Soviet airline, Aeroflot.

Faced with unruly Czechoslovak citizens, the Kremlin replaced the popular Dubček. The new Moscow-approved hardliner instituted purges reminiscent of the days of Stalin. Social reforms were revoked, police persecution increased, and central economic planning resumed.

"Families crossed to the Americans in 1946," Luboš said, sitting quietly at the kitchen table while mulling their options. "Access to the west is blocked, and radio signals are jammed."

"Rebellious girls in our school traveled by train through Hungary to Yugoslavia carrying just their občanský průkaz cards." Searching for advice, Marcela asked, "How can teenagers run away with only a school identity card? A note said they were visiting friends. The parents are worried sick and ask the teachers for guidance. Is Yugoslavia an alternative for us?"

"My mother and Jan steered us from the Balkans. They believed southern Slavs were untrustworthy. Freedom lies in West Germany and Austria."

"I would miss my family."

"Let's not mention this in front of your mother. We will wait and see whether the tough talk of our new leader comes true."

As the words were leaving his mouth, Luboš was planning a getaway.

Jan had told him he had been a strong boy on the winter trek. But as a young man he was trapped in the society and listened, as recommended by Jan. For Luboš, the years of passivity were over: it was time to be a man. A beautiful girlfriend and a thwarted future brought out his repressed instincts.

During his week of unmonitored night shifts, he rigged the newest bus, No. 505, with a lever on the cargo door latch to open the baggage door from the inside. Also, he created a secret opening from the baggage compartment to the plumbing area below and behind the toilet. The space was large enough for two people, barely. The modification was ready in May.

Luboš told Marcela his perilous scheme for a new life in West Germany.

"Didn't you say we would wait and see?"

"Loving you this winter isn't the same as loving you last summer. At work, people are irritable, the music and spirit in the clubs are dull, and you share stories of the more rigorous indoctrination in school. We are at a crossroad. We will be more Russian than Czech. I escaped before, and I'm prepared to try again."

"Have you forgotten that pain and loss? You are the only one who survived."

"My mother decided. Jan decided. Now, it is my turn. We will go to Frankfurt in West Germany."

"Why West Germany?"

"Democracy and more Americans."

"I need more time."

Marcela anguished through the night worrying how her sister and mother would be affected. Yes, I love Luboš, and he loves me. Can a truck mechanic find work in a strange country speaking a foreign language? Will we suffocate under the toilet? Is it that dreadful here? Marcela lay down by her mother and did not sleep.

Following days of internal debate, Marcela conveyed at their next rendezvous, "I am ready for our dreams somewhere else. Repression will get worse, and our brief taste of freedom is gone. Tell me when."

They waited weeks for the stars to align—Luboš on a day shift and his bus, No. 505, scheduled for the 0600 departure to West Germany. He worried that a co-worker would discover the jury-rigged door latch or the modified access panel. The schedules were posted a day in advance; his responsibility was to position each bus. Finally, the day arrived.

He reviewed the details one last time. "Don't drink because we will be cramped for five hours. In Frankfurt, the driver will open the baggage door and unload the delegate's bags. Before he shuts the door, I will open our panel enough to verify it is safe to leave. If clear, I will pull you out. I won't know which way to run, but we will run to a uniformed customs official or policeman and ask for asylum. The delegates will grab us, and we will scream and resist."

"I won't let go of you."

Luboš grasped the weight of the burden he had been to Jan, who had promised Nadiya to lead her son to safety. He offered a silent prayer of thanks to the former soldier who made his life with Marcela possible.

The point of no return was at hand. Luboš hid Marcela in a dark, secluded spot that he had reconnoitered weeks earlier. He walked past a sleepy man from the night shift who yawned and asked, "Hey Luboš, why this early?"

"I came here to sleep," he answered with a cheerful laugh. "Just kidding."

"Ha, ha, don't get caught."

"I will be wide awake. I'll be your guard." Luboš waited for the man to lie back on the conference room couch. Returning to escort Marcela, he recalled how twenty-five years ago, he feared Germans. This dreary morning he was leading a bolt into West Germany.

"Let's go."

No more words were required. He gripped Marcela's hand to scramble in the dark through the maze of silent behemoths. Their clothes were soaking more from nervous sweat than the light summer drizzle. She slipped on the oily surface, but Luboš didn't let her fall.

Kneeling in the wide and low baggage chamber, he demonstrated the operation of his door latch and access panel and told her, "Lock the panel after I leave. I will knock several times for you to open and then push in. I love you, Marcela. I will return in an hour."

She squeezed below the toilet into the plumbing compartment. Luboš lost sight of her as he tried to close the panel. Marcela trembled in her wet blouse and would not release his hand.

"Please, I have to go. I love you."

"I love you. Come back.

"I will." Only then did she relax her grip. In slow motion, her wrist, hand, knuckles, soft fingers, and fingernails slid from sight. He waited for an eon until she locked the panel.

Chapter 24: Bus to Freedom

Luboš had informed his boss that he was sick with the flu and might leave in the middle of the day. Bus drivers started their engines, and delegates boarded Marcela's bus. Luboš ambled over and was about to squeeze into the baggage hold when his boss called to him.

"Luboš, go to the next bus."

"I'm getting a light bulb for this bus," Luboš protested.

"Forget that. Come here."

"The parts..."

"Luboš, the buses are late, get over here."

He had parked 505 in a remote location to prevent a misstep, and he had no alternative. Luboš had to respond to the boss. There was no time to put a nail in front of the tire. Luboš was crushed. He let his arms sag and dropped his wrench. The bus shifted through its gears. He watched the red taillights drive out of sight.

He fell to his knees, his face white and his heart trying to pound through his ribcage. In an instant, the high expectation of slipping away to a democratic country was shattered with the truth that he, and Jan, had failed. At least Jan had said, "I will find you."

"Hey, Luboš, what's going on?" the boss demanded, aggravated at first, and then baffled. "You look like shit."

Luboš was speechless. His brain was chaotic. What have I done to Marcela? If she panics and cries out loud, they will bring her back.

"Bohdan, move him out of the bus lanes."

"Hey, are you drunk?" His buddy asked as he half-carried him.

Workers crowded into the break room to hear Luboš weakly say, "Bad flu."

"Real bad. You shouldn't have come in early."

"Okay, okay, let's move on," the boss directed. "We have to send out the Frankfurt bus."

Luboš was stunned and claimed, "West Germany just drove out!"

"No. That's why I called you. The head Party member insisted on No. 505, and we swapped it. 505 is going to Vienna."

"What?" exclaimed Luboš, the muscles of his body stiffened as in a grand mal seizure.

"Luboš, are you sick? Hey, Bohdan. After West Germany leaves, get him to a doctor."

Darkness enveloped him, and his head spun. He was in shock until he regained some sense. He had to leave. "Bohdan, I'll be okay." Luboš ran, stumbling, from the room.

Luboš had been hesitant to step out of his passive life, and he took himself to task for jeopardizing Marcela. Alone, she was heading to the wrong country. Does she believe in me now?

Miluše and Marcela had worshipped in the Basilica of St. James. Luboš entered the cathedral for the first time and prayed: "Dear God, please listen. Protect Marcela and lead her to safety. Let me suffer so she may be free. Amen."

Chapter 25: Marcela Alone

The drain hose for the sink passed between Marcela's legs, the toilet pipe pressed painfully against her side, and her head was canted to fit between the wall and underside of the bowl. She had expected the space would be miserably tight for both of them; she found it dreadful for just herself. She understood why Luboš had advised against wearing earrings. One spot of light illuminated the insides of her sanctuary behind and under the toilet. She was unable to turn her head enough to see the release latch. She found it by feel but hesitated to lock herself inside. She had second thoughts. Only after Luboš insisted, "Please. Hurry up," did she close the latch.

Confined in the cold cavity, her lips quivered. Her lover would join her in a moment to calm her. Marcela was excited about her new life: inside, she carried beautiful tidings. Once in Frankfurt, she would tell Luboš the terrific news: "I'm pregnant. We will have twins!"

The diesel spun and clattered to life. It rumbled its tune, and Marcela lost track of time. Petrified, she awaited Luboš while delegates boarded the bus speaking German and Czech. Suitcases were thrown next to her panel. There was no knock. The cargo door slammed shut, the bus lurched forward, and the engine ran high, low, and high as the driver shifted gears.

To avoid screaming, Marcela bit her hand long after she tasted blood.

Chapter 26: The Secret Police

The Party leader in Vienna on No. 505 called frantically at mid-morning to recount that a woman emerged from the belly of the bus and sought asylum. He explained to the StB that the delegates wrestled to return her, but she would not let go of the leg of an Austrian border patrol guard. Communist officials in Prague activated contingency procedures, and, alerted to the modification to the bus, the StB quickly arrested all workers at Prague Transport.

The detained men were blindfolded, handcuffed, and roughly brought to StB headquarters. Each was a suspect and intensely interrogated in different rooms. They denied knowledge of bus modifications, although several told of Luboš's unexpected early arrival at work, his distress over 505's reordered destination, and his "bad flu." Questioners forced Bohdan to divulge the name of the girlfriend.

Where was Luboš? He wasn't in his room or a doctor's office. By early afternoon he was the only person unaccounted for. He had no alternate strategy, no stores in a hideout, no compatriot, and no means to remain safe.

The StB interrogators developed a profile of their missing man: a Czech, quiet, former soldier, hockey fan, and fisherman with a girlfriend named Marcela Burešová. Every government asset in Prague hunted for Luboš; by mid-afternoon, they found him slumped over, drinking a lager at a pub a block from the Sportovní hala.

In a stupor, the memory of Marcela's hand and fingers at the hidden compartment consumed him. He did not resist. They manhandled him through the back door of No. 4 Bartolomějská Ulice.

The StB knew only the name of the woman. Pressure from the Communist hierarchy drove the interrogators to find answers quickly. Who was he, who was she? How did this happen at the Party's transportation facility? Is he involved in a conspiracy of malcontents?

Luboš feigned ignorance. The impatient StB men escalated their interrogation to beat the information out of him.

After midnight, Luboš was dragged, thumping down the steps to the lowest level of the basement where prisoners were said to be shot. The way the door slammed shut, he knew he was in a soundproof room. If offered a cigarette, he would be at the end of his life.

He rolled his head and blinked his eyes as a new inquisitor in a clean uniform walked around Luboš's metal chair. "So, are you ready for more intense questioning?" The interrogator growled as he rolled up his sleeves and softly slapped a truncheon onto the palm of his hand. Luboš glimpsed the man's red knuckles and a bold, red tattoo on his forearm.

Luboš's work clothes were wet from his blood and the water thrown at him. His wrists and shoulders cried for release from the tight bindings. He shook uncontrollably in the cold room and vomited on his shirt and pants.

"Look at me," the new voice boomed.

Luboš's eyes were unfocused, and his brain was addled. "Hold up his head," the interrogator told his beefy assistant. "Do you recognize me, you bastard? Splash him. Do you remember me now?"

"No."

"You will remember this day if you survive. The last time we met, I called you Comrade. I suggested that were you to discover unlawful activities, you should contact me at the StB on the top floor. Ha, tonight we meet in the basement. Do you remember me now?"

The face was blurred, but Luboš remembered the forehead marked by distinct creases above the eyes and the gravelly voice. "Yes," he managed. The coarse official who had recruited him to spy on his co-workers now controlled his destiny.

"I committed a serious mistake. You are the devil. I remain your case officer, and you will not embarrass me a second time. Perhaps you forgot my name. It is Černy. We are no longer comrades."

Černy swaggered around the room, brushing his cigarette stained Stalinesque mustache with his forefinger. Stalin's tactics and mien were back in vogue.

"It is a grave time for you wreckers who surfaced during the misnamed Prague Spring, Our 'normalization' policies are much stricter now. You have told my associates about your youth in Bohemia and the man you call Uncle Jan, but not much else. You have been a companion of the woman in the bus. You are the only one who is tight-lipped. Do you think we are dumb? You are sitting in a metal chair. Ha. It is easy to clean up. You will disclose everything sooner or later, your choice."

Luboš did not know if Marcela was safe, and he had already paid a bloody price for bravery. The interrogator was correct. To confess and stop the beatings was his decision. I won't jeopardize her, Luboš resolved. I will hold out.

Černy's arrival raised the beatings to a higher level. They caned the bottom of his bare feet. He wailed but laughed inside. Frostbite had damaged those nerves; the pain wasn't as effective as his tormentors expected.

"Wake this imbecile," Černy shouted to his subordinate, and the water splashed again. "The loyal Soviets told us you spent much time in one of the buses. They said you were lazy and sleeping at four in the morning. Did you modify a bus?"

"I did." He was powerless. Why endure more abuse for information already known? Still, he was resolved to avoid mentioning Marcela.

"Keep going. Why did you destroy state-owned property?"

"To leave Czechoslovakia."

"With a woman." sneered Černy. "You will be an informant—on yourself. Keep talking. Who are your collaborators?"

Luboš owned nothing more to give except faint moans.

"Playing tough? I have a rude awakening for you," a gleeful Černy added. "This woman, Marcela Burešová, was trapped in the baggage compartment. She surrendered to our delegation and was immediately returned to Prague. She is in this building. Too bad your tooth fell out. You won't be worth looking at if you ever see her. Also, here is her sister, Zuzana Burešová, who will be tainted by your crimes against the state."

This information defeated Luboš. He did not care about the torture, denying Černy the pleasure of his brutality.

"Get him out of here!" exploded Černy. "Send him to our special room. He will find his tongue."

Luboš recognized hell. It wasn't the Soviets or Nazis, or yesterday's beatings. Until today, hell was the cold winter when he was ready to die, but Jan would not allow him. "This is hell, fuck you!" he shouted back at the blinding lights and the sound megaphones penetrating him. He rocked back and forth, same as a crazy man.

"I'm not a believer," he told the wall. "Is that why you gave me one good year and the rest full of conflict?" He searched the room for a way out of hell—a sharp piece of glass, the edge of a metal tray, or a belt to commit suicide.

When alert, he feared for Marcela and Zuzana's interrogation and shouted, "God, keep them out of the basement." Guards regularly slid open the Judas hole to see whether he had battered his head on the wall.

In the morning, Luboš was returned to the basement. Černy asked if he was ready to talk.

The prisoner was semi-conscious and mumbled, "What about Marcela?"

"I ask the questions. Did you have a chance to clear your head last night? To have a chance for survival, start now. Do you understand?"

Luboš feared another day of torture. He was a broken man and replied, "Yes." Through swollen, bloodshot eyes he saw the pile of papers, his already prepared confessions

"Tell me everything."

Luboš recited once again the fabricated story Jan told in Nováky and ended with how he alone modified the bus. To ease her imminent torture, he insisted that he coerced Marcela. Černy pestered him to identify accomplices, unable to imagine that one man could execute the escape. He tried to force Luboš to implicate his boss, fellow shift workers, roommates, and especially Zuzana. Černy would be applauded for unveiling a conspiracy. To pursue a high-ranking Party member was treacherous, while the reward would be promotion to colonel.

Černy eventually grasped the fact that if he continued the interrogation, his detainee would die. He announced, "You piece of shit. I have your confession for numerous crimes. Your trial will be a spectacle."

The word "trial" stunned Luboš and implied a glimmer of hope. He imagined a future and mouthed, "I might live."

Dazed, Luboš asked, "Where is Marcela?"

"Why give a damn, you will be dead after the trial." Černy sneered and directed his assistant to release the remaining depot detainees.

In the cellar of the StB, Luboš kept control of nothing except self-blame for putting Marcela in jeopardy. Crucially, he did not disclose his Ukrainian origin.

Luboš healed slowly in solitary confinement cell No. 6, hearing the occasional sound of a single gunshot from the cellar. Steel doors slammed behind him as he limped two floors upstairs to meet prosecutors who refined his coerced confession. Handcuffed, he asked the guards the whereabouts of a woman in custody. They were stone-faced.

Luboš met in the bugged room with his advocatura defense counselors, who offered no guidance except "Plead guilty, renounce your errors, and you might live." When he asked about the fate of Marcela, they slammed their briefcases shut and walked out of the room.

Czechoslovak trial and prison policies had relaxed after Stalin's death in 1953, but, after the failed Prague Spring, Luboš was snared in reinvigorated state terror. Televised stage trials, absent under Dubček's leadership, resumed as the country faced the retraction of liberties. The Communists punished harshly to discourage dissent.

The prisoner entered the courtroom's glass-enclosed dock the morning of the trial wearing the provided sloppily tailored suit. His white shirt was of a collar size so large that he resembled a cartoon character. The bruises had subsided, but the stitches on his face, covered in makeup, itched, and he repeatedly brushed the cuts. He wasn't paying much attention as the extensive list of charges was read. He perked up when the prosecutor paused, deepened his tone, and read a new charge: aiding the defection of a Czechoslovak citizen.

Marcela was in Austria? The camera recorded Luboš bolting upright at the reading of the last charge. For weeks he had believed she was a fellow prisoner at the StB. He whispered for the cameras, "Černy, you bastard. She is a free woman. I win this battle."

Witnesses, some from work, some he had never met, denounced him in lie upon lie. Their forced condemnations were as fraudulent as his forced confessions. Luboš held no animosity. Absent was a denunciation from Zuzana who, somehow, had avoided coercion.

The orchestration of the daylong trial ended in his plea for clemency. Luboš peered into the camera, displaying the vacancy of his missing tooth. He read his extensive confession in a lisp: "I fell victim to the revisionist propaganda of Alexander Dubček ... I ask the Court to accept my true confession ... I admit my full guilt for treason and treachery ... In the presence of the workers who criticized me, I surrender to your denunciations ... I have betrayed the Communist Party and the country and beg to reclaim the support of our heroic workers."

Pushed hard from Moscow, the Czechoslovak courts imposed harsh sentences, especially for political prisoners. Aware that Marcela had defected, Luboš was reconciled to his fate: hanged from the gallows.

The prosecutor repeated the confession, and the judge announced the court's ruling. "Based on the confession of Luboš Novák, and in accordance with articles of the Civil Procedural Court of the Czechoslovakia Socialist Republic, Luboš Novák is found guilty of all offenses and is sentenced to twenty-five years of corrective labor at Kamp No. 12."

Only hard labor at a notorious prison?

"Luboš lives and Marcela lives," he mouthed in Ukrainian to the camera. In disbelief, he searched the courtroom for Černy. Hands loosely shackled and hidden below the glass enclosure, the convicted prisoner put his left fist into his right elbow to salute the bastard symbolically. He purposely had not walked by this building for fear of the brutality inside. Now he was a witness and a victim.

Convicted prisoners were held four to a cell, and second-termers described Kamp No. 12 as a huge open-pit quarry near the East German border. It was a former Nazi labor camp, unchanged since 1940. His cellmates had confessed on camera, and he learned that though trials were recorded, they were not necessarily shown on television. There were too many convictions to broadcast in the developing purge.

Luboš expected Austrian intelligence would learn of his trial and share his fate with Marcela. His defense attorney delivered a disappointing revelation, however. Television and radio transmission of his trial were preempted by historic political show trials and condemnation of the dissident, Václav Havel.

Chapter 27: Pilnost je Svoboda, 1969-1988

Luboš reached Kamp No. 12 with twenty other political prisoners after a two-hour trip north packed on the metal floor of a stifling, windowless military truck. Recidivists described the brief induction process, the daily routine, and the gritty, gray, stone dust they would grow to hate. Most were silent, dwelling on their crimes or crimes of the state to condemn them.

From the vehicle they were unable to see the denuded shoot to kill zone surrounding the prison, the entry arch that declared "Pilnost je Svoboda," [Diligence Is Freedom], the tall fences, the rolls of barbed wire, the watchtowers, the guards restraining fierce dogs, and the assortment of dreary barracks spread across hectares.

The truck skidded to a stop, the rear ramp clanged down, and guards yelled at them to climb down and form a line. Luboš was blinded by the sweep of searchlights from high towers. Tightly packed front to back, the prisoners moved into the dingy reception room where they were told to strip naked and proceed to sanitation. They were run through a delousing shower, their clothes fumigated, and their heads shaved.

In 1945 Russians had shaved his head. This time, Czechoslovaks shaved him, and the humiliation was no different. He was the cleanest he would be until his release, if he survived that long. Next, he stood naked while the "doctor" evaluated him for manual labor by inspecting his hands.

"How old are you?"

"Thirty-five."

"This man goes to the quarry. More to eat."

A trustee handed him a blanket, tin bowl, and work clothes of heavy canvas pants, waistcoat, mittens, cap with ear flaps, mid-calf boots, socks, undershirt, and heavy long outer coat. The man absently said, "The clothing must last a year. If it doesn't fit, trade. Remember the number on the bottom of the cup."

Guards guided the quarry selectees to a barracks and told them to enter and keep to the schedule of their work brigade.

Less than an hour after he reached the camp, Luboš stepped deeper inside his prison. The door slammed shut and he stood frozen. Oppressive odors filled his nostrils. The expansive wood-frame building was poorly lit. He couldn't discern if one area was better or worse for his first decision—where to berth. Double-tiered bunks met the low ceiling. Luboš scanned the heads, eyes, and beards of the prisoners lined up side-by-side, resembling logs on flat wooden planks. The inmates fell silent and hunched up on their elbows to gauge the new men. The only sounds were hacking coughs.

Luboš was cowed, but now he had to demonstrate confidence and strength among these strangers. He was the first to step forward on the creaky wood floor between the tiers. They evaluated him as he hoisted his bundle of clothing to a bare space and climbed up. One by one, the remaining new prisoners filed past and selected their spot. Murmuring resumed.

It was an idle time after evening roll call. A man confidently lumbered to Luboš and said, "You have good boots, and they gave you work boots." He was plump and full in the face, suggesting he worked in a kitchen or administrative office. He wore clean clothing and had the facial expression of a man who was relaxed in the prison environment. He was the power in that area of the barracks. "I will offer you ration coupons in exchange for the boots. What do you say?"

154

Luboš could only guess the worth of a ration card. He had heard that if a formidable person makes you an offer, common sense dictates that you accept it. Another prisoner might have put forth a proposal, yet they deferred to him.

"What will a card buy me?"

"At the canteen they have tea and smokes. You will want those things, and you don't need the boots. What do you say?"

"The ration cards, let me see them," Luboš said as he considered bargaining for more.

"Sure. Here they are. What do you say?"

"Okay." Luboš elected not to alienate this person. "What's your name?"

"They call me 'Big.' " He licked his fingers to count the wrinkled ration cards.

Still holding the boots, Luboš said, "Where are you from? I grew up in Smižany."

"Welcome to splinter village. I was born in Košice, not far away. What is your name?"

"Luboš." He handed the boots down to Big and placed the ration cards in a pocket. The prisoners viewing the transaction waited for Big to return to his space.

Luboš judged the exchange a fair value after he replayed the scene. The big shot should be pleased by the transaction. He is a Slovak, the inmates know I was the first to walk and claim a bunk, and I wasn't a pushover.

He lowered himself to the floor to hear a man on a lower rack mimic him. "Hey, you. Dith you thay your name wath Luboth?"

"I'm Luboš," he growled and dragged the man who had mimicked his lisp onto the floor and pummeled him until other prisoners intervened. Luboš stepped back, inhaling deeply and exhaling until the adrenalin wore off. He rubbed his hands together, stretched his arms, and rolled his shoulders to determine if he was ready for the next fight. No one came to the defense of the beaten man.

Luboš stood a minute to establish his presence further and then climbed up to his rack. He had confronted bullies in the army. There would be no more wisecracks about the lisp caused by his missing tooth.

Amid the coughing and snores of bone-tired men, Luboš calmed down by thinking of his first coffee date with Marcela. He tried to stay alert in the dangerous setting, but he dozed fitfully.

Luboš awoke to a commotion and followed his bunkmates to the prison yard to stand in formation. He examined his tin bowl bottom. Etched at the bottom was his identification: N 122542. Scratched out was the previous owner's number. The guard called out the last name, and a prisoner replied with a first name and number in a tedious process. When the roll call was complete, they broke for the food line.

After he drank the flavorless gruel and ate a portion of the 100 grams of black bread, Luboš followed the line to the outdoor toilets and back to his plank bed. His mittens and hat were gone, stolen, and probably already traded for cigarettes, the prison currency.

Luboš was boiling inside for his stupidity. He was incarcerated with criminals and needed to think like one. At the wail of sirens, the men formed outside, and he marched his newly issued boots into the future.

Luboš had no training for the dangerous work of swinging a sledgehammer at iron spikes set on stone. A worker could easily hit a leg or a hand or have a stone chip cut an eye. Two men worked together, one clamping a pincer tool longer than his forearm to the spike and the other man hammering until a chunk of rock fell. Luboš's exposed shaved head made clear that he was new. The experienced man, too skinny to fill his canvas shirt, asked, "How new are you?"

"This is my first day."

"Watch me." Only his salt and pepper beard, nose, and eyes were visible under his cap, and they exuded toughness.

Luboš held the massive pliers, and the seasoned man grunted and moved Luboš's hand slightly on the tool to reset the spike a quarter turn after each strike. Holding the spike was more dangerous because an inaccurate swing of the hammer would break an arm or crush a hand. Hammering required more exertion than holding. At mid-morning, they switched positions.

Luboš prepared his first swing as if he were bashing Stalin's statue. It was forceful but misguided. The hammer bounced off the spike and landed on the stone. His workmate made eye contact for the first time and snarled, "If you miss again and injure me, you will die before roll call." They stared at each other, one with the power and the other with none.

"Did you watch me when I hammered?"

Luboš was silent.

"Are you mute? Did they cut out your tongue?"

Luboš paused and pointed his finger to the vacancy in his mouth and said, "I'm recovering from the interrogation." Unsaid was his altercation the previous night.

The workmate, painfully familiar with the ordeal prisoners had already endured, softly said, "Okay, follow me." The gruff man changed his voice to that of a professor. That day began the new man's survival lessons for years to come.

"This is how you swing the hammer—less chance to miss. We are not the outside, where one might exceed quota. If we do, they increase our quota. If you are hurt and don't work, they feed you less. If you die, they don't care. Find friends from your home area and stay close to them if there is trouble. Where are you from?"

"Smižany."

Marching back at the finish of the workday, Luboš said to him, "Thank you."

"Congratulations on surviving until roll call," the man replied pleasantly.

The first night set a solid tone. He had demonstrated strength, which was confirmed by Big, the organizer. "Hey, Luboš, these boots fit nicely. When you wake up, your hat and mittens will be on your rack. Nice work last night. He is an ass. I threw him out." The boots he had traded away were clean, in contrast to his scuffed and sandy pair.

The din of hundreds of men hammering metal onto metal and the smell of unwashed men would not leave him. The next day he hand loaded broken rock into a wheelbarrow and rolled the rubble along narrow boards rising to conveyor belts at the top of the quarry.

The first weeks were physically and emotionally exhausting as Luboš adjusted to pervasive gray dust, roll calls, inadequate sustenance and sleep, dangerous working conditions, and the constant worry of whom to trust. Luboš continued to watch his surroundings, trying to form alliances that would help him survive the next two and a half decades. He never mentioned Ukraine, and he never responded if his native language was spoken.

Twice a day, an erect gray-haired prisoner walked past Luboš's rack. Prisoners deferred to him as they did to Big. His eyes and lips seemed to smile with inner tranquility. Luboš asked who he was and was told he was called "General."

"A general? Why is a general here?"

"Anyone is here, even priests."

Chapter 28: Life and Death in Kamp No. 12, 1970–1980

Thousands of expendable prisoners under a century of masters had chiseled and hammered at the pozary granite, gouging deeper and deeper into the earth. Diesel-powered crushers sorted the granite pieces to a uniform size. A prisoner directed the distribution onto dump trucks—trucks driven by outsiders who delivered stone as far south as Prague. Despite the danger, high-risk smuggling was commonplace. The illegal trafficking depended on which prisoner loaded the trucks, and that assignment was prized.

Luboš learned that the General was the organizer of army veterans and partisans. Some had fought the Germans on the Western Front or been prisoners of war. Communists persecuted them solely for their exposure to Western values. Whatever the reason for incarceration, their military experience bonded them—there were no informants. The General looked after his men, who held the privileged location near the stove in winter and windows in summer. Luboš mentioned that he had been in the army, which brought an introduction to the veterans. The General asked, "Where was your unit?"

Luboš recounted his conscription and location on the border at the Hungarian Revolt.

"I remember Highway 17 well. We will talk about it. Move your things to an empty sleeping space in our corner. The windows will offer ventilation."

"Yes, sir. Thank you."

The brigade of men frog-marched to the pit in pairs, leading to the only pleasant time of his day. At the guard's command, "Halt," Luboš was at the edge of his deceptively quiet, open-mouthed quarry. Night dew had settled the dust, and he sucked in the clear air. The mandatory silence offered rare free time. Scanning the horizon, he might recall Jan, who had asked him, "How many kilometers to the next ridge?"

Morning visibility was excellent, and he contemplated life in the blue-gray Krkonoše Mountains. They shimmered as if they were unreal. Sadly, his horizon was the barbed wire, 100 meters distant.

That was the only time during the workday he didn't have to watch his footing or the spike or the wheel of the wheelbarrow. The guard broke his trance with the order to get to work, and hundreds of prisoners spread out hefting a shovel, pick, or hammer and descend to the place they had finished digging the previous day.

When the steam whistle marked quitting time, the exhausted laborers climbed out of their hole and lined up again. The dust bloom from the dynamiting, drilling, and crushing blocked any view except the watchtowers. Prisoners coughed and choked from the powder they had created. Luboš was too tired to see past the prisoner in front of him. When he learned that Czechoslovakia won the 1972 bronze medal in ice hockey, he didn't care.

The fiasco of his escape attempt, the beatings, and the endless prison sentence put Luboš in long-term shock. He didn't think or reflect. He just endured the day, as his mother had during her final winter.

The best opportunity to relax was after evening soup and roll call. The General held court with old soldiers sitting on the two levels of the sleeping boards. It was their unique place where they played Durak, gambled, and smoked. The first rule was to leave the misery of the prison with a joke.

Ridicule was their way to say "Fuck You" to the system. Following a hearty laugh, they would proceed to any topic that came up, from stealing food from the kitchen to how to seek revenge on a cruel guard. The underground samizdat copy of *Darkness at Noon* by Arthur Koestler was read aloud at night. The evening ritual ended as they quietly sang ballads about their Czechoslovak heritage, a woman, or a lost compatriot. Luboš introduced Slovak songs he had learned from Petra.

The evenings were a ritual for the men to maintain a mental reference outside the barbed wire. *The Good Soldier Švejk* had been smuggled in, and they shared humorous anecdotes of army life and their current circumstances. The General's brotherhood appreciated the opportunity to briefly return to life elsewhere and laugh.

They didn't laugh about the system that put them in prison, often for crimes never committed. If given an opportunity for retribution or to challenge Communism, they would.

The General was a tough man who had survived extensive combat against the Nazis and twenty years of brutal labor, inmate subterfuge, and diseases. However, Kamp No. 12 and age seventy became too much for him. His lungs were lined in silica, and his response at roll call became inaudible. Despite medicines stolen from the dispensary, he collapsed and was placed in the ward for doomed prisoners.

Luboš visited in the evening carrying snacks from the canteen and told familiar stories, making the General laugh and then cough uncontrollably. Since his incarceration six years earlier, Luboš had looked to the General as his backbone of internal strength. When he died, Luboš was devastated to lose another mentor.

The General's loyal second, Ota, became the organizer. He and Luboš arranged a respectful service in the barracks. A nationalist partisan leader in the Krkonoše Mountains during the war, Ota's clenched jaw and firm voice carried the same authority as the General. He was equally savvy about the inner workings of the camp to protect his mini tribe.

Day in, day out, year in, year out, the rigorous labor drained Luboš. His diet was unchanged, the heating was no better, the rats were widespread, and Luboš had to be vigilant. His face wrinkled, his hair turned gray, and quarry thunder stole more of his hearing. His cough was worse than Miluše's.

The only difference from one day to the next was the prisoner turnover. Scores died natural deaths, others were killed trying to break out, some completed sentences, and unruly behavior sent the worst to a uranium mine to die more quickly.

Luboš had no family or friends outside. He received no letters, packages, or money. To whom would he write? To Marcela, wish I were there? To Zuzana, asking for a pardon? To Miluše, to send strudel?

Communication to the outside was unlikely, so Luboš floated over the barbed wire. *Will your mother cook bream tonight?* He wasn't delusional. He connected to Marcela to keep sane. His imagination helped him endure his reality.

Will your mother ski tomorrow? To make love on a wide bed. . . .

Except Marcela was across the border.

During his ninth year in the camp, a dynamite detonation dislodged stones, and Luboš slid into a crevice. His foot was trapped for hours until fellow prisoners extricated him. The cuts became infected and healing was painful. He limped at each step. Ota arranged his reassignment to a job repairing the diesel engines of the large stone crushers. Luboš joked to himself that he was a constructor of Communism and deserved awards. Oil on his fingertips, he painted imaginary medals on the inside of the engine covers and snickered.

Did I tell you? I traded cigarette rations to have "Marcela" tattooed on my chest. I must go now. I kiss you.

And Luboš returned to Kamp No. 12.

Chapter 29: Revenge, 1981

Newly convicted prisoners arrived in a padlocked truck, passed under the arch, and were assigned in the same manner as Luboš's arrival twelve years before. The men were scrutinized. A fellow conspirator, an acquaintance from your village, or a criminal associate might turn up. Recognizing a person whose head was newly shaved was difficult.

Survival required continual awareness—of the granite stone face where you worked and of people. Luboš noticed an unshaven man wearing his cap pulled low in the summer heat. The man walked away when approached. Luboš was eager to learn about him. Who did he hang around with, and where did he work?

Luboš pointed out the detached man to Ota. Word came back through spies in the administrative office that the man's files were restricted. He was a loner. Luboš and his accomplices waited to corner him in an area of the latrine not visible to the guards. Ota sidled up, and when at his hip, he stomped down on the loner's boot with his full weight.

The prisoner called out but was grabbed from behind.

"Speak quietly. What's your name? Where are you from? My friends are curious," Ota demanded.

"What the fuck are you doing?" the trapped man asked. "Get off my foot!"

"Shut the fuck up. I ask the questions."

At the mercy of the threatening group, he replied in a strained voice, "My name is Vinko. I'm from Prešov."

"I'm from Prešov, and we stick together. Have you been avoiding us? Perhaps you aren't from Prešov. What was the damage when the Germans retreated in 1945?"

"I don't remember," the man replied, his face contorted in pain.

"What street is the Church of St. Nicholas on?"

"I can't remember. I must leave."

"Not yet. You have no records in the administrative files. What was your work? Why did you end up here?"

"In Prešov, I was a smuggler and was caught."

"Yes, yes, you are caught. The Nazis exacted retribution from Prešov, and everyone knows the Church is on Hlavna. You aren't from Prešov."

"I was young, and my family worshipped at a different church."

"Bullshit!" shouted Luboš. "I didn't recognize the bearded face, but I know the voice. You are the Černy who beat me to a pulp at the StB." The three furrows on Černy's forehead arched up in fear.

"Is that true, you were an interrogator?"

Ota was about to ask a question, but Luboš fumed, "You laughed when you knocked out my tooth. I can't hear shit after you blew out my eardrums. Your lies tore me apart. Fuck you! You were on the top floor of the StB. Comrade Černy, this is your cellar!"

"What are you saying? My records will be delivered soon."

"Records?" Luboš was spitting mad. "You have powerful enemies. They sent you here, satisfied that, of the thousand prisoners pounding rock into sand, some will get even. You won the battles. We will win the war. Today, I'm your case officer."

The prisoner's eyes swept for an alley to bolt.

"Roll up your sleeves!" Luboš bellowed. "Roll up your sleeves!"

Černy twisted free of Ota's boot and dashed for an opening. One of the waiting partisans slammed Černy's face with a board. He collapsed on the ground, streaming blood.

Ota knelt, rolled up the right sleeve of Černy's limp arm, and looked to Luboš. Luboš pointed to the other sleeve, and there it was: the red tattoo of the Czechoslovak coat of arms—the lion's head replaced by a skull. "What's next?" Ota asked.

"For him, torturing was pleasure. Rumors fly. Spread the word he is from the StB and see what happens."

The next morning Ota eased to Luboš's sleeping spot and smirked. "He won't answer roll call. A tooth for a tooth."

Chapter 30: Hope and Slow Change, 1984

Repression within Czechoslovakia remained unchanged since the 1969 normalization, but the world was changing. Clandestine copies of Yevgeny Yevtushenko's *Heirs of Stalin* and Václav Havel's letters from prison circulated. Increasing protests in Poland, where Lech Walesa was leading an independent union, and the elevation of Pope John Paul II of Poland, provided opportunity for change.

Our hockey team won the silver medal. The bad news—Russia took the gold. The new camp administrator played the game live on the loudspeakers. You should have heard the boos. Even the guards were angry at the Russians. Over the years, these imaginary chats with Marcela occurred less frequently.

A new political prisoner with a fifteen-year sentence for espionage and anti-Soviet agitation was assigned to Luboš's barracks. He was a charismatic, confident, cigarette-smoking journalist who had run afoul of the government in his role as a reporter and spy. Tall, slender, and upbeat, he sang in a clear voice, and the men welcomed him. He wasn't perceived a threat and assumed a spot near Ota at the evening confabs.

Appreciating the crucial guidance he had received early on, Luboš offered suggestions to ease the newcomer's transition to prison. Luboš learned that Martin had been a Party member allowed outside Czechoslovakia on assignments for the Communist newspaper, *Rudé právo*.

He was suspected of disloyalty, tried as a traitor, and confessed for his family's sake. Instinctively, Luboš trusted the newcomer.

166

He told Martin of his own transgression—modification of a bus in Prague that enabled the getaway of a young woman in 1969. He briefly described how he attempted to flee with her.

Martin was astounded to follow a piece of the story and listened attentively. He recalled the uproar in Vienna in 1979 when he was a journalist. The capital's newspaper *Kronen Zeitung* had published a news article about the tenth anniversary of a daring pregnant woman seeking asylum in West Germany. The article celebrated her welcome in Austria.

The Czechoslovak ambassador had protested, saying the story was propaganda. Martin wrote press releases for the ambassador and letters to the editor to create a false narrative.

Luboš didn't share the woman's name with Martin. Luboš couldn't picture the color of her hair or the shape of her breasts. After fifteen years in prison, she was a faint shadow of a love story.

Martin led Luboš to a private area and asked, "Was her name Marcela?"

"Why do you say Marcela?" Luboš demanded.

Martin related his duties at the embassy and how his task was to delegitimize the story. The essence of the article was her assimilation in Austria as a schoolteacher with boy and girl twins and her Austrian husband.

Luboš's mind was running too fast and in all directions. He sat open-mouthed until he demanded, "How old were they?"

Martin, surprised at Luboš' abruptness, couldn't guess and said a picture of the four of them accompanied the article.

"How big were they? Were they little?"

"They were not babies and not in their teens."

"Was Marcela pretty?"

"Yes." In an instant, she was back in his life.

"Marcela, were you pregnant when I hid you on the bus? I cannot sleep. I kiss you again and again."

167

Martin had been effective in challenging the newspaper article; in prison, next to Luboš, he was ashamed for his role in discrediting the story. Martin was empathetic and patient as Luboš pestered him for details.

The decade brought relaxed rules for relatives to send money to prisoners for cigarettes, clothing—and bribes. Ota arranged for Luboš to become the contact for trafficking operations. The drivers of the large dump trucks—who were not prisoners—and the guards were amenable to payoffs. He worked deals trafficking items the truck drivers brought in, selling at enough profit to pay off the guards. Luboš had wrangled enough money and coupons to bargain for anything, even new boots.

Luboš was desperate to learn more about Marcela. He persuaded Martin to ask a former colleague from the *Rudé právo* to search their files for a copy of the 1979 story from the Vienna newspaper. The truck drivers were intermediaries in this intrigue and upped their fees. Luboš paid without hesitation.

The newspaper story, written in German, was eventually delivered, and Martin translated the text. The children, named Lida and Libor, were ten in 1979. Luboš was shaken. The names begin with "L." Luboš smiled, certain that Marcela did this for love for their father. Libor means free—a perfect choice for the baby. Wilhelm and Marcela? Did she love the man?

Luboš was slow to fully absorb the article as he focused on the twins and Marcela's marriage. Several times Martin read the article describing her new life. The Viennese reporter had inquired how she planned her flight. She responded simply, "Leaving Prague was difficult."

Did Lida figure skate? Did Libor play hockey? Were they good babies? Ota, our army boss, has given me responsibility for our smuggling here—I am a capitalist speculator, ha, ha.

His thoughts ran far and wide, but he was in prison.

Marcela was beautiful in the newspaper image. He hadn't considered her marriage to someone else or, especially, falling in love. He held a copy of the article and read between the lines. Luboš had found Marcela, his son and daughter, and a renewed dream.

Chapter 31: Zuzana, 1987

United States President Ronald Reagan's June 1987 challenge in Berlin, "Tear down this wall," resonated with the prisoners. Graffiti supporting the Polish labor union Solidarity was painted in hidden places, and sympathetic truckers delivered resistance leaflets. Liberalization enabled by General Secretary of the Soviet Union Mikhail Gorbachev's Glasnost, openness, in Soviet countries gave hope for freedom. The early release of younger prisoners due to the labor shortage in Czechoslovakia was encouraging.

Jan's last words drove Luboš, "I will find you." To find Marcela, he needed to communicate with her sister, Zuzana Burešová. Although Marcela wasn't a believer, Zuzana had tolerated her sister's independence out of respect for their mother.

Luboš knew only a paper fragment of Marcela's life in Vienna. He asked Martin to use his newspaper contacts to obtain the addresses of Zuzana and their mother to write for a fuller picture. A month passed before the smugglers provided Zuzana's address and information that Miluše had passed on. Luboš grieved for Miluše, who raised two daughters during the war and watched them pursue divergent paths. Marcela's departure, without a kiss to her mother, must have pained Miluše.

Since the Communist coup in 1948, Zuzana had performed well in positions of increasing responsibility. At the time of Marcela's escape, she was director of the Presidium of the Central Committee of the KSC. Her expertise was recruiting and training. She was proud that in the late 1960s, Czechoslovakia maintained the highest percentage of Party members of Soviet countries. She was not adversely affected by the escape. Not surprisingly, Luboš had not written her, or anyone. Guided expertly by Martin, Luboš wrote in his best hand to a woman whose career he may have ruined:

Dear Zuzana, I ask forgiveness for difficulties in 1969. The StB tortured me to implicate you. I recently discovered Marcela has a boy and a girl born in 1969 and a husband. I hesitate to ask you—am I their father? Luboš, Kamp No. 12.

The note was sent via a smuggler. Luboš hoped the looser prison policies would permit a reply. His note didn't ask for favors, only information. How much could Zuzana do? How much would she agree to do? The unknown was killing him.

After three months, he was resigned to continued cluelessness of Marcela's children.

Chapter 32: Correspondence

Finally, news came: an official envelope from Zuzana's address at the KSC, unopened by the censors. Luboš held the sealed wrapping as if it were gold, or Miluše's goulash, and read it in a solitary place.

Dear Luboš, these 20 koruna banknotes are for your necessities. I will give your address to Marcela. Zuzana

He pondered her minimal response. He shared the brief letter with Martin, who said, "You could have no letter, no money, no offer toward Marcela. You have a good reply and good expectations."

"You are reassuring. I hope you are right. And Zuzana remains a Communist official and not in prison."

Unknown to Luboš, Zuzana had been a staunch proponent of Communism until cracks in the system widened. Václav Havel, Lech Walesa, and Secretary Gorbachev influenced her year by year to re-evaluate her values and adopt more liberal ideas—and actions.

Zuzana's letter to Marcela provided more than Luboš's address at the prison. She opened the door to end the sisters' seventeen-year silence and encouraged her sister to write Luboš if Wilhelm approved. The same day she wrote separately to Wilhelm asking to reunite the sisters.

Liberalized communications in 1987 enabled exchanges between the sisters and these crossed.

Zuzana wrote to Marcela: *After you left Czechoslovakia, Máma was disoriented, and neighbors shunned her. The StB interviewed me, but I was cleared. I have been upset with you. No more.*

Marcela wrote to Zuzana: *I was selfish to leave and cause so much pain for you and Máma. I should have apologized, but I was ashamed. I apologize now and ask for your forgiveness.*

Marcela's first post to Kamp.No.12 was delivered a month later. He read and reread it: *Dear Luboš, At my side is my husband, Wilhelm, who has looked after Lida and Libor and me. Yes, you are their father. You will be proud of them.*

Although the letter was short, he imagined a new beginning: she is running to him, he sweeps her off her feet and hugs and kisses her and—and nothing.

He accepted its significance without the daydream.

Martin assisted Luboš as the displaced lovers exchanged tentative letters, each unsure how to progress. As a courtesy, Marcela shared with Wilhelm the mailings she sent and received. She couldn't do otherwise to an honorable man. He was a supportive husband to Marcela and a fine stepfather. However, he understood from the day they met that his wife had been committed to Luboš. Wilhelm did not protest.

Marcela's informative letters described the children's education and hobbies, her position at their school, and Wilhelm. She didn't go beyond mundane expressions.

Luboš wrote short letters and described the prison in words to pass the censors. Luboš got it: Marcela had moved on. For him, if he completed his sentence, Lida and Libor might be a small fragment of his life. Marcela's neutral tone seemed to place their love in the past—no more fantasies about a large bed to make love.

Marcela understood the awkwardness of their correspondence and was bursting to tell him more. She spilled her innermost emotions in one poignant letter—one she didn't divulge to Wilhelm—sent via Zuzana in uncensored mail.

The special letter maintained that she never stopped loving him and that she raised the children to revere their father. Marcela's letter continued: *In Vienna, I feel guilty watching our twins grow up while you are far from me. They are sad not to call their grandmother, Babička. Lida and Libor idolize you and are accomplished in languages, as you will see. They are excellent students, and we will be proud of them. In Austria, they say Communism will collapse, and then we will meet. Wilhelm is a gracious stepfather and husband who has supported our communication. I am deceitful because I will send this letter without his knowledge. I imagine a life for us in Prague would be better than the life I live. Love always, I kiss you, Marcela.*

Luboš was certain he smelled Marcela's perfume. The letter was magical for Luboš, raising the possibility for more "bright" years. It was the sole message she sent, or could send, that declared, "I kiss you." Was her declaration a revival of her love, and was she offering a path for them?

"I imagine a life for us in Prague would be better than the life I live. ..." a prisoner read loudly, mocking Luboš. He had stolen the precious letter. The man was unable to finish the sentence. Luboš withdrew his always-handy shiv, a sharpened screwdriver. In a split second he had to decide, should I kill him? What would Jan do? Kill him, and the guards might kill me. Instead, Luboš stunned him by a head butt to his nose. The man fell to the floor, and Luboš beat him bloody and pounded the shiv into the man's hand so hard that he was pinned to the floor.

Luboš backed off to his bunk, panting loudly and eyeing the room, awaiting the judgment of his army band. Except for the muffled cries of the man locked to the floor, the matter would not leave the barracks.

Luboš read her missive over and over in a quiet spot and reluctantly burned his link to the Prague Spring. He let it burn his fingers as a reminder of the last picture of his father.

He was embarrassed to write poorly. And what was there for him to write about, life in prison? He couldn't say, "I kiss you," mindful that her husband would read it. They were like two magnets pulled together in love, realizing that, by a slight twist, they are pushed away by reality.

❖ ❖ ❖ ❖ ❖

Friends in the highest places had steered Zuzana through power struggles and purges. A visit to Luboš in prison by a senior Communist officer would be a distraction and might upset her efforts. She dared not give him false hope.

Luboš, Spring is coming. Stay out of trouble.

He received this curt advice from Zuzana and asked Ota to arrange a transfer from the trucks and replace him as head smuggler. Dumping a wheelbarrow of stone off the boardwalk would mark one for haranguing while misdirecting a truck off the narrow road would result in solitary confinement. Luboš focused on his work at the engine maintenance shop.

Optimism was rising in Central European countries in the late 1980s. Would those visions wither as in 1956 and 1968? The responsible governance Luboš's Ukrainian family sought, and Marcela found, was a possibility in Czechoslovakia. A Communist and a Czech, Zuzana endeavored to prepare for the future. However, senior Party members adhered to the strict "normalization" policies.

In her opinion, that policy had backfired as indicated by low morale and the declining percentage of active Party members. Zuzana was a reformer who walked a thin line. How could she prepare the Party for change and not be ostracized? On a tightrope, she asked her confidant to direct that Luboš's re-education was complete and arrange his early release from prison.

The timing was excellent. Under the guise of overcrowding and the high cost of incarceration, long-serving political prisoners were placed on parole and released. Luboš was one of them.

The paperwork for the release of the selected prisoners was hastily completed. Camp administrators arranged for their discharge the next day. Luboš said goodbye to Martin, Ota, and his army pals and was sequestered that night to keep him safe from resentful prisoners.

At noon he walked beneath the entry arch. He stopped and looked back to read for the first time the rusted wrought iron words, Pilnost je Svoboda.

Part Three: Change Is Coming, 1988–2014

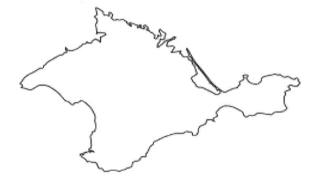

Crimea

Chapter 33: Luboš Is Released, 1988

Dipping his left shoulder in sync with the awkward swing of his right leg, Luboš limped fifty meters on a straight course toward Zuzana, standing next to the gray Škoda Favorit. He was halfway to her before she recognized him among the whiskered, newly released men wearing identical brown prison garb. She expected him to appear somewhat different, but not that old and thin.

She approached him with arms outstretched, but he shied away. He was unprepared for this moment or any moment outside the barbed wire. Zuzana persisted and gave him a long hug and began crying. He returned the embrace and sobbed. They were unwilling to let go until silica in his lungs forced choking coughs.

"I smell bad and look bad, but inside I feel safe and free. At least free of the barbed wire." Luboš leaned back as Zuzana reached over him to buckle his seat belt, something new to him. He savored her perfume. Then he sneezed, unaccustomed to any pleasant fragrance.

"I arrived chained in a truck. Today, I dirty your auto and leave in comfort," Luboš said with a laugh, trying to find suitable words for an outsider. Luboš had forgotten about his missing tooth and hoarse, lispy speech. Zuzana was shocked.

As a high-ranking leader of the Party, Zuzana had access to a Škoda, a modest Czechoslovak auto, and led a privileged life. Her collared dark red blazer, black slacks, and broad leather belt lent an imposing aura. Her styled brown hair held a sprinkling of gray. Zuzana had aged well, keeping her trim frame and avoiding the chunky image of middle age. Luboš furtively glanced across and imagined her sister.

"You appear alert," Zuzana said, aware that he was observing her.

"If you aren't alert in prison, you won't finish your sentence. One day I'm a prisoner with six year's sentence remaining, and the next day I'm released. Thank you for picking me up on short notice. You didn't have to sign for me. Your KSC connections were adequate."

They scarcely talked at the onset of the two-hour drive south. Luboš was tranquil for the first time in decades, observing fields of corn and soybeans and listening to a cassette tape by the Plastic People of the Universe. He surveyed the buttons and knobs, and with Zuzana's approval, he amused himself by running the tape forward and backward time and again.

Though the air-conditioned car was comfortable, Luboš asked for fresh air. Zuzana pointed to the switch on his door. He ran the window up and down repeatedly. His curiosity satiated, he held his mostly bald head in the wind stream—causing her hair to blow this way and that.

"Did my letter asking you to stay out of trouble confuse you?"

"It was a signal. I didn't show it to my friend Martin, and I burned it. I guessed, comply with camp rules."

"I feared you might try an escape."

"Not me. I limp worse than my father. Those who attempted died on the second row of barbed wire. The inside perimeter of Kamp No. 12 was my home. I only dreamed of the hills outside." Luboš was fifty-four years old and wasn't confident he would fit in the modern world.

"Did that road sign read Kadan?" Luboš asked, ruminating on his disappointing search for Jan thirty years earlier.

"We are avoiding the major highway and taking country roads. Kadan is fifty kilometers west. In a minute, you will see the village of Kojetice where Máma labored under the Nazis."

"We intended to go together, but, you know, she escaped."

Ignoring the reference to her sister, Zuzana replied, "You have a room to yourself. I purchased clothing for you. We will proceed at your pace for these days and weeks."

"Thank you. Tonight will be a test: a soft bed and no roll call."

"What would you choose to do first?"

"Leave these prison clothes and wash in a shower."

"You will have a bath."

"That's a luxury. I will have trouble adapting to hot water," Luboš quipped, trying to envisage a bathtub. "I'll have trouble adapting to everything."

"I will help you."

Zuzana stopped the Škoda outside the clothing factory. Silence prevailed. She thought of her mother stealing fabric from the Nazis and stifled her tears. Luboš thought of Marcela. Zuzana continued in heavy traffic at the outskirts of Prague and slowed for citizens overflowing the sidewalks, standing stoically in a queue for whatever the government store placed on the shelves.

"The longest lines were at that store. Are conditions better or worse now?"

"Worse. Gorbachev's initiatives were well intentioned but gave the entire Soviet Union inflation and shortages. You may have heard in prison of his Perestroika, market restructuring, which has disrupted production. Fortunately, I have access to the Tuzex stores."

"Yes. Stores for 'our own.' " Luboš remarked with disdain. Zuzana held her response, conscious that only Party functionaries and those with foreign currency were admitted to such stores filled with imported merchandise and fresh produce. Long lines for inferior goods were all he had known. Zuzana faced no lines.

Weaving home through Prague's narrow streets, she pointed out landmarks in the dwindling daylight. Luboš identified familiar sights and said, "The sun sets, but Prague isn't warm and sunny to me."

"Together, we will remedy that impression. And here we are," Zuzana announced, relieved the day had gone smoothly.

"It's the same apartment," Luboš said, sitting in the car, readying himself for his transition.

"An effort to move me failed."

"After your interrogation?"

"Yes."

"Marcela and I walked by frequently. She chose not to invite herself in. You were different. She never uttered an unpleasant word about you. Just that politics blocked a friendship beyond skating and dinners at your mother's."

"The system doesn't unite us. Can you walk the stairs?"

"I'll climb slowly."

On the steps, Zuzana advised, "The apartment might be bugged. We should be careful about what we say."

"Is it bugged for you or me?"

"If they weren't listening yesterday, they are listening today."

She unlocked the door and ushered Luboš into his new surroundings. The accommodations were spacious, and he detected the same aromas from Miluše's cooking twenty years before. He paused at the modest kitchen to his left and bent over to put his nose in the colorful bouquet.

Zuzana turned on the radio playing music of Czech composer Antonin Dvořák and said, "When we talk, I will run water in the sink."

"Government hasn't changed much, I guess."

"Enough to release you from prison."

She led Luboš through the open parlor to windows and floor to ceiling drapes at the far end. Zuzana's bedroom was on the right, and she opened the door to his bedroom on the opposite side. "Welcome to your room. I will take your clothes tomorrow."

"Throw them out. They are the wrong size," he chuckled. Luboš paused at the single bed with coverlets folded aside, bedside table and lamp, four-drawer bureau, closet, and rocking chair. At the window open to the summer night, he asked, "Which direction does the window face?"

"To the south."

"Ah, toward Marcela," he said, smiling.

"You have a real closet," Luboš noted, swinging the heavy walnut doors back and forth and opening each sliding drawer. "What do they call this furniture?"

"An armoire."

"My closet in the dormitory was cardboard."

Zuzana didn't reply and shooed away her cat, who was sleeping on the newly acquired clothing. She explained how to operate the tub handles and gently said, "Your first wish is granted. Take your time." She eased the bedroom door shut behind her.

Luboš carried no effects, like his arrival in Nováky with Jan. He hesitated to stuff his repulsive clothes into the clothes hamper.

For the remainder of the evening, everything was new. He cut his summer stubble with sharp scissors, shaved at his bowl, and savored his long bath. The hour was eerily quiet except for the hot water dripping into the tub.

He emerged from the bedroom in a wave of humid air that fogged the mirror over the fireplace mantel. He wore the clothes purchased for him and patted toilet paper onto the nicks on his face from the sharp razor. He plunked down on the straight back chair at the black lacquered table. She set his favorite dark lager on the embroidered runner.

With one hand and then two, Luboš repeatedly twisted the warp threads, searching for the right words.

"I'm sorry to nearly wreck your life," he forced out. His face gripped in his hands, he wept into his fingers, his elbows punching his knees.

Zuzana touched his shoulder.

He regained his composure and noticed that Zuzana had freshened up from the hot afternoon. Her hair was brushed and parted on the left side by a silver barrette. Wearing a hint of perfume, a freshly laundered blouse, and an encouraging smile, she looked like Marcela might look. He stifled that notion.

"I might have been released with no one to greet me, riding a bus to nowhere. Instead, I'm collected by an attractive woman in a brand-new auto and escorted to a beautiful home."

"The rest of your life commences today."

"You are my only family."

"You have family in Austria."

"I forget. You are my only family in Czechoslovakia."

He finished his beer and asked for another. "What would I desire the first night out of prison?" Luboš rubbed his scarred hands and leaned back to answer his question. "A lager, a ripe pear, a hot bath, a woman, or a pistol to shoot the judges who put me in prison. That and more. I asked the question over the years, and, of course, it was a joke. Last night it was real. For my first night, I long for security."

The cat sauntered in like she was the queen of the building. She raised her tail straight up, rubbed along his new trousers, and jumped onto his lap, startling him.

"Tippy Toes, off," scolded Zuzana. The cat looked dismissively at her and the new friend.

"Do you have mice?"

"No!"

"We did not name the cats at the farm."

"Sorry, she has poor manners. I will take the cat."

"It's okay. The cat is fine. Is it a he or a she?"

"She is female."

"She is purring. Tippy Toes is quite a name."

"Black except for a white spot on her chest and the white booties on her feet," Zuzana said, pleased Luboš wasn't upset. "She is elegant—a Cinderella."

"She is a princess. Cats ate mice at the farm, and they were never inside."

"Tippy Toes never goes outside and might remain on your lap for a long time."

"She is comforting. I'm in no hurry. No one is telling me what to do," he said until he caught himself. "No. You are telling me what to do."

"I will assist without pushing. I bet you are hungry. I have smoked mackerel and kulajda soup for you."

Luboš slurped soup faster than a prisoner until he raised his lips from the bowl and realized he was safe. His hostess ladled out more soup, and this time he sipped from the spoon, savoring the flavors and aromas.

"I have been running like the river, to or from somewhere. Jan and my mother said it was freedom. I don't know what that is, but today is better than yesterday."

With no specific goals for reentering life in Prague, Luboš proceeded one step at a time. He rubbed his newly shaved face. "My mother cut my hair with glass, Jan cut my hair with a dull knife, another prisoner cut my hair with a piece of metal, and today I cut my own hair while looking at a mirror. Ha. I look pretty bad. What's the style of sideburns these days? Are these too long or too short?"

"Our first trip tomorrow will be to a barber. Ask him."

"These clothes are nice, too nice. I'm not comfortable in them."

"I'm sorry they are big. I guessed your size."

"It isn't the size," Luboš said, stretching his back to free muscle kinks. He stood to walk to the crowded sideboard. "Sure, I'm a smaller person than the last time you saw me. They stole my soul and my tooth. I'm not ready to act normal wearing a vest on the street."

"Your soul is right here. I am your friend, and together, we will bring you back."

"Is this porcelain collection Miluše's?" Luboš asked, studying the face of a figurine and recalibrating his life. She gave him the liberty to ask questions and did not overwhelm him with her responses.

"It is."

"What kind of flower is this?"

"It is an orchid."

"Yes, I remember. Marcela admired orchids." He was restless and moved past the upholstered soft burgundy couch and armchairs to straighten his legs and further ease his back pain. The drapes waved rhythmically in the cool evening breeze. Luboš brushed them aside to view the brightly illuminated spires of Prague Castle across the Vltava. "I fished from the downstream side of the bridges to see the Castle."

"The view is magnificent. The Vltava should bring back pleasant memories of Marcela."

"All memories of her are pleasant. We didn't argue, although she thought I drank too much pivo at the hockey games." After several minutes holding his place at the window, Luboš turned to see his reflection in the mirror and Zuzana behind him.

Her barrette blinked at him. The hint of mascara and eyeliner accentuated her sharp sky-blue eyes; a matching silver broach on her lapel held his gaze. The lady was attractive. Nevertheless, he saw Marcela.

He returned to pictures of the Burešová family and her Communist Party activities and asked, "Is this the last picture you have of Marcela?"

"No. Máma took the last photo of the two of us." Zuzana opened a drawer and rummaged through unframed pictures. "Please don't be offended that these pictures are hidden. Marcela is out of the country and more or less forgotten, and you are not. Besides, I learned of your release just last night."

Luboš cradled the picture in his hands. "She told us to smile. We had resolved to leave. We appear sad because we left without a last farewell to her—ah, your—mother."

"She was despairing. One daughter is a criminal in a foreign country, and the other is complicit and interrogated by the StB. They brought her in but didn't grill her."

"I wanted to suffer instead of you."

"Enough about misery. Tomorrow you will discover the kitchen and television. Let's take a walk." She refreshed his nighttime bearings until the church bells of the Basilica of St. James Cathedral struck midnight.

Late in the morning, Luboš arose to find rohliks, honey, and slices of cheese next to the refrigerator and a note saying, "Be back soon." He was turning the television's rotary knob through the three government channels when she returned from the Tuzex store. He exclaimed, "The television has color. Even the soccer match is in color."

"It's a Sony Trinitron made in Japan. You snored louder than thunder. You slept soundly your first night?"

"Please forgive me. I was absorbed in the television. I forgot to say 'thank you' for bringing me here. There are no social manners in prison, just rules."

"Did you sleep well?" she asked again, becoming accustomed to his lisp, as she put the string grocery bag on the kitchen counter.

"Yes and no. Sleep interrupted by awful thoughts. Prisoners sleep with one eye open. Last night I shut both eyes."

Luboš wasn't ready for the sudden transition from the rigid life to his swift release. He felt guilt for his release while innocents were trapped in prison. Neglected buildings lined by black stains from pollution were dreary. Diesel soot filled the air, and the city lacked color. Stalin's poplar trees dangled dead limbs. Noisy scooters whined, and even the apartment unnerved him by its clatter of a fax machine and bells and tones sounding from kitchen appliances. He had imagined a happy release from prison, but he was overwhelmed. His constant companion, Tippy Toes, soothed him.

Zuzana and Marcela spoke in the same slow rhythm. Zuzana enabled Luboš to assimilate slowly and didn't schedule daily obligations. Luboš slept in his bed or on the couch, dropped his clothes on the bedroom floor, overate, and watched boring TV.

Three days of decompression were enough, Zuzana forced him, wearing his preferred dark, check-patterned shirt and black pants, to go on slow-paced walks to the river, churches, parks, and plazas to reintroduce him to Prague.

"Did your father say, 'Listen to the birds' in this garden?"

"Yes, every week in the springtime. I suppose you learned most everything about us."

"I'm a listener, same as all Czechs, and Marcela was outspoken. What about her?"

"Who knows? She will be amazed when she receives your next letter from Prague." Zuzana almost added "as a free man," but, of course, they were in Communist Czechoslovakia.

On the first of these strolls, Zuzana recounted her experience and how difficult the arrest was for her. Luboš was reluctant to bring up the aftermath of the escape. He was glad when she initiated it.

"Černy attempted to trick me by reading your false confession that I aided my sister. I was angry at the two of you, and I was isolated. However difficult it was for me, it was far worse for you. I knew of your boyhood strength, and any accusations against me were from your torture. I refused knowledge of your plans or any involvement. A long-time colleague was aware of my detention and demanded to see me. I convinced him of my innocence, and after two days of tough interrogation, I was out. On the day of my release, Černy apologized."

"He was a real bastard trying to force me to inform on you. You are a tough lady."

"You are a tough man. The entire episode shook me. My friends high up helped me remain a low-profile person instead of becoming a non-person and forgotten. I excused interrogation overreach as your fault and not the failure of the state. A perpetrator of crimes should be punished, but forced confessions are wrong. Even after my arrest by the StB, the serious faults of our state were unclear to me."

"Who is the man in your pictures?" Luboš asked after the walk.

"He is the one who protected you and me."

"After Dubček was replaced, Marcela and I planned to leave. We worried you would be disciplined. We were selfish."

"You were, and I was angry. From the outset, I wasn't in favor of Dubček easing central economic planning. My friend and my resistance to change in 1968 saved me. Party members who aligned with Dubček were purged. Your first letter was a rude awakening, and I was glad to receive it. I could have written Marcela, but too many years had passed. That is my inadequate excuse. Our communication last year was a positive change to my life.

"Don't judge me full of forgiveness," Zuzana continued. "I didn't forget Major Černy and his overstep of authority. When the opportunity came, I trapped him in a series of lies that led to his downfall. The ultimate punishment was his sentence to Kamp No. 12."

"Černy tried to be invisible. We found him after a month and then he was gone. I'm not proud, but it happened. If I have a nightmare, he is there."

"I'm not smug over the demise of Černy, but I have no regrets."

Chapter 34: Transition

Zuzana continued her Party assignment as liaison to international organizations, including the International Red Cross. Luboš reacquainted himself with Prague. Despite the drab view, he became comfortable with the outgoing friendliness and confidence of the younger generation.

His correspondence to Marcela from Zuzana's address was a new wrinkle. The tone continued to be business-like as he mentioned his medical rehabilitation. Marcela was encouraging about his release, yet not effusive. Each understood the boundaries of their communication. He was frustrated to be released from prison but unable to see, or have, Marcela.

Luboš was thankful for Zuzana's support—her leadership—since she seemed to know him better than he knew himself. She gave him a broken casting rod from a flea market to get his attention. Consequently, he bought a new bamboo pole with a soft handgrip and eyelets for the line. His mood improved when he provided bream to cook for dinner.

She kept her charge immersed in privileged medical appointments, which he accepted without guilt in partial payment for his incarceration. The bone spur was removed, and he was fitted for hearing aids and prescription glasses. After weeks of dental appointments for his new bridge, he was comfortable in his new image.

Zuzana brought Luboš back to the Prague Transport Enterprise to meet the boss, the same one who had called him away from Marcela's bus.

"Hey, Luboš, I heard you were released. You look good. I'm relieved to see you." He was grateful Luboš had not implicated him or his co-workers during Černy's torture sessions.

"Each day is better. You have new oil change bays for the buses. Ah, and a color television in the break room."

"We pitched in to watch the Olympics last winter. We jinxed our team and didn't win a hockey medal."

"Yeah, sixth place is no place. Tell me about your interrogation."

"All of us were arrested quickly. We were separated, and I assure you, we were shitting bricks. I stated that you were sick, and you were upset about the destination to Vienna. They suspected you quickly. They were impatient and assumed that an accomplice modified 505. They didn't find one and released us the next day. They kept us under surveillance until your conviction. They forced our ridiculous statements denouncing you as a thief, a wrecker, and—and absurd schemes. You had a hard time, I'm sure."

"Yes. I expected to die. The fabrications were laughable. I'm glad no one else was dragged in."

"Luboš," the boss said earnestly, "Solidarity changed our attitudes. In 1984 Bohdan started a tradition. At Sparta home games and Olympic hockey games, the guys from 1968 offer a toast to you. You did what a few of us only imagined."

"Bohdan was full of ideas. I am honored that you remember me favorably."

"When the season opens next fall, we will meet you at a game for na zdraví."

"I'm always ready for na zdraví. Where is Bohdan?"

"He is in Bulgaria at a Black Sea resort town called Sunny Beach. He goes for his annual vacation."

"The Black Sea and Sunny Beach is a confusing combination."

"Bohdan goes on a boat or lies on the sand. He comes back covered by jellyfish bites and sunburn and can't work." The boss laughed and said soberly, "They accused me of running a ring of laggards. I was removed from the Communist Party and demoted."

"I'm sorry you were caught up in my predicament."

"It was a short-term problem. Remember bull-necked Černy?"

"I can't forget his voice or his evil eyes."

"My replacement sold spare engine parts on the black market. Černy caught him. Within a year, I was boss again."

"Černy was caught too," Luboš was pleased to say and changed the subject. "Did they reinstate you in the Party?"

"They did. I don't go to meetings and don't pressure others."

Zuzana heard the exchange and clenched her fists. Her efforts in enrollment were waning, along with her ardor for the cause.

"Do you have friends who might hire an engine mechanic? I have a place to stay and will show up to work."

"Give me a few days."

Not long afterward, a friend of the boss hired Luboš to be a truck mechanic. The friend, the owner of a small family enterprise, relied on instincts learned avoiding German dragnets and applied that experience to avoid taxes in the Soviet economy. Luboš was paid in counterfeit coupons.

The employees were not Communists. Peter, a straightforward activist, gathered underground newspapers and grumbled about the oppressive political system. He wrangled an illegal radio, listened to broadcasts of the Voice of America, and stirred underlying resentments amongst his trusted friends. Every segment of society held grievances. The wretched prisons were filled with innocent men and women. On the outside, the young, the old, workers, professionals, and intellectuals were equally discontented. The year 1989 was ripe for change.

❖ ❖ ❖ ❖ ❖

Zuzana's two-bedroom apartment was appropriate for a prominent Party member. Unless they were discussing hockey, fishing or Tippy Toes, they sat talking with heads together at the kitchen table to frustrate listening devices. She turned up the volume of the classical music and ran water. Regarding current events, Luboš realized she was more open-minded than an ideologue.

"Marcela smoothed my rough edges," Luboš said in his imperfect delivery.

"She was a talented schoolteacher. She was the artist, and I was the patriot. Máma watched us grow apart politically. Still, we loved each other. Only when I was blindsided was I enraged."

He hesitated and then asked, "You decided not to marry?"

"I never decided anything." She rose to pour two beers and relocate Tippy Toes from the countertop to Luboš's lap, her preferred napping spot. "I graduated from Charles University in 1948 and approved of the election. I was passionate about the Communist reforms and too engrossed in my socialist duties."

"For forty years, you didn't meet a man to marry?"

"It's not that simple. I met a delightful man, a married man who loves me. I love him and am happy to be his mistress."

"Is he the man in the pictures on the bookshelf?" he asked, stroking the purring cat.

"Yes. The two of us are at Party functions. You can see us aging," Zuzana said, shuffling the pictures. The most recent was in color.

"You are older but not old. If Marcela has taken these twenty years as well as you, she will be as beautiful."

"You are kind to say that," she said, blushing and confused by the compliment. "I walk to work and take the waters once a week."

"Did Miluše ever meet him?"

"She did, at a reception he and his committee hosted. I was going to tell her of our relationship because she nagged me about marriage. But lung cancer weakened her, and I delayed."

"He must have been a powerful man."

"He is, alive and well. He put pressure on Černy's boss to back off, or I would be a 'former,' ostracized from the Party and work. At your sentencing, he kept you from the uranium mines."

"That would have been a death warrant. I want to thank him?"

"That won't happen. He works in the background. I will tell him how obliged you are."

"Am I jeopardizing you in the Party?" Luboš asked as he placed the cat on his lap again.

"No, I'm in a protected position. Our system is at war with its people. We judge for them, and we do it poorly. We should evolve. I'm trying my best to promote leaders who are ready for the next decade."

She paused, sipped her pilsner, and said, "I have grim news."

"Oh?"

"You asked me to find what happened to Jan."

"Yes?"

"Jan Novák returned home to Bohemia with that assumed name. And then he disappeared. No Novák or Czernek fit his description. The forced expulsion of Germans in 1945 was violent and often lawless. Even though he was Bohemian, he could have been caught in the disorder. Local armed volunteers made their own rules and did not keep records."

"That's why he didn't find me," Luboš moaned. "I'm the only survivor.

"Luboš Novák. My first and last names are both wrong. I'm named after Jan's father and the city where we surrendered. Uncle Yarik said there would be surprises, and they keep coming. I feel like my insides don't belong to my outside.

"Zuzana, I have to tell you about Dmytro." For one hour, he recounted his woeful story.

195

Zuzana did not let him flag. "You are even stronger than I imagined and certainly as strong as Jan expected."

A year after his release, Luboš was impatient to meet his progeny and fully understand Marcela's one revealing letter. Written communications between Vienna and Prague were inadequate.

Zuzana suggested that her sister take advantage of the country's temporary family reunification program, which granted émigrés a short duration visa to legally return to see relatives. Because Marcela had not engaged in "anti-Czechoslovak or anti-socialist activity" while in Austria, she was eligible.

"We force them to flee the country, then they pay the state to see their parents before they die. We are doing something wrong."

"Who is 'we'?"

"The Communist government. The program fees are exorbitant. It is a ploy to bring foreign currency into the country and not a humanitarian gesture from the state."

"I'm floored to hear your comments."

"So am I."

Chapter 35: Wilhelm's Family in Prague, June 1989

Wilhelm first met Marcela at a Sunday Mass in Vienna in 1970 as she struggled to manage two babies. She attended the Catholic Church, where he was a leader of the finance council. Over time, they courted. She was an attractive, educated woman with a riveting history. He admired her deliberate style of speech while she learned German, and he appreciated her patience as he learned Czech. The Austrian Red Cross provided aid for her transition to an open society, and she enrolled in education courses to qualify for a school position.

Wilhelm was a dignified investment banker who wore a jacket, tie, and vest every day of the week. His head of blond hair was striped in silver, and he was a presence in social and philanthropic circles. For Marcela, he and the church offered stability. For him, marriage was an opportunity to be a stepfather and husband. They wed when Libor and Lida were age two.

Wilhelm understood his guardianship position, hoping Marcela would come to love him as much as she had loved the father of her twins. Wilhelm thrived as a responsible husband and doting stepfather. They sent the kids to Sunday school, and Wilhelm avidly supported their ice hockey and figure skating youth competitions. Marcela, in her formal gown, proudly held his arm when they mounted the steps to the opera to greet their friends.

Yet the memory of Luboš lurked. The Austrian Consulate had told her of the trial and prison. She had wept, aware of his misery but helpless. When updates provided by the Red Cross stopped, she had shifted her attention to the toddlers and her new life with Wilhelm. Marcela regularly sang the praises of Luboš to her children, while secretly fantasizing thoughts to share with him, albeit less and less frequently:

Libor was constantly hungry and bit my nipples when he nursed. He eats more than a pig and he outgrows his clothes quickly. . . . His name means free. . . . Lida sketches and is quite talented. . . . My school is excellent, and L & L will enroll next year. . . . My happiness is only skin deep. . . . If I cannot live in the past, I can recall it. . . . How can I have peace while you struggle?

Lida and Libor speak German and Czech and are learning Ukrainian. They call you Táta or Tatínek. You called your father Tato, but the Czech is better. Libor is a real terror on the hockey team. He is a dedicated brother and attends Lida's figure skating events. They know you, except for your voice and touch. They are proud of you.

Your son will be a big shot. With degrees in business and engineering, he will conquer the world. L & L love the University of Vienna, and twice a year Lida leads a forum on contemporary art. Their professors think Communism is on its last legs. You and I believed that in 1968.

The delicate balance of Marcela's occasional flashbacks to Luboš tipped off-scale when her past summoned her. Zuzana's letter, followed by the first letter from Luboš, rejuvenated Marcela. Simultaneously, Wilhelm worried that an unseen prisoner jeopardized his eighteen years of marriage. Ever the gentleman, Wilhelm agreed to the correspondence. How could he deny his wife the opportunity to reconnect with her sister and the father of her children?

198

In multiple ways, Wilhelm had created the family. He paid for most expenses, allowing Marcela to save her earnings. Deferring to his wife, he spoke Czech to his stepchildren. He gave principled guidance, provided a healthy home, and pampered his wife. Nonetheless, a proposed amnesty visit to Prague might test their relationship.

Police and security agencies, including the StB, assured KSC official Zuzana that her sister would not be detained if she met only family members. The train travel permit from Vienna was for just one day.

A thorough search of their passports and goods at the border check point went smoothly. At the train station Marcela, Wilhelm, Lida, and Libor crowded into a yellow and white state-owned taxi, aware that the driver would report all conversations. They arrived at Zuzana's apartment for tea at four. Each was quiet and tense, concerned for different reasons.

Laden with gifts from Vienna, Wilhelm cautiously led them up the stairs. Marcela thought of the last time she saw Luboš in the belly of the bus when she said, "I love you." There was equal apprehension inside—for Zuzana who might regret arranging the meeting, and for the high hopes of Luboš, who feared that a real relationship with Marcela was unachievable.

Wilhelm and Zuzana had arranged a short reunion full of contrasts. Marcela had fled twenty years earlier while her sister stayed. Wilhelm was stepfather to the teenagers and husband to Marcela, while Luboš was the father but not the husband. The introduction of these long-separated relatives would last just a moment, and then Wilhelm would conduct his family back to a free country.

Zuzana greeted them at the door and gave a tentative hug to Marcela. Past her sister, Marcela caught sight of Luboš across the room. The former lovers rushed into their open arms. Luboš, recovering from foot surgery, almost lost his balance. His nineteen-year-old twins and Zuzana merged with them, and they all sobbed, arms entwined, including Wilhelm at the fringe. They backed up a step. Marcela stood tall and proudly said in Czech, "Luboš, this is your daughter, Lida, your son, Libor, and my husband, Wilhelm. Zuzana, it has been too long."

"Too long, but not too late," Zuzana replied, holding her sister's hands firmly.

Marcela was as attractive as Luboš expected—hair parted on the side, fewer shades of gray than Zuzana, pleasing makeup, and wearing his favored perfume. Sandy-haired Lida and brown-haired Libor were taller than their father and embraced him again. Marcela was unable to hug him the way she desperately desired.

Zuzana guided the guests to her couch and chairs and turned up the volume of Czech composer Antonin Dvořák's "Slavonic Dances," which was playing loud enough to interfere with government eavesdropping. After serving tea she began, "Well, we have much to catch up on. Our letters had to be circumspect, but now we can speak freely."

Lida and Libor were excited to start. Unlike the others in the room, they held no mixed feelings. The thrill of meeting their father echoed in their words.

"We planned a special visit," Lida said. "I debated about which flowers to buy until Libor said, 'Get bunches of them.' My brother selected the sweets."

"I thought, 'What would Táta prefer?' Probably everything. At a Czech confectioner, we bought every chocolate in the store. Tatínek, which is the best?"

Luboš marveled at the fragrances and chocolate flavors.

"I haven't tasted all of them, Libor, but dark chocolate with orange cream inside is the best so far. "Tomorrow, I will eat the rest for breakfast and have the answer."

They laughed. Merely saying his son's name gave him goose bumps.

Vases of purple iris, Lida's flowers, and a platter of baked bream cooked by Luboš topped the sideboard. Zuzana encouraged her guests to fill their plates.

Clicks of forks on porcelain and teacups set on saucers awaited renewed conversation.

"Luboš, your bream is delicious," Marcela said to break the silent period. She hungered to repeat his name again and again.

"It is freshly caught at the Legion Bridge, cooked from Miluše's recipe."

Reminded of the days with Marcela at that bridge, Luboš slumped into an armchair, He was confused over what might come next, and was silent. Zuzana's windows were open, but the drapes didn't rustle on the hot summer afternoon. Wilhelm tugged at his starched shirt collar. Luboš wiped his brow with the handkerchief Zuzana had placed in his pocket. The room was quiet except for the clatter of plates moved about and Zuzana's encouragement to sample more of their mother's favorite pastries of kolache and tredelnik.

"I'm ready to smile again," a revived Luboš announced. "This is the best day of my life."

Luboš was too shy, too embarrassed, to hold a steady gaze at Marcela. He longed to brush the lobe of her ear, stroke her fingers, and look at her the way he had during the bright years.

She, too, was unable to study him and distractedly described significant events of the past twenty years. Nervously, she turned her bracelet round and round. I will respect my husband, she thought, yet she played with the watch dangling from her gold chain necklace. The sentiment of her special letter of the previous year was adequate in her view to show her true love. It was enough, for now.

"Luboš picked the iris today," Zuzana said, handing her sister a tiny container the size for an engagement ring wrapped in a purple ribbon, "and here is something special for my sister. I polished them yesterday."

Marcela opened the box, removed the tissue paper, and burst out crying, her face scarlet. Lida comforted her to no avail.

"I'm sorry, Marcela, I expected they would bring tears of joy." At a loss, Zuzana said, "Maminka gave her these ski earrings. I chose a bad time."

All eyes were on Marcela, and her eyes were on the mirror, looking at Luboš. Zuzana glanced towards Luboš, contorted, chest held high and pained as his coughing fit filled the room.

Marcela, with Lida at her side, calmed down before Luboš, attended by Zuzana and Libor. Wilhelm didn't know how to comfort his wife. The tension eased when Luboš said in an unsteady, wheezing voice, "My cough is my continuing malady."

"Luboš," Marcela said after she recovered, "I pray it improves."

"Zuzana sends me to the best doctors. Please don't worry."

Marcela dabbed her eyes with her handkerchief and apologized. "I was overcome. Excuse me. I miss Máma."

"You both skate," Zuzana said to Lida and Libor to shift forward. "It has been forever since I skated. Someday we will skate together."

"And Máma too," Lida added.

"These pictures and stories," Libor said to his father as he gave a photo album to their father, "of our sports and extracurricular activities will bring you up to date. We are happy to give them to you."

"Ohhh," Luboš said proudly, "I'm impressed that they write newspaper articles about you. Your mother and Wilhelm must be proud."

Libor was the President of the United Nations Youth Delegate Programme at his school. He discoursed about democracy in Austria until he saw his mother frowning at him and Zuzana looking at the floor.

The chatter continued after Zuzana passed Miluše's old photo album of the sisters' youth. Sitting closely on the full sofa, the sisters and twins cried softly, touching the pictures and reminiscing about grandparents and great-grandparents.

"This is the last picture of our father," Zuzana said, "taken in Wenceslas Square before the army took him."

"I think I was five," Marcela added, "I remember the hot chocolate."

"Now I see Máma's Máma," Libor said.

"Your Babička baked the best strudel," his mother said proudly.

Marcela turned the page to the Vienna newspaper article of the tenth anniversary of her arrival in Austria. Wilhelm backed away to take pictures of the tea party. Luboš became withdrawn again. Talk was strained; Dvořák's "Dances" filled the vacuum.

Ringing church bells signifying 1800 brought Zuzana and Wilhelm to their feet. The chimes dictated their departure. Wilhelm was anxious to leave for their long train ride home and said to the real father, "Lida, Libor, and I appreciate your difficult journey. You are a resolute man."

Luboš marshaled his strength and haltingly said, "Wilhelm, thank you for bringing your family. I am overwhelmed to meet Lida and Libor and see Marcela."

"Aunt Zuzana, can we stay longer?" Lida couldn't address her plea to her father. Vater was Wilhelm. Táta was Luboš.

"Your letters filled in our missing years," Marcela whimpered to her sister. "You have arranged this day to reunite us—and for Luboš to meet his children and Wilhelm. Luboš, you suffered for the three of us. We can .... "

Marcela's face lost color and the ability to address the future. Restraining her tears, she recovered enough to say, "Thank you, Zuzana."

Zuzana, fearing she too might break down, grasped her sister's hands and moved to the stairs for the scheduled taxi pickup.

Wilhelm bade goodbye to a damp eyed Luboš. Words were few. After the two men shook hands and tears and hugs all around—Marcela and Luboš no more and no less than the rest—Wilhelm led his Viennese family down the steps. Marcela was the last to squeeze into the taxi. She paused to look back and see Luboš blow her a kiss.

Chapter 36: Reflection

The tea had lasted less than two hours. Luboš was exhausted. He and Zuzana collapsed into the armchairs, trying to absorb what had happened. The door Zuzana had opened was ajar, but he couldn't see to the other side. Luboš spoke first.

"I received one beautiful letter from Marcela. I talk and say nothing. Her eyes, I hardly look at them. I lied when I said this was the best day. I wish I knew what she started to say: 'We can....' We can what? I wish I knew what she thought when I kissed my hand."

"I have no solution for you and Marcela. She has the same constraints. Can she kiss you as in 1969 with Wilhelm right there?

"You didn't realize that she wore those earrings for our first date. I didn't let her wear them in the bus because they would have cut her face in the tight compartment. That morning she left them on Miluśe's kitchen table."

"Oh my. That explains why she lost control. The afternoon turned sad, and I regret making the gift."

"How could you know?"

"Marcela will either talk candidly to her children, or she will tear her herself up. I'm here for you."

"And one more thing. On our first date, she wore a watch on a necklace. It was a signal."

"Well, you can guess that was her intent."

Luboš was not educated, but he was astute. He had maneuvered to stay alive as an observer, taking what was possible and not all that he wanted. He wanted to erase the miserable years in prison, have Marcela, and assume the role of father. Was that too much to ask?

"Today is the longest day of the year, the solstice when my flight began," he continued, stroking the sleeping cat. "Lida and Libor—I love them. Our meeting proves a path will be hard to follow, but I will dream Marcela is there."

"It's possible."

Preoccupied, Luboš, his head held low, cleared the table. He didn't select another chocolate.

"Time for a walk."

The two strolled aimlessly until the sun set over the Vltava.

After several days of contemplation, Luboš wrote a short letter of love for his children, affection for Marcela, and high regard for Wilhelm. Restrained letters continued during the summer and fall. They did not tell the full story.

He imagined a rekindled love; did Marcela? The idea was sense and nonsense. How can an ex-lover expect to abscond with the woman he hasn't seen for years, and take two children from the husband who has been devoted to them? His ideas were outrageous and impossible. And persistent.

Chapter 37: Death Throes behind the Iron Curtain

The mechanics at work addressed each other as "comrade" to show their contempt for the system. Peter and Luboš were the most forthcoming of the tight cluster of eight complainers. Peter collected inflammatory leaflets contesting the one-Party rule. "Hey, read how Solidarity won the Polish elections," he said and handed them to Luboš.

"Let's spread the word," Luboš said. "My friends don't belong in prison."

Luboš and Zuzana had already discussed the protests and her predicament in the Party. He stuffed flyers under his shirt and left them on her kitchen table under *The Good Soldier Švejk.* In an unguarded moment, he mentioned broadcasts of the Voice of America that described the Soviet collapse in adjacent countries. She was attentive to his summary.

Restrained letters between Prague and Vienna continued, without mention of political events.

Free elections in Poland in June signaled the downfall of Communism. Hungary followed in the summer by opening borders to East Germany. Citizens of Estonia, Latvia, and Lithuania staged a protest that couldn't be ignored. Two million formed a human chain across the Baltic States to demand independence from the Soviet Union.

Ignoring the changing landscape, Czechoslovakia was the most repressive Soviet country. Demonstrators were in danger. Zuzana, cornered by her allegiance to the Party and her recognition that the Party had lost its legitimacy, supported a move, even an abrupt step, from Communism.

"I'm on the wrong side of this fight," Zuzana said emphatically. "The suppression in 1968 was okay to me, but how did I miss our declining system? Starting in 1979, clues from Václav Havel and the Pope were obvious. I reassessed my position, even more so after the Soviets lied about the Chernobyl nuclear disaster a few years ago. I try to alert my superiors to get ahead of the flood. They don't listen. They have a grade school education and are promoted for punishing dissidents. You and Marcela had the guts to leave."

"Are you considering leaving the Party?"

"Mark this day, September 1. This is Maminka's birthday, and the day I resigned from the Communist Party. She would be proud of me. The government doesn't work for the people. The people work for the elites. With your help, I saw the regime through different eyes and stopped lying to myself. I don't believe in the fiction of Communism. It is a failed experiment."

"I am amazed. You have made an abrupt turn. Marcela will be glad to hear of your decision. "

"I will write and tell her in a way that will pass the censors. She was forced to teach false doctrine, and she acted by fleeing."

"Do you worry about your safety?"

"No. The Party has more challenges than my departure."

The truck mechanics didn't view themselves as revolutionaries, but during the fall, they pushed for change in what became the Velvet Revolution. In the streets, the challengers to one-party rule in Czechoslovakia grew more confident. Would new liberties permit a closer relationship with Marcela? Will she choose him again?

Luboš and his emboldened friends moved from passive complaining to attendance to active participation in the protests.

"I'm tired of listening. I'm on strike and going to Wenceslas Square," announced Luboš. "Who else is coming?" Luboš and Peter led them out, and the boss followed, locking the sliding overhead door.

In Vienna, Marcela, Wilhelm, Lida, and Libor were entranced by the television coverage leading to the dramatic announcement on November 9, 1989, that the Berlin Wall was open. East Germans flooded across the border to West Berlin, signaling the demise of Communism.

Luboš and Zuzana joined thousands, then hundreds of thousands, in Wenceslas Square to challenge the Party. Luboš feared the dissent would founder, yet the crowds grew larger and were not suppressed by police.

Accompanying Marta Kubišová, they belted out her "Prayer for Marta" in Wenceslas Square and applauded Václav Havel when he stood at the Melantrich Balcony on 24 November 1989. Luboš jangled his keys and yelled, "Havel na Hradl," [Havel to the Castle] until he lost his voice. The impetus for democratic change built, and the populace was ultimately rewarded by the stirring 29 November declaration that the Communist Party had relinquished control of the government.

From different vantage points, Luboš and Zuzana had witnessed the first days of the forty-one years of Communist rule. With common mind, they witnessed the last day. His spirits soared. This political change was beneficial for Czechs and him—and Marcela.

Marcela and Wilhelm followed the events in Prague on television and celebrated with the rest of the free world. She was thankful for Luboš's freedom and thrilled for her Czech twins and all Czechs.

Tears streaming, Marcela sang the ever-popular "Prayer for Marta" that she and Luboš sang in 1968, sure he was singing alongside her: "Let peace remain, settle on this landscape...." The jubilation and triumph were overwhelming. Marcela believed the future could include Luboš.

Chapter 38: The Velvet Revolution and Tragedy

Lida and Libor arrived home after celebrating with friends at the Michaelerplatz to find a scribbled note telling them to go to the hospital. En route, they were hushed, realizing something terrible had happened to their mother.

Wilhelm, pale and disheveled, was hunched over on a bench in the corridor. Lida and Libor sat beside him, each holding an arm. In a subdued voice, he recounted what happened. "We watched Czechoslovak history, world history, unfold. Marcela stood for hours, arms clutched to her chest, singing the songs with the protesters, crying in joy until she collapsed on the floor. She gave no warning. I called for medical assistance. Her heart attack was fatal."

Lida spoke in broken phrases, her tears falling on Wilhelm's jacket. "I don't understand. Today is the day to live for."

Celebration in Prague continued through the night, but Luboš and Zuzana's euphoria was shattered when Wilhelm called at seven. Zuzana crumpled onto a chair, her unblinking eyes wide open, the phone at her knee.

Luboš hesitated, then removed the phone from her tight grip.

"This is Luboš." He listened. He was silent. The color drained from his face. He kept the phone to his ear, listening to the dial tone long after Wilhelm said, "I must go."

Zuzana eyed Luboš and, despite her grief, understood that she was the hardy one once again. She was the anchor to enable Luboš to overcome another tragedy. In keeping Luboš upright, she was doing the same for herself.

"I have lost a sister and will be forever sad about those lost years. We will endure this trial together." Zuzana was a tactician maneuvering through life. She became Luboš's guide to honor her sister and her family.

"My father, my mother, Jan, and Marcela died too young. Now I am dying. I couldn't change my circumstances, but I overcame them. After this phone call, I may not try."

To prevent Luboš from sinking into despair, she called Lida and Libor and asked them to speak to Luboš. Throughout the following day and night, the youthful, positive spirits of Lida and Libor battled alongside the reality of Marcela's death. His children were stunned as much as he, and the three of them affirmed a durable bond.

For Zuzana, quitting the Party was both unnerving and liberating. She was optimistic that her international liaisons would lead to fruitful employment in coming months.

Zuzana urged him to go to church and familiar streets the next day. "Mingle with the joyous Czechs still celebrating the change of government. Join me."

Inevitably, they went to Miluśe's street. "Máma lived there. Too much smoking, but she protected us from the Nazis."

"Marcela and I went often."

"Marcela was thirty-six when she met you, and Máma knew what occurred. She was glad her daughter loved a kind man."

"I dreamt that Marcela and I would come together."

"She couldn't offer an expectation, but the two of you would have become one."

"The ending happened too soon."

❖ ❖ ❖ ❖ ❖

The seven-hour rail journey across the open border to Vienna to bury Marcela was solemn. Luboš and Zuzana had been with her for only minutes in twenty years. "Last

211

summer Marcela came to Prague. My children came to Prague. I go to Vienna, and there is no Marcela. Too much sadness in my life. What's the point?"

"The point is Lida and Libor. You are fortunate to have accomplished children."

The service marked a celebration of Marcela's life, but not for Luboš. He craved to celebrate the life of twenty years earlier and the reunion that he imagined.

Lida and Libor sat beside their father with Zuzana next to Lida. Wilhelm sat next to Libor. Lida relaxed her grip on her father's arm, stood up, and walked to the pulpit to honor her mother. Mixing Czech and German, she ended her eulogy: "…You do not know them, and Libor and I recently met them. Their sadness is more than we can imagine. Luboš, our father, faced tyranny head-on so that our mother, Libor, and I can live free. Zuzana, our aunt, brought us together. We love them. … "

Lida was unable to continue and returned to the pew to Luboš's trembling arm. Although most in the congregation were not fluent in Czech, they understood.

Marcela's short visit to Prague in June had set Luboš in emotional turmoil. He now feared an extended stay in Vienna for the same reason. Comforting words from family friends offered no comfort. In the antechamber, he spoke privately with Libor and Lida. They asked him to stay the night, the week, but he wasn't ready. Zuzana would have stayed but agreed to return to Prague.

"You are blessed to have Lida and Libor," Zuzana said to comfort him on the train back to Prague. "Everyone in the church loved Marcela, and Lida placed you by her side. They love you too."

❖ ❖ ❖ ❖ ❖

Czechoslovaks were excited and confused at the upheaval of the Velvet Revolution less than a week earlier. Zuzana expected to keep her quarters and was confident a suitable work opportunity would develop. Daily, one of the twins called to reassure Luboš and themselves. They were a year from graduation. In a gracious gesture, Wilhelm suggested that Luboš relocate to Vienna. Luboš felt a move was awkward and declined. He sought comfort on the river and asked Zuzana to accompany him. She didn't—the bridges were Marcela's domain.

Luboš needed Libor and Lida more than they needed him. Zuzana urged the twins to persist. When she reminded Luboš that Austria was the family's destination of the migration in 1944, he agreed to a short stay in Vienna.

Lida pressed her case the first day. "You and Máma tried to leave in 1969. You have met setbacks, but the time to finally arrive in Austria is now. Come here, come and stay. Be involved in our future." They rejected his excuses until he agreed to relocate to a compact apartment in Vienna, paid for by Wilhelm.

He returned to Prague to see Peter and friends and to pack his few belongings. Sitting in Zuzana's stiff kitchen chair with Tippy Toes balanced on his legs, he reviewed his recovery while in her care and finished saying, "I owe my recovery to you. Thank you."

"The International Committee of the Red Cross has hired me, and there I will use a velvet touch and not a hammer. Enjoy what you have." Luboš didn't realize that he had been Zuzana's guide as much as she was his.

Chapter 39: Life Is a Kaleidoscope

Except for his nagging cough, Luboš moved to Vienna a new man. The dentist, the surgeon, Zuzana's cooking and counsel, and the encouragement of Lida and Libor brought him strength for life's next stage. His letters from prison had inspired admiration and love, and his children were thrilled to have him in their city. Wilhelm was a loving stepfather. Luboš added a positive dimension. Once rivals, the men were devastated by the loss of Marcela and shared a unique companionship as both supported Libor and Lida.

Zuzana periodically called her extended family in Vienna—pleased that she had encouraged Luboš to relocate, yet confused. Her Prague apartment seemed empty, and she missed cooking for him and guiding him through his new freedom. She reflected in solitude about the revolution that eventually freed Czechoslovakia at such a high personal cost to her loved ones. Before Zuzana fell asleep in her armchair, she told Tippy Toes purring on her lap, "The Party surrendered. Luboš and I celebrated for only six hours. Six hours."

A week after his introduction to Vienna's neighborhoods and schilling currency and German phrases, Luboš summoned his courage. While Wilhelm was at his bank, Luboš was compelled to ask his children for details of Marcela's solitary bus escape.

214

Lida and Libor had dreaded this moment. Their mother had shared her terrifying experience when the twins were mature enough at age fourteen to come to grips with the sadness.

They described her holding back her sobs in the bowels of the bus, her fear of miscarriage, the facial cuts from the baggage compartment latch, the torn sleeve from the driver trying to pull her from the Austrian border agent, and the lengthy mending of broken bones in her hand.

Luboš stared out the window.

Nightmares returned to Luboš, but Lida reminded him of Marcela's resilience as a free woman in Austria. Lida told him that he had already suffered at her death. Please don't suffer again.

The twenty-one-year-old students were finishing at the University of Vienna. Talented and ambitious, they excelled in summer internships that continued during the school year. Their schedules were hectic, yet they set aside time for their father. Lida especially fancied taking him to museums and galleries to give him an overdue classical education. His favorite was sculpture—possibly influenced by his years in the prison quarry.

An underlying question nagged Luboš: what were Wilhelm's responsibilities during the war? There were no pictures or any discussion of those dreadful years when Austria was cooperative with the Nazis and then under Russian administration until 1955. Luboš never asked or answered the question.

Although his health was stable, Luboš was worried about venturing into the liberated world, just as he was cautious as a young man in Prague. He was awed by the wealth and glamour in Vienna and tagged along with Wilhelm and his talented children as an awe-struck foreigner. He was shy in the society he was thrust into, but he was at peace, blessed, and devoted to his children.

Absorbed in his studies, Libor welcomed the diversion of his father's pleas to fish together. The son bought colorful lures and the latest spinning reel and rod combo for what might be the perfect gift. Luboš was stubborn and preferred using long, imported bamboo poles on the Danube River, but finding bait was difficult. After seeing the local's success using modern gear, he relented. He found he preferred the cork grip, lures, and active motion of casting and developed his skills.

Their preferred location was at the Steinsporn pedestrian bridge, where the mud-colored water swept around the support columns. Luboš brought home too much pike, turbot, and catfish for them to eat. Libor saw recreational anglers catch and release and suggested that his father keep what he expected to cook and return smaller or less savory fish to the Danube. The idea appealed to Luboš, who, until now, fished to survive. At either apartment, Luboš prepared fish in butter and lemon, a recent discovery for him. Lida had learned cooking skills at her mother's side and served tasty Czech dishes for the foursome.

Luboš was reluctant to revisit painful memories, but over time, he shared his experiences with Lida and Libor. He talked for hours about their mother, the trek, his parents, and a little about prison.

Luboš recounted courting Marcela and their optimism for a life together. "Until I met your mother, I passed the day asleep. In Czech, we call it Švejkism—not expecting much and not giving much, just getting along."

"Ah," Libor lit up. "We studied Švejkism last year and how to motivate employees. The professor taught that Communist workers have a poor work ethic."

"Yes, we met our work obligation, our quota, and not much more. I changed after I met your mother. I bought clothes to impress her, I worked harder, and I would have been promoted except for … you know."

The dissolution of the Soviet Union in 1991 inspired enthusiasm for entrepreneurship in former Iron Curtain countries. Libor's professors encouraged him to apply his education and live his ambitions. The parents of one of his economics professors, Dr. Evetov, were Ukrainian White Russians who fled from Simferopol, Crimea to Austria after the Bolshevik Revolution. Longing for the peninsula described by his parents, the professor encouraged Libor to consider Crimea.

❖ ❖ ❖ ❖ ❖

Luboš and Libor cast in the Danube for salmon and dreamed of landing a trophy sturgeon. Young Libor had played junior hockey, and when the season opened, they attended Vienna Capital's games. Slovakia and the Czech Republic amicably split in 1991, and Luboš was guarded about the 1992 Winter Olympics. The team was still Czechoslovak, but all but three players were Czechs. Luboš considered the team to be Czech.

Luboš prepared to spend a month glued to Wilhelm's remote control color Sony television. Wilhelm cheered for the Austrian team until they were eliminated and then rooted for the Germans, who finished in sixth place. Luboš was cheering for a steady winner while Libor caught the Czech hockey fever. The Czechoslovak team was outscored by only one opponent in the weeks-long games and earned the bronze medal. Another Olympics had consumed him.

Although late in life, time Vienna gave Luboš unhurried circumstance to find his bearings. A favorite destination for Luboš was the library where he read general interest magazines. His German was rudimentary, but he read what he could and absorbed the pictures and descriptions. He learned the truth about Stalin, World War II, Communism, and the Iron Curtain, as well as difficulties facing democracies.

Luboš had been in the thick of major world events, but he had limited understanding of the context. He became a regular at the information desk, asking for translations or clarification of topics that interested him. The principles of freedom as described by the Voice of America, his mother, Jan, and even Marcela became tangible.

At last, the future looked bright. No more tyrants.

Winter and spring passed at a feverish rate as the twins completed their exams and theses. Lida submitted marketing research on selling art to newly wealthy investors. Libor's was titled, "Collapse Yields Opportunity in Planned Economies."

Luboš and Wilhelm proudly attended graduation ceremonies for Lida in the morning and Libor in the afternoon. At home, following the university receptions, Wilhelm spoke first. "The commencement speakers mentioned the changes near our borders, including the conflict in Chechnya. The commerce practices in these countries are different. The adjustments will be fascinating to follow when they compete with the West."

Lida served lemonade, and they sat down to rest. "Zuzana called again. She is sorry to miss our graduation and apologized a thousand times. Her friend must have been a special person."

"Her influential companion, who I never met, died suddenly," Luboš said. "He saved her from a forced confession and saved my life. I would have returned to Prague for his funeral, but I couldn't miss this special day,"

"Aunt Zuzana has helped me understand the Crimean financial situation," Libor added. "She has long-range ideas for the Czechoslovak economy and is optimistic about their move to free markets."

"She will be a positive influence for necessary changes in an open society. We are proud of your accomplishments. Your mother prepared you well. Na zdraví."

"Na zdraví."

Wilhelm returned to his office, and in a relaxed moment, Libor winked at his father. "Vienna has been your home for two years. Have you noticed the pretty women?"

"There are attractive women here, yes."

"May I introduce you to Máma's friends from church?"

"No, thank you."

"Or not from church?"

"They won't speak Czech. I'm content watching you prepare for your future."

"Okay, Tátinek," Libor granted, using the familiar term for daddy.

In Prague, Zuzana busied herself in Red Cross initiatives in the new Czech Republic, but the loss of her lover created an emotional void. Former Communist colleagues were unappealing, and at age sixty, she deemed romance a thing of the past. Three years after her sister's death, she wondered if the man she knew so well and knew her so well would re-enter her life. The decision was not hers.

Job opportunities for graduates were limited in Vienna. Each twin contemplated moving to different cities or even different countries. Fortuitously, Marcela had required that they learn languages, and their options were broad. Lida worked at an art gallery and was attentive to all facets of the business. Libor interned as assistant to the owner of a construction firm to complement his academic training. Wilhelm indicated early in their job quest that, although he was supportive of the next step for his stepchildren, he would stay in Vienna.

They devised a plan to remain together. Libor, already inclined to Crimea, introduced Lida to Dr. Evetov, who described his recent trip to the capital, Simferopol, to meet his relatives. The pleasant weather and expectation for democratic leaders, he assured, would be ideal for their initiatives. Dr. Evetov convinced Lida to evaluate for herself.

Autonomous within Ukraine, Crimea was recognized for its Communist resorts, home for famous artists and writers, and strategically vital for Russian naval bases. Wilhelm paid for the siblings' trip to scout cities with artistic influence and for seaports on the Black Sea suitable for a modern seafood-processing factory, an idea that Libor had included in his university thesis.

"Crimea is beautiful," Libor gushed to Wilhelm and Luboš upon his return. "There are hills for hiking, open farmland, cultural pursuits, mild winters, and best of all, the fishing is excellent. Look at this brochure."

"The pictures look nice," Luboš said. "The flag on the cover is simple, bright, and not dreary. The blue reminds me of your mother's eyes."

"It does. The blue on the Ukrainian flag symbolizes the sky and streams, and the yellow color of wheat represents prosperity. We met officials who say investments are needed to replace decrepit factories. They say the Cold War is over."

The two dreamers were ready during a time when the world seemed prepared for them. Independent for one year, Ukraine sought to balance nationalism and Russian influence. With sad memories of Ukraine, Luboš hesitated to move east, closer to Russia.

"The war is over," he remarked skeptically. "What about the peace? Nightly, the television news has a segment on the challenges in the former Soviet Republics: civil wars, inflation, ruble devaluation, shortages, crime, and unemployment. Russian soldiers to the southeast encroach on territories of Georgia. They are sparring in Moldova right now. Dr. Evetov shows a picture I don't see."

Libor was ready for these questions and countered with assurance. "Here is what I have been told about the problems and solutions: Ukraine is changing from rubles to coupons, the government is selling enterprises to new investors, residual communists are in disarray, and parliament in Kyiv is passing laws to ensure democratic and capitalist policies.

"Dr. Evetov introduced us to influential men who will facilitate our immigration. They will obtain our documents." Libor neglected to acknowledge the combative presence of Russian soldiers in disputed former Soviet states.

"You taught me to fish on the Danube," Libor continued, sensing Luboš wasn't persuaded. "I envision efficient farming and harvesting of all species thanks to ideas conceived on the Danube with you. Not one fish at a time, but thousands of fish that my company will grow and process. I will have trawlers at sea, anchored fishnets full of juvenile trout, a refrigeration plant, packing machines, and trucks to deliver our products."

The twins convinced their father that Crimea was far from the tentacles of Moscow and, as a peninsula, was distinct within Ukraine. The name Black Sea sounded ominous; Libor explained that the name described the dangerous navigation that mariners had faced centuries earlier. The idea of going to the seashore grew on Luboš, especially since mountains had been cruel to him and his family. Relaxing after watching a hockey game on television, Libor convinced wary Luboš that vast waters to fish and a horizon uninterrupted by turmoil awaited him in Crimea.

On reflection, Luboš said to his children and Wilhelm, "Last week at an art gallery, Lida asked me to peek into the tube of a kaleidoscope. I twisted the cylinder, and my, it was confusing. At the next kaleidoscope and the next, I was amazed. I thought of my troubled almost sixty years and imagined my mother and Jan and Marcela coming and going." Luboš paused and said, "I have been in the wrong place most of my life. Crimea will be the place to start over."

"Crimea will be right for us," a relieved Libor said. "Before we leave Vienna, will you go to Prague to see Zuzana?"

"No. My one request is that our plane doesn't stop in Moscow."

"Feodosia is as far from Moscow as the moon," Libor quipped.

"But not far from Russia."

Chapter 40: Immigration to Crimea, 1992

Uncomfortable wearing his only suit, Luboš addressed Wilhelm at the farewell dinner at his exclusive club, "You and Marcela raised two exceptional children. I missed their first twenty years and came to Vienna at your invitation. Thank you. They ask me to join them for their adventure, for which I am most grateful. They will be solid citizens in the new Ukraine."

Wilhelm was an exceptional parent. He had helped raise the babies, paid education expenses, supported their sporting events, and loved Marcela without reservation. In his late seventies, he elected to remain close to his doctors rather than move to Crimea. Despite Lida and Libor's encouragement, he was determined to stay in Austria. He had mastered his responsibilities as stepfather and was content to follow their progress from a distance.

"You are their hero," Wilhelm complimented, "and they need you beside them. You and I are blessed; your turn is now." He added with banker's caution, "They are young and ambitious. Watch over them."

Lida and Libor selected Feodosia on the south coast of Crimea, enthusiastic about launching their dreams and a new generation. Haunted by memories of Stalin, the Nazis, and Communism, Luboš was ready to end his odyssey, expecting to be free of despots. Carrying bank lines of credit and wire drafts from Marcela and Wilhelm's accounts, Libor and Lida brought their father back to his birth country.

Luboš was observant of every aspect of his first journey by air. The massive airport, the hefty fees for

222

overweight baggage, the security checks, the new carry-on bag for his medicines, and the polite attendants dazzled him. He kept his head pressed against the window on the nonstop trip from Vienna to Simferopol except when he ate his snack or sipped the Coca Cola. It was a journey to a sea-girt land, overdue peace, and an optimistic future with his children.

"Are you a family vacationing together?" the border official asked at the kiosk in the dark and sterile immigration hall.

"Please excuse me, we are learning Russian," Libor answered in Ukrainian.

"Are you a family vacationing together?" he asked in Ukrainian.

"Yes.

"Same last name. Why two Austrian passports and one Czech?"

"We were separated before our birth," Libor said, expecting increased scrutiny for their second entry to Ukraine in two months. The agent was puzzled by the reply but didn't call for a supervisor.

"You," he said, peering at Luboš over the new burgundy-colored document. "This is the first Czech Republic passport I have processed. Your form says you were born in Czechoslovakia."

"Yes. Kadan, Bohemia. It is my first passport," Luboš said tentatively in Ukrainian, unable to disclose his actual birthplace.

"The three of you speak Ukrainian?"

"Our father insisted we learn the languages of our neighboring countries," Libor said, giving a complimentary look to Luboš.

"What cities did the two of you visit in Crimea?"

"Yalta, Feodosia, and your capital. We weren't permitted near the large port at Sevastopol."

"Yes, Sevastopol is a closed city. Were you in Crimea for commerce or pleasure?"

"Vacation."

"Your vacation was quite rushed," the agent said, checking out Lida, Libor, and back to Lida.

"It was. This time we will relax in Feodosia."

"Your form is marked tourists," the agent noted, flipping Lida and Libor's pages again and again. Do you have arrangements for ration cards?"

"Austrian schillings were accepted," Libor replied, aware that devaluation was a sensitive subject.

"Yes, foreign currency is desirable and doesn't drop from inflation." The officer continued to study the documents and refer back and forth to his computer screen. Perhaps he was waiting for a handout. The lack of progress confused Libor, but not Luboš, who was ready to give the officer an envelope of schillings to ease their entry.

"You are early. Tourists fly in next month."

"We want to tour Crimea with our father. It is less expensive now."

Their entry was a ruse. The instructions of their hired facilitators were straightforward. Enter Ukraine as tourists and apply later for residency. The fixers were well connected and charged a princely sum, payable in US dollars, for arrangements leading to legal immigration and dual citizenship.

Luboš had been unsure of the plan. The open-ended questions reminded him of the interrogation by Russian officers in Nováky forty-seven years ago.

"Will you take him to Yalta?" the inspector said, his eyes still darting between the twins. "We are famous for Yalta. The Livadia Palace is our biggest tourist attraction. The American President Roosevelt stayed there in 1945."

"We will go," Lida said nervously.

"You might apply for entry to see the war museums and monuments in Sevastopol."

"We will try that," Libor replied with growing concern about the scope of the questions.

"You are twins. Which one was born first?"

"I was," Lida answered.

"My twins are girls." The agent paused, closed the three passports, and handed them to Luboš. "Go to the left and collect your bags."

"Thank you," a relieved Luboš said on behalf of the nervous trio.

They were in!

"The sea didn't seem wide from the air," Luboš complained, sitting in the front seat of the hired minivan for the two-hour drive to Feodosia. "Now, I'm back in Ukraine, and I see only sharp hills to my right."

"They are volcanic. Please wait," Libor replied enthusiastically, sitting next to Lida behind their father. "We will leave these winding roads at the edge of the mountains. The winter wheat will be harvested next month, and these sunflowers are recently planted. The sunflower is Ukraine's national flower. The yellow fields will dazzle you."

"The soil is rich," Luboš said quietly.

"We will pass through a forest," Lida added to improve his mood for a new adventure, "and wildflowers bloom at the side of the road."

The driver pointed out a monument to the Great Patriotic War along route P 260. The Black Sea teased, exposing itself for a moment at turns on the top of hills. After the driver proudly mentioned that he was a retired Red Army officer, Luboš stopped asking questions. The vision Libor and Lida had described appeared in the next hour as they wound down the mountain road entering flat land outside Feodosia. Luboš straightened up in his front-row seat.

"Oh, look. The water is so blue and so big. Here is the sea I was expecting. You were right, Libor."

"Feel the humidity," Lida said, sitting impatiently at the edge of her seat.

Luboš swung his head back and forth, evaluating the entry to the city. Fields of green soybean shoots, smaller plots fenced by tree branches, outdoor markets, individual houses, family-run stores, and finally, the residence, met his approval.

Libor had rented the first floor of a large pre-Bolshevik two-story home on a narrow cobblestone street. In Communist days three years earlier, six families were jammed in. The Ukrainian owner, great-grandson of the original owner, reclaimed the property, and after extensive renovations, lived on the upper floor. Fronting the street was a low stone wall that enclosed a vegetable garden. Grapevines grew on a pergola over the front door.

They stepped into the comfortable accommodations of an expansive parlor, three bedrooms, and two bathrooms. The wooden Communist-era furnishings were mixed with a softer couch and armchairs appropriate for an Imperial Russian dacha. The new, blue-patterned carpet in the main room stretched from the front entrance beyond the fireplace to the back door and smelled of glue, unlike the antique Turkish rugs in the bedrooms. Striped beige and yellow curtains warmed the room and covered the patina of the unpainted window trim. New kitchen appliances and bath fixtures completed the modernization.

Lida loved classical music. The first items she opened were her cassette player, numerous tapes, and speakers. Smetana's "Libuše" filled the disordered room as the trio hustled about, stowing their pre-shipped possessions. After two hours of unpacking, Lida plopped into one of the soft velvet chairs with frayed piping and said, "I'm tired. I'll go to the market tomorrow. Libor, please take Táta around our city before dark."

The primary destination for Luboš was the broad shoreline. He learned in coming days the three routes: the meandering course along their cobbled pedestrian street fronted by mature sycamore trees, the scenic way in sight of the shore along the rows of tall Italian cypress and budding poplar trees, and the short, noisy route through the congested commercial street past the village green and municipal buildings.

Each route ended at the railroad tracks, meters from the beach. Freight cars laden with salt, limestone, and grain, rumbled by the loading dock and filled the air with their odors and dust. The industrial and cargo storage areas of the port lay to the east. The fishing pier jutting into the sea protected the arc of the shore.

"Remember I mentioned a neighborhood the Greeks called 'Quarantine?'" Libor asked on their return to their new home. "Well, this is it."

"Every place has a past. The buildings are sad and need paint, but we have these trees to keep the temperature down, cafes, and no traffic on our narrow street. Vienna and Prague were too fast-paced. Feodosia is a promising change, especially the clear waters."

Because the produce at the neighborhood market was disappointing, Lida suggested they eat at an outdoor cafe where a sole musician played a lively kobza and sang Ukrainian ballads. The "cooperative" restaurant, encouraged under Gorbachev's Perestroika efforts to reconstruct the economy, was empty of patrons. Luboš was pleased to hear Ukrainian tunes and studied the singer's finger movements, considering whether to play the instrument again. Luboš shared stories of Yarik and Alya, who had filled the old farmhouse with music and song.

Father read the Russian language menu for their first evening and, with little confidence, ordered their meals. Lida raised a glass of her too sedimented Massandra white muscat, and Libor and Luboš held up their local Krim beers to salute their future. "Na zdraví," they said in unison. Luboš added, "Here is my toast for 'no surprises.' Next year we will toast with Czech Becherovka."

The trio was mindful of the contradictions of a Czech toast, drinking local wine and Russian beer in the new country of Ukraine. The siblings reviewed their embarkation in their city and readied themselves for their challenges.

Luboš was subdued after the toast as he recalled the disruptions during his fifty-eight years. He yearned to be ignored by governments and the liberty for his children to pursue their goals. As a ten-year-old, he was a follower. As a citizen, he was a listener. At Marcela's escape, he was the leader. On his first night back in Ukraine, he had earned the right to be a follower, anticipating a slow-paced life at the shore.

Sort of. Luboš wasn't merely going to watch TV and fish. The youthful zeal of his children called for a steady hand. Now that Luboš had found them, he was committed to guide and support them.

Both recent graduates landed with limited hands-on experience and unearned confidence. Unlike their soft and measured mother, Lida and Libor rushed to jump-start their careers. Enthusiastic investors and speculators detected opportunities in newly opened countries, and the family's timing was perfect for integration into an environment greedy for a version of capitalism.

The twins' charismatic personalities were a curiosity in somber Crimea, which struggled to adjust to the opportunities and uncertainty of democracy and capitalism. Lida and Libor, and to a lesser extent Luboš, strolled the streets of Feodosia, absorbing the culture clash.

Their shoes, trousers, shirts, jackets, and sunglasses were more current and European than the Russian-influenced styles, and the émigrés stood out. The distinction was a benefit in their interaction with bankers and lessors who anticipated a profitable, maybe greedy, relationship with the neophytes.

Lida and Libor conducted their initial fact-finding in Ukrainian and stilted Russian, learned from their Russian language immersion course in Vienna. They found Feodosia was significantly more Russian than Ukrainian. Right off, the pair had to dispel the expectation of taking a business template smoothly from Austria into a wary system. Even the terms "business" and "company" were suspect.

"I understand enough Russian," Luboš said when asked about registering with them for the language course. Although Uncle Jan had warned him in 1945, "to survive, forget your Ukrainian language," the vocabulary and accent slowly returned.

"You read the restaurant menus," Lida complimented her father, "and at the market, you read the Russian labels."

"Let's say I was lucky. The waiters aren't too confused, and the labels on the cans have pictures."

"Ukraine is supposed to be the breadbasket of Europe," Lida complained to Libor. "That abundance was a century ago before the Communists and before restructuring. There isn't much to choose from in the market. Dinners of canned spaghetti each night are unhealthy."

"What will I shop for in Simferopol?"

"Okay, brother," Lida replied in a false laugh, "here is my list of items we need: slipcovers for the armchair, microwave oven, fax machine, television—all from a western manufacturer. Oh, and a floor lamp."

"And size 43 shoes for me," Luboš added. "I forgot to purchase them in Vienna."

Karbovanets, the name from Nazi rule when Luboš was a child, were currency coupons replacing the Russian ruble. Issued to tackle inflation and shortages of food and merchandise in Ukraine, they underscored the bleak economic situation. The return of Karbovanets was an unpleasant reminder of German occupation.

Dr. Evetov had misjudged Ukraine's privatization schemes and dependence on a planned economy. The dissolution of the Soviet Union had severely disrupted commerce, and businesses closed. Workers were let go, unpaid, given scrip, or given a portion of what they manufactured. Scarcity and economic irregularities were novel to Lida and Libor. Luboš chose not to mention his previous caution.

Father and son acquired furniture and valuables from desperate hawkers on the streets. Keeping in mind the scant treasures his family abandoned, Luboš felt guilty benefiting from societal troubles and paid fair prices. He bought a six-string kobza and Matryoshka dolls for Lida and Zuzana. The dolls brought him both joy and sadness.

The Feodosia community welcomed the Viennese immigrants as boosters of the local economy. The facilitators fulfilled their promises for permanent residency applications. "Will you turn in your Czech passport and claim Ukraine as your birth country?" Libor asked.

"I lied when I applied for the Czech passport. Will changing to a Ukraine birthplace cause trouble?"

"The war caused so many dislocations, the lawyers don't expect complications. You might be eligible for a Ukraine pension."

"Good, I can retire my invented story of growing up in Bohemia. Ha, and receive a pension for running away from the country. My journey from Ukraine and back is complete, but I will still cheer for the Czechs."

Chapter 41: Lida and Libor Chart Their Paths

Lida was an attractive, slender young woman with flowing hair who stood out for all to notice. She carried her mother's genuine smile and firm handshake to negotiations and social events. As a student, she fit in. In Crimea, Lida was confident enough to push forward her new contemporary art gallery proposal. A thin scarf around her neck in all seasons and, invariably, a fashionable small purse held at her waist, Lida set a measure for attire in the same manner as Wilhelm, who was the best dressed for all occasions.

Her enthusiasm could not be restrained. Assisted by Libor, she leased a vacant former Catholic church to fulfill her dream. Appropriated in 1920 for Party offices, the former house of worship had been restored in a Gorbachev-inspired project. The economy had ground to a standstill after the Soviet dissolution, and the building had been empty for two years. The location was prime, near city hall, and across the street from the always-crowded Aivazovsky National Art Gallery.

"Tomorrow, I sign the contract documents. Help, I have a frozen brain. What should I name my gallery?" she asked her father and brother, standing in the vestibule.

"The space is huge," Luboš said warily. "How will you find enough artwork to sell and pay for the rent?"

"The lease cost is low. In Vienna, I learned how to display art. The art galleries here are missing the market. It's a stretch, but you wait."

"I hope you are right," Táta replied, unconvinced and wary that Lida, with her unproven skills, was overconfident.

"Maybe something Crimean or something Ukrainian?" Libor put forward.

"Does such a name limit the gallery?" Luboš questioned. "You are an optimist. What about a worldly name, maybe 'Modern?' "

"What names stand out?" her brother asked.

"I thumbed through the dictionary and gave up."

"It should be about why you have the gallery," Luboš continued, "and the future."

"This name sticks," Lida said with some hesitation, "and follows what you said: 'Promise Gallery.' "

"That is an excellent choice," Libor said. "Promise for today and the future."

"The name is fitting for a former church. We will grow together."

Lida walked the length of the nave on the squeaky hardwood floors to judge the best natural lighting locations and to envision carpentry improvements. Outside, she measured for the size of the Promise Gallery sign and wondered whether to add, "Lida Nováková, Proprietor."

"Now that you have your gallery name, I have one I favor for the seafood plant." Libor announced: "Sea and Shore Industries."

"Oh, you have chosen a powerful name," Lida said.

"These names express your visions," Luboš added. "Let's celebrate these milestones."

❖ ❖ ❖ ❖ ❖

Confusion over the language, unfamiliarity with the city, and efforts to get their careers underway filled their frantic spring. Over time they outfitted the apartment, taking care to create a homey kitchen and dining area. Luboš had placed a small Junost color television on the white Formica counter. The aluminum foil on the antennas brushed them when they walked near. Four rickety chairs at an ancient,

232

scrolled, oak dining table were crowded adjacent to the sideboard.

Luboš prepared fish, and Lida sliced vegetables picked from their front yard. Lida referred to aged, scribbled cards to cook her grandmother's recipes. Through the kitchen window, Lida kept track of neighborhood happenings.

Lida discovered a market carrying acceptable foodstuffs and announced, "Now that we are getting organized, we will return to our Sunday dinners, same as Máma's."

"Ah, yes, and Miluše's," Luboš said in Czech. His favored language competed with the Russian the twins were studying.

"I will buy the desserts," Libor offered before he was assigned vegetables.

"Please clean the fish at the pier," Lida said to her father, who nodded in agreement.

"My job is to net, prepare, and grill carp or trout or any fish that bites the hook."

Viennese and Czech dishes were a source of pride for Lida, who added, "The aroma of Máma and Babička's breads, seasoned cabbage and onions will fill the kitchen."

Adjacent rooms and balconies for administrative offices and work studios complimented the spacious main sales and display area of Promise Gallery. High ceilings, innovative lighting, meticulous placement of art, and rich colors greeted inquisitive purchasers. Artists working in the newest materials and concepts sought to display their artwork at Lida's gallery. A year earlier, they were selling at flea markets to pay for groceries.

Lida gave them an opportunity for financial stability. Her gift was to appreciate talent and develop a following for the artists under her wing. Word spread among the newly wealthy Russians vacationing in Crimea that paintings, sculpture, glassworks, and photography at Promise Gallery were of high quality and bound to appreciate. They bought passionately, confirming its success in the first year.

His sparse white hair cut short, his cheeks drooping more flesh, and his belly challenging his belt, Luboš was a worn man, but he was not worn out. He walked about Feodosia wearing clothes from Austria until he chose to appear more local. His mechanical skills were needed in Feodosia to repair the unreliable vehicles built in Eastern Bloc countries. He found work at a service station on Otava Street. He knew the tricks to squeeze extra kilometers out of almost any truck, bus or auto, and the appreciative owner shared his tools.

The business was privately owned and a comforting place to go since the Ukrainian owner had lost relatives under the Communists. He had maneuvered in the underground economy before the Soviet breakup. At the introduction of capitalism, he avoided paying taxes. The employees empathized, complained, played Durak, and said "comrade" in jest. Russian was the predominant language in Crimea but not at work, where one of the men had survived a decade in the Gulag. Luboš earned a wage based on his mechanical skills and proudly contributed to the household budget.

Part-time mechanic and leisure time fisherman didn't fill his days. Luboš loitered around Promise Gallery seeking tasks. Touch-up painting, repairing a damaged easel, or assembling a display case kept him busy. Luboš was comfortable in work overalls or his angling garb, but Lida envisioned her father in a more substantial role.

"I'm the youngest business owner in the city and besides, a woman," Lida explained at home as she sipped her favored Pinot Gris Massandra wine and he a lager. Her art gallery was well received by collectors and artists and also envied by the criminal elements that flourished after the Soviet structure collapsed.

Whether by a loose pack of local young men or the more forceful Ukrainian mafia, Promise Gallery was pressured to pay racketeers for protection. The militsiya, the corrupt Ukrainian police, and the State Security Service, the

DSO, were not trusted counterbalances. They, too, expected protection money.

"Wealthy men come to acquire paintings, be a business partner, and invite me out. Other men dressed in black come and just hang around to establish their presence. They congratulate me and offer to keep me safe from undesirable situations. They are the undesirable situations. I need you here as the mature man on the floor, so people won't take advantage of my inexperience."

"The eyes of men follow you. Are you suggesting more than a bouncer?" Memories of brutal fights in prison ran through his mind.

"No. I have two tasks in mind: something upscale and a real-life buffer. Some men discuss western politics or capitalism or how to earn money. They see their friends investing in art and guess Promise Gallery has high profits."

"Do they want to become the owners?"

"They aim to invest, and I do the work. I call them slippery. If you are here, controversial conversations won't happen, especially about privatization. You fish early and fix trucks until lunch. Will you spend afternoons here? I want to sing your praises as my father and my colleague—a man who is worldly and loyal. Clients will talk more about art and less about their yacht.

"The second part is more difficult. If I ignore these soft threats, they will escalate. They can knock over a display or break a window and much worse. The militsiya won't care. I will spread the word that you are a man who has been to prison and familiar with violence."

"Coping involves money. Better a payoff than having your church burn down. My friends at the garage will have some ideas. Do you have schillings or dollars?"

"Both."

Wearing his new work wardrobe, Luboš treasured the opportunity to be a significant presence in his daughter's life. Conveniently, his activities were fifteen minutes from the gallery unless his arthritis flared up. Cleaned up after gutting the fish and a morning turning a wrench, Luboš would report wearing a dark crew neck shirt, double-breasted black blazer with gold-colored buttons, black Levi 501 jeans that he paid too much for, and a woven black leather belt. During his quasi-hippie days with Marcela, Levis were treasured. Lida regarded him as distinguished in his unofficial job, which she called "the master of the floor."

Lida trusted her father whenever he asked for an "advance." He disbursed the funds to the undesirables, while she remained aloof. His aspiration in Vienna to follow the rules conflicted with post-Communist reality. At least Lida paid taxes.

The Czech language had been a challenge for Luboš. Although his native tongue flowed comfortably, his Ukrainian accent was from the north, and misspoken Czech and Slovak words slipped into his speech. Nevertheless, his confident manner projected stability on the floor.

At one of the artist's receptions, an intoxicated man was reluctant to leave. Luboš said to Lida, "Let me know if he bothers you."

"He is just flirting and not serious. You are on top of everything. I will pay you to be my Czech and Slovak art consultant."

"I'll be your unpaid sculpture consultant to pay my rent."

"You don't have to chip in, thanks to our inheritance from Máma. By the way, I asked Zuzana to visit. Is that okay with you?"

"Of course. She can come to your gallery and listen to the wild music."

"I prefer classical music, but my—our—customers prefer the newest musicians. She should come to see you."

Waving his hand to brush off her suggestion, he said, "Friends at work, fishing with Libor, cooking fish for you, and learning from the lecturers at your exhibitions are all I need."

"Okay, Táta, just trying. She will come to my art gallery."

Lida's invitation was a spur-of-the-moment decision, and Zuzana readily agreed. As the day approached, though, she had second thoughts and canceled.

❖ ❖ ❖ ❖ ❖

Libor had nervous energy and grand visions for his new aquaculture and fish processing company. Taller than Lida, he carried the imposing build of a hockey player. His thick brown hair combed back, he was chiseled handsome, well dressed, and confident. Bright blue eyes identical to his mother were restless and swept the room for his next pursuit. His sharp features complemented his crisp speech, which was less accented than Lida's in their new tongue. Libor bought an older Lada, a temperamental Russian car, and spent weeks, at times, accompanied by his father, searching possible sites for his factory.

Crimea resembles an island, and the rocky coast has few safe harbors. The peninsula's best port lay at Sevastopol, home of the massive Russian Black Sea Fleet. The dissolution of the Soviet Union a year earlier put enormous stress on Ukraine-Russian government relations as they testily negotiated ship allotments and disposition of nuclear armaments. Sevastopol was a restricted military stronghold and unavailable to commerce.

The most suitable port near the Sea of Azov was Kerch. The sea was farther from Black Sea fishing grounds and constricted by the Kerch Strait separating Ukraine from Russia. Although the cost of land was lower, Libor deferred to his father's objection, "On the Sea of Azov, I see Russia."

The port city of Yalta, notable for the Yalta Conference of 1945 between President Franklin Roosevelt, Prime Minister Winston Churchill, and Premier Joseph Stalin, had collapsed economically after the Soviet breakup. Real estate values were low and fishing vessels of government enterprises lay idle.

They walked the empty space between the seawall and rusted cranes and forced their way into vacant structures to inspect. The flawed Soviet economy had supported the local fishing industry, but not capitalism.

"The port is run down," Libor said, sitting in his Lada overlooking weeds growing in the parking lot and trawlers leaning off-kilter along the bulkhead. Libor deliberated how to initiate his grand proposition. He asked, "What about Yalta?"

"The docks and warehouses are neglected," Luboš replied, trying not to unduly influence his preference for a Feodosia location.

"The buildings can be modernized," Libor responded, envisioning new trawlers delivering their haul on conveyor belts to his bustling new processing plant. "From these foundations, someone will restore them and succeed. Why not me?"

"Perhaps others see obstacles that you overlook."

"I updated the estimates on my thesis to reflect a more damaged economy. Even so, the revised numbers show that my strategy is workable."

"I worry about beams falling on us."

"You worry too much, Táta."

"Perhaps you don't worry enough."

"Or we might demolish these and build to my specifications." Libor usually appreciated his father's comments, but he was bent on his vision of Yalta and ignored subtle remarks.

"You have a high-powered team of bankers and fixers in Feodosia, and the railway is closer to the warehouses."

"Feodosia has limited opportunity for expansion. These ships have been inspected. I can find a suitable site here. My new employees will relish the promise of a real paycheck. You land one fish at a time. I will be a commercial fisherman with new equipment, new processing techniques, new transportation—new everything."

"Yalta will meet your requirements then," Luboš said doubtfully, conceding the inevitable.

238

Ignoring any reservations, Libor chose Yalta, 120 kilometers and more than two hours from Feodosia. Libor hired local contacts at substantial expense to initiate discussions with newly created government agencies. Overcoming planning obstacles, Libor presented his undertaking to banks in Yalta and to his guarded father.

"You picture a smaller business," Libor said.

"I'm a stranger to large projects. Your banker will lend all the money you ask. He is encouraging you to refurbish those old trawlers that last sailed when Gorbachev was boss."

"Payments are not due until a year after we start construction."

"The three outfits where I've worked were cash only," he said to his son, who wasn't paying attention. "They were illicit and didn't have loans or pay taxes. The owners paid bribes when necessary. If business slowed, he paid us when work picked up. A bank loan is different."

In less than two years, flush with a generous line of credit backed by his mother's inheritance, Libor broke ground for the factory and new docks. It was the largest project in Yalta since the Soviet dissolution. Libor and Lida were enviable young entrepreneurs making waves in an open and aspiring Crimea. Both rushed into their projects oblivious to their lack of experience.

Chapter 42: The Fisherman and the Garage

Luboš never thought to revert to his Ukrainian name, Dmytro, when they first moved to Crimea. By now, he deemed himself a Slav living in Ukraine, a Czech to his bones, in his acquired tribe. Libor asked if he would return to visit the farm where he grew up.

"I wouldn't recognize it. The Poles, Communists, and Ukrainian partisans kept fighting for that corner of Ukraine. My family fled west to avoid the past. I traveled east with you and Lida. I'm done traveling. I have my Ukraine passport, which I will never use."

Distressed by the economic conditions and Russian presence, Lida and Libor renewed their Austrian passports and opted not to apply for dual citizenship.

Luboš considered searching for his father's military records. He shivered when he wondered how Anton might have died. After cursory inquiries in Simferopol, he learned those records were in Moscow and were incomplete. Luboš would not fly to Russia.

Luboš preferred to use his bamboo pole around the support pilings of the pier. His rod and reel were best to cast while wading off the beach. Unsure of the sea conditions, he would bring both. Any day that he walked to the shore was a quality day.

Lida had infrequently fished with Luboš and Libor in Vienna and never in Feodosia. Although Libor was often in Yalta, he was keen to fish with his father on Sundays, followed by family dinners.

240

Typically, Lida's soup and vegetables were ready first, and they lounged about while Luboš prepared his bounty.

"Are the permits coming along?" Lida asked, eager for an update on her brother's week.

"The energy permit is the hardest. The new gas utility is disorganized and unwilling to commit to digging a new natural gas line."

"Otava Street lost gas for three days," Luboš added, "and the gas association ignored the owner."

"Talk about problems; new construction slows our traffic here. Tourists were detoured from my gallery after a crane carrying the new war monument blocked downtown for a day. Is Yalta congested?"

"Only at the palace. Tomorrow I will fish with Táta and not waste the day in Yalta."

"You will see the plaza cordoned off at the monument."

"Is it the statue of the soldiers and the bayonet that was pictured in the newspapers?"

"Yes, Feodosia Landing, 1941." Parliament in Simferopol finally found the money for the installation."

On Monday morning, the two men walked on the quiet pedestrian street past the monument and to the pier. "I will have a fantastic industry, just not at this pace. Don't tell Lida that I am worried."

"I won't mention it. What will solve your problem?"

"I'll ask my banker for advice," Libor posited as he baited his hook. "They have a stake in my success; together, we will expand."

"Last week you asked for a delay in the payments. How did they respond?"

"They are working with me on an extension. I have funds from Máma, but Lida cautions me."

"Can you spend only your share?"

"So far, that is the case." Libor said, hefting the full wicker catch basket.

❖ ❖ ❖ ❖ ❖

Quickly accepted as the best fisherman at the pier, Luboš was reluctant to explain his techniques in his mixed Czech-Ukrainian dialect. His fellow fishermen preferred to speak Russian. They asked about his accent and his Czech name, but his poor Russian and his hearing loss from the quarry were his excuses to ignore them. He set his pole, sat on a bench, and gazed out to the sea with Marcela in his daydreams.

Salinity gave an added pleasant flavor to the drum, shad, mackerel, brown trout, and carp caught and cooked in too much butter. Despite recognizing the value of catch and release, Luboš was compelled to bring most of his haul home. To have more fish than he could consume was a luxury. In his new homeland, he shared with the owner on the floor above and his pals at work.

Artem was the unofficial leader of the mechanics. "Hey, Luboš, I will stir the kindling. What are we grilling for lunch?"

"Sorry, I'm late. A few brown trout are this week's measly meal. Someone go down the street for dumplings." The resident cat wove among them.

"Did you bring the wrong bait?" Artem wisecracked.

"No, my favorite spot on the pier was taken."

"Do you need some beef? We can go with you," Artem said, standing up, one arm raised to flex his substantial muscles. Olive skin and brown eyes set under thick, unruly eyebrows portrayed the image of "Don't mess with me." Artem's memories of the peacetime Soviet army were dismal, whereas Luboš was proud of his service in the Czechoslovak army.

Artem had relocated from Lviv in Northern Ukraine and had witnessed the CCCP freight cars overloaded with pathetic exiles transiting to Siberia. A widower anticipating a reduced Russian influence, he migrated in 1990 to Crimea's warmer climate. The weather was pleasant, but his welcome less so. While playful and upbeat among friends, he was prone to arguments with Russians.

"Artem, you remind me of Bohdan, a friend in Prague. He was of full loony ideas and always on thin ice."

"He is my friend, and I haven't met him. He was smart enough to avoid crossing the wavy line of trouble and no trouble."

"No action required on the pier. They might foul my lines on purpose. Sorry, no fish next week."

"Are you mad at us?" Artem kidded and turned over the trout filets.

"No, the doctor will dig for skin cancer on my cheek. For years she advised me to wear a hat and stay out of the sun. Lida tells me that every day."

"We will bring you one of Libor's fish sandwiches from the cafe."

"Not this year."

Chapter 43: Return to Vienna and Prague, 1995

Wilhelm had visited his stepchildren only once, a year after they immigrated. "I called Wilhelm, and he sounded tired," Luboš said. "He hasn't recovered from his illness."

"The doctor is worried about pneumonia," Lida responded. "Libor and I will go to Vienna."

"Because we are not far away," added Libor, "we will see Zuzana in Prague. Will you meet us in Prague and show us where you and Máma fished?"

"No. Too many tourists line the bridges, and the ugly Žižkov TV tower was built next to Babička's home," Luboš replied. He wasn't going back to Vienna or Prague. Vienna was the city of his offspring, but it was too rich and fashionable for his taste. For him, Prague was Communism, Marcela escaping on the bus, and the StB. Yes, Zuzana was there, but that slice of his life was in the background.

Wilhelm had waited for their return, made his peace, and was ready. He died at ease in his sleep days after the twins returned home. "Wilhelm was grateful Marcela picked him," Lida said in her call from Vienna following the memorial service. "He said the three of us gave his life a significance that had eluded him. Wilhelm admired you and asked me to thank you for sending Marcela and two babies to Vienna."

"Vater wanted to visit her grave," Libor added, "but the doctor didn't allow it. Libor and I laid flowers on Máma's headstone and said a prayer."

"He was a loving stepfather to you and friend to me. I am glad you cheered him at the close of his life." Tears falling on his shirt, Luboš said, "I should have gone to visit Marcela and say goodbye to Wilhelm." Deep down, that wasn't true. Luboš was concentrating on the present more than the past.

The twins spent time with friends and their professors in Vienna until later in the week, when they were ready to deal with the will. Law books lined the walls of the conference room where files of Wilhelm's account summaries were spread out on the polished walnut conference table. Two lawyers greeted them to explain Wilhelm's estate. His finances were as neatly organized as the handkerchief in his breast pocket, and they were substantial, reflecting fifty years as a prosperous banker. There was no trace of his dealings before 1955. His letter to his stepchildren was minimal except to "keep most of your money in schillings in Vienna."

Wilhelm had recently placed his assets in money market funds. They viewed the windfall through different lenses. Lida's gallery was profitable, but Libor's loan payments were onerous.

"Vater didn't discuss investments," Lida began when the siblings were alone. She undertook to protect her economic security without overly offending her brother. "These account balances are huge. You can see how conservative his bonds and mutual funds were before he became ill. From his grave, he is saying, 'Be prudent.' "

"Now, I can sell my Lada and move to a larger apartment."

"I won't make any big decisions for a month. Later I might add a second gallery location."

"My obligations are immediate. I don't have that luxury."

"Please don't buy the biggest Mercedes in Crimea," Lida jested, dressed in her fashionable new suit.

"I can choose what to buy. Thank you."

"Máma's gift supported us. Your half is gone."

"Thank goodness I didn't ask for your assistance. The processing works are almost complete, and I will pay off the loans from this inheritance."

"Táta believes the trawlers are too old and costly. To have all the pieces operating on the first day may be premature. Ships are expensive to operate."

"I hear you," he said, without hearing her.

"Máma's gift was placed in one account, and that worries me. You take more risk than I do."

"Risky, yes, but we will feed the entire country and make a profit. Her gift was enough to lease your church. My plans are bigger."

"We have different needs and visions. I propose we establish separate accounts."

"Separate accounts are fine," Libor replied, relieved that her signature wasn't necessary for his disbursements. "Except for the trust fund, I will wire most of my funds to Feodosia. It'll comfort my bankers."

"I'll invest my schillings here in Vienna," Lida said, hoping that her brother would be more conservative when his company produced revenue.

"Remember the inflation of the Karbovanets? Next year Ukraine will introduce the hryvnia, and our lawyers expect currency devaluations to continue. Here is my suggestion—transfer the minimum to Feodosia."

Zuzana welcomed her niece and nephew to Prague a week after Wilhelm's death. Her parlor décor was unchanged since their short visit under amnesty six years earlier. "Lida, your mother sat on the couch when she visited—please sit here," Zuzana directed. "Libor, your father sat on the chair under the mantelpiece—please sit there."

Attired in clothes only Vienna offered, Lida and Libor were contemplative as they scanned the room and grappled with memories of the reunion tea party. Nattily dressed in a bright yellow blouse, navy blue blazer, and dark pleated skirt, Zuzana was thrilled that her niece and nephew wished to visit her.

"Is this the same cat that purred for Tatínek?" Libor inquired after the cat jumped on his lap and flexed her claws on his pant leg.

"Yes, Tippy Toes. I hid her during the tea because she leaps onto tables. She is a loving cat and loves table scraps. She is my best companion."

"I was so nervous I didn't look around," Lida said while tugging the gold pendant on her necklace. Zuzana moved to the kitchen to pour iced tea, while Libor rose and placed the cat on Lida's lap.

Holding a framed picture from the sideboard and tabletops, Libor observed, "These are amusing pictures. Here is Luboš sporting long sideburns and Máma in a tie-dyed T-shirt—1968, I bet. They were a lively pair."

"It was their hippie period. Too bad the hippies didn't last longer."

"Were these pictures here?"

"No, I hid the pictures of Marcela and Luboš together. I wouldn't embarrass Wilhelm."

"Embarrassing for Máma. Check those pants. The pictures in the photo album brought tears and, oh my, the ski earrings."

"Is this older man in a suit the one who saved you and Táta?" Lida asked.

"Yes. More than once he intervened on our behalf. I miss him terribly."

"Vater was slow to walk the steps to meet you. He told us that several weeks later. Of course, none of us imagined what to expect."

"I was hesitant to open the door and Luboš more so. Does he dwell on Marcela? How is he adapting to Ukraine?"

"He has his Ukrainian pals," Libor said, "and his fishing gear."

"After prison and after Marcela died, he was a guest in need, a friend, a relative. I was stunned over everything at the Velvet Revolution, but if I kept Luboš alive, I too would live. He was depressed. I kept his head above water."

"Those telephone calls raised his spirits. And he moved to Vienna at your insistence," Libor added.

"Yes. He left this apartment, and he left me. I was lonely."

"I disagree with Libor," Lida interjected. "He talks with me more than Libor. He is lonely in some ways. Imagine the sadness he has encountered. Still, he isn't interested in women. Losing Máma still pains him six years later."

"Really, after six years."

"When she died," Libor said, "Máma was wearing the ski earrings you gave her. They were her connection to him. We hide them."

"Don't tell your father."

"Why did Máma die of a heart attack?" Lida asked. "You are healthy, and Babička didn't have medical issues."

"I cannot imagine her stress. Did she ever tell you about the secret letter she sent to Luboš?"

"No," Lida and Libor reacted in unison, inclined forward in anticipation.

"She sent a letter to me to send to Luboš and didn't show it to Wilhelm."

"Keep going," Libor said, impatient to hear.

Zuzana detailed the intrigue of that single impassioned missive. "It was the link that gave them the possibility for their reunion."

"I suppose she couldn't tell us," Libor said, "you know, her loyalty to Wilhelm."

"The revolution gave her a new choice—Wilhelm or Luboš. She would have told you someday, but...." The three of them paused, and even Libor reached for his handkerchief. "But she died too young. The stress probably killed her."

"In a way, she told us," Lida said. "She was cool, perhaps cold, to Wilhelm after we returned to Vienna. I ignored her new temperament as anxiety that would ease. She may have made a mental shift to Táta. I feel guilty that I didn't notice and offer comfort."

"Don't take any responsibility," Zuzana said, consoling Lida. "She may have harbored a return to Luboš. Just imagine her emotions that night standing next to her husband."

"I miss her so."

"I didn't ask you this over the telephone," Lida asked the next day. "Why did you cancel your visit last year?"

"Meetings came up."

"We expected to show you our new home and a warmer climate," Lida continued, unsatisfied with Zuzana's evasion.

Zuzana didn't amplify her response. "I will go to Crimea."

Life wasn't simple for Zuzana. The words in Marcela's secret letter to Luboš were imprinted in Zuzana's mind—as a witness. How could she compete with what was equally imprinted in his mind? Would she go to Lida's Promise Gallery, or Libor's factory, or Luboš's fishing pier? Or Luboš?

Her dismay was well founded. After Luboš had moved to Vienna, his concentration shifted away from Zuzana and Prague—his past. He had not expressed an attraction to her, and he wasn't inclined to change.

"How are matters for you?" Zuzana asked Libor, changing to a new thread.

"The construction is complete." With an appreciative glance at Lida he said, "I have a cautious team and we will not buy the ships. The next step is to purchase the special nets for fish farming. The locals believe I will steal their jobs and their fish, but I will buy their harvest at a fair price."

"I meet young men at Rotary Club meetings who have recently opened new businesses. They are as confident as you. I can't believe it: me, the Communist making lunchtime appearances at the Rotary: how attitudes change.

Next semester I return to Charles University for courses in marketing. I missed an intellectual education when I attended in 1946."

"Zuzana," Libor congratulated, "you will be the class spokesperson. I considered Rotary in Yalta, but I spend all my time arguing with city officials about permits."

"Feodosia doesn't have a Rotary. I should start one."

"You should. Guess what? I have been nominated to be the first woman member at the Prague City Rotary Club, the largest in the Czech Republic."

"A nice tribute to you," applauded Lida.

"It is a tribute to the Prague Rotarians."

"When Lida and I first arrived in Crimea, we did our best to understand the makeup of the country and our peninsula. Deep disagreement about nuclear weapons on Russian ships and the number of soldiers persists, but the mood changed after the signing last year of the Budapest Memorandum on Security Assurance.

"It was important news that Britain, the United States, and Russia assured the integrity of our independence. Still, I don't know how the British or Americans can protect Ukraine, especially Crimea."

"That conference was big news in Prague newspapers and television. The Russian shadow falls over borderland countries, wherever the sun shines. Former countries of the Soviet Union like the Baltic countries, the rest of Georgia, and Belarus also must have clear protections of a security agreement that will be honored by the signatories."

"Well said. You should run for office. Picture this, 'Vote for Zuzana Burešová, the next mayor of Prague.' "

"You're teasing me," Zuzana said modestly.

"In Crimea," Libor added, "the former Communists unfastened the red stars from their lapels but kept the red stripes on their backs. And they are elected. The success of our Ukrainian democracy is years away."

"The Czechs will lead the way for Ukrainians. Now we will visit the famous sights of Prague and the less famous sights—Hunter's Island, our mother's apartment, and your father's bus company. Tomorrow, Lida and I will skate and shop, and Libor will have coffee with Mila Hellerová, a friend who is a music professor at Charles University."

Chapter 44: Lida and Libor in Business, 1998

Independent Ukraine had entered the treacherous era of capitalism. Laws written by the Verkhovna Rada in Kyiv provided the framework to sustain the country's democratization. However, their enactment favored the well-connected who could buy state-owned operations at huge discounts.

In this environment, Lida's gallery succeeded while Libor's undertaking wrestled against barriers. Promise Gallery was the only dealer of contemporary art, and the Aivazovsky National Art Gallery funneled collectors to her gallery. Her enterprise was a mandatory destination for the limousines of the oligarchs, and she regularly transferred funds to Vienna.

In contrast to Feodosia, the powers in Yalta were not receptive to new initiatives. Although he was adequately funded and adhered to the modern principles from his education, Libor had been too optimistic and naïve. The entrepreneur struggled. He faced a crisis six years after he entered Crimea and three years after the seafood factory was complete. Revenues were low, and his loan balance was rising.

"Wherever I turn, there is a stumbling block," Libor lamented, sitting in a construction trailer in sight of the idle conveyor belts that awaited replacement of damaged pulleys. "Electricity fails suspiciously, a permit request for expansion is misplaced, and the nets at the fishpond are cut loose by rivals. My professors follow my progress and offer advice regarding the setbacks. Dr. Evetov even flew in to investigate. He presented academic suggestions, which underestimate the turbulent reality.

"I have a few reliable workers. The rest aren't trustworthy and might be delivering drugs. I don't care where the ships go in the Black Sea if they bring back plenty of fish."

"You better care. The DSO or the mafia can squeeze you. Both are brutal."

"I don't know if that is today's problem or tomorrow's. Today's problems are my suppliers pay no attention to the contract. I'm hesitant to smooth the construction with illegal gifts. I give courtesy money to the electrical inspector, yet he continues to find faults."

"You bribed him, but maybe not enough. My boss pays for protection, and so does Lida. I give extra to the doctors for an appointment. Do you pay and keep your business, or not pay?"

"Prominent people buy from Lida, and officials don't bother her. I'm at the whim of bureaucrats. We are outsiders here. Prison is unappealing, especially for a foreigner."

"Lida has friends high up who buy from her. On her behalf, I deliver some money. You pay your team of consultant's substantial fees. They ought to give the incentives?"

"I'm paying them for advice and guidance."

"Are they giving you worthwhile advice," Luboš persisted. "Are they are driving new BMWs instead of paying the electrical inspector? Or the plumbing inspector?"

"The owner of the older processing enterprise must be laughing."

"Are you running out of money?"

"I have funds." Libor was hesitant to detail his money woes. "My schillings in Vienna saved me from devaluation at the introduction of hryvnia two years ago."

"When I spent a week with you, we went to the Livadia Palace. It's a historic place, but the guides were lazy and hardly talked. Lida has two employees; they are paid a commission, and they are conscientious. You have Švejkism, same as Prague in the 1960s. I have proven friends at the service station. Our pay is okay. We are Ukrainian. Hire Ukrainians."

"The bank will call the loans if I let the Russians go."

"You are on thin ice. Who has the power—the worker, the criminal, the entrepreneur, or the banker?" Luboš asked.

"Thus far, not me."

❖ ❖ ❖ ❖ ❖

Libor's capitalist initiative, launched soon after Ukraine's independence, foundered in his company's seventh year. The criminal threat from the mafia and corrupt business, political, and government leaders of the country was overwhelming.

Libor faced the reality of construction sabotage, graffiti warnings on his new Ford, and personal threats of violence. Complications in Yalta forced him to shutter Sea and Shore Industries. Not surprisingly, the local oligarch who led the underground campaign against Libor bought the company at auction, easily acquired all permits, and restarted the operation, further enhancing his portfolio.

"My venture was a debacle," Libor said to Luboš and Lida as he pecked at his potato pancakes. "I misjudged my skills and underestimated the entrenched forces against a minor player. I'm disappointed to tell you that last week I wired for funds to pay off my loans."

"That was a good idea. Clients at the gallery ask about your troubles."

"I avoided bankruptcy, which is best for both of us."

"Do you have much inheritance remaining?" Lida asked, but promptly added, "You don't have to answer. I'm sorry to ask."

"I'm not broke."

"Chasing a new adventure requires foresight to predict where you are going. Think of my family in 1944 or me and Marcela in 1968."

"That doesn't reassure me," Libor replied.

"You are young and smart. You will be fine. Navigating in the Black Sea is a challenge. Lida rode the waves to shore. You went aground in a storm."

"My gallery was painless, and the money floats to me? I worked hard to grow Promise Gallery into a premier destination for artists and collectors."

"You warned us of Dr. Evetov's unrealistic view of Crimea," Libor said. "Are you saying I failed to anticipate these problems? Regardless, you were right."

"I don't mean to make you angry," Luboš replied defensively. "Devaluation and then inflation of 1998 brought investors into Promise Gallery to protect their wealth but disrupted the operations that Sea and Shore Industries relied on. The Mercedes and their bull-necked chauffeurs lined up outside Promise until the oligarchs drove off to steal the troubled companies. Lida's supporters were your adversaries."

Neither was happy with his summary, but it was hard to contradict.

"I need a break. We need a break. I have a friend who offered to take us fly-fishing in the hills. Your spinning gear is perfect, and the countryside is beautiful. Will you go with me?"

"Too much hiking."

"Or we can board a charter boat in Feodosia and troll in deeper waters. Please go with me."

"I'm set in my ways. No, thanks."

The success of Lida's Promise Gallery contrasted with Libor's fruitless efforts. But the twins held no lasting envy or grudges. They were relieved their testy disagreements were behind them.

During his seafood experiment, Libor had negotiated with commercial and government entities in fluent Russian. He was well regarded for his engineering competence and perseverance. After a short job search, the largest construction conglomerate in Yalta welcomed his technical skills.

The presence of Russia's Black Sea Fleet within the territory of an independent Ukraine created an ongoing controversy over nuclear weapons, division of ships and piers, and long-term leases in the Port of Sevastopol. Libor's firm was the lead contractor for the repair of dockyard facilities. Officials of both countries disputed the responsibilities, costs, and quality of the projects. Biased television and newspaper coverage hardened the positions of both sides.

As a recent émigré, Libor was brought in as a neutral to arbitrate. He patiently modified the demands of all parties and accommodated their disputes, enabling his company to finish the harbor undertaking.

"That was a frenzied month in Sevastopol," Luboš proudly said to his son. "Every day, you were on television and in the newspapers."

"I'd rather be an engineer in Yalta and avoid sitting a kilometer from hundreds of nuclear missiles and between quarreling admirals and politicians. It was unsettling, especially because ruffians loitered around our hotel, leaning against their motorcycles, to pressure our company officials."

"We missed you," Lida said, "and your tula gingerbread."

"I'm ready to go to the fishing pier tomorrow. I hope no one recognizes me."

"We will go early and watch hockey in the afternoon."

Unsaid by Libor was his relief to have dissolved Sea and Shore. He was content to work on projects that didn't further drain his inheritance.

Bitterness from the divisive television coverage spilled over into the Crimean bars and pubs during the 1998 Olympics, shown live from Nagano, Japan. Artem and other garage employees supported Ukrainian and Czech teams. Cheering for a Russian competitor brought threatening scowls and shoving from Russian fans.

256

The games were the second Olympics following the amicable separation of Czechoslovakia. Luboš was apprehensive. Will the Czech team excel? Luboš could cheer for Ukraine or Austria, but, of course, he chose the Czechs. Artem carried no competing country allegiance: when the sky-blue and wheat-yellow jerseys of the Ukraine team were on the ice, he was cheering for Ukraine.

"Hey, Artem," Luboš announced to his confidant the next morning. "If the Czechs win, there will be a fight. I'm not going back to that bar. Bring everyone to Lida's."

"Yeah, the Ruskies are rotten losers."

Luboš, wearing his red and white hockey jersey, provided snacks and beer for the noontime party at Lida's to cheer against Russia for the final match. The apartment resounded in shouts and groans in the tight game until the lone score gave Luboš one of his finest days. His Czechs shut out the Russians 1-0 and won the gold medal.

Chapter 45: Family

The new century brought romance to Lida after she met Serhii from Donetsk, an industrial city in the Donbas region of Eastern Ukraine. Half a head taller than Lida, he was an attractive man with glossy black hair brought straight back. He was intense and gestured with his hands in wild motion, leaning close enough to make one uncomfortable. Penetrating eyes, full eyebrows that angled with his mood, and an unruly mustache that didn't hide a scar from a fight in a hockey game, ensured that Serhii was the center of attention.

In sales settings, he aggressively convinced potential buyers to purchase his construction equipment. He was the free-spending top salesman for his importer. Since Lida spoke excellent Russian, they were compatible chatting at his fast, animated pace. Serhii, sporting gold chains around his neck and the pinkie ring of his championship junior hockey team, charmed her during high-spirited nights in the city.

"You said our brand-new backhoe loader was cute next to our bulldozer. Cute no, powerful, yes. We have older ones in the back lot. Do you want to drive one?"

"Drive? Where can I drive it?" Lida answered with a laugh. "They are huge."

"I meant to operate it. We have a field where customers dig a ditch, move a pile of dirt, or plow a road. I demonstrate to buyers how to operate the controls. Then I watch them dig a hole. It will be fun for you."

"I might break it. I'm not a customer."

"You are a special customer, ha, and I will offer you a special deal."

"I gave your boss a bargain on a painting he admired."

"He is a bastard," sharp-tongued Serhii declared. "I'm his best salesman. I'll have his job next year."

A popular lady, Lida met wealthy buyers but was repelled by their pretentious airs. She dated but was unable to find a man to sustain her interest. Her thirtieth birthday party was a shocker when she read the humorous cards her friends gave her about growing old and over the hill.

She ran her fingers on the crow's feet trailing from her eyes, looked in the mirror to see silver streaks in her hair, and took the cards seriously. Serhii was in the mix of suitors. She reassessed this stage of her life, musing of a family. She found him confident and hard working in the daytime and lively and fun in the evening. Lida delighted in both faces of Serhii, and they dated frequently.

"You and Serhii are regulars now," Luboš said, having returned from Artem's pub for Lida's specialty of holubtsi, stuffed cabbage rolls.

"Yes, I hope we don't wake you when we come back."

"Are you the last to leave the party?"

She stopped slicing the carrots and asked, "What do you mean?"

"Nothing. I'm glad you have a companion." Luboš was irritated because Serhii sat in the soft armchair that he snoozed in. Without asking, he changed channels of the new Samsung widescreen TV to watch Russian stations. He emptied his ashtrays only when they overflowed.

"We won't stay out late."

"That's okay. Artem found a room for me. You deserve your privacy."

"You don't have to move, Táta," Lida answered, sure that the move was best for all.

"It is time. You redecorated in lighter colors and appear ready for change." Luboš thought Lida drank too

259

much. He was certain Serhii did, but he didn't criticize his daughter's choice of friends. Luboš moved Lida and Libor's photo album and his hockey trinkets to the furnished room to infrequently play his kobza.

Promise Gallery was profitable, and Lida saved prodigiously. For what? The temperate winter climate was pleasant, but the tourists were gone, and art enthusiasts weren't buying. Each year was the same. Sell art from May to October and buy art in the off-season when the artists were anxious. Waiting for spring was tedious, and Lida was restless.

"Do you recall this opera?" she asked after she pressed the play button on the cassette player and sat at her end of the comfy sofa holding another glass of Pinot Gris. The trio listened while the fragrances from the simmering beetroot filled the kitchen. Important issues were debated at her dinner table, especially this Sunday evening.

"Hmmm," Libor hummed, searching for the name of the opera their mother shepherded them to as teenagers. The overture continued until he said, "Ahh. Do we have an announcement coming?"

"Excellent, Libor. Tátinek, this is "The Bartered Bride" by our Czech composer Bedřich Smetana."

"I'm partial to the dancing strings," Luboš said in his simple interpretation.

"This isn't an announcement, only a question. What if I marry Serhii?"

"You can choose any man in Crimea," Libor said after a short deliberation. "If you choose him, that is fine by me."

"Dumb question—has he asked you?" Luboš asked.

"To a degree. We meet every day and are moving in that direction."

Luboš added, "When he comes here, he is pleasant. We are passionate about hockey."

"That was too easy. Nothing more to say?"

"Well," Libor said, "have you dated him long enough?"

"A few years are enough. He treats me well. His company thinks he is responsible. You know of the ancient Ukrainian sentiment that a girl won't marry unless she can serve delicious borscht."

"Is my sister superstitious? No wonder we have borscht every week."

"I smell it. I taste it. Your soup passes the test," Luboš said, sniffing the air. "Marcela and I were together for a year and a half, but we weren't mindful of marriage. I suppose we should have. Lida, you have answered your question—he is the one. Your marriage is the best way to bring in the new century."

"Thank you for your encouragement. Now I can respond."

Lida and Serhii's wedding opened spring in Feodosia with the most elegant party in memory. Aunt Zuzana was the matron of honor, and Luboš was the proud father of the bride. Luboš was Zuzana's formal and restrained companion for the weekend.

"You are quick with a smile," Luboš remarked before she returned to Prague.

"Thank you. We have much to be cheerful for."

"I mean, when the situation was low for me in Prague, your eyes said happy, and your smile, and then your words. I counted on your pleasant disposition, same as Marcela."

The weekend was magical for the newlyweds and Zuzana until it collapsed when Luboš mentioned Marcela. Zuzana was crestfallen but not caught unawares. Luboš was sorry to have mentioned Marcela, but not enough to apologize to Zuzana or admit his faux pas to Libor. To correct his misguided comment, he invited Zuzana to fish with him the next day. Zuzana declined. She was upset by the Marcela comment, and fishing was Marcela's link to Luboš. Zuzana would be on uneven ground.

❖ ❖ ❖ ❖ ❖

The recession of 2001 affected Serhii's equipment sales. His income fluctuated, and the young couple relied on Lida's earnings. Restless, he asked Lida to move to Eastern Ukraine, where he could count on financial security and could assume responsibilities in the People's Democratic Party, an offshoot of the Communist Party, where his Russian parents were leaders.

"You will manage nicely in Donetsk. The city is larger than Feodosia, and my parents will obtain the best location for a gallery."

"I have excellent artists who live here. They are my friends."

"Brilliant artists are in Donetsk. Find new friends," he said, throwing his hands to the ceiling.

"We went last year. It was dreary."

"My parents aren't good enough?"

"I didn't say that," Lida replied, staring at him with her hands on her hips. "You bring up this topic frequently, and it goes nowhere. There is no reason to move."

"I can earn more money in the East," Serhii persisted.

"This poor economic spell will change. My sales are picking up, and so will yours."

Libor and Luboš joined the husband and wife at Lida's Sunday meals. Ten years of pleasant family and work concerns migrated to discussion in Russian of political issues. Czech was no longer spoken when Serhii was at home. He reoriented the dining room table and sat in his chair farthest from the kitchen. The tone was restrained with the new male head and the four of them speaking Russian. Serhii did not pitch in for meal preparation. When he determined that the meal was complete, he was quick to push his chair back, move to the comfy armchair with his leg dangling off one arm, and turn on his preferred television channel.

Libor moved to the couch one Sunday and mentioned new government contracts and recently hired employees.

"My boss and I submit proposals to your company, but they don't return phone calls or buy," Serhii said.

"I don't coordinate the purchases," Libor replied quietly. "We will buy road-grading equipment. We are in negotiations with subcontractors, and they will buy equipment next summer."

"On television, they blather about economic growth. I don't believe it or the politicians. I believe in our—my—Russian hockey team. Good night, I will be at my Russian pub."

"He gets that way," Lida said in Czech after Serhii departed to his noisy bar to talk hockey and politics with friends. "He has been upset for a week. He watches the disputes between the political parties for the election next month and gets so angry he might throw his ashtray at the television. The elections and hockey are too much for me."

"In two months," Libor said confidently, "spring will come, and we will have survived. Stop worrying."

"Thanks for your encouragement," Lida replied angrily. "You come once a week."

"We support you," Luboš cut in. "Libor wasn't mean, just optimistic. Buyers will fill Promise Gallery, and he will sell again."

"I'm not worried about Promise. I'm worried about Serhii."

"Last night at his bar, Russia beat my Czechs in a tight game. We got a little hotheaded. Fairly normal for him."

"It's okay for him to yell at you and me? Are both of you against me?"

"No, Lida," Luboš replied. "Sometimes, I don't say the words correctly. We are on your side. He should treat you better than a princess. For me, it's 2002, and I get wound up in Olympic hockey. It is my 'four-year plan.' The Russians play again, and he will become angry, even if they win."

"What should we do?" Libor said. They moved to sit next to Lida, who was moping on the couch. "How can we help?"

"I'll be okay."

Serhii came home drunk after the Russians lost to the Americans. After a few days, he settled down, and he and Lida muddled through the rough stretch.

As Libor predicted, equipment sales returned, and Serhii earned record income in 2002 and 2003. His confident demeanor and lively spirit returned, making Lida's Sunday dinners pleasant. Libor had been promoted to director of engineering, Luboš worked when he wanted, and stability reigned as Serhii fished with Luboš and Libor. And Lida longed for a baby.

"The doctor says I will be too old to have a baby," Lida shared with her brother and father after her husband walked to his bar. "Serhii is so-so on a baby, but I'm ready. What are your opinions?"

"A little one would be nice," Libor said, imagining a baby in his arms. Libor was a workaholic at his new job, and although he dated, either he lost interest, or the woman lost interest.

"You have responsible employees and Táta at Promise Gallery," Libor continued. "You paid for the wedding and the rent when Serhii's income dropped. Will his finances be trouble again? He is a big spender."

"Spender?" Lida replied, exasperated and tugging at her scarf. "Are you criticizing Serhii? You spent Máma's gift and most of Wilhelm's inheritance. My best year was in 2003. The gallery pays for everything. I have enough in Vienna to buy out the owner of this house and Promise."

"I'm sorry. I don't want you to have my money issues."

"Neither do I."

"Money shouldn't be an issue," Luboš chimed in to defuse the issue. "I'm concerned that he sides with intense Russian friends."

"They don't come here, and I'm not bothered," Lida answered, avoiding eye contact.

"I don't have a wife. I won't advise about babies."

264

"Your mother and I didn't intend to have babies." Luboš drew his son and daughter to him for an extended embrace and said, "Now, look at my two babies."

At last, Luboš would have a baby to hold.

Despite Serhii's ambivalence about the pregnancy, Maksim was born in the winter of 2004. The parents were joyous watching the baby sleep and coo. Serhii was proud to have proven his manhood. He took easily to Max in the crib.

Luboš bought a maple dining room table for Max's hook-on highchair. A leaf allowed expansion for more grandchildren.

Lida thrived at home, caring for Max while her trusted staff managed the gallery. Libor's former room was decorated in the soft blue color of Ukraine, and Luboš, now called by the Czech name Deda or Dedeček—grandfather—by Lida, was thrilled to have a grandson.

The twins' businesses and the whole of society changed after high-speed Internet finally reached Crimea. Lida expanded her client base and Libor accessed reduced material costs for the construction company.

While Serhii was home tending to his infant, his work contemporaries learned to increase sales opportunities online. By the spring, they were adept at marketing to contractors of government road and bridge projects, and they garnered most available sales. His employer increased quotas, but Serhii failed to redouble his efforts. He wasn't paid end-of-the-month and end-of-the-quarter incentive bonuses typical of a capitalist economy.

Worse, at work, he followed extremist websites on the Internet. He spent too much time watching RT, the new Russian language television network, and insufficient time being an admirable employee, father, or husband. When Lida turned off the television, he turned it back on.

Serhii had two periods of high equipment sales, but he failed to prove his skills in the new, fast-paced system. He preferred the work stability under Communism. He was always angry over biased Russian news programs or the rapid changes in his industry.

"You are fortunate to have Max," Luboš advised one evening. "You should be happy."

"The world is going to hell. Look at Kyiv," Serhii said, tapping his pinkie ring obnoxiously on his beer bottle. He picked at the label with his thumb until it fell onto the floor or between the cushions.

"Max is about to walk, enjoy him. He doesn't know what the television says."

"Well, he's lucky to miss the politicians making promises they can't keep."

Serhii turned more irritable when fractious elections in the Ukrainian presidential contest forced a revote. He ignored his nine-month-old toddler. He argued at home and at work about the political situation.

"Fascists are fomenting this so-called Orange Revolution," an incensed Serhii announced at the Sunday dinner. "They fake stories, and people believe them, even you."

"Voter fraud was rampant," Libor disagreed quietly. "Parliament responded."

"They respond to the influence of the CIA," he exclaimed, pounding his fist on the table and bouncing the bottle.

"Communists stole the Czechoslovak election in 1948 through voter fraud," Luboš inserted.

"How do you know?"

"Everyone knew. Some right away, some forty years later."

"So what?"

"Spend less time online," Libor said, trying to offer a solution, "and you won't get this angry."

"You should be angry," Serhii said, pointing his brown-stained cigarette fingers in Libor's face. "I look at podcasts that tell the truth. This re-vote will wreck the country and your company. I'm leaving for my pub where people listen."

"He leaves your table in a huff," Libor said after the back door slammed shut.

"After his income dropped the first time," Lida replied as she cleared the table, "I expected him to recover. I'm not so confident this time. He won't trim his beard or wear a respectable shirt. He is financially dependent on me, and his anger at politicians is driving him crazy. The bar that he goes to is full of malcontents, fellow travelers of the Party of Regions."

"That party is full of hard-core Russian conspirators and thugs. I wish they would just disappear," Luboš said. "Does he have a weapon?"

"Not that I know of. He goes to a shooting range or into the country with them to shoot. I can smell the gunpowder on his clothes."

"They are a bad influence," Libor added.

"I looked for support to handle his whims, and I've found strength in the emerging Eastern Orthodox Church. I attend when both of you are fishing."

"I give you support," her brother said defensively. "We give you support. We help in every way we can."

"The Church offers me spiritual comfort. Right now, I listen. We will see where religion takes me."

"Before I was born, my parents attended festivals of the Ukrainian Autocephalous Orthodox Church. I don't know how devout they were, but they prayed when circumstances dictated. If religion helps your soul, I am in favor."

"I was hesitant to go and hesitant to tell you, but I'm glad you approve."

"These are complicated times," Libor said. "How is Serhii with Max?"

"He doesn't pay attention."

"Probably good for Max. I'm near."

"Thank you, Tátinek."

"Should I move back?"

"I am okay," Lida replied weakly.

❖ ❖ ❖ ❖ ❖

Even more vexed after the January 2005 presidential re-vote was validated, Serhii was fired from his job for insubordination. He was surly at home and in the clubs, and at one Sunday dinner, he lost control.

"I'm sacked a week before Max's birthday," he let fly, pouring another glass of vodka and flipping through his favored television channels. "They are a cruel bunch of robber capitalists."

To avoid Serhii, Libor busied himself, Luboš pan-fried trout, and Lida set the table.

"This country is broken. You will see!" He fumed, waving his hands. "You are Austrian. Maksim should be Russian, in Russia."

"Max is Ukrainian," Lida countered.

"I should have returned home to Donetsk last fall. Goodbye." Uninterested in a reply, he picked up his already packed bag and stormed out.

Luboš and Libor sat stunned until Libor asked, "Has he threatened to leave before?"

"Yes. I hoped the Christmas holidays would soothe him. Thank goodness he didn't take Max."

"You worried he might?" her father asked, taken aback by Serhii's admonition. "He doesn't seem to care."

"I did worry," Lida said, slumped on the couch and relieved that her husband had departed.

"The television is off for a change," the grandfather said, walking to lift Max from the crib.

"Serhii was too much. I didn't tell you that I called the militsiya. At least they recorded the complaint. Simple things like choosing the colors of the nursery made him angry."

"I would have moved back had I known. You were brave to stay with him."

"Even naming Max was a fight. Both of us fancied the nickname Max. Serhii insisted his birth certificate read Maksim. Maxim is pronounced differently in Czech. I chose Maxim to respect you. He insisted Maksim sounded Russian and wouldn't give in. I call the baby, Max, never Maksim."

"Will you change his name? My name was changed."

"That saved your life in 1945. No name change is called for in Ukraine, though I will change the door locks. Marrying him was a mistake."

"You have a happy toddler and a loving family."

Relieved that Serhii had broken contact, Lida relished the return to normalcy at the evening meal. She moved the dining room table closer to the kitchen, and Luboš sat at the head with Max's chair at his right. Lida reupholstered her father's soft armchair in white cotton, trimmed in the red and blue piping of the Czech hockey team. She placed it so he could snooze in the afternoon sun. Friendly conversation resumed, and the focus shifted to Max.

Luboš mused about his destiny to be fully involved in the upbringing of a young child: I am here for Max and Lida. He thought of Uncle Jan, who assumed responsibility for a young Dmytro under life-threatening conditions, and Wilhelm, who provided for the young twins. They did their best, and so would he.

Luboš gladly stepped in as a loving advocate. He reduced his hours at the repair facility and Promise Gallery and fished less frequently. Dedeček was a common sight around town pushing Max in the pram at a modest gait to shady parks.

Lida's contested divorce was approved after reports to the militsiya and Serhii's outbursts in court proved he was a danger to his family. The court ruled in Max's best interest. Serhii was ordered to avoid contact with Lida or Max. Serhii's final words to the judge were, "Russians have long memories."

"That chapter of my life, our life, is over," Lida said to her father after the courthouse confrontation. "How did this happen? Why didn't you caution me?"

"If I influence your decision," Luboš answered, not sure there was an appropriate answer, "I'm the goat if a problem develops. You are a smart woman. I watch at your side, not over you."

"Okay, Tátinek. I ask you to intercede if you see a problem in the future."

"I will speak up."

"Thank you. I'm ready for a change. Do you care if Zuzana returns? She has visited just once. She should meet Max."

"Go ahead and ask her," Luboš said passively.

Chapter 46: Zuzana Visits Crimea, 2005

"You might appear tough at work sporting your two-day stubble or that dreadful beard," Lida prompted her father, "but you look much better clean-shaven."

"The beard was terrible and brings bad memories. Fine, I will shave for you."

"Really, for Zuzana."

"Okay, for both of you."

Zuzana lugged her oversized bags across the airport tarmac and waved at Luboš and Lida before disappearing to customs and immigration stations. Half an hour passed until she emerged wearing lightweight slacks and a purple-hued sweater for her return to temperate Feodosia and her introduction to Max.

"My, you look lovely," Lida welcomed. "Max is waiting to perform for you. We have been saying 'Zuzana' to him for days."

Initial greetings were upbeat, and Luboš carried the heavy bags. Joking, he asked Zuzana, "Did you bring food for the week?"

"Ha, not food, but I have spices and gifts. I'm relieved that the import tariffs were lower than expected."

"The real gift is that they didn't confiscate anything."

Zuzana and Lida hovered at the crib as Luboš sang gibberish in various languages to entertain Max. Lida and Zuzana smiled at Deda's antics and the baby's reaction of giggles and bubbles forming on his lips. Lida patted her face and Max's to point out their similarly shaped chins and noses.

"Put your finger in his hand," Luboš suggested.

"He is squeezing me," Zuzana said, animated by the pressure. "He looks at me as if he knows me."

"He is a smart baby. He sees the similarities of his mother, grandmother, and grandaunt. Listen. He is saying Zuzanananana, or something."

"Max is talking Luboš talk, a language of wisdom only the two of them speak," Lida jested.

"You hear, he already knows languages," Luboš remarked in mock approval and handed the naked baby to the visitor. "You saw my and Lida's impressive diaper change technique. Now it's your turn."

"Wait. This is my first day with Max. I'm new with babies," Zuzana replied in hesitation, arms outstretched while holding Max.

"We will be at your side."

Zuzana laughed, watching year-old Max waddle precariously and plop on the floor. She listened to his baby noises and developed a language to compete with Luboš's.

For the first time since reading to her little sister before the war, Zuzana read a children's book to Max. She and Lida pushed the pram down the narrow street to the pier where Luboš had filled the catch basket.

Luboš didn't eat at restaurants full of rowdy Russians. Each night, he grilled, Libor brought pastries, and Lida and her aunt coddled Max. On the last night, Zuzana put on Lida's apron to prepare an entire Czech meal.

"You cooked the same dinner for Libor and me in Prague. You are a master chef."

"Miluše, your Babička," Zuzana said in baby talk to Max, "taught us to spice the rationed cabbage or whatever she scrounged during the war. She was a creative cook."

"After my release," Luboš said, reenacting the scene for Lida, "Zuzana heated the kulajda soup. I set my nose above the china bowl and inhaled. It was not a tin cup. It was not gruel. I breathed in and closed my eyes. I held a real spoon. I was in heaven. I ate so fast I tasted only potato. In the second bowl, I savored the mushrooms and dill and

272

vinegar. That soup is a favorite memory, along with Marcela, of course."

A chill settled in after mention of her sister's name. Once again, he disturbed a moment that should have been only about Zuzana.

"We speak Czech," Luboš added awkwardly and unconvincingly, trying to salvage the situation. "Max will learn Czech."

"A favorite soup for me also," Zuzana said in a pensive tone. In a more upbeat voice, she said, "Correcting your medical issues was troublesome, and here you are, seventy-one years old and still working."

"Your doctors in Prague repaired most of me. I need my hearing aids and spend too much time in the sun. Thankfully, my perpetual cough bothers me less."

Zuzana turned to offer her collection of house gifts and said to Lida, "Beautiful music fills your home. I brought you a paisley scarf and a compact disc player, actually two CD players. One is for home and one for Promise Gallery. These Smetana and Dvořák CDs will put buyers in a good mood."

"So, you are a smuggler," Lida said, as she smiled and wrapped the scarf around her neck. "I have heard of these new music machines. My cassette tapes skip and are embarrassing to play in the gallery. A perfect gift, I mean gifts,"

"For you, Libor, a concert CD by my cello-playing young friend, Mila Hellerová." Zuzana jested, "Do you remember her?"

"Of course. I called her last night to tell her how happy we are to have you here. I heard her perform during my last trip to Prague. We wished you would join us for the performance."

Although Lida had introduced her brother to attractive contemporaries, his involvement with women had been intermittent and short-lived. Lida was thrilled to see that Zuzana's matchmaking was a success.

273

"I'm not a chaperone. Besides, you were going to those dungeon bars to dance in the smoke and crowds. Who is next? Ah, little Max. Max gets these bedtime books and Crayola crayons that aren't available here."

"Thank you, Max is an excellent artist. After we read to him at night and leave the room, he rambles on."

"And for Luboš...."

"Let me guess—it's a compact disc," he said playfully and slowly unwrapped the slender package. "Oh my, a CD by The Plastic People of the Universe. And look, the musicians are old. I might recognize the songs. Marcela sang each one."

Startled a second time at the mention of her sister, Zuzana noted off-handedly, "Of course the musicians are old."

Max was stirring, and Luboš was glad to place him in the baby carrier on his chest for a solitary walk around Quarantine.

Zuzana's successful efforts to strengthen Luboš after prison and after her sister's death led to friendship, nothing more. Neither could overcome the memory of Marcela, and he hadn't tried.

"Creating a Rotary Club is a challenge," Lida said to her aunt to shift from Marcela for a moment. "The men want it to be a men's club."

"Don't give up," Zuzana replied, and shared suggestions based on her experience.

Discussion of the Rotary was Lida's way to put Zuzana at ease to see if she held affection for Luboš. Lida did not ask that question in Prague. However, in her home, she said, "You were devoted to Deda after his prison release, almost a wife. Were you ever attracted to him, you know, after Marcela died, or after your mentor died?"

Zuzana didn't expect a deeper relationship with Luboš, but she did have hopes. She had made subtle overtures over the years, but he never acknowledged her beyond gratitude for tending to him—as a family member.

At her age, she peered into the mirror and saw the spinster aunt of Lida and Libor.

"You know where his heart is, and I loved another man."

"I didn't hear 'No,' " Lida persisted.

"I cared for him, yes, as a dear friend," Zuzana sighed. "I have white hair and am seventy-four."

Chapter 47: Max Grows Up

Luboš hadn't been given much in his seventy years, and he didn't consider himself a victim. Others had suffered worse. Judging the perils of the age, he didn't believe he was owed much either. What he had, he had won the hard way, and his account was square.

Lida asked how he was so mellow inside.

"Your mother asked the same question. I listen and try to get along. Why waste your time tormenting yourself over the past? Marcela's death was the ultimate test for me, but I listened to Zuzana: that you and Libor were my future, and it would be a good future. I leave the dreadful episodes to an occasional nightmare."

He was content to fish alone or with Libor, work at the garage and gallery, discuss hockey, and softly guide his family.

The sweet life in Feodosia continued to improve with Max's birth. Luboš held the baby and thought, this I deserve. Lida's child has found me. He won't experience the loss and sadness I saw. No child should face that upheaval. Luboš daydreamed that disputes in Ukraine and Serhii's most recent court challenge would be mastered, and the boy's biggest disappointment would be an empty catch basket.

After diapers, walking, talking, and preschool, in a blink sandy-haired Max was fishing with his grandfather. In every season for more than a decade, Luboš walked alone, and later with Max, to a fishing spot in Feodosia. Approaching the Genoese Fortress protecting the seaport,

Luboš looked for the wind direction of the blue and yellow Ukrainian flag to choose where to fish: the pier or the beach.

Max liked to run up and touch the massive walls and slide down the grassy slope. In nasty weather, they walked the short distance past the city green to the pier, where Max threw rocks at the seagulls.

The grandson's favorite was the beach, where he gathered colorful fish-trap buoys broken loose in storms to add to his collection. He wiggled his feet in the coarse sand and watched older boys and girls swim to the blue and white striped lighthouse of the Feodosia Memorial, seventy meters from the shore.

Luboš was emotionally linked to water, starting with the pond, the rivers, and the sea. He lived for the slap of waves on the concrete pier in Feodosia, the rhythmic sounding of the seaport channel bell buoys, and the breeze on his face. Stormy clouds sailing by or cloudless blue skies, smooth waters or turbulent waters, all were his good fortune in Crimea.

"Max, can you keep a secret?"

"Yes, I have plenty of secrets," exclaimed the six-year-old.

"Well, here is the best one." Luboš opened his shirt to uncover a crude tattoo made from cigarette ash ink spanning his chest.

"Cool, Dedeček. It says 'Marcela,' my Babička. I didn't know old people had tattoos."

Knowing Max was a talkative, happy participant at family meals, Luboš reminded the boy, "This tattoo is our secret, right?"

"Yes, Dedeček, for sure."

The duo was inseparable, although Luboš might nap while watching cartoons with Max. But not during their favorite—*The Adventures of Pea-Roll Along*. Deda said, "Aunt Alya said I would meet a princess. And I did, your Babička." Young Max glimpsed the pictures of Marcela on the mantel.

Luboš walked Max to and from school, and, for a time, Max was proud to brag to his second-grade classmates about his Deda's twenty years in prison to defeat the Communists. After Russian students bullied Max, he didn't mention that background again.

Progressive school administrators introduced English language study. Luboš was proud that his grandson was in the initial class. Russian parents were incensed by the affront.

"Boys paint the hammer and sickle on their schoolbooks," Max confided as they walked to the beach, "and they tease me because I'm better at English. They start fights."

"You are a tough kid and can take care of yourself. Your family has a gift for languages, and the Russians are jealous. If the war had lasted two more weeks, I would be an Austrian or an American speaking English."

"It's a hard language to learn. The teachers don't care."

"There is a reason for that," Luboš kidded. "The teachers are Russian, and they finished behind the Americans at the last Olympics." He added, "In ten years, you will attend a university, perhaps in America."

Luboš couldn't figure out why Max must have the latest toys. Deda whittled a horse and fish for him, saying to Lida, "What else does a youngster need?" For Christmas, Lida bought the boy a digital camera. Max took pictures of fish, sunflowers in summer, his Deda asleep on the bench at the pier—everything, and Max uploaded them to Lida's computer. In addition, she gave Luboš a mobile phone. It was usually turned off or the battery was dead.

Luboš would bundle up Max on a sunny winter morning to fish for drum, shad, and mackerel. On summer days, they sought mugil, carp, and perch. For a treat, they would stop for ice cream from a vendor's motorized pushcart at the foot of the memorial, Feodosia Landing, 1941. Dedeček described the rickety horse-cart of the itinerant photographer who had taken photographs at their pond.

278

"This monument was erected when we arrived here in 1992. Waving his arm across the broad plaza, Luboš said, "The granite base we sit on was laid, and the crane bringing the statue hit a pothole. It swung wildly, and the soldier's bayonet broke tree branches."

"The soldier's rifle is bigger than me," Max observed, looking up to the arm of the statue. Holding his cone at an angle, he dripped ice cream onto his shorts.

"After the Germans conquered Crimea, the Soviet army landed at our Feodosia pier and beach and held off the Nazis for three weeks."

"Our beach where we throw the nets for minnows?"

"Yes. Now we cool off in the shade of the trees and eat ice cream. Times have changed."

"Was your father in that battle?"

"I don't know."

At Lida's urging, Zuzana returned to Feodosia for Max's seventh-year birthday party. Lida's ulterior motive was to sway Luboš to accept that Zuzana was more than Max's grandaunt.

Luboš had learned, with Zuzana's prodding to "Enjoy what you have." That was his goal since he moved from Prague. Luboš wasn't oblivious to Lida's hopes for Zuzana, but he did not hold Zuzana as more than his former caretaker. He was content and unwilling to risk change.

Zuzana was aware of her niece's efforts. For her, the short visit was to see Max, Lida and Libor. Disappointed by Luboš's passivity, she flew home shortly after Max blew out the candles.

As Max grew and ran around as any child, Luboš was slowing down at an equal rate. He accepted his limp and gait from recurring bone spurs and pictured his energy transferred to Max. The boy was prompt with his chores of tending the owner's garden and cleaning the house so that he could play with friends or go fishing.

279

Max was thrilled at the first strike and the challenge to land a fish into Luboš's net. Bamboo fishing poles had been suitable for young Max until his skills and enthusiasm deserved better equipment. For his eighth birthday, Luboš bought him the latest lightweight spinning rod, reel, and tackle gear. Max carried his small tackle box, holding the same baits, lures, hook, floats, and weights as his grandfather. Max strutted around in his stylish sky-blue pork chop hat with a yellow band and his new angler's jacket of numerous pockets.

Casting a new rod and reel is challenging. Fellow fishermen scattered when Dedeček taught Max how to cast.

"Wow, that was wild," Luboš exclaimed in Czech, his default language, after Max's new spinning rod flew out of his hand and landed behind them at the edge of the pier. "Max, it has a slippery handle. Next time, grip tighter."

"Sorry," Max answered in Czech. "Glad the hook didn't snag anyone."

"They ran away," Luboš laughed. The grandson was attentive and learned how to bait the hook, select the best lure, and not cut his fingers. He learned where to cast and how to recognize the bobber dipping or the line tensing.

"Did I tell you about talking to fish?"

"No." Max paused to hear another fantastic story.

"Uncle Jan and I fished on a frozen lake with a Slovak who talked to fish." Luboš relished retelling the pleasant parts of his past to his grandson.

"Do fish hear? What do you tell them?"

"He spoke softly to them, politely asking them to bite the hook."

"Do you talk to fish?"

"I do, and sometimes they listen."

Curious about Uncle Jan, Max asked, "How many uncles do you have? Uncle Libor, Uncle Jan, and Uncle Yarik are different ages."

"And Uncle Jozef in Slovakia. I asked the same question. Jan was a German deserter and like a father. 'Uncle' is a term of respect for an older person who is a member of our family."

"Isn't a deserter an evil person?"

"That depends on why a person leaves. Jan couldn't remain a German soldier because the Nazis were on a quest to conquer the world and were killing innocent people. He sneaked away from the army and convinced my mother to flee to avoid the battles. We trusted him."

"But your family died in the mountains," a confused Max asked, holding his rod, the line looped around his bait basket.

"We may have died if we had stayed in Ukraine. My mother and Jan did their best."

Fishing can be a sedentary sport, waiting for the tug of the line. Max would ask his Deda to watch over his fishing gear to chase seagulls swooping and diving, attempting to steal their catch or bait. In the distance, patrol ships of the Ukrainian Naval Forces sailed in and out of the off-limits inlet.

From the pier, Max saw cheerful kids his age sailing small boats at the neighborhood sailing club. At his request, Lida enrolled him in a beginner clinic for nine-year-olds in the tiny Optimist prams. Soon he was either riding his bicycle from Quarantine to the sailing center or fishing every day.

"Be careful. The wind stirs quickly here. Pop-up storms have blown my bucket off the pier."

"Uncle Libor taught me to swim, and they teach us how to right the boat if we capsize."

"Okay. If the sea turns dark, go to the beach."

"You watch us all the time. You worry too much," Max said while walking to the little sailboats.

Max was the echo of Luboš at age ten: active, diligent, polite, and smart. But unlike his grandfather, Max had grown up in a safe environment.

To Lida's delight, Max cleaned fish at the pier, and when he was tall enough, he prepared them at the sink. Max insisted after a productive day, "I caught more than Uncle

281

Libor. I will cook tonight." Precocious, he entertained at dinner, rambling on about his day at school, fishing, sailing, or goofing off with friends.

Deda's best days were Sundays, when Libor met them in Feodosia at the shore. Grandfather had closed the circle, fishing with his father, son, and grandson.

Luboš was grateful for this late in life gift— guardianship of a child.

❖ ❖ ❖ ❖ ❖

After Max ran to play outside with his friends on their skateboards, Libor assured Lida, "I will take tomorrow off to help you and Dedeček dispute Serhii's latest motion."

"Thank you. The judge expects both of you by my side. I'm frightened of Serhii."

Chapter 48: Father and Daughter Discuss Zuzana

Luboš hadn't thought of his father in years, and only rarely of his mother or Jan. Luboš lived in the present until the present was interrupted.

Lida poured a glass of wine and lowered the volume of Gustav Mahler's "Adagietto." She sat at the kitchen table, spinning the stem until she initiated an awkward conversation "You are sturdy enough to keep up with Max."

"I don't try," he replied, a lager in his hand, before breading his latest drumfish. "He zooms ahead on the narrow streets and comes right back."

"Are you pleased Zuzana will return? It has been too long."

"Sure. Winters are mild here. On her last visit, she walked him to school. He is growing, and she will see him sail a boat. She cooks her Czech goulash and makes strudel for Max. She will be amazed at how big he is."

"Tatínek, you are hard-headed."

"About what?"

"Zuzana is keen to cook for you. You should take her on a date."

"A date? I'm almost eighty." He wiped his hands and turned off the burner.

"Are you too old to express affection to someone other than Max, me, and Libor?"

"Fine. I will drive her to the hills, and we will hunt mushrooms for her goulash."

"Sit down with her. Listen to the birds. Collect flowers in bloom. Say, 'I'm glad you returned to Feodosia.' "

Luboš was silent, and Lida bored deeper. "You are unwilling to see in Zuzana what you loved in Máma. She is your excuse not to love Zuzana. She comes to see her family. She is our family."

"Love? What are you saying?" Luboš responded uncomfortably and walked to the back door.

"Bring her closer."

"Have her move here? Move to Prague and leave you, Libor and Max? We are set in our ways."

"The visit is about Zuzana. Right?"

"I will think about it."

"Well, think about this! Who could imagine your mother loving Jan, and he loving Nadiya?"

The sunlight behind him left only his silhouette. Her father slowly turned around and lowered his head.

"In Prague, Zuzana saved you—twice." An exasperated Lida advanced, "Why not you and Zuzana?"

Recalling the connection between Jan and his mother confused him—and resonated for him.

"You care for her. I'm sure you do. Give her flowers and look into her eyes. Not the same way as Máma, but a way that makes plain she is special. Who says love has an age limit?"

Lida walked to him at the window and held his gaze until he understood.

The edges of his lips turned up in a slight smile. Yes, he did understand. He held his daughter's hands and kissed her on each cheek.

"Wildflowers, many wildflowers. Thank you."

284

Chapter 49: Zuzana Returns to Feodosia, Autumn, 2013

Luboš anticipated Zuzana's visit in a new frame of mind, especially since she had asked to fish with Luboš and Max. Lida had tipped off Zuzana.

"I'm seventy-nine years old," Luboš proudly said to Zuzana, sitting in the passenger seat of Lida's car. "I help Lida, work two days a week at the garage, and can pass the driving test. Do you trust me to drive to pick mushrooms?"

"I guess so. Lida trusts you driving her BMW." Zuzana asked mischievously, "Will you scare me? Should I hold onto the seat?"

"No, I drive cautiously. We are only twenty kilometers from the Karadag Nature Reserve. You have the directions on your fancy telephone. Don't let me lose my way. My father taught me to recognize poisonous mushrooms. We will pick morels for your goulash and will lunch at a restaurant at the shore."

"Sounds romantic."

Luboš didn't answer. He was nervous. He drove to the area in the Reserve recommended by Lida. They found the morels deep in the forest, and he limped about picking until his rucksack was full. They emerged into a meadow of multi-colored leaves blown about in a gust of wind. Luboš wandered toward end-of-season flowers.

"Pick blooms that have long stems. The red ones and these tall purple ones are my favorite. My mother stuffed them between the boards of our farmhouse."

"Flowers give hope, even for a short time," Zuzana suggested.

The view along the winding drive from the park to the shore was spectacular. "I see why Lida organized picnics here. Now you are a naturalist?"

"My boyhood name, Dmytro, means earth lover. I'm not normally a nature person, except for today."

At the restaurant, Luboš asked for a table at the edge of the patio and a glass of water. Sunglasses perched on her nose, Zuzana sat facing the bright blue waters and dramatic volcanic formations offshore.

"That arch in the sea is called the Golden Gate," Luboš said knowingly.

"Just imagine how sailors have marveled at it over the centuries."

Her white hair danced in the breeze, and she spread her lavender colored sweater over her shoulders, snagging an earring. Luboš untangled it, lingering for a moment with his fingers on her ear. He stretched his arms into his ribbed short-sleeved sweater and maneuvered his arthritic legs under the table. He cocked his wide-brimmed hat over his craggy face. When the waiter brought the water glass, Luboš asked about local beers.

"I'll have a lager, and the lady will have a pilsner."

Luboš relaxed after sips of his beer and straightened up, gathering his nerve. "Isn't this a nice day?" he said, grasping for a way to lead off.

"It is a beautiful day. Will you put the flowers in the water glass?"

"Oh, yes. I forgot. What are their names?"

"The purple ones are hollyhocks. Purple was Máma's favorite color and mine and Marcela's."

"Ah, your family favored purple. These flowers are for you."

"Thank you. Are you anxious?" Zuzana asked in an encouraging tone.

"Do you remember my first day out of prison?"

"Every minute."

286

"You reached over me and buckled my seat belt. Your perfume was the best fragrance in twenty years." He coughed several times and cleared his throat.

"I knew you were sneaking glances at me."

"Since then, I avoid those glances. It was simpler to shy away. I'm looking now, with Lida's encouragement. You have beautiful eyes—better than the sky."

To allow some time-space, they each stared at waves gently rolling toward them.

"Lida tells me I'm living in the shadow of Marcela," Luboš continued.

"Both of us live in her shadow. Lida said that I am holding back. Are you holding back?"

"Probably." Lowering his head in embarrassment, he added, "I have a secret. I see her name every day. 'Marcela' is tattooed on my chest."

"The same day you revealed your tattoo to Max," Zuzana giggled, "he told Lida, she told Libor, and he told me. Max was then sworn to secrecy, for real."

"Ohhhh," Luboš said, at first chagrined, and then promptly laughed. "He is a rascal."

"We presumed you would tell us when the time was right. You have chosen a good time. I thank you."

Luboš had practiced for days. The ending was clear, but he was unsure how to get there. Meanwhile, Zuzana patiently waited.

"Well, here I go." Fortified, he shifted to sit directly across from her, laid his arms on the picnic table, folded his hands, and began, "Regard for Marcela kept me from thinking we were a couple. You are a companion, the guide who saved me. I put you in a compartment of a friend and not a partner.

"Besides, I was a physical wreck—mostly bald, limping walk, ragged cough, and skin etched by dust. I was old too early and considered myself boring. And you were committed to your lover. I had nowhere to go except my children, work, fishing, and then Max. I was content."

287

"Today, you are stalwart and keep up with Max. Neighbors admire your devotion." Zuzana complimented him with her head canted and a sparkle in her eyes, "You are more vigorous than younger men."

Revived, after finishing off his beer, he continued, "My mother and Aunt Alya told me I would meet and dance with a princess. I took too long to recognize the second one: you."

"Possibly an elderly princess."

"You are the beautiful eighty-year-old princess I wish I had recognized earlier."

"Eighty something years," Zuzana proudly interrupted. "Marcela wore makeup. Me, a little, and the wrinkles show."

"Even better, a beautiful eighty or so years and a few wrinkles. I missed twenty years of a full life, a life I didn't pursue despite Lida and Libor telling me time and time again. I will wake up fully, to you."

The waiter, patiently waiting for a break, strode to the table and announced, "Madam and Sir, have you made a selection?"

They fumbled for their reading glasses, scanned the menu, and ordered two fish specials.

"And what does waking up mean?" she prompted.

"That, that we become a couple," he forced out.

"You are brave to share this. It's complicated when you are young, and some may say ridiculous at our age."

"Is this conversation ridiculous?"

"No, no. Not at all. Now, my turn." Luboš eased back, and Zuzana squared before him. "When I brought you back from prison, I saw the man you describe. But I pictured you differently, as the man Marcela loved and Máma approved of. At your departure for Vienna two years later, you were healthy in body and mind. I didn't think of you as more than, as you say, a friend. My mentor died the next year, and I tell you, there were times I wished we were together."

"I kept you away by my thoughtless comments. They broke out. They protected me."

"From what?" Zuzana asked.

"From you and me."

"Lida visited me in Prague three years later, and we had the same talk about my living half awake. I didn't have children or grandchildren to keep me busy. I was lonely. I was stubborn and told her you were simply a dear friend. It was my way to stop the questions. I worried that since you loved Marcela, was I her substitute?"

"Lida and Libor recognized we are equally stubborn. I wish I had had enough courage to recognize this years ago."

"So, have we resolved anything?"

"Yes. To be together."

"Does this mean we are in love?"

"Yes." Luboš confirmed, "Yes." Luboš rested his shaking hands on hers.

"I love you too."

"Your touch is comforting." Her eyes closed, and both leaned forward to kiss on the lips.

Chapter 50: Libor Moves On, December 2013

Their commitment was firm, but the timetable and location for Zuzana and Luboš to settle were elusive.

"I thought we would have decided by now," Luboš said by mobile phone to Zuzana in Prague.

"Moving to Crimea seemed sensible before the demonstrations began in November. I wanted to tie up loose ends here, but now, I'm not sure."

"We will get through this noisy time, just like Wenceslas Square and our Orange Revolution. You should see all the fish Max catches."

"I will. After the Red Cross Christmas Gala that I chair, we will take another look."

Kyiv marchers took to the streets in November after President Yanukovych broke from signing the European Union Association Agreement. The promised westward political and economic orientation was in jeopardy. Militsiya and government corruption, flawed elections, human rights, and the lurch back to Russia were central to the complaints. Demonstrations in the Maidan escalated in breadth and intensity after excessive police suppression.

Libor was unsettled, watching the month-long protests. He feared the pull of progressive forces would not give the success of the 2004 Orange Revolution, which had reversed a fraudulent election. Since the governmental challenge started, his spare hours were fixed to the television, the Voice of America on the Internet, and calls to his

290

girlfriend in Prague. Would the rallies and riots force President Yanukovych to make concessions to enable a credible democracy with a European slant? Libor ran out of patience.

"We have talked about and around my complaints," Libor said, motioning his sister to join him at the couch. "My business collapsed when competitors sabotaged me. Construction at my company is shoddy; when I find deficiencies, they ignore me. If a crane falls and kills someone, they will come for me. My Russian boss would laugh at me on my way to jail. Every day I sense fair warning."

"What's on your mind?" Lida crossed the room to turn off Bedřich Smetana's Czech proud *Má Vlast*.

"I'm forty-four years old and restless. I've gained too much weight. My hair is thinning. Furthermore...."

"Stop! How old do you think I am? I look in the mirror and wonder what happened. You depress me."

"I started this conversation poorly."

"Agreed. Will it get any better?"

"Probably not."

"Go ahead."

"Crimea is unstable, at least for honest work that requires government approval. You have succeeded because you earn substantial money and don't need banks and government licenses."

"I lease my gallery and, sure, Táta makes required advances. He tells me the government authorities are pressing him more and more. I give Táta what he needs, reluctantly, and some paintings here and there. I have limited interaction with authorities, and I'm not bothered. So?"

"I interviewed at Charles University when I visited Mila last month. They have offered me the position."

"Why didn't you tell me?"

"I told Táta."

"Why not tell me?"

"No good reason. I'm trying to figure things out. He thinks I will be a good professor, but I should find a better job here instead—to keep us together."

"Are there jobs?"

"None I would accept. To teach challenging courses is a life-changer."

"And?"

"And Mila and I are compatible, probably in love. The curriculum is Business Principles in the Post-Soviet."

"You can stay with Zuzana. Will you take it?" Lida asked, shaking her head side to side and holding a tissue to her eye.

"Only if you approve," Libor said, putting his arm around her. "Your gallery sales haven't declined in this turmoil. You will be fine."

"Fine financially, but I'm apprehensive about Max. Serhii doesn't give up. Are you giving up on Crimea?"

"I suppose so."

"I don't have the luxury of abandoning Promise Gallery. I can't just get up and leave. Besides, I have mandatory counseling after the Olympics, and the court date for Serhii's appeal is in March. You have been a reliable brother to accompany me to these hearings. I will miss your advice."

"Your lawyers have acted well for you. The judges have determined he can't restrain his temper. The court should continue his restrictions."

"I'm less confident this time. A new judge partial to Russia will preside. Serhii's latest scheme is that I'm a foreigner discriminating against a Russian father."

"Oh. A different tactic," Libor sighed. "We can't afford to ignore it. I'll hire the best lawyer to join yours."

"I will require the best. I believed going to church would help in times of stress, but the protests, Táta falling in love, and now you are too much."

Lida slid to the end of the couch. She walked to the window. With her back to her brother, she watched Max weed the garden. After a prolonged silence she acknowledged, "You have your life to lead. This is your decision."

"It is our decision," Libor said, hoping his sister would support him.

"Táta helps with Max, but he is pretty old. You moved to Yalta twenty years ago, yet you were close. You come to dinner on Sundays."

Lida bought and sold art with her sound judgment of the market. She made decisions promptly in business; here, she reluctantly yielded to the inevitable. "All right. If Mila and Prague are the future, you must commence a new life. I love you. You have my blessing."

"Thank you."

"Max will be sad. The three of us will be sad. They will be home in a moment. I must stop crying. When will you leave us?"

"Before the New Year."

Chapter 51: Confrontation, February 2014

Luboš' twenty-two years in Feodosia were the most stable in his life. He and Zuzana were in love, Lida was established in the community, Libor had embarked on a new career, and Max was a joy. Despite the uproar shown on television, Deda had overcome hardships in a tumultuous century.

"Libor called," Lida said when her father returned to Promise Gallery. "He asks if we saw Alexander Zaldostanov carry the torch in the opening ceremony for the Socchi Olympics. Zaldostanov was the leader of that bike gang that tried to intimidate him during the Sevastopol naval port negotiations."

"I worried about Libor then. And remember two years ago when Putin rode a motorcycle around Crimea in the Night Wolves rally? The leader of a violent bike gang is a leader in last week's parade? What a disgrace.

"He is playing tough guy to the die-hard Russians. I don't trust him. At least the streets in Feodosia are quiet." Father continued, "Everyone is inside either watching the Olympics or the troubles in the capital."

"He has completed his lesson plans, and winter semester starts next week. He moved out of your bedroom at Zuzana's. He and Mila leased an apartment."

"Zuzana is a good match-maker. She has been kind to our family for a long time."

"She thrives when she is with us. What are you and Zuzana doing about your relationship?"

"We text and call, but seeing the mess in Kyiv, we will wait a while. This is peculiar: a bloody revolution in the capital against Russian influence at the same time the Russians celebrate the Olympics 500 kilometers from here."

"I'm anxious about Kyiv and Crimea. Please keep your cell phone charged and on."

Luboš didn't tell his daughter that Zuzana was also concerned about his safety and had asked him to come to Prague. With the tumult in Ukraine, Luboš wasn't ready to leave his grandson and daughter. But he was tuned in to undercurrents in Feodosia and Crimea. and daily he reviewed precautions with Artem if Kyiv-type violence imperiled Crimea.

"Did you have buyers today?"

"Not even lookers," Lida replied as she placed a recently delivered sculpture on its pedestal. "Young men wandered around the square and snapped up all the pastries from the bakery. They don't look like tourists."

"Olympic fever has seized the city. You ought to close and watch the games with everyone else."

"Fine idea. I should have locked the doors last week."

"Tomorrow afternoon Max and I will watch my Czech team play the United States. Tomorrow night is a critical game when the Russians play Finland. The bars will serve half-price vodka. I will go to Artem's Ukrainian bar where we root against the Russians." To avoid confrontation, Luboš wore his white and red Czech hockey jersey only at that bar or in his home.

"They are already crazy. I will write a 'Closed' sign for the door. When do the Olympics end? When do we reopen?"

"Today is the eighteenth. The last hockey game is Sunday, 23 February, also the closing ceremony."

"Okay. I will write 'Closed: Reopening 24 February 2014.' No, wait. That is a Monday. I will stretch my vacation and reopen for the weekend, Thursday, 27 February."

"What about the boy? How is Max handling the Russian nationalism?" Lida asked on the way to retrieve him from school. "You and I are either Czech or Austrian to most people here. Max has a Russian father. I hope they don't bother him."

Luboš didn't answer.

"I cringe when customers mention the protests," Lida continued. "I'm petrified of a posting on my Facebook page that will affect the gallery."

"Artem does that Facebook thing, and he tells me the Euromaidan posts are worse than a brawl in a hockey game."

❖ ❖ ❖ ❖ ❖

First Secretary of the Communist Party of the Soviet Union, Nikita Khrushchev, had administratively transferred Crimea to Ukraine in 1954. Even though they had relinquished the governance of Crimea, the Russians stayed. The unhealed wound to Russian sympathizers remained. Tense exchanges in the bars, coffee shops, and city halls around other cities in Crimea exposed the raw divisions.

Despite the winter of deadly confrontations elsewhere, Feodosia had been peaceful but on edge. The controversies were acknowledged but did not disrupt the routine of the anglers on the pier, with these exceptions: the bench fishermen discussed how to apply for a Russian passport and voiced their support for reinstalling the statue of Stalin.

Luboš tuned them out.

Memories of Stalin's Great Famine of 1932–1933, notorious as the Holodomor that forced death by hunger of millions of Ukrainians, were resurrected on supportive television channels. The Ukrainian Genocide instantly became a volatile issue. Provocative Russian TV commentators hit back and blamed the starvation on Fascists, the same term they applied to Euromaidan protestors.

The all-day news coverage of the capital's demonstrations brought Luboš back to Wenceslas Square in Prague in 1989, when the chains of Communism were cast off. Videos of protestors toppling statues of Lenin and Stalin in the Euromaidan gave Luboš comfort. He slapped his hand as if he had a crowbar. For months, the dissenters in Kyiv's Independence Square had risked their lives.

They ultimately achieved victory when, early on the morning of Saturday, 22 February 2014, the Verkhovna Rada stripped presidential powers from Yanukovych. Fearing for his life prior to a vote for impeachment, he fled to Karkiv, then Crimea, and eventually Moscow.

"A pleasant wake up to you," Luboš announced enthusiastically to his sleepy daughter. "This coffee tastes better than usual. Yanukovych is gone. Parliament voted to remove him while we slept. The television shows joyful revolutionaries filling the Maidan: no army, no snipers."

"What a relief," Lida said, dressed in her slippers and bathrobe. "Those protesters are heroes. The only place for us to stand to celebrate in Feodosia is in front of our television. You and Zuzana stood in Wenceslas Square. Máma stood in her Vienna apartment."

Lida and her father froze. "Oh my, what did I say?" They stepped toward each other for a long embrace.

"This time is different, Lida. All of us will be okay," Deda asserted, unwilling to bend to the sadness of Marcela's death. "In Wenceslas Square, we rattled our keys. Now they wave their mobile phone flashlights."

A man of the present, he added, "I'm relieved the suspense is over, and we can move on. The USA hockey team plays for the bronze medal tonight."

"You want to watch? The United States beat the Czech Republic."

"Sadly, we are out of the medals. I'm hoarse from cheering for the Czechs. What else can I do? The best of the week was the Russian loss to Finland two days ago. After work, I will watch a hockey game."

"Today is Saturday. Isn't the garage closed?"

"It was, but our local politician browbeat the owner into repairing motorcycles from mainland bikers."

The tide might have turned in Kyiv, but not in Crimea and Eastern Ukraine. Russian language TV stations intensified their attacks on the legitimacy of Parliament's decision and described the events as a coup by American puppets. Ukrainian channels countered by replaying scenes of Yanukovych's gaudy palace and dead citizens killed by snipers. Russian supporters in Sevastopol were at odds with protestors in Simferopol, who marched in favor of the new Parliamentary decrees. The drumbeat of fiery words and threats allowed no compromise.

Lida ignored the unrest. After Yanukovych fled, Lida imagined a stable future and abandoned the television to read her stack of books during her short vacation. Luboš celebrated at work and waited for a sunny day to fish with Max.

During the week, Max had flipped channels to watch Olympic recaps. Luboš followed the positive developments in Kyiv on Ukrainian language television channels. At the closing ceremony four days earlier, they had watched Vladimir Putin, smug and unsmiling despite the success of the Russian athletes. He had won the lion's share of medals but lost Yanukovych and Ukraine.

By Wednesday night, Lida was restless, lounging on her couch reading mystery novels set in Vienna. She remarked, "A week off is too long. We will have to dust high and low tomorrow."

"Not me. Max will skip school, and we will go fishing." Luboš was emotionally exhausted from the drama akin to the Velvet Revolution. Optimistically he said, "These months of angry scenes show our free spirit and offer opportunity. We have five days of peace in Kyiv; justice will prevail."

"Are you worried about Russian sympathizers in Simferopol blocking parliament?"

"No. Anti-Russian protestors in Kyiv saved our country. The same will happen in Crimea. I will join them if needed."

Mother and son prepared for bed, and Luboš fell asleep as optimistic as when he last sang "A Prayer for Marta" in 1989.

But for President Vladimir Putin, the military commanders in Crimea, and the Russian zealots in Feodosia, the debate was over. His one-party, one-person autocratic rule was intent to "recover lost glory" and return Crimea to its place inside the far border of Russia.

Days before the Socchi Olympics closing ceremony, Putin had surreptitiously added equipment and thousands of soldiers to Russian bases to execute a stealth invasion. The assault would replicate the seizure of territories of Georgia in 2008. While the eyes of the world were on the Russian Olympics, Putin's eyes were on Crimea.

On Thursday morning, President Putin followed the progress of his masked, insignia-free Special Forces and surrogates as they deployed from the bastion at Sevastopol, airbases throughout Crimea, and warships on the Black Sea.

Chapter 52: Get Out of Ukraine!

The greatest victory is that which requires no battle.
Sun Tzu, *The Art of War*

Repelled by the resolute soldiers at the pier, Luboš gave up plans to fish and headed home past the monument, Feodosia Landing, 1941. Blocks away from the village green, penetrating squeals of loud music blasted his hearing aids. The song playing over and over was "Back in the U.S.S.R." by the Beatles. Luboš reminisced of the Vzorkovna bar of the bittersweet Prague Spring.

His pleasant memory of rock and roll music with Marcela vanished when he saw armored vehicles lacking national markings block the side streets. Was his country occupied again and so easily? He did not fathom the lyrics, perhaps neither did the ruffians, but Luboš would learn that the U.S.S.R. and Russia differed little, and he was back in Russia.

Pickup trucks, the Russian Federation Tricolor hand-painted on the doors, powered loudspeakers. The City Hall balcony draped blood-red flags of the star, hammer, and sickle. Those flags had been absent for twenty-three years.

The pair was unable to bypass scores of rough-looking men wearing motorcycle leathers. Bottles of vodka underfoot, they burned boards of picnic tables in a firepit to keep warm. Shreds of the blue and yellow Ukrainian flag smoldered. Machine guns behind sandbags were not aimed

at the sea. They were aimed down city streets and directly at
Luboš and Max. In contrast to the disciplined, uniformed
Russian men they had faced minutes earlier, these men were
rowdy and eyed the fishermen. There was no minder.

❖ ❖ ❖ ❖ ❖

The leader continued shouting, "Are you deaf, old
man? Get out of Crimea! Get out of Ukraine!"

Unsure of his strength, Luboš put his scarred hand
on the boy's shoulder and turned away from the gang.

"Look at Máma's gallery!" Max cried. "Where is
Máma?"

Luboš's heart raced as they walked past the smashed
windows of Lida's art gallery, fractured sculptures on the
floor, and the sign, Lida Nováková, Proprietor, in pieces on
the sidewalk. Shards of glass crunched under their shoes.
The bakery next door where they bought pyrophy dough had
been looted.

"She is home," was all Dedeček could say and hope
for. Large paintings were stacked neatly against a truck,
awaiting their disposition.

Motorcycles with saddlebags embroidered in "Night
Wolves" images blocked side streets—the same motorcycles
that Artem and Luboš had recently repaired. The tough-
acting bike owners in full leather had shrugged off the
obligation to pay. The boss didn't bother to complain to the
militsiya.

Luboš rethought the recent days in Feodosia. The
hotels and bars had been packed with young, boisterous men
whom he assumed were simply watching the Olympics. Of
course! After the closing ceremony, they dispersed to their
deployment sites. They had infiltrated the city in a quiet,
well-planned invasion and were manning the weapons.

Luboš's thoughts drifted. He wished to have a
picture of Libor and Max carrying a string of trout. It was
too late to learn the kobza or fish from a charter boat with
Libor.

For a second, he started to relapse to Czech Švejkism. Could he wait for the Americans or the British to honor their commitment under the 1994 Budapest Memorandum to maintain Ukraine's territorial integrity? Jan did not find me, but I find him when I need him. Luboš had confidence in his emergency plans and snapped out of his funk—for Max.

When Dmytro began his odyssey and fled Ukraine, he was Max's age. His peasant family had not bowed to totalitarianism. What could Dedeček do?

"Luboš!" Artem hailed, out of breath. "I've been looking for you. I need to tell you something. Hi, Max. I need to speak to your Deda for a minute."

"This mess is bad for us Ukrainians and especially for you."

"Why me?"

"Serhii is here wearing one of those dark green uniforms of what they call a self-defense force. He is poorly trained and keeps his finger on the trigger of his Kalashnikov."

"Holy shit! Where and when?" Luboš exclaimed and stopped in his tracks.

"Keep moving. Two hours ago at one of the main roadblocks. He didn't see me."

Max, already distraught, overheard the men talk furtively. Artem pulled Luboš towards Quarantine.

"He stopped a Navy truck with sailors in uniform and forced them out with their hands held above their heads. He confiscated their weapons, locked them on the truck and kidnapped them. Our First Infantry Battalion in Feodosia is surrounded. I heard the Russians blockade our Ukrainian ships in Sevastopol. You, Lida and Max should scram the way you planned. Now."

"We are the wrong tribe here, more so starting today."

"You should worry about revenge from Serhii."

"He is a mean bastard. Serhii was a follower, now he is a messenger for Putin. I thought I was done with tyrants."

"We don't have much time—any time. He isn't simply checking identity cards. He will take Max, and you and Lida are in the way."

"Artem, you are a good friend. Okay, I will talk to Lida and call you."

"Mobile phones are dead. I will meet you at Lida's in thirty minutes." Artem prodded Luboš to move faster and disappeared to a side street of Quarantine.

Luboš threw the worthless rods to the cobblestones and trudged on, hoping he was in a bad dream. At least daybreak stops a nightmare. He hummed the Ukrainian national anthem. His family fled Ukraine seventy years ago. He reassured himself, "This time, I am Jan."

"You are Jan? Uncle Jan?" Peering up and holding onto the crook of his Deda's arm, Max insisted, "I don't want to see my father."

"Do you like Zuzana?" Luboš responded evasively.

"Yes," answered the puzzled boy.

"You are a strong boy. It's important you speak Czech," Deda said, confusing Max even more. "The fishing on the Vltava River is excellent." Luboš was steadfast. He stared straight ahead and pulled Max the way Jan had dragged him in the final days of the trek in 1945.

Lida stood at the doorway, holding her mobile phone in one hand and the television remote control in the other. When Luboš approached the threshold, she grabbed and held Max to her chest. RT flashed scenes of the Russian federation flag flying over Sevastopol, Simferopol, and Eastern Ukraine and the apparent triumph of the invasion.

"Only Russian television channels are on, and it is all bad news. Ukrainian channels have static. Where have you been?"

Luboš ignored her question. "Lida, sit down." He spoke urgently as his chest heaved. His eyebrows froze high above his eyes. He relayed his encounter with Artem, his preparations, and plan.

"Serhii scares me. Artem said we should leave; where to?"

"First, from this apartment. Next, from Crimea. We don't have much time. Then Prague."

"To Zuzana?"

"Yes."

"This is too quick. I cannot think straight. You have seen this before—what should we do?"

"I watched my mother consider alternatives with Uncle Yarik. Wait for the battles between the Germans and Russians or flee. Once again, escape is our only choice. Artem will be here in a minute. I will call Zuzana."

"Libor gave up in December. Now it's our turn to escape."

"Max, put on your boots. You too, Lida."

He feared the telephone landlines would be dead.

"Zuzana, is that you?" Luboš voiced, an octave higher than normal.

"Yes, Luboš."

"I'm ready to return to Prague, and to you." Luboš imagined he detected her perfume. "Will you take Lida, Max, and me?"

"I've been waiting for you."

"Princess, I'm sorry I took this long."

The back door squeaked open. The threesome turned in fear and then relief—it was Artem.

Luboš took Max and Lida, one in each hand, and said, "Let's go!"

Acknowledgements

My sincere thanks to friends who have encouraged me: Ron Ball, Indulis Pommers, Al Cinquino, Mimi Ribot, Charlie Heller, Jen Nicholson, John Yahner, Terri Boddorf, Jim Reese, Lynn Auld Schwartz, the Key West Writer's Guild, and friends in Ukraine. Books by Anne Applebaum have presented the era in which Luboš lives. My wife, Kathy, is a wonderful supporter and guide.

About the Author

Ward R. Anderson is a retired Naval Aviator who piloted attack aircraft from the USS Ranger. He then flew for a major airline to cities in Europe, where he could not pass up a museum. A photographer, he is on the Board of Directors of The Maryland Federation of Art. He and Kathy live in Annapolis. They have sailed, raced, and cruised extended passages to the Caribbean, Canada, and Maine waters dodging lobster floats. Research included visits to Ukraine, Slovakia, The Czech Republic, Germany, and Poland.

Escape From Ukraine is a timely reminder of Russia's undeclared wars and a glimpse into the future of Russian neighbor states. The resolve of NATO, the European Union, and the United States may be tested as President Vladimir Putin consolidates power.

Made in the USA
Middletown, DE
21 March 2022

63017714R00191